DECEIT OF THE EMPIRE TRILOGY

BOOK ONE

TO SKIN A LEOPARD

KD NEILL

'"To Skin a Leopard" (Deceit of the Empire Trilogy, Book One) by KD Neill is hands down one of the most riveting and well-crafted books I've read in a long time!'
(5 stars) *Nicola Flood*

'I would love to read more from KD Neill in the future as he has a true gift for creating a well-thought out story and bringing memorable characters to life and I feel like I have more understanding of this part of British/African history. (4 stars)'

Layla Messing

Very, very, very good. It's not often that I start reading a book and it consumes me right away and forces me to re-prioritize my life for a little. "To Skin a Leopard" by KD Neill is not a quick read by any stretch…. There are too many important events and experiences here to gloss over so the author takes his time in carefully developing the various storylines from the different perspectives of the main characters, so that we the readers are thoroughly invested the whole way through. This is an edgy, powerful ride through a fascinating time in South African history, one which I had never known about, the 'Xhosa wars', where the natives fought against the invading colonial forces.
A great start to what looks to be a very promising series. (5 stars) *Tabitha Parks*

Really glad I took a chance on this one, and I can't wait to read more from Neill in the future. This is a first of a series and I'd recommend it for older readers of historical fiction/action/romance. (4 stars). *Megan King – Goodreads.*

KD Neill's literary voice and writing style is absolutely perfect for this genre, and I am surprised to see that this is his first (and only?) book? I looked to see if he's done others and didn't see any which makes this effort even more impressive. (4-5 stars) *Samantha Ryan*

There is an erotic element I wasn't expecting, but it was fun. There are just so many elements to this book, it is truly on an epic scale. But impressively it doesn't get too confusing, and all came together to create a fresh-feeling book that was out of the ordinary and kept me completely invested throughout. (4-5 stars) *Cale Owens – Goodreads.*

It is engaging, fast paced, believable, surprising, sad, intense and heartwarming… all the qualities I look for in a good book, and it delivered an emotional win in the end. (4 stars). *Cody Brighton – Barnes & Noble.*

An intimate look into some fascinating historical times that isn't really covered in modern textbooks or in fiction, but it tells such an intriguing tale of survival and resilience. Would recommend to fans of historical literary fiction and (erotic) romance. (5 stars) *Stacy Decker – Indie Book Reviewers.*

Not only did I really enjoy reading this, I actually feel like I learned something more about this time period that I didn't know before. The flow was perfect, the romances believable and the thrilling plots keeps us hooked right until the end. (4-5 stars) *Essie Harmon. Goodreads.*

KD NEILL

KD Neill, musician, composer, singer, songwriter, arranger, producer, entertainer and author was born and raised in Scotland and started playing and reading music from the age of eight.

Later in life the company he worked for needed two engineers to work in their branch in South Africa, he applied and emigrated on a two year plan, but fell in love with Africa and stayed there for more than half of his life. He now lives in Scotland.

Follow Kenny on facebook… Kenny D Neill

Tweet Kenny… @kd_neill

Instagram: Kennysa01

Website: www.kdneillbooks.com

Email: kdneill@kdneillbooks.com

Copyright

2017 Copyright: K.D. Neill.
The right of K.D. Neill to be identified as the author of this work has been asserted by him in accordance with the Copyright, Designs and Patents Act 1988.

All rights reserved.
No part of this book may be reproduced, stored in a retrieval system, or transmitted, in any form or by any means, electronic, mechanical without written permission from the publisher.

Cover design by K.D. Neill
Cover Image by Freeimages.com/Odan Jaeger
Map illustrations by K.D. Neill

ISBN-13:
978-1544718705

ISBN-10:
1544718705

Foreword

I lived and worked in parts of Africa from 1977 until 2010, mostly in South Africa, and wherever I worked, I tried to read as much as I could about the local history.

When I was working in the Eastern Cape I took a great interest in the Xhosa wars of the nineteenth century, and often visited the museum in East London and the museum and central library of Cape Town.

Reading the history of this period gave me an insight into the trials and tribulations of the settlers, and especially the native tribes fighting to keep their land and take back their freedom.

This book was inspired by actual events, which took place in the Eastern Cape, mid-nineteenth-century that caused a devastating loss of life to the Xhosa people. This is a book of fiction and apart from the old ancestral chiefs all the characters are fictional.

It is necessary to explain the use of certain words that appear from time to time in this book.

The word *'Kaffir'* is an Arabic word meaning 'unbeliever'. Arab slave traders hunted and captured Africans before the Europeans arrived in Africa. They used this word to denote Africans and, over time, Portuguese explorers adopted the word, as did British and Dutch explorers. The idiom continued to be used over generations until eventually, it became an offensive and abusive term as racial hatred grew.

This word, as with *'heathen'* and *'native'*, were words commonly used as part of the terminology of the day by colonials and settlers to describe the local people. I do not mean any insult or disrespect to anyone in any way by using these words in this novel.   KD Neill.

Eastern Cape: 19th Century

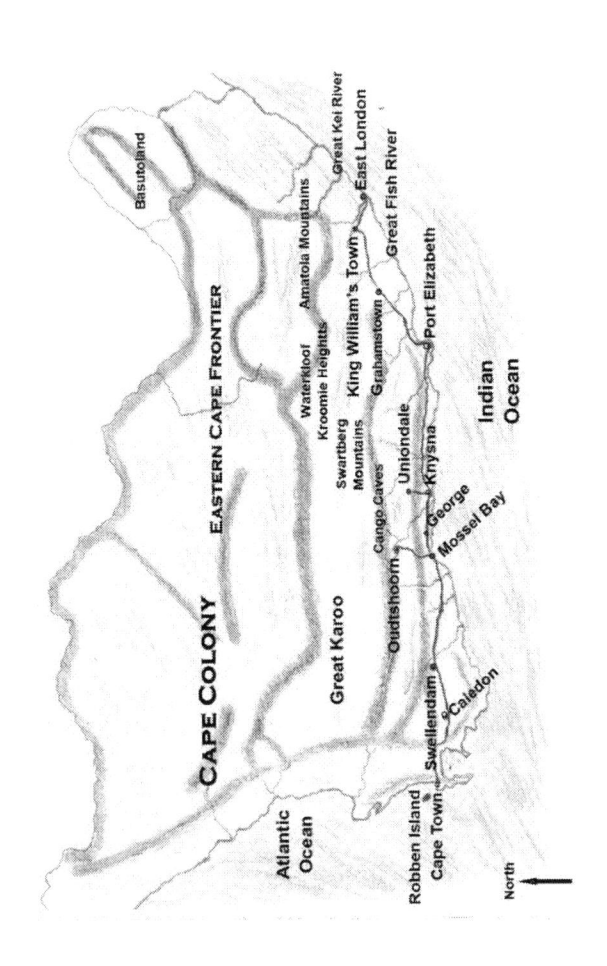

Cape Town, South peninsula: 19th Century

Chapter One

May 1855

Liverpool

Jamie Fyvie boarded the coach in Glasgow almost two days before, enthusiastic and eager to be travelling. Now arrived in Liverpool he climbed down from the mail coach and gratefully stretched his limbs.

He retrieved his luggage and managed to hail a hansom cab, instructing the driver to take him to the Royal Park Hotel on Admiral Street.

After the cab driver had helped Jamie to carry his meagre belongings into the hotel lobby, he approached the reception desk unsure of the procedure of signing for his room, as he had only ever done it once before at a lowly tavern in Glasgow.

That was where his journey had begun after he had decided to take up a Government offer of land and work in the Cape Colony on the southern tip of Africa.

The letter he received from a Mr Hugh Armstrong at the Government's Immigration Department was a bit strange, to say the least. It said he was booked in at the Royal Park under the name of Mr Trevor Black, and to register under that name. He would explain why when they met up.

The well-dressed young man behind the reception desk helped him sign in as Trevor Black and showed him to his room, placing Jamie's small, worn trunk and a large, equally worn valise on the floor, then handed him his key and a note.

'It's from a Mr Armstrong. He said to give it to you as soon as you arrived and to inform you that the room has been paid in advance,' the clerk said before departing.

The clerk made his way back to the foyer and approached a man sitting in a comfortable chair. He asked him if he wanted any refreshments.

'A pot of tea, please.'

'Right away, sir,' then, in a quieter tone, he added. 'The second one has arrived.'

The man nodded slightly. He was a well-dressed man with a woollen cap hanging on his knee.

Jamie opened the note and read:

Dear Mr Jamie Fyvie,

Go to a public house by the name of Rigby's, in Dale Street, and find a fellow passenger there by the name of Iain McColl. He is booked in at the hotel under the name of Steven Rattery. He has very light reddish hair and a ruddy complexion. He looks like he doesn't like anyone, but introduce yourself and I will be along later. Please keep all this confidential. All will be revealed when we meet.

Regards

Hugh Armstrong.

Jamie looked around the room, not really taking in the view as he glimpsed through the large sash window, wondering about the mysterious note and the intrigue that lay behind it.

Picking up his valise he walked across the paisley patterned carpet to the large brass bed, unpacked and arranged his clothes in the wardrobe and his few toiletries in the cabinet below a wash basin and water pitcher.

He looked at his reflection in the mirror hanging above and wondered again about the note and what he was getting into.

That was the most uncomfortable coach journey I have ever been on, he thought. *I was sure my kidneys were going to fall out through my arse the seat was so hard.*

After bathing and changing into fresh clothes Jamie left the hotel walking west on Admiral Street, on to Windsor Street, left into Upper Parliament and down to Strand Street, then turned west once more and headed up past the Salthouse Dock.

It was hard to believe he was actually on his way to Africa.

Liverpool was a very busy port city, built chiefly with huge profits made from the lucrative slave trade of the previous century.

That business was good was evident by the number of wagons, drays and hansom cabs traversing the streets, and the omnibuses ferrying people throughout the town. *I've never seen so many work horses in my life,* he thought watching with wonderment at the huge animals pulling vehicles around the streets. He glanced down at the roadway. *I've never seen so much horse shite either.*

Eventually he turned right into Water Street, which

became Dale, and on to his rendezvous.

Rigby's tavern frontage comprised two large bay windows, made up of small square panes of glass separated by a wide, heavy wooden door. The tavern was on the ground floor of one of a few imposing buildings on the street.

He pulled the door open and walked in through a cloud of tobacco smoke and made his way to the bar. The room was dimly lit with candles and oil lamps as the late afternoon daylight faded, but his eyes adjusted slowly as he approached the bar.

The walls and ceiling were stained a yellowish brown from years of the patron's smoking habits. Working men stood around murmuring, some in deep conversation, some sitting at tables laughing, one or two drowning their sorrows and some near the hearth of a warm coal fire in the centre of one of the walls. There was a pleasant, cosy feeling about the place.

He turned to the barman and ordered a pint of ale. Taking a couple of deep swallows of the beer to slake his thirst, he cast his eye around in search of his travelling companion.

As he was taller than the average Scotsman, he could easily look over the heads of the other patrons to survey the room.

Jamie had shoulder-length fair hair and stood at six foot four inches with square shoulders and a strong muscled body. A square jaw framed his long handsome face, and more than one lady had commented on his high cheek bones, kindly mouth and full lips. His hazel-green eyes scrutinised the pub's customers.

He looked toward the end of the bar and noticed a man with reddish-blond hair looking at him as if sizing him up.

Jamie lifted his tankard and wandered over to introduce himself.

'Excuse me, would you be Mr McColl?'

'I am Iain McColl, although I don't get called *Mister* McColl very often.'

Iain McColl's eyebrows and eye lashes were almost white-blond, creating an eye-catching contrast against the red of his hair, the reddish ruddy complexion on his round face and piercing blue eyes above a wide nose and thin mouth.

'You must be Jamie Fyvie,' said Iain, standing up almost as tall as Jamie and extending his right hand. 'How did you recognise me?'

Shaking hands Jamie said. 'Armstrong's note said to look for a red-faced grumpy-looking bastard.'

'Is that right? 'cause he left me a note saying, *look for a tall, simple looking bugger, looks like a lost fart in a storm,*' said Iain laughing.

The two men took an instant liking to each other.

'So are you staying at the Royal Park as well?' Iain said.

'Aye. It looks very comfortable and I've never seen such a large bed before, made of brass no less,' said Jamie. He leaned over to Iain to keep his voice down. 'The change of name is a bit strange though.'

'Aye, that is strange, but I'm assuming your letter says the same as mine, that Armstrong will reveal all at the meeting. After all, the hotel is a wee bit expensive for a couple of migrants, don't you think?

'That's just what I was thinking on my walk over here. I would like to know what's going on. Anyway, so where are you from?' inquired Jamie.

'I'm from a picturesque wee village called Clydebank, in Glasgow to be exact, and you?'

'Well away from the big city. New Lanark on the upper reaches of the Clyde River.'

'Aye, I've heard of it. Isn't there some kind of textile mill next to a village, with a school and doctors in attendance for the locals who work there?'

'You're well informed, Iain. Do you know what Hugh Armstrong looks like?' asked Jamie, looking around the bar. 'I was very young when I met him, I wouldn't recognise him. Have you ever met him?'

'I remember meeting him once, years ago. I don't think I would know him if he walked through the door right now,' Iain said thoughtfully.

'Don't ye think it's a bit strange that we've both met him but don't really know him and that he is helping us get away to South Africa?'

'Aye, it is strange, but we'll find out what's going on soon enough when we meet with him.'

'Can I get you another beer?'

Iain waved to the barman. 'I don't see why not, I'm not going anywhere soon.'

'Do you have any idea when we sail for Cape Town?'

'No idea.'

A loud voice behind Jamie shouted. 'Hey lads we've got a couple of sheep-shagging Jocks here.'

Jamie turned around.

'Come down to England to find some real women then?' The agitator said in a thick Liverpool accent to the laughter of his two friends and the interest of those within earshot.

'Aye,' said Iain as he stood up next to Jamie. 'We heard you boys couldn't satisfy the good ladies of

Liverpool so we came down here to show them how real men do it.'

The three troublemakers stopped laughing and the leader said. 'Oh yes?'

Jamie slapped his leg and shouted. 'That's just what your wife shouted when I was shaggin' her last night.'

'It must run in the family,' Iain taunted.

The whole pub went into an uproar, then the mayhem started.

The ring leader of the trio made a swing at Jamie who easily parried the blow and punched him in the solar plexus, dropping him where he stood. Iain did not wait for the other two trouble makers to take a punch at him, he hit the second one with a left jab swiftly followed with a straight right under his nose, as he was heading for the floorboards the third one tried to grab him around the head but Iain head-butted him with a Glasgow kiss bursting open his nose and he fell back with his hands now on his face.

The barman appeared with two other handy looking chaps.

'Right! Enough of that if you want to fight then take it outside.'

'They threw the first punch,' said Iain guiltily.

'I know. I saw and heard everything. That big one, the one that was mouthing off, I've seen him around. He runs with a bad bunch that work off and on the ships; they won't be coming back in here.'

After ejecting the trouble makers into the lane at the side of the pub, the barman went back to Jamie and Iain and pointed at a door behind the bar marked private. 'When you finish up your beer we'll go through there. Mr Armstrong is waiting for you.'

The boys looked at each other and Jamie said. 'Alright, but how do you know Armstrong?'

The barman winked. 'Hugh and I go back a long way.'

The boys followed him through the private door, which did not go unnoticed by a man sitting at a table on the other side of the pub. He was fairly well dressed with a woollen cap hanging on his knee.

'This way,' said the barman locking the door and leading the boys down a long corridor into a small office where a severe-looking woman was shuffling some papers.

'Rosemary will look after you from here, I'll be seeing you lads later.'

'Right. Thanks,' said Jamie looking at Iain with some confusion.

The lady introduced herself.

'I am Rosemary Porter, Mr Armstrong's assistant,' she said smiling.

'I'm Iain McColl and this is Jamie Fyvie,' Iain said, looking like he was going to bow.

'Yes, I have been expecting you both. Please come this way. Mr Armstrong is waiting for you.'

They went into a large warm room with well-worn leather chairs and a sofa to the left in front of a coal fire; a dining table straight ahead; and to the right, a writing desk in front of wall-to-wall overloaded book shelves. In the chair behind the desk sat Hugh Armstrong.

'Hello! I am glad to see you both made it here,' said Armstrong, coming around the desk and shaking hands.

He was of medium height with a slight paunch, his brown wispy hair sat atop a face old before its time, the bags under his eyes revealing more than a few sleepless nights. He wore a high-collared white shirt and black tie under a tweed jacket and waistcoat, with a gold watch chain across the pockets.

'Welcome, welcome. Sit yourself down.'

The boys sat in the chairs in front of the desk. Armstrong sat in his, lit his pipe and said. 'You are, by now, wondering what is going on and why I am being a bit evasive,' he said drawing on his pipe.

'We did wonder a bit, yes,' said Jamie.

'Well then, let us get straight to it as time is not on our side.

Armstrong blew out a plume of smoke and said. 'I work for the government and as far as anybody is concerned my job is to get immigrants to the colonies. The cover gives me the scope to travel without drawing attention to myself. I say *cover* because my real job is as head of a clandestine department, a secret service set up to protect Britain from foreign governments and other secret organisations who would steal our state secrets, sabotage us and try to bring down the country and the Empire. You need to be aware that my department is not governed by the normal legislation or laws of the land. We infiltrate companies, organisations and foreign countries, gather information and use it against our enemies. Sometimes we make people disappear, but we also help a lot of people and save British lives. Other Government departments are not sure of our existence yet, or that we are known — or not known — as the Secret Field Police.'

'So you have permission to kill people if you have to, without telling anybody?' said Jamie.

'Actually, yes,' said Armstrong, 'but I do have to answer to a superior.'

'So, you do have to answer to a higher authority?' asked Iain.

'I do. But now you are wondering why I am telling you all this and, believe me, there is so much more to tell but I cannot tell you anymore… unless of course you both agree join us.'

Jamie and Iain looked at each other.

'So that's why you changed our names at the hotel? To protect our real names and our identities?' said Jamie.

'That is correct. I want you two to join the service to work covertly and help us put the bad men in jail … or in the ground,' said Armstrong. 'Like I said, we are short on time for we need to implement certain operations. It is a bit of a surprise to you, I know, but think on it while I carry on. I have wanted to recruit the two of you since you became of age. Your fathers were loyal agents to the Secret Service and great friends to me, as were your mothers. They were all assassinated by the ELOS.'

'The ELOS?' asked Jamie.

'The ELOS is the name we have for a ruthless and very secretive organisation that likes to think it will enlighten the people of the world, please bear with me, I need to give you both some more information then I will tell you what ELOS stands for and what their agenda is. Fifteen years ago your fathers were working on an operation which was about to expose a spy ring and bring down a powerful aristocrat who is a highly placed elder within the ELOS in London. The spy ring was destroyed but unfortunately we still do not know who the aristocrat is. It was regrettable that your parents were all together when the assassins waylaid them and murdered them with a salvo of musket fire. After this happened I decided to have you both placed with your nearest kin in separate safe houses. For both your information I will give you a brief history of each other.

'You, Jamie were taken from Edinburgh to New Lanark to live with your Aunt who worked as a bookkeeper in the cotton mills, there, you went to school and were eventually apprenticed to the smithy. You worked with different metals, repairing wagons, machinery, and were taught to maintain the looms in the mill and how they worked.

'Iain, you were taken from Glasgow to live with your godfather and his wife in Dumbarton, where you had your schooling and were apprenticed to Denny's shipyard, where you worked with all types of wood, building boats and ships and also repairing wagons and the like.'

Jamie said. 'So one of us is a carpenter, the other a blacksmith, and we could join to form a company, which could build anything from a pitchfork to a wagon?'

'Precisely. The whole point of this was to eventually establish the two of you as businessmen when you were old enough, to have your own companies, or company as you have put it, to train and recruit you into the Secret Field Police; that is, if you want to do be recruited. You do have a choice. But the world has changed over the years, and the British Empire has expanded, especially into India and Africa. Do you remember the army sergeant who visited you two or three times a year and taught you how to box?' Asked Armstrong.

'Aye,' Jamie and Iain said together.

'He taught me to fight,' said Iain.

'He taught me to fight as well,' said Jamie. 'How do you know him?'

Armstrong smiled and looked at the boys.

'What! That was you?' said Jamie. 'You sent him to

teach me — us — to fight?'

'Aw, I don't believe it!' exclaimed Iain. 'How did you manage that?'

Armstrong threw up his arms, palms out in submission.

'Wait! Wait. Let me tell you the story. When you reached your teenage years I arranged for the sergeant to spend some time with each of you every now and again over the years, to train you to box, or *fight* as you call it. Apart from being in the army the sergeant was a bare-knuckle boxer but had to retire because of his health. The service recruited him for certain jobs, which you do not need to know about, and in between these jobs he trained recruits, you two included.'

'Well, he certainly showed me how to fight, and fight dirty as well,' said Iain. 'I remember him saying, *there's no such thing as a fair fight, Iain. Sometimes you have to fight dirty to win. Don't ever forget that lad.*'

'He was right about that,' Jamie agreed. 'I've been in a couple of scrapes where you use the first thing that comes to hand to hit your opponent.'

'So here you are,' said Armstrong. 'I visited you both only once in your early teenage years if you remember, and I have been watching over you ever since, not only because you are the sons of my friends but to offer you a future in the service of your country and keep it safe from very bad people who would see us fall. You need to decide if you want to do this and that is why I have brought you here. If you don't want to do this you can still go to the Cape Colony – god knows, they need good people out there – or go back to Scotland and carry on where you left off. I want you to join us and go to Cape Town. It's a simple yes or no.'

Iain looked at his new friend. 'What do you want tae do, Jamie? I think I would like to find out who the big man with the ELOS is. If he was responsible for my mother and father's death, I know where I want tae go and what I want tae do.'

'I've already made up my mind to go and settle in the Cape colony, Iain, and I would also like to find out who this ELOS aristocrat is as well. I've come this far, so I might as well keep going.'

'Aye, what would the English do without us? Might as well show them the way,' said Iain.

'It looks like you have two new recruits, Mr Armstrong,' said Jamie.

'I am so glad to hear you both say that. There is a lot to discuss and a lot of information we need to give you. Firstly, Rosemary will draw up your paperwork. Secondly, we will start your training, I say *we,* because I want Bradley Fairbrother to be here for this briefing as well, as he will be involved, not only in your physical training but also your mental alertness to the unseen problems that you may encounter along the way.'

Armstrong crossed the room, opened the door and gave an instruction to his secretary and within minutes Fairbrother knocked on the door and entered the room at Armstrong's command.

He was a stocky, thickset man with muscled sloping shoulders and a cannon-ball head covered with short-cropped, sandy-coloured hair. His bushy eyebrows and moustache were his prominent facial features.

'Bradley here is going to train you in firearms and knife fighting and maybe even a bit of fencing, although there's not much call for using swords any more. He's going to teach you how to be aware of your surroundings and how to interpret situations and look at people in a different light. Get comfortable everyone and pour yourselves a drink and a large sherry for me. I need to give you a lot of background as to what we are facing in the South of Africa,' said Armstrong.

Bradley and Jamie were sitting comfortably in soft leather chairs; Iain stretched out on the couch with a cigarette.

Armstrong propped his elbow on the corner of the huge fireplace, took a sip of his sherry and placed it on the mantelpiece. He lit his pipe and sucked it into life, then started his story.

'Because of recent events, which have just come to our attention, this operation now has two phases. The first phase is the most important as it involves the security and the well-being of this country and the Empire; it is about certain individuals both here and in the Cape Colony who have, and are still, infiltrating and undermining the British Government. The second and newest phase suddenly forced upon us is about a hidden treasure buried by the Knights Templar, but both phases involve the ELOS, the organisation I mentioned earlier.'

'What, where and who are the ELOS? How do you know of them?' asked Jamie.

'All in good time. First of all I need to start with the second phase of the operation which has just come to light. What I am about to tell you is a shortened account of a letter and journals pertaining to the Knights Templar, which were discovered hidden in a deceased freemason's house in Edinburgh.

'The order of the Knights Templar was a monastic warrior order whose sole mission in life was to protect Christians on their pilgrimage to the Holy Land, and to keep Muslims and Islam out of the Holy Land. They were a very rich organisation and had a powerful, financial hold on European countries, especially France. The Knights had been forewarned, through their network of agents, that King Philip IV of France was building a case of heresy against them, based on charges of colluding with Islamists, made by a disgruntled Knight expelled from the order some months before. The French King was insanely jealous of the Knights' great fortune and was deeply in debt to them because of his war with England. He saw this as a way of ridding himself of his debt and filling his coffers with the confiscated fortune of the order.

'The King put pressure on the Vatican to back him, with promises of a share of the orders' assets. You see, 400 years earlier, the then Pope, gave the Knights his blessing to pass freely throughout Europe and Christendom. After receiving this request from the French King, Pope Clement, who was a relative of Philip, was loathe to break tradition with the Knights, knowing the charges were blatantly false, but politically and financially he had no choice but to excommunicate them and order all Catholic countries to arrest and detain any and all Knights Templar. Being forewarned, the Knights moved all their assets from their headquarters in Paris down to the coastal town of La Rochelle, which was a Templar port on the west coast of France, where they anchored their fleet of ships. The bulk of the fleet sailed for the only country which would receive them – Scotland – simply because King Robert the Bruce had been excommunicated as well.

'But four ships of the Knights Templar broke away and sailed south, and that is what we are interested in, because history tells us the Knights disappeared into Scotland and later, parts of Europe and the Americas, but there is no mention of any Knights sailing southwards. Now keep in mind this was almost 500 years ago when those four ships sailed south, then eastwards past the great Rock of Gibraltar into the Mediterranean Sea, heading for the island of Cyprus to meet up with another two ships sailing from the island of Arwad, off the coast of Tortosa, which is now part of the Ottoman Empire. The crews of the six ships loaded the remainder of the assets and relics from their Mediterranean headquarters, securing them safely with the treasure already aboard the ships from France. The journal also indicates the preservation of clay jars containing scrolls found in the Holy Land sometime in the past.'

'If those scrolls and relics do exist and are uncovered, the historical implications could be exceptional,' said Jamie.

'Yes they could, Jamie. But, depending on their content, they could also be catastrophic,' said Armstrong. 'Carrying on, the six ships sailed south from Cyprus to Egypt, to the east of what is now Port Said, where wagons, camels and horses were waiting on the beach. The Knights' influence was extensive; they had helped many people in the Holy Land, some employed by the order. These friends and the crews, which included some of their finest warriors, took days to transfer the precious cargo and prepare the supplies and beasts for the trek south over the desert to the Red Sea to a small harbour just south of the town of Suez, where they were met by other brethren. The cargo and supplies were transferred to four large and one smaller dhow owned by the order, then under cover of darkness they set sail down the length of the Red Sea. Everything and everyone on board was appropriately covered with Islamic markings and disguised as Arabs. The supplies on board were sufficient enough for them not to have to stop until they were past the Gulf of Aden and into the Arabian Sea, where they anchored off the island of Suqatra to restock with provisions and water. From there they sailed south off the east coast of Africa to the Indian Ocean, where they were attacked by a fleet of small dhows from the slave market island of Zanzibar.

'The Knights and their ships were well armed and they fought off the pirates with the loss of one ship and a few of their warriors. They sailed on past the island of Madagascar off the port bow and then turned west along the southern coast of Africa, where they encountered very wild coastal weather. Battered and tattered they had to find a secure natural bay to make repairs and resupply with water and food. One of the captains' spotted a slight, vertical opening in the cliffs between two giant heads of rock. He glimpsed a lagoon on the other side of the natural entrance and with another storm looming he signalled to the other ships to follow him in between the jagged rocks and through the narrow channel into the lagoon.'

'So this lagoon, is it now part of the British Cape Colony?' asked Jamie.

'We think it must be Jamie, but from what I can ascertain this is, or will be, part of a bigger picture,' said Armstrong.

'I think we're all intrigued to hear the rest of the Knight's journal,' said Iain.

'Yes indeed. The captains and crews were old hands and they guided their vessels between the heads and through the channel into a huge, peaceful lagoon, or estuary, as it turned out to be. It was surrounded by lush foliage on high hills footed with sandy beaches along the shoreline. To the north-west a river ran into the lagoon, teeming with bird life such as ducks, egrets, water fowl, herons and fish eagles, along with numerous other varieties. The captains ordered the anchors down and along with their respective crews they stared in wonder at the magnificent panorama that surrounded them.'

'The attention to detail is quite remarkable,' said Fairbrother. 'One can build a picture in the imagination from the description you are giving us.'

'As I said at the beginning, this is the short version. The writer's attention to detail would take far too long to read out. However, let us continue. The Knights decided to stay in this protected paradise and over the years they built a small settlement on the eastern shore of the lagoon. They sent out scouts to find an appropriate place to conceal their treasures; a place not easily discovered even by chance. Such a place was found but the location is not mentioned in the journal. They had water, wild game, they planted a few crops and bartered with the indigenous Khoisan people, and over the following years they built wagons and nurtured growing herds of oxen there. And when the time and the season was right they loaded up their supplies, their tools, as well as the treasure with the relics, and cut a path inland. Then, they disappeared!'

'So that was the end of the journals?' said Iain.

'Basically, yes. The details in the notes become very vague, we think – in fact we know – some pages are missing. There is also a single mention of the safe-keeping of holy relics or scrolls and, as we know, the Knights are rumoured to be the guardians of the Ark of the Covenant and the Holy Grail, although there is not shred of evidence to support this, so the doyens think this is pertaining to the aforementioned scrolls.

'Now, obviously the Knights did not take any women with them as they were a celibate order, so over the years the men died off and, from what we can deduce from the journal, many of them died of disease and illnesses they picked up and succumbed to in the environment they had decided to settle in. Only three survivors made it back to Europe after many, many years, and eventually one surviving Knight made it to Scotland as a very old man.'

'And I presume there is nothing in the journals saying where he went to?' said Jamie.

'No. From what we can ascertain from the scraps of the journals, from the four remaining dhows the Knights built a smaller ship, which the survivors used to make their way back to civilisation, and we think many of them were left behind, probably too old to go on.

'On the long journey back they left clues at different locations to guide searchers to the next clue, and eventually, to the secret location of the so-called *treasure* and maybe holy relics. Or so the story goes.'

Jamie stood up to stretch his legs and asked. 'Where did the journals come from and how do you know they are from the Knights?'

'One of our men was murdered for these journals,' Armstrong said, shaking his head. 'He was a partner with a firm of solicitors in Edinburgh, and was working for us secretly because his firm was involved in many legal transactions with highly placed individuals in business and in Government. He informed us of the discovery of a note with a symbol and instructions with clues to an incredible treasure hidden in Southern Africa by the

Knights Templar. His firm was appointed as the executor of an estate of a deceased Freemason, and during the clearing of the house a young post-graduate student employed by the firm, described by our man as being very inquiring and nosey, took an old bible from a bookshelf and a note fell out of the book. Seeing the student start to read the note he went over and took it from him. After reading the note and realising its significance he discovered the bible was, in fact, a Freemason edition from the Grand Lodge of Scotland in Edinburgh, and immediately left the house to report to us.

'From what we can deduce, our man was followed by the student who later broke into his house to steal the documents and murdered him. We looked into the student's background and discovered he had been placed there by his master and controller who we knew as being a member of the ELOS. Now, unbeknown to the thief, our man had gone back to the deceased Freemason's house and made a thorough search which uncovered the journals describing the perilous journey the Knights had made so long ago. The thief was also not aware that he had painstakingly copied every word and symbol from the note and the journals.

'The student has subsequently disappeared without a trace, no doubt murdered by his own people, not just for botching the theft but for drawing attention to himself with the murder of a prominent solicitor.'

'So the ELOS have the note and the journals and would no doubt like to have their hands on the treasure, if it is there,' surmised Jamie. 'But what they don't know is that there is a copy in our possession and the very fact that they are willing to go to this much trouble and kill for it, has got the attention of the British Government.'

'Very good, Jamie. Can you imagine what the ELOS could do with a vast amount of wealth like that? It does not bear thinking about, but we have to keep ahead of the game and beat them to the prize.'

'How are the Freemasons involved and how did the deceased mason get the journals?' asked Iain.

'He must have inherited them. The Freemasons are a secretive organisation which rose from the ashes of the Knights Templar, supposedly. There is a degree in Freemasonry, which elevates a member to the status of a Knights Templar, but obviously it is symbolic only,' said Armstrong.

'Jesus, how many secret organisations are there?' said Iain.

'You would be surprised. Anyway, we needed to move fast,' Armstrong said worrying his pipe in his fingers. 'With the clue from the journals we despatched two men to find the next clue which was in a Templar grave on an island in the middle of Loch Awe in the west of Scotland. The two agents hired a boat from one of the locals and after much searching found the island with the grave, which had the corresponding symbol as that on the letter: a knight on a horse holding a shield with a cross on it. They opened the grave and found the next clue in a gold box and as instructed duplicated the script and symbol after which they returned everything as they had found it. When they returned to the mainland they were informed that there were other individuals looking to explore the small islands of the loch, so they settled down to wait, and sure enough, two individuals rowed a boat to the island and found the grave. When they came ashore our men followed them back to an address in Edinburgh, presumably to pass on the clue to their contact. We then followed them to London and to their controllers. This operation has given us extensive information on certain individuals within the ELOS who are being closely watched as we speak.'

Iain asked. 'So who are these people, who controls them and where are they based?'

Armstrong knocked the ash out of his pipe against the fireplace and proceeded to refill it with the shag from his tobacco pouch before answering.

'Nobody knows who they are or who has control and they have no base or headquarters. We only know of a small number of their lackeys, such as the men we followed from Scotland, who carry out their dirty work and who would rather die than give away any information.'

He lit his pipe and sat down in the chair next to the fire.

'What I am about to tell you does not leave this room and you will be hard pressed to take in and indeed believe it. A secretary working at the office of the Secretary of State for the colonies attracted our attention a while back. We put him under surveillance and discovered he was removing classified documents in a secret pocket sewn into the back of his jacket, taking them home, copying them, and then returning them the next day. We broke into his house and found a substantial amount of stationary, quills and inks, obviously for copying important documents. In his fireplace we found a partially burnt scrap of parchment, which said; *By order of the EnLightened OneS, the Elders of ELOS.* The mention of The Enlightened Ones worried us as that title had only been used in the past by an ancient order called the Illuminati. They had not been active for many years, which obviously made us wonder why they were using it. We detained the secretary and after days of interrogating him he seemed to go a bit mad, and said, *the old men of the Illuminati are done. We; the sons, have taken over and I, as you will eventually, will answer only to the Elders of the ELOS.* From what our interrogators squeezed from this individual, one of the old Illuminati family heads who wanted the order revived had passed on his secrets to his son, who in turn contacted the first-born of the other families who made up the elite of the order and with those who joined him created the ELOS, which is a short word for the **EnL**ightened **O**ne**S**.' Armstrong wrote it down highlighting the letters E–L–O–S.

'This organisation is directed by a handful of unknown people controlling governments and industries of Europe and America, most of whom are unaware they are being manipulated. These unknowns are beyond wealthy and well hidden in society. People such as Carnegie, Rothschild and the Kings and Queens of Europe do not even come close. The ELOS want power, they want Africa with its mineral wealth and, we believe eventually, world domination. They want to hold the power over everything and everybody.'

The astounded audience sat and looked at Armstrong, who was relighting his pipe and threw the taper in the fire as they absorbed the information just related to them.

Jamie and Iain looked at each other as if to silently say; *this is really, really hard to believe.*

Armstrong could see them trying to come to terms with the incredible information he had surprised them with.

'A few of us in the leadership of the Government's

secret committee have mulled over this information for a long time and through discreet investigation, sound logic and long debate have come to the conclusion that the ELOS are making a concerted effort to gain a foothold in Africa through the Cape Colony and because of their infiltration of both governments could take control of the army and the Royal Navy. The ELOS want the Templars' treasure in order to fund their subversion of Southern Africa.'

'If what you say is true,' said Jamie, 'how do you fight an unknown, unseen enemy with the considerable resources they command? I mean, they must have a network of spies from here to… well, from here to the ends of the earth.'

'And we don't know who they may be, where they are positioned and also, who do you trust?' said Iain sitting upright on the couch.

'You don't trust anybody. That's why I brought the two of you into the service. You are unknown and out of the mainstream. You have never been linked to any Government office, official or agent.

'Fairbrother here,' nodding at him, 'and I are the only people who know about you two and I answer only to the Prime Minister.'

Chapter Two

Kroomie Heights, Eastern Cape

'These mountains, these hills and valleys are our very existence. Here, the spirits of our ancestors are alive and among us,' said Samkelo, King of the Xhosa Nation, the paramount chief of the Xhosa and chief of the Gcaleka clan.

A round-shouldered, tall man with a rounded face, low forehead and heavily lidded eyes. He had a long flattened nose above a full-lipped mouth and, like all the Xhosa men, tight curly facial hair and a deep bronze, almost black, complexion.

He had inherited the chieftainship at an early age due to his father's murder by a British officer.

In the hut with him were the other chiefs and their respective pakati, the advisers to the chiefs of the tribes that made up the hierarchy of the Xhosa Nation.

They had avoided the army patrols and entered the Kroomie Heights secretly; the stronghold from where the war chief, Mzingisi and the Ngqika clan had been expelled by the British invaders years before, after the British had invaded the Cape Town settlement at the turn of the century and defeated the Dutch to take back the

Cape colony.

The Xhosa chiefs, each wearing a leopard skin kaross, the cloak symbolising the rank of a Xhosa clan chief, had gathered to devise a plan to rally the Xhosa people and rise up in an effort to fight, defeat and banish the white men from their great land forever.

Running on an axis from west to east the strategic fortress that was the Kroomie Heights rose up from the plains below to oddly shaped flat lands, above which a large plateau was accessible only through a narrow ridge, from where the land fell steeply away on both sides to magnificent gorges and valleys, locally known in Afrikaans as *kloofs*.

To the west of this ridge was the Waterkloof, carpeted with rich forests of assegai-wood, iron wood and yellow-wood trees, bounded by the plateau to the north and the Kroomie in the south. The western end of the Waterkloof opened into Bush Nek, which was in another kloof with a wagon road running north from the plains in the south.

From the east side of the ridge, was a continuation of Waterkloof, known as Fullers Hoek, which opened up into yet another kloof further east called the Blinkwater, that also ran north from the plain.

There on the steep slopes in the dense bush of Fuller's Hoek was Mzingisi's Den, the stronghold of the Ngqika tribe of the Xhosa people. They were back here in defiance of the Great Queen of the white invaders, and in defiance of the man who had robbed them of their freedom, their existence and their rich lands; the conqueror and Governor of Cape Town and Kaffraria — the respected but hated Sir Garry Smyth.

'We need guns and shot and powder,' said Mzingisi.

'Spears are useless against the guns of the white men. We are cut down like the meilies at harvest when we fight them. How can we get these guns when the English patrols are everywhere from Cape Town to the Amatola Mountains, and their great ships with guns that fire musket balls as big as my head sail along our shores?'

One of Samkelo's pakati, a man called Misumzi, asked for permission to speak.

Samkelo waived him forward. 'Speak Misumzi, what have you to say to this?'

Keeping a respectful profile he said. 'Just before I started my journey here to be part of this council, a man of mixed race was brought in to my kraal by my trusted warriors. He asked to talk to me of a matter of great importance and when asked to explain he said; *Only to Misumzi – tell him it concerns guns, many guns.*'

The gathering bristled at the mention of coloured folk.

'They are dogs without ancestors, not Xhosa nor Khoisan nor white men. They fight alongside our sworn enemy, the Mfengu levies, with the English,' said Samkelo, whose hatred for these peoples knew no limits. 'When we drive the white man from our land, the Kat River settlement of the coloureds will be burned to nothing, and all who live there will perish under our assegais: man, woman and child. Those people are born only because the white men have taken our women, Koisan and Malay women as well, to satisfy their lust. They are servants to the English, who care nothing for their offspring from any of these people. The Kat River settlement was created to protect them, but soon they will die or be servants in the Xhosa kraals, and along with the dung-eating Mfengu, they will be no more.'

Mzingisi said. My spies tell me the people of the Kat River settlement are in rebellion against the British and are deserting in great numbers, also the Hottentots of the Cape Mounted Rifles are deserting in great numbers as well. They want to join us in the fight against the British because, like us, the Xhosa, they have been unfairly treated by the English and want more freedom to buy and sell land and cattle as we do, we could use them to strengthen our fight with the white men.'

Mzingisi looked at Misumzi to continue.

'I met secretly with this coloured man, Williams,' said Misumzi suddenly full of importance. 'He is the boss boy at a great house in Cape Town belonging to an Englishman who speaks for a number of white men in the Cape Colony and in the land of the great white queen. They are also in alliance with the Boers to the north who want the English driven out of Africa. They will supply guns and powder to the Xhosa to help defeat the armies of the English.'

'How will these guns find their way to us?' Samkelo asked.

'He says they have people secretly placed here and in the great white queen's kraal far away in England that can make this happen,' Misumzi replied.

'Why would the white men trust this coloured with these secrets? I feel betrayal here,' said Mzingisi.

'He says they told him to tell me these things so that we would know they speak the truth.'

'At what price to the Xhosa?'

'They want the land to the west and south of the Great Fish River, including Cape Town, and free passage to the north in order to trade with the Free State of the Boer Government, as they want to negotiate a treaty with them. All the land to the east and north-east of the Great Fish River will belong to the Xhosa nations once more, all the way to Port Natal, which would be ours when the English are driven from there as well.'

Mzingisi, a powerful man, short in stature, was the war chief of the Xhosa, a tactician and an intelligent general, and a respected and energetic leader. He shook his head, looked around the gathering and said. 'The English will send more great ships and more armies with more guns, I have seen them do this many times. They will corrupt the people here with promises of new treaties, gold and land, as they have done in times gone by, and then take them away again as they have done to me and to all who have listened to their treacherous words and lies.'

Misumzi was a tribal seer and a trusted pakati to the chief, held in high regard within the clan and trusted by the people. He was always listening and definitely not trustworthy.

He was thinking about the money Williams had offered him to get the chiefs to take the offer of the guns, and that offer now seemed to be slipping away. He threw his arms open to the gathering around him and preached. 'You are the great chiefs of the Xhosa Nation and with these guns we can hunt down and kill our enemies. Our Sangomas will make a muti to protect us from the English guns.'

Samkelo raised his hands for quiet and said.

'Misumzi, you will tell the coloured we will think on the white man's offer but tell him this; if there is any treachery he will be the first to die a painful death.'

Misumzi retreated back in line with the pakati.

'What of the English armies?' Samkelo asked.

'Smyth and his soldiers are in King William's Town. They have sent out patrols to the Kroomie and Amatolas.' said Mzingisi. 'They are looking for us.'

Chapter Three

London

'We have been fighting these bloody savages for over fifty years,' fumed Earl Harold Greyson, the Secretary of State for War and the Colonies in Whitehall, London.

'Now we're fighting them again because of Smyth's egotistical arrogance; they have not forgotten how he humiliated not only the paramount chief, who was made to kiss Smyth's boot, but all the Xhosa chiefs and peoples,' he lamented to Edward Carrington, assistant to Greyson.

They were sitting on opposite sides of Greyson's large desk in his yellow-wood panelled office surrounded by volumes of books and documents on long floor-to-ceiling book shelves.

Carrington leaned across the desk. 'Surely, after all this time, the natives are not still holding a grudge toward Sir Garry?'

General, Sir Garry Smyth was, at that moment, the Governor of the Cape Colony.

Earl Greyson looked at Carrington sternly. 'These people never forget; they live by their myths and legends. It has been my experience that natives throughout the

Empire do not forget these histories nor the atrocities we commit. Whatever it takes we will end these wars once and for all. We will send more forces and destroy the Xhosa warriors, we will make treaties, if we then have to break these treaties then so be it. We will lay down our law, which will be enforced with violence if necessary after which we will cut off the heads of the snakes.'

'The snakes?' asked Carrington.

'The Xhosa tribes are the snakes and the chiefs, adorned with their fine leopard skins, are the heads of those snakes.'

'The Government will never allow you to carry out this kind of campaign. The public would be outraged, not to mention the opposition stirring up support to stop it.'

'Oh, but we are the Whigs in Government; the liberals; the democrats who want to be fair to everyone, including the natives in our colonies,' Greyson said sarcastically. 'We want to civilise these barbarians.' He shouted, slamming his hand on the desk.

Carrington jumped and looked at Greyson with a mixture of surprise and fear.

Greyson took deep breaths to calm himself, and said softly. 'Neither Government nor the public will know anything about it until it is too late. This Government simply cannot afford to carry on pouring money into the Cape Colony. It is going to need all its resources for the campaign in India. So these Kaffir wars must cease, quickly and finally, and the Xhosa must never be allowed to rise again.

'However, having said all that in support of the Government, when this war is won and the Xhosa natives are destroyed by the victorious British army, which will be led by one of our ELOS elders who have already infiltrated the cape government, Britain's focus will then be pointed at India, but our focus will stay in Africa. The ELOS will spearhead a long-term commitment to take over southern Africa, infiltrating and using the British infrastructure and war machine to annex the Boers in the Free State to the north of Cape Town, and the Republic of South Africa to the north-east. The Zulus in the south-east will fall under our guns soon enough, or should I say, the *British* army guns, although they might take a little more persuading. This will take careful planning and years to complete, but we, my friend, we will rise through the ranks of the brotherhood of the ELOS, and be remembered as the instigators of this bold mission.'

Greyson leaned forward and whispered in Carrington's ear. 'We will do this with the help of the *second* Government, which is us and we are, after all, the ELOS, are we not?'

Carrington winced. 'Have a care, sir; we should beware of eavesdroppers and prying eyes.'

'You worry too much, Edward. Come, pour us a glass of port and let us sit in more comfortable chairs, then we can discuss the field outing to Scotland.'

Crossing to the leather chairs on the other side of the room Greyson said. 'We have to move quickly. The Tories are sure to win the next election and our plans must be in place before then.'

'All these plans we have made will all be for naught once the Tories take power, how will we see it all through?'

'Edward, governments change but the ELOS remain in place, no matter who is in power. We, as the liberal Government, cry out for equality for all, especially in the colonies for the illiterate native, whilst behind the scenes we plan to absorb them into the Empire and destroy their culture. When the Tories win the election they will have to carry out what the previous administration has bequeathed them. It is simply brilliant. It is our secret society that makes the Government work: we are the power; we merely change our affiliation every few years.'

'Perhaps the news from Scotland will change our fortunes in Africa for the better,' said Carrington pouring the drinks.

'As you know I have been rather busy with affairs of state and I did order this mission to go ahead some time ago, so I need to catch up with what has happened,' Greyson said, 'give me the concise version of the events in Scotland, leading to where we are now. Are we to find out where the fabled Knights Templar treasure is hidden or is it all hearsay?'

Carrington placed his glass upon the rosewood table and gently cleared his throat.

'Well, it does appear that the Knights spirited away some of their wealth, so it just has to be found, if indeed, it has not been found and plundered already. Following the deciphered clue from a letter, stolen by one of our foolhardy subordinates, who is now deceased, our agents went to Loch Awe, close to the west coast and secured a small boat to row out to an overgrown island in the middle of the loch. There they found a number of graves of the Knights Templar which were hidden away so as not to be desecrated. The agents recognised the graves by the broad swords engraved clearly in the tops of the lids.'

'When did our agents return?' asked Greyson.

'They arrived back in London two days ago. It took them a considerable time to find not only that particular island, but also to find the grave with the correct symbol on it.'

'Which symbol would that be and how did they recognise it?'

'This particular seal was *Knight on the Horse,* which could have been St George: a single knight on a horse holding a shield with a cross on it.'

Carrington took a sip of port and continued.

'The agents broke into the grave and discovered a small gold box which they opened and inspected. They resealed the tomb and returned with the gold box to Edinburgh, where it was given to our agents from London, who, as I said, have just returned.'

Greyson got up from his chair and wandered over to the window. He stared out at the rain-swept London Street and thought, *yes, and I will be debating the contents of that box and the next step in the search for the Knight's treasure with the Elders of the ELOS very soon.*

He looked at Carrington. 'Do you believe there is any truth as to the existence of this treasure, Edward?'

'What I believe is of no consequence sir, the question is, do we pursue the clues?'

'How are we to believe this legend to be genuine?'

'Apparently, only one Knight from that journey made it back to civilisation, although a few did try to leave Africa together.'

'So how did the legend come to be known?' queried Greyson.

'It was quite by chance. A member of our order was working with a firm of solicitors involved in winding up an estate outside Edinburgh. He found a letter hidden in a masonic bible. When he began reading it a senior colleague, a solicitor, took it from him. The agent followed the solicitor to his home and decided to wait for a while then go back to break in to the house and steal the letter. Unfortunately he was discovered and in the ensuing scuffle the solicitor was killed, but the letter was recovered after a search. During that search, however, other documents were discovered detailing the journey to Africa and back to Europe by the surviving Knights and the sole survivor. Our agent then turned all the letters over to his elder.'

'What about the dead solicitor?'

'Well, you can imagine the furore surrounding his death and the investigation as to who killed him.'

'You mean to say our man did not try to conceal or get rid of the body?' asked Greyson incredulously.

'Suffice it to say our man will never be available to testify, the idiot. What the whole content of the documents is I do not know as they were sent to the senior Elders of the ELOS.'

'You have done well Edward, and I thank you for seeing this business through to this stage on my behalf. We must be vigilant and stay ahead of the game. As you know there is only one punishment for failure in our organisation as our man found out.'

'Indeed,' Edward Carrington said nervously.

Chapter Four

Cape Town

She was coming out of the drug enhanced trance and, although she was not immediately aware of the abuse being inflicted on her, she began to sense that maybe something was wrong. But her abuser, who was naked except for the belt around his waist, wasn't ready to let her back into the real world, not yet.

She had been fed the drug, or muti, as it is known in Africa, for days now, just enough to keep her in a trance-like state and talked into believing that all was well. He withdrew his engorged erection from her — the muti was good for physical as well as mental adaptations — and took himself in hand, using the other to extract the bottle containing the muti from a leather pouch tied to his belt. The muti was made with ingredients found only in the tropics of Africa.

He stopped massaging himself and ran his hand over the girl's lithe, brown-skinned body and squeezed her pert, firm breasts as she looked up in bewilderment. She was strong-willed this one; not like the others. He could see the realisation of what was happening beginning to dawn in her eyes. He ran his hand up to her chin and eased her mouth open, then poured two drops of the muti into her mouth.

She was forced to swallow the vile-tasting potion as he held her mouth closed. He replaced the bottle in the pouch and returned to her open legs, loosely secured by the ankles with leather straps, as were her wrists. The straps were attached to chains secured to iron rings embedded in the stone wall behind the padded table, conveniently built to the correct height for penetrating his victims.

At the opposite side of the room in the vast four-roomed cellar another young coloured girl was kneeling in front of a chair between the legs of a second abuser. The only reason she was still alive was because she knew how to pleasure him, bringing him to climax with her hands and her mouth just at the right time by listening to what was going on the other side of the room, never daring to look at the scene which was about to unfold behind her having been warned never to look, on pain of death.

She had knelt before him and performed oral sex on him on more than one occasion but he would tire of her eventually.

She must try and find a way out of the cellar soon, but it was hopeless, it was always locked and she was in her own cell when not cleaning up or satisfying her captor.

The abuser behind her pulled the semi-conscious girl to the edge of the table and pushed her legs back. He rammed his erection into her and she screamed in excruciating pain, the blood streaming out as he kept thrusting inside her.

'Scream, heathen, scream! Nobody can hear you

down here,' he shouted, enjoying every moment.

She was returning from the trance, the pain was bringing her out of it. She looked up to watch him unsheathe a huge, gleaming panga from his belt and raise it above and behind his head. She tried weakly to kick her legs but he held her as the restraints limited her movements.

As his orgasm started he slashed down with the panga, first into one breast and then the other, the razor-sharp blade slicing the flesh to the bone. The girls eyes widened and she screamed again even louder as he started hacking and hacking at her young flesh, the blood running in rivers while his orgasm continued. Suddenly she stopped screaming and convulsed. She died with her lips curled back and teeth bared, her eyes wide open.

Covered in blood and sweating with exertion, her attacker stopped his violent assault and stepped back, grunting and panting like a wild animal.

Behind him the other man was ending his own orgasm. He looked down to see the young girl's mouth and hands keeping busy. She kept her tongue moving all the time, her fingers massaging his genitals to keep the pleasure going for as long as possible. He had never experienced orgasms such as she gave him.

This man knew he could not do the killing himself but he could not resist the perverse pleasure it gave him to see it being done by someone else.

The killer's grunting had slowed to heavy breathing. He half-stepped forward and propped himself up with both arms over the mutilated body of the young girl.

When he eventually got his breathing under control, he started to undo the straps on the body.

'When we finish up here we need to talk upstairs

before you leave,' he said to the other man. 'The meeting with the Boer went well I am pleased to say. He said, dragging the body to the trapdoor in the floor at the far end of the cellar as he had done many times before. It was an iron door and could only be lifted by someone with strength.

He pulled back two bolts, swung the trapdoor up and back until it propped against the wall. Then he kicked the body over the edge into the black hole that fell away into a deep ravine from the underside of the house where the cellar was hidden.

The house was built with the indigenous rock found on the slopes under the flat mountain towering over the principal town of Queen Victoria's, African Cape Colony. Cape Town.

The bodies would never be found as the nocturnal creatures that prowled the mountain would eventually devour the remains.

'Yes, the meeting turned out better than planned,' the other man said as he placed his hand on the girl's head in front of him. She knew to wait with her head down, eyes closed, keeping her fear and terror under control until she heard the iron trapdoor slam shut and the killer leave.

Her master said. 'You can go now and make sure the rooms are cleaned properly.'

She fetched the buckets of water left inside the inner door and cleaned the blood from the table and the floor, washing it down towards the trapdoor, the filthy red fluid escaping through the drain holes in the corner of the floor where it met the wall.

When she finished up she went to her room in the cellar and washed herself down, dressed in a clean linen robe and closed the door. There was always a new, single candle beside fresh food and water placed there by her master before he left, locking her door and the inner and outer doors on his way out.

She settled on her makeshift bed and wondered about what the other man had said about a meeting with the Boers.

Her thoughts turned to the hopelessness of her plight. She wanted her family and her home, her own bed; she knew she was not going to see them again.

'The Boers have a gold mine,' James Storer declared to Nicholas Banbury.

'How can that be possible and how do you know this?' asked Banbury.

Both of these men held senior positions in the Cape Government and both were minor members of the ELOS.

Storer poured two glasses of red wine from the small Buitenverwachting wine estate in the Constantia area. He had washed the blood and sweat from his body and changed into a smart suit of clothes. His previous position had been Colonial Secretary for Van Diemen's Land, now officially Tasmania in Australia, but he had clashed with the governor there because had not agreed with Storer's brutal acts against the convicts under his control, which he had carried out under the guise of a staunch religious firebrand handing down the wrath of God. So he had been conveniently offered the post of Colonial Secretary of the Cape to begin the ELOS's conquest of Africa.

Storer was a handsome man with thick wavy black hair and an almost Latin look about his face, dark eyes and a roman nose. Tall and confident, he exuded the persona of a man in power.

He handed his companion a glass of wine without

even mentioning what had just happened in the cellar as though it was an everyday occurrence and said. 'I know this because our elder in the Boer elite has informed me.'

'So let me get this clear,' said Banbury. 'An adventurous Boer went prospecting and discovered a gold seam and our agent found out about it?'

'Not only did he find out about the mine he persuaded the Boer elite to let him invest in the venture and bring in another partner,' said Storer. 'He has also informed me that since he and his partners have taken over they have enslaved blacks to mine the gold; they are keeping it very hush-hush. It's a very small operation at the moment but they want to expand it.'

'Yes, but how can this be true James,' said Banbury. 'We would have known before this if they had found gold, you cannot keep something like that from getting out to the ears of the public.'

Banbury was the Colonial Administrator of the Cape and attached to Storer's office. Older than Storer, his slightly greying hair was cut short, he had washed and changed as well into a sensible suit of clothes which hung on slightly sloping shoulders and a substantial paunch. He had a pock marked face with a brown grey moustache under a large protruding nose, his eyebrows looked very similar to his moustache.

'Well, we have it on good authority from our elder, that this is the case, they will pay in gold to buy slaves to increase their production,' Storer replied. 'Not only that, they have struck a bargain with certain companies that control Mozambique, the Portuguese colony in East Africa, to supply ships to sail down to the Eastern Cape and pick up slaves and take them back through the port of Lorenço Marques. From there the Portuguese will take their share of the cargo, as slavery is still rife up there, and the Boers have a short journey to the Republic of South Africa.'

'Are you suggesting we start selling slaves?' Banbury said in disbelief, realising what Storer was indicating. 'You cannot be serious, James. We will never be able to get away with something like that even with the help of the ELOS.'

'The Boers want their slaves but they are not fools, Nicholas. They will not start warring with the local black tribes by trying to enslave them. They need the blacks to wet-nurse their children, look after their farms, clean their houses, and yes, they have their concubines as well. They are a hypocritical and detestable people,' he said with venom. He waved his hand in the air. 'So, they capture or purchase blacks from elsewhere and they are treated with contempt by the local blacks.'

'The Boers have never forgiven the British for outlawing slavery and they continue to use the kaffirs as their slaves to this day,' said Banbury.

James Storer turned to look through the large bay window overlooking Cape Town. 'There are plans afoot to further disrupt and infiltrate the Colonial Government here. We are set to bring in thousands of guns to arm the Xhosa tribes and incite them to drive the white men out of their land. We know the Government in London will send troops to bolster Smyth's army and eventually try to crush the Xhosa once and for all. But Smyth will not succeed; he's a spent force and has inferior officers. The elders in London will see to it that he does not receive the fighting force or the equipment he needs to defeat the Xhosa, then; when he fails, he will be replaced by one of us.'

'The fighting has already started. Smyth's armies are in the Kroomie Heights looking for Mzingisi, as we speak. The Government will have to send more troops,' said Banbury.

Storer turned and looked back to Banbury with a strange look in his eyes.

'There has been another development, which has emerged conveniently to help us rid this region of the Xhosa troublemakers. Before I left England to take up my post here I made the elders aware of an old acquaintance of mine, an American southerner who is in Britain trying to drum up support for the Confederates for their inevitable civil war with the Union. He is looking to bolster the Southern States slave population. We have, between us, devised a way to remove whatever is left of the Xhosa natives from the Cape after I have finished with them. You see, I have a plan which I will finalise with our masters when I go to London; a plan which will induce the Xhosa clans to self-destruct. We will use our position in the Government to bring about their destruction in the Eastern Cape and the survivors expulsion as slaves to the American south, and hopefully to the Boers in the north.' He went over to Banbury and gripped his shoulder. 'I am empowered to tell you our long-term plan because I will need your help. Because of our position in Local Government we are well placed to manipulate and influence certain orders going out from Cape Town and coming from London, which will be sent by the elders in the government there.'

'Such as? Let me guess,' Banbury interrupted as he stood up, the vision forming in his mind. 'We can manipulate the British army but crucially, the Royal Navy, to be elsewhere when the slave ships arrive to take their cargo.'

'Exactly,' Storer exclaimed. 'The correct procedure to replace a governor in the colonies is to seek permission by writing to the Crown, but that is not going to happen. The Colonial Secretary in Whitehall is, as you know, the elder, Earl Greyson. He will, without going through the usual procedure of asking the Crown's permission, send a letter of dismissal to the idiot Governor Smyth, who will be replaced by one of us, and the new governor will clean up the Xhosa tribes and chiefs. They will be hunted down, imprisoned or killed. By that time we will have infiltrated most offices of Government both here and in London. We will then implement the plan for total annihilation of the Xhosa culture, details of which you do not need to know at the moment. The British Empire will eventually annex the entire Cape region. Natal is already ours, taken from the ever retreating Boers. Basotholand to the east and Bechuanaland to the north, but more importantly, the Boers will be brought to heel in the Orange Free State and the Transvaal Republic of South Africa. After that… well, after that we carry on north through Africa.' He started to get even louder as he saw the vision in front of him.

'When do you leave for England?' Banbury inquired, bringing Storer back to reality.

'I have been summoned by our masters, Nicholas; that is, our Whitehall and our ELOS masters. So when I sail will depend on when I can secure a comfortable berth on a decent ship and on how far we get with our plans. I need to take them a report of our progress which will please them, especially, Earl Greyson.'

'Does that mean I will have to make arrangements for a further delivery before you go?' Banbury said, referring to their ghastly activities in the cellar.

'Yes. See if Williams can find us suitable candidates at short notice. The question is, can we still trust him to supply the girls?'

'Williams is in too deep to cross us now. He would hang if we were exposed. Besides, who would suspect two highly placed Government officials of even touching local girls?' said Banbury.

'You are aware, Nicholas, that our elders cannot be aware of our transgressions in the cellar. They would view it as putting our plans in jeopardy and would not condone it at all. Do you understand?'

'I understand, James; we have to look after our interests and each other. Yes?'

'Indeed. What of our new policing force? Are they getting nosey and asking questions about the missing girls?'

'Naturally, the locals are up in arms about the missing girls, but the police force is a ragged affair, made up mainly of raw recruits and Irish officers who have left their regiments and decided to settle here. Most are layabouts and drunkards and not too bothered about a few missing coloureds. Besides, they are too busy tracking down bandits who are rustling and stealing cattle and goats and whatever other animals, and getting their rewards from the farmers for recovering the stock. But there is one member of the force asking questions with a bit more enthusiasm than the rest,' Banbury said.

This got Storer's attention. 'Who? What's his name?'

'Sergeant Brian O'Donnell, but he won't worry us. If he gets too nosey he will simply be transferred to the Eastern Cape frontier.'

'Has Williams managed to contact the Xhosa and dangle the carrot?' Storer asked.

'He has, but nothing has been relayed back to us yet. He says they cannot refuse the offer of guns as their hatred of the English is so strong they will do anything to be rid of them.'

'I want a full report as soon as possible and I want Williams to ask his contact with the Xhosa what the feeling is about the white men – us – who are going to be left behind after the English are driven into the sea. And what kind of... I think the word *partnership* comes to mind... do they have in mind.

'But that's not going to happen, is it?' Banbury asked with a knowing look in his eye.

'Of course not, but we need to plant the seed of cooperation, to let them think that we will help them before they kill us all afterwards.'

'The stupid heathens won't know anything until it is too late.'

'No, Nicholas,' Storer said angrily. 'Do not underestimate the heathens. They are not stupid. They are a proud and noble people, just not as civilised as we are, but they are naive and desperate to move back to their homelands taken from them by the treacherous English, who have been making promises to them over the decades and never keeping them.'

Banbury bristled at the rebuke.

'At this stage we can only surmise who will be left standing in the event of an all-out war,' said Storer. 'The British Government will not let these natives take away their foothold in Southern Africa, no matter how much it costs, but the threat of the Xhosa must be eliminated so we can annex all the territories to the north and east.

Although, the inevitable war will cost a fortune, London will send troops in force and get it finished as quickly as possible, but the campaign will be led by one of our own elders whose identity will be disclosed to me when I arrive in London. When this is over the Xhosa Nation will be eradicated once and for all.'

Chapter Five

Kroomie Heights, Eastern Cape

The Xhosa war chief, Mzingisi, along with his two brothers, Sandla and Xolaxola watched the 600-strong British troops of the 74th Regiment followed by the survivors of lessor tribes which made up the Mfengu Levies, all led by Colonel William Forsyth, ascend the summit plain of the Kroomie Heights.

They walked in single file, hacking their way through the dense bush across the pass leading to the plateau and some trees, grateful to have some shade from the blazing sun.

When the troops emerged from the pass Forsyth ordered them to make camp and posted sentries to watch the dense forest which bordered this part of the plateau, spreading down into the Waterkloof to the west and into Fuller's Hoek to the east, where Mzingisi and his warriors were gathered.

Mzingisi did not want them to get settled on the plateau as they would then have the advantage of the tactical high ground to attack into the Ngqika clan stronghold after the sunset. He would position some of his warriors at the entrance to the pass by which the troops ascended, giving the appearance of cutting off their retreat.

'Sandla, take some warriors to the pass leading up to the plateau and be ready to attack, I'll join you shortly.'

'Is this wise my brother? The British are camping and cooking food. We could attack them now and chase them off the mountains.' said Sandla.

'Remember what was spoken about the guns. We need to be cunning until we decide on more guns. We would be cut down in great numbers,' said Mzingisi. 'I have a plan to lead them into a trap, so go toward the pass and let us find out what they do. We need to draw them into using the ammunition they have with them. If they do nothing, send some men to taunt them. I will send warriors on to the plateau and test their defences.'

In the British camp a young captain saw Xhosa warriors emerging from the bush near the entrance to the pass and called out. 'Colonel! Mzingisi's warriors are moving toward the pass leading to the plateau, sir.'

'Let them stay there. We need to rest the men. It's too hot by far. We will make an advance once the sun goes down,' said the Colonel.

From his position at the entrance to the pass, Sandla sent a few warriors to wander around the perimeter of the plateau. The soldiers ignored them, until Mzingisi signalled his warriors to stage a mock attack from the bush bordering Fuller's Hoek, running at full speed, some firing as they ran.

The soldiers, who were relaxing, dropped what they were doing and it was a mad scramble to retrieve their guns, but the captain quickly took control and formed a skirmish line with fixed bayonets, the Xhosa charge suddenly stopped. The Highland cry went up and the troops charged with fixed bayonets and drove them back, but only temporarily.

Colonel Forsyth immediately sent his small force of mounted troops to secure the entrance to the pass and ordered the main column to form a line up the left side of the plateau and curve around to the right as a defensive measure, but suddenly, hundreds of Xhosa warriors leapt out of the bush along the full length of the western border of Fuller's Hoek, screaming their war cry, and attacked the main column, again firing what guns they had but to no great effect. The Colonel also set up a skirmish line and the steady fire of the troops halted the advancing Xhosa. This went on for thirty or forty minutes and after a while the fighting became subdued.

Mzingisi could not understand why, after all the years of conflict in the Cape region, the British continued to fight in the bush with the heavy uniforms they wore, with bandoliers and objects hanging from belts and from their backs. And why did they wear those helmets as they tried to negotiate the dense bush?

He had witnessed their uniforms torn apart and their skin gouged deep into the flesh on the large acacia thorns, as they battled through thick webs of creepers and vines. The bush here was thick with undergrowth and enormous roots protruded from the ground and hidden crevasses. They were totally at the mercy of Xhosa warriors who could move through the bush with ease having no cumbersome garments to hamper them. This was their fighting ground.

Mzingisi could see that he needed to stir the blood of his warriors to regain the advantage. He called to his other brother. 'Xolaxola, send some warriors to fell some small trees across the path going down through the pass to the plain. Tell them they must keep silent and stay under cover of the bush.'

Xolaxola did as ordered, then returned to his brother's side for further orders. 'Sound the gong for our warriors to retreat, then go and bring the white man's clothes and my horse,' said Mzingisi.

Years ago, Mzingisi had understood the need for a bugle in the ranks of soldiers. During a raid on a splendid farmhouse, he had come across a dinner gong, which could be heard at a fairly long distance and now used it to recall his warriors. He had also taken some white men's clothing to wear and was about to put it to good use.

Xolaxola came back with the items as instructed and Mzingisi started to dress in the British clothing.

'But what are you doing my brother?' asked Xolaxola, bewildered.

'I need to show our warriors that I am fearless and that the British guns do not scare me into running from our land. I need to mock the enemy. Go to Sandla and tell him to ready his warriors to attack when the soldiers are caught going down through the pass.'

Xolaxola smiled and ran off.

Mzingisi mounted his horse and turned to his warriors. 'Today we fight for our freedom. Today we fight the British invaders to win back our land, these mountains. Fight bravely, my brothers.'

He rode his mount out of the cover of the bush and on to the plateau easily within range of the British muskets. He rode up and down the plateau urging all the warriors. 'Come to me my brothers, you are Xhosa. Come and I will lead you to drive the invaders down to the sea.'

As he rode backwards and forward, tens of hundreds of Xhosa warriors emerged from the forest and the dense bush. Mzingisi then dismounted and with his assegai in his hand he shouted.

'This is our hunting ground. Do not be afraid of the white man's guns. Together we will silence them,' Mzingisi continued his rallying cry.

In the British camp Captain King and Colonel Forsyth and indeed all the troops heard the eerie sound of the gong and watched as the Xhosa fighters melted back into the bush.

When the Xhosa chief rode out onto the plain they looked on with confusion at the black man, dressed in European clothing ranting away in the clicking tongue of the Xhosa language from the back of a horse. The confusion soon turned to concern when Xhosa warriors started appearing again from the bush and then the concern turned to fear when hundreds more surged forward behind Mzingisi, chanting as they ran on the spot.

'Sir, we cannot repel another attack. The skirmishes have depleted the ammunition stocks,' said the captain.

'I am aware of that Captain. That must be Mzingisi on that horse and he is rallying his men for another attack to take the pass.'

Forsyth now realised the reason for the Xhosa retreat. They had done their job well, baiting him into using up his ammunition, he had been cleverly outmanoeuvred by the wily old fox, Mzingisi. *There will be no victory here,* he thought. Indeed, he was in the most precarious position. 'Captain, order the bugler to call the troops to retire. We will have to get down through the pass to regroup on the plain below.'

Mzingisi heard the bugle and saw the soldiers retreat to the pass leading to the ridge and knew victory was within his grasp.

'They are running, they are defeated. Go after them!' he cried.

Anticipating the British retreat through the pass, Mzingisi moved his warriors further down in the forest and they began to fire into the retreating soldiers.

Meanwhile, Sandla and his hidden warriors emerged from where they had retreated to when the mounted troops appeared to guard the pass and attacked the unfortunate troops waiting to enter the pass.

The British troops were holding their own as they fought their way into the pass. They continued fighting on bravely until the soldiers in the lead halted as fallen trees barred the way. The soldiers coming behind them started to bunch up and stop, which immediately panicked the Mfengu levies bringing up the rear. The Mfengu did not want to be caught by Xhosa warriors: they were bitter enemies, and they would die a terrible death at their hands.

When Mzingisi saw the single column had halted he signalled his warriors to attack in greater numbers. The Mfengu saw them coming and in their terror, broke ranks and rushed down the path, scrambling over tree trunks, wailing like banshees and firing in all directions. They barged into the troops and crowded the skirmish lines whose constant gunfire was now unable to keep the Xhosa warriors at a distance.

The big, physically impressive, blood-streaked Xhosa warriors leapt through the musket smoke screeching like devils. Like demons from hell they fell on the soldiers, especially the Mfengu; blood lust taking over; all reason gone.

The fighting was now a free for all, hand to hand with bayonets and assegais from both sides stabbing and slashing. Men cried out in anger and pain as they ran, fought, ran again, wrestled and killed and maimed. The dead and dying from both sides were left behind as the desperate, heaving mass slipped and crawled on blood and entrails down the path on the ridge until, at long last, it opened up on to the plain, where the surviving soldiers retreated from the fighting to regroup and form up in their companies.

As instructed, the Xhosa warriors did not pursue them, Mzingisi knew if the British had any ammunition left they would decimate his warriors on the open ground. They melted back into the bush and through the pass to the forests of the Waterkloof and Fuller's Hoek, back to Mzingisi's den, the fortress of the Ngqika clan, elated with the joy of victory.

Colonel Forsyth was devastated. They had suffered many dead and many more wounded. To his captain he said. 'The British army has been defeated by loin-clothed natives with spears and shields.'

'They had guns, sir,' said the captain looking for an excuse.

'They had a few guns, Captain, and certainly not as many as we could shoulder. We will go back to King William's Town and report to the general that we need to return to the Kroomie Heights with a much larger force and show these bloody savages who are the masters.' Forsyth said bitterly. 'Tend to the wounded and let us go and report our shame.'

Mzingisi and Sandla were still delirious with victory as they watched the British army trudge away from the Kroomie Heights.

Mzingisi picked out one of his best runners. 'Go with the speed of the antelope to our great chief, Samkelo, and tell him what has happened here today. He must tell Misumzi to meet with the coloured, Williams, and tell the white traitors we will accept the offer of guns in exchange for their demands. After today the British will come back with vengeance in their hearts, with more men and more guns; they will seek revenge and hunt us down. We must be ready for them.'

Mzingisi looked on in disbelief at the retreating army. *Everything has changed. Maybe the white men are tired of fighting,* he thought. *No, the Xhosa warriors are stronger. We will arm ourselves and bring more warriors. We will kill the white men and take back our freedom.*

Chapter Six

July 1855

Cape Town

She heard the outer doors of the cellar being unlocked but did not think anything of it as this happened frequently. The door to her confinement would be unlocked and her food and water left outside the door.

Under strict instruction, she would wait for the sound of the outer door being locked, which was the signal for her to open her door and take her food and water into her cell. She would wash herself, change and place her soiled clothing and old plates outside her cell, then she would knock on the outer door, go back to her cell and close it.

This time, however, she could hear subdued voices and knew they had found another victim.

She pressed her ear to the space at the top of the door and heard the sounds of the body being arranged on *the death table*, as she had named it, and the sound of straps and shackles.

She knew instinctively that this was her last time before she died. She slid down the door, her hands on the floor on either side of her, panic taking over. *No, no, no!*

Stop! Keep your wits together! She told herself. She looked around yet again for some kind of weapon but there was none. Besides she could not stand against two grown men, one with a panga. They thought she had not seen it.

The voices grew slightly louder.

'I will be away for a few weeks,' she heard Storer say to Nicholas Banbury. 'Are you going to keep that girl in here for all that time?'

'I never actually thought about it until now. I suppose we will have to throw her to the lions tonight,' said Banbury. 'I will not be here while you are away.'

'That's the smart thing to do, Nicholas, so let's have our fun and then be done with her.'

Her door was unlocked and she walked past the disorientated girl lying on the table. She disrobed before kneeling in front of Banbury. He felt her breasts, squeezed and pulled her nipples then pushed his fingers into her sex. Whilst he was doing this she was masturbating him, getting him hard. He pulled her up and turned her around and she reached below to guide his erection into her. He gasped at the pleasure of it as she eased up and down, contracting her muscles to make it feel tighter.

She pushed herself down as far as she could so he could feel himself deep inside her. She had to keep him satisfied to stay alive. Then, she heard the door unlock, so she slipped off him and knelt between his legs, massaging his testicles and using her mouth on his hard shaft, while Storer started the abuse at the table.

She went through the whole scenario, the screaming, the hacking and her master came in her mouth, but this time he grabbed a handful of hair and held her head on him.

She heard the other man drag the body and push it into the hole in the floor but he did not close the trap door. That's when she knew her time was up. She heard the other man coming back, she let her master's penis fall from her mouth and she bit as hard as she could on his testicles. Banbury got such a shock he did not actually scream, but let out a stifled yelp.

'Are you not done yet?' asked Storer, mistaking Banbury's voice for the sound of pleasure.

Banbury let go of the girl's hair. She jumped up, ran around the corner and down the passage. She shoulder-charged Storer, who was walking back from the trapdoor, bowling him over off his feet, taken completely by surprise. She grabbed her clean change of clothes as she ran past her cell and jumped feet first straight through the trap door.

Storer got to his feet and shouted. 'Christ almighty! What–?'

He rushed back to the trapdoor and looked into the black void as though expecting the girl to be sitting there looking up. He ran back to Banbury whose face was white. He was clutching his testicles. 'She... bit... my... balls!' he said in a slightly high-pitched tone.

'I'll cut off your balls, you bloody idiot,' ranted Storer. 'She's jumped through the trapdoor into the ravine.'

'She won't survive a fall like that,' said Banbury, recovering his voice and looking down to see if he still retained his manhood.

'Get Williams and ride up the ravine as far you can then walk the rest of it and make sure she is dead, you bloody fool!' Storer was furious.

Chapter Seven

London

'The contents of the gold box have been scrutinised but the clue that was left in it does not tell us where to start in order to find the next clue,' said Earl Greyson nervously.

Earlier that evening Greyson's carriage had taken him north of London where, at a predetermined meeting point, he had transferred to a windowless carriage and driven for, he thought, about an hour and a half before it stopped. He had made this journey before, always to different locations; always fine houses or country mansions.

The carriage stopped adjacent to a wide doorway. He stepped out and a butler led him into the large library of a stately home. He never ever saw the route he travelled nor the outside of the property he visited. Nobody ever spoke to him except for the elder giving him instructions.

He was now seated behind a winged, high-backed leather armchair, plumes of cigar smoke rising into the air from his unseen host.

'History tells us,' the high Elder of the ELOS said from the chair, 'that the Knights Templar amassed large amounts of gold, coin, precious stones and historical artefacts. If there is such a treasure and it has not been plundered after all these years, the clues were never going to be easy.'

'The search, I believe, should start in the Cape Colony, elder, as the letters indicate that the Knights Templar settled for a considerable time somewhere on the Eastern Cape coast, between Cape Town and Port Natal. Since the clue is a riddle of sorts, I will, with your permission, send it to our elder in Cape Town, who would be in a better position to find the locations mentioned in the riddle and therefore lead us to the whereabouts of the Knights treasure. After over 400 years the clues could be more recognisable and easier to find,' said the Earl wondering if he was being too forward.

'You will not have to send the clue to Cape Town as the elder there is coming to England. You can deliver it in person along with the documents I am about to give you, but yes, I do agree with you; only a local person would have the knowledge to decipher the clue. It would be very beneficial for us to uncover a localised pot of gold.

'But this treasure hunt is secondary to our main objective, which is to exterminate the Xhosa threat, sell off the survivors to the slavers and mould the future of Africa as we see it. Have all the preparations for the removal of Colonel Smyth as Governor of the Cape been finalised?'

'They have sir. The latest despatch I received from Smyth was disappointing to say the least. He sent in a force of Highlanders 600-strong under the command of Colonel Forsyth to root out Mzingisi and his Ngqika tribe from the Kroomie Heights. They were defeated with thirteen dead and fourteen wounded. Mzingisi still has his den in Fuller's Hoek. I have convinced the cabinet that Smyth is a liability and must be replaced, although the Duke of Wellington was not convinced,' said Greyson.

'Well, that's no surprise as they are old comrades and good friends.'

'I anticipated the Duke's resistance and I asked him what he thought about Sir Gerald Cuthbert as a replacement for Smyth, and as Cuthbert had previously been an Aide de Camp to the Duke he reluctantly gave his backing for Cuthbert to be installed as the new Governor of the Cape.'

'Good. Cuthbert is one of the best people the ELOS have overseas and we will be in a position by that time to sanction any strategy he wishes to use. Cuthbert will be ruthless and he will, given time, put an end to the wars in the Eastern Cape,' said the unseen elder. 'After Cuthbert has cleared out the Ngqika strongholds and subdued the rest of the Xhosa clans, he will be replaced with another of our own, Sir George Whyte, Governor of New Zealand at the moment, who is being groomed for the sole purpose of governing the Cape Colony. Once he is installed, we will then execute our final plan to put down the Xhosa Nation for ever. Where is Smyth at the moment?'

'He is holed up in King William's Town directing the war against the Xhosa, especially against the Ngqika tribe in the Kroomie Range and the Amatola Mountains.'

'You will send a despatch to Governor Smyth, dismissing him from his post, and informing him that his successor, Sir Gerald Cuthbert, has been chosen and will be en-route shortly. Smyth will step down as soon as his replacement arrives,' said the elder. 'He will then do a formal handover with Cuthbert. Make sure you state your displeasure and exasperation at his feeble attempts to bring the natives to heel.'

'I will draw up the despatch when I return to Whitehall and start the procedure through the Crown for approval,' said Greyson.

'No, you will not send it to the Crown for approval. That will take far too long and it is guaranteed that there will be an objection. Do not concern yourself with the Crown procedure. It will be taken care of. The cabinet are already aware of the situation; you will send the dismissal directly to Smyth with the appropriate letterhead and seal. After all, you are the Under Secretary of State for the Colonies, are you not?'

'Yes, elder. I will see to all these matters and report to you with my progress,' said Greyson.

'Open the drawer in the table next to you. You will see sealed documents there, one addressed to you. Take them out.'

Greyson removed the documents from the drawer. 'I have them, elder.'

'As I said, I have sent for our elder in the Cape Colony, who you know to be fairly high up in government there, through our manipulation of course. His name is James Storer and he will be arriving in England in the next few weeks. You will see your instructions in the documents. Make sure he receives the documents personally.'

'They shall be delivered as ordered elder,' said Greyson.

'He will give you a report on the progress of our operation in the Cape Colony and the progress he has made with the Boers in the north. He will also give us the dates when he is to visit our American cousin in Liverpool, and the approximate date of when he plans to sail back to Cape Town. That meeting is crucial to our plans in Africa. You, in turn, will give him an up-to-date report that you are ready to execute our plans from this side. From there on you will liaise directly with Storer, keeping me informed until this phase has come to fruition. Is that clear?'

'Yes, elder, that is clear.'

'As you know, the Government's Secret Field Police Force is keeping a vigilant watch on any movement of ships and exports to South Africa. But we are also being vigilant in throwing them off the scent and feeding false information whenever we can, attempting to find out who is working for them and we may have obtained some good fortune.'

'And what good fortune would that be, sir?' asked Greyson as he watched cigar smoke waft up to the ornate ceiling.

'We have discovered an individual, a retired drill sergeant, who has been seen entering and leaving the back entrance of a Government building. We believe he has been travelling up and down the country to different locations, in order to train operatives within this Secret Service, but our man who is following him reports that he always disappears when he gets to his destination, and then we pick him up in London again. This fellow's name is Bradley Fairbrother. He has been followed to Liverpool, where he has, we think, been meeting with Hugh Armstrong, the head of the Secret Field Police, and two other unknown individuals who we have yet to identify. We have tracked them to a location in Dale Street, a public house, the name of which is in your documents. We are reasonably sure this is a front for the Secret Service. The two unknowns are probably recruits.

They are staying in a hotel on Admiral Street. Keep them under discreet surveillance then hire some locals to disable them, or make it look like a mugging gone wrong and kill them. Our intelligence says there is a lot of activity in Liverpool and it is too much of a coincidence that it is happening at the same time as the meeting with the American. You will be the liaison with Storer in Liverpool until he sails for Cape Town. Keep me informed of any incidents, even the slightest detail that arises.'

'As soon as he contacts me I will deliver his report immediately, elder,' said Greyson.

'The success of this venture rests squarely on the shoulders of two individuals: you and James Storer. Timing is crucial for our vision to succeed. If it fails the consequences would be grave indeed. That will be all.'

'Yes, elder. I will be in touch through the usual line of communication,' said Earl Greyson, very aware of the veiled threat.

Chapter Eight

Liverpool

Iain poured himself another whisky from Armstrong's drinks cabinet. 'Anybody else like one?' he asked? Nobody did. 'So now is the time you tell us what we are going to be doing, and then we start school.'

'That's right,' confirmed Armstrong. 'But first we will take a look at the clue and the sketch of a ceremonial seal that was left in Scotland. Our best academics have looked at it and they think after almost 480 years the clues will be weathered, or overgrown or, perhaps, easier to discover. So it would be best to start in Africa, presuming there is any treasure there, of course.'

Armstrong spread the clue on the table.

It read;

As the south-east wind howls o'er the Bay of Whales,
The tables' cloth is lost in the gale.
The southern crags hold the Elephant's Eye,
Where the mountain echoes the eagle's cry.
Find the seal the lamb is there,
To take ye on to who knows where.
The morning sun will light the eye,

There to see the way or die.
Find the way for the powers that be,
Lest you lose the heart in thee.

'Jesus, that's a bit scary, don't you think?' said Iain.

'The words in the clue and, as you can see, the hastily drawn sketch of a ceremonial lamb, were copied from the original to help you to discover the next step, if there is one. All of this has yet to be proved, so I suggest that when you arrive in Cape Town, get to know the locals and you can start asking discreet questions about the metaphors in the clue. You may be searching for something resembling the lamb or the inscription on the Knights seal. Who knows? But for now, let us concentrate on what we have to do here first. You will start your training, and once we think you are ready, your first directive – or should I say secret operation – will be right here in Liverpool.'

The following weeks were gruelling to say the least. The boys left the hotel every morning as though going to work and were picked up by a hansom cab at different locations by waving down the same cab in the employ of Armstrong, which took them to a large house in a private estate on the outskirts of Liverpool.

They were drilled physically and mentally by Fairbrother, on disciplines such as loading, firing and reloading a new percussion cap gun, after which they were taken into the arsenal to choose their weapons. Jamie chose two over and under percussion pistols with hammers on both sides of the barrels. Iain picked out a blunderbuss rifle and an identical blunderbuss pistol a quarter of the size of its big brother, both with barrels made of a brass alloy that would not rust. They came with appropriately sized bayonets. They were taught to ride a horse and handle horses and wagons. Although they had done this before, they were now shown how to do it better.

The sergeant who had taught them to fight all those years ago even made an entrance to brush up on their fighting skills.

'Oh, this is murder,' complained Jamie.

'I know what ye mean. I feel like somebody's been whacking me with the flat end of a shovel. My whole body is aching.'

Armstrong would arrive at the training site or the classroom every now and then to check on their progress and at the beginning of the fifth week he invited Jamie and Iain for dinner in his rooms behind Rigby's.

After dinner they retired to the lounge area for drinks and Armstrong said, 'You are almost ready for your first assignment lads. I want to show you something.'

They went over to his desk and looked at an architect's plan of a large mansion located in a wealthy suburb, most of which, like Liverpool, had been built with the illicit proceeds of slavery.

'This mansion belongs to one Chester Karl Primeaux, a very wealthy land owner from America, the Southern States.'

Jamie said. 'From what I gather from the newspapers there is a bitter argument brewing between the north and the south in America about the abolition of slavery in the south. Is he a southern sympathiser?'

'That he is, Jamie. He says he is here to raise money for the Confederate cause but he is actually here to buy guns, and…' He paused for effect by pointing his index finger in the air, 'he is also trying to buy slaves. We have first-hand knowledge that he is talking with certain individuals who are known to be running slave ships from the east coast of Africa; more specifically, from the island of Zanzibar. He wants slaves to bolster the Southern States' productivity, slavery was never abolished there, which is why the Americans may be heading for civil war. I don't know if you know this, but Liverpool was more or less built on slave trade money and is still very much connected to slavery.'

'But slavery has been banned for years now,' said Iain.

'What do you think, Iain? The slavers were just going to say that's fine we'll find other cargo to move? Certainly not. This is huge money for these criminals. All they are doing now is making more money to pay informants and bribes.'

'But surely the navy has had a hand in curtailing the activities of these slavers, sir?'

'For every ship they rescue ten get away. It will never stop. These poor African wretches are condemned for ever to be subjected to this despicable trade in human suffering.'

They sat and reflected for a few moments and then Armstrong said. 'Anyhow, you two will break into his house and find any correspondence or evidence that he may have, to find out who he is talking to in order to transport the slaves and, more to the point; when they are to be moved, where he is buying them and who is selling.'

'So how do we plan this?' Iain asked.

'According to information we have received, within the next few weeks Primeaux is having a party which will start with luncheon and carry on into the night. That is when you will break in, when it is dark and everybody is full of drink and trying to grope somebody's wife or husband, or trying to get themselves groped. These fundraising parties are for invited, wealthy guests only and they are all in the same clique. Anything goes when it comes to changing partners and they are well guarded by Primeaux's henchmen who, by the way, are ruthless.'

'Is he part of the ELOS at all?' asked Jamie.

'No, we don't think he is, but we think he is being manipulated by a certain individual by the name of James Storer who is the Colonial Secretary in the government of the Cape Colony. We know he has, in the past, met secretly with Primeaux. We also know that Storer is a low-ranking elder in the ELOS, and like Primeaux, he has a preference for abusing young girls; the younger the better.'

'But why would or how could James Storer sell this American, slaves from Africa? He is a Government official in South Africa, well away from the slave trading from the east of Africa,' said Iain.

'Iain, the ELOS will have infiltrated the Boers in the Orange Free State, north of the Cape and especially in the Republic of South Africa. They still have slaves there despite the ban and their slaves are bought from the traders in the east. Storer, we think, is a go-between with a Dutchman whose family is connected to the ELOS in Holland, but as far the slaves are concerned we don't know when and where this will happen. You two need to find this information,' said Armstrong.

Armstrong could see the boys' confusion and said. 'I can see you need to ask me questions. Ask me or tell me what you think and I'll answer you as best as I can, or tell you I like how you are thinking… or not.'

Jamie spoke first. 'I can see that the slave trade has

to be dealt with and that the treasure, if there is one, cannot be allowed to fall into the wrong hands but I am not sure where we come in,' pointing at Iain and back at himself.

'The ELOS has infiltrated the British Government at all levels. We don't know the extent of this or how high it goes, and this applies to all Her Majesty's colonies as well. It is our job to weed them out and deal with them.' Armstrong sat in his chair and relit his pipe. 'This will be an ongoing fight; we catch or kill an ELOS operative; they recruit another two. Part of your cover in the Cape will be to get yourself known in the social gatherings of Cape Town. There will be parties for the wealthy elite, formal balls and banquets for which you will have invitations, I will see to it that you have the wealth to qualify for these invitations. There is also a clique of people in Cape Town, whose identities are closely guarded and they, like their counterparts in England, also hold private parties where anything goes. James Storer, we believe, is the leader and organiser of this clique in the Cape. One of you fine young gentlemen has to penetrate this happy band, find the enemy and use them or destroy them.'

'Use them as in find any signed letters or information and use them to blackmail them for names, places and dates?' said Iain.

'Torture is allowed as long as you don't get caught. Make no mistake; these people will have no compunction about torturing or killing you when it comes to protecting their objectives. For them failure is a death sentence, so do not think for one minute they will hesitate, because they have everything to lose.'

'If you look at it like that, then you are of course right

in what you say,' said Jamie.

Armstrong again relit his pipe and said. 'You ask where you come in, well that is simple; you need to stop the ELOS arming the Xhosa tribes. Thousands of guns of all shapes and sizes are being produced for, perhaps, an impending American civil war and we have to keep up supply to our own armies across the world. A large quantity of these guns has been diverted and we think they are to be shipped to Southern Africa to instigate a war.'

'Guns for slaves?' said Jamie.

'Right! It's cheaper and faster to take slaves from South-West Africa to the east coast of America than from the east coast of Africa,' said Iain.

'Exactly, but how they are going to achieve this we do not know, and as time is against us we need to act sooner rather than later,' said Armstrong. 'You two can have a day off tomorrow: we will meet in due course for a briefing on the operation. You might want to see if you can find alternative accommodation to move into after the raid; somewhere as close to the docks as possible. Remember to keep a low profile and try not to get into trouble, please.'

'Don't worry, sir, we will be good boys,' Iain said, winking at Jamie.

The boys slept late the next day and after a huge breakfast of fried bacon, eggs and sausage washed down with mugs of strong tea they decided to go and look at Liverpool and have a few ales along the way.

'That hotel needs to get tattie scones and black pudding,' muttered Iain.

'Maybe the cook's too lazy to make them, besides I

could not eat another thing, I'm full,' said Jamie.

In the late afternoon, after visiting one or two public houses along the way, they came across a wee place close to the docks called Monaghan's Tavern, which had an adjoining boarding house and run by Molly Monaghan and her family.

'This could be a good place to stay over before we set sail,' said Jamie sipping his ale.

'You may be right. We'll mention it to Armstrong,' said Iain eying up the barmaids.

Just then somebody sat down at the upright piano on a raised platform at the side of the pub. He was joined by fiddler and guitar player and the party began, dancing and singing like there was no tomorrow.

Later on the two barmaids joined in and it was evident they were from the same family as Molly. They were fresh-faced, green eyed young Irish lasses looking to enjoy themselves with two dashing young men.

The four young people danced and laughed under the watchful eye of a smiling Molly.

Also watching them was a fairly well-dressed man sitting at a table sipping a beer, a woollen cap hanging on his knee.

Jamie and Iain decided not to be too late.

They were standing outside the tavern saying goodnight to the young ladies and one of them said in her fine Irish brogue. 'My name is Maggie, by the way and that is my cousin Marie, are we going to be seeing you boys again or is this just a short visit?'

Jamie glanced over at Iain and he said. 'We came here to find work and we have, so we'll be staying around,' he lied easily.

The two couples kissed goodnight and Jamie and Iain walked off.

It was cold and a light drizzle of rain started to fall. The boys huddled in their overcoats as they made their way back to the hotel.

'Well that was a damn good night, wasn't it?' remarked Jamie.

'Aye, we are definitely going back for more of that before we sail but we need to be careful Jamie. No loose tongues.'

They turned into Windsor Street which became Admiral. The rain was pelting down now, the wind blowing squalls up the street.

'Christ, what a night! I'll be glad to get to my bed,' said Iain loudly over the noise of the rain.

But Jamie was peering into gloom ahead of them and could have sworn he saw a head disappear back into an alleyway. It was late and the streets were deserted because of the weather.

Jamie put his hand on Iain's arm and leaned into his ear, 'I saw someone ducking into the lane up ahead.'

Iain immediately looked around and could see two figures walking up behind them.

'Trouble!' he shouted over the noise.

They kept walking and started to cross the street when another two figures emerged from the alleyway ahead on the left, carrying pick-axe handles. The boys stopped and looked for a way out but there was none and no open doorways.

'Aw shite!' said Iain. 'They picked the right spot for an ambush,' said Jamie. 'The two at the back look to be carrying coshes. Let's go for them first and then take our chances with the pick-axe handles.'

They turned and ran straight at the two thugs at the rear who stopped in confusion. They were supposed to be attacking them, not the other way around. The boys were armed with dirks, Scottish stabbing daggers, at the ready in their hands as they closed in on the thugs.

'You can run or fall where ye stand, ye pair of bastards,' shouted Jamie over the noise of the weather.

The villains lunged in swinging wildly, one caught Iain above the right elbow as he tried to deflect the cosh. The blow caused him to drop his knife so he punched his attacker with a left to the jaw. The villain staggered slightly and slipped on the wet surface giving Iain a chance to scoop up his knife as the cosh came down towards his head. He blocked the blow with his left forearm and grabbed the sleeve of the jacket and pulled the villain toward him.

Suddenly, there was a sound of a gunshot.

In the split second Iain had his opponent's arm straight out he stabbed the knife up to the hilt into the villain's armpit, then let go of the sleeve and pushed him away pulling the blade out as he fell away.

'Jamie!' he shouted turning around.

Jamie was standing over the other villain whose blood was being washed away by the rain. Jamie had rushed at him and stabbed his attacker in the groin.

Another shot rang out.

The boys ran to the side of the street and, flattened against the wall of a shop, they tried to see who was shooting and at whom. They moved slowly down the street, leaving the villains at the rear to their fate. As they drew parallel with the lane on the opposite side of the street they could see two bodies lying in the gutter, the pick-axe handles beside them.

Cautiously they approached the bodies looking around the street and buildings.

Jamie checked the bodies.

'They're dead, Iain; one shot each in the head.'

Iain tried to see down the lane but it was impossible. The rain was getting heavier.

'I can't see anybody. Christ! I cannot see a thing. Who are these people?'

'I recognise these two. Remember that punch-up in Rigby's the first time I met you?'

'Aye.'

'They're the ones you floored. Maybe the other one is back there.'

Jamie looked back at the other two bodies back down the street and could see a lantern swinging back and forth in the gloom and then he heard the piercing shrill of a police whistle.

'Iain, we have to get away from here.'

'Aye, right now. We don't need the police.'

'The hotel is just along the road but we should go down the lane. We need to get into the hotel without being seen.'

They found the rear entrance of the hotel and sneaked in through the staff entrance at the back and up the stairs without any trouble.

Jamie stripped of his clothes and dried himself, then went to Iain's room.

Iain was a bit pale when he opened the door. Jamie pushed past him. 'Jesus, Iain. I think we just killed two men and caused another two to die and we did it without even thinking, without any compunction at all. Is that what we are now? Killers with no remorse?'

'They came at us, Jamie, and I don't feel sorry.'

'Aye, I suppose that's true. But I just wonder if it will get any easier in the future, after the deed is done.'

At the north end of the lane four streets away a man with two spent percussion pistols in his coat pockets was walking into the shadows; a fairly well-dressed man wearing a sodden woollen cap.

'Are you sure you weren't seen going into the hotel?' asked Armstrong for the third time.

'Definitely not. We have our keys with us all the time anyway so we don't have to go to the reception. We slipped in through the back and up to our rooms. There was no one around,' Jamie reassured him.

'And you did not see anyone loitering in the immediate area.'

'With all due respect, sir, but how many different ways would you like me to give you the same answer? The rain was so heavy you couldn't see a bloody thing, which was probably a good thing for us.'

'Yes, yes, you are right, of course. We cannot afford to have this operation compromised. The police are knocking on doors along the street and they will be asking at the hotel if anyone came in at that time.'

It was late morning and they were sitting around Armstrong's desk in his rooms behind Rigby's bar.

Armstrong said. 'The other worry is who shot those two thugs and why did they help you. I mean this is a serious business if they can just shoot people out of hand like that.'

'What happened to the other two?' Iain asked.

'One bled to death, the other is comatose and in a serious condition in hospital,' said Armstrong.

'Which means if he wakes up he can tell the police

who stabbed him.'

'That is not your worry. He won't be talking to anyone.'

Jamie and Iain glanced at each other.

'I will contact my sources on the street to try and find out who our mystery executioner friend was.'

'I think we've found suitable lodgings that would suit us,' Jamie said. 'We were at a place called Monaghan's last night and we got friendly with the owner. They have a boarding house next to the pub, but the good thing is it's a local and full of Irishmen, so any strangers would be scrutinised immediately and it is close to the docks.'

'Yes, I think that would work. I know of Molly's place; in fact it's perfect because I plan to have you both on a ship bound for Cape Town as quickly as possible after you break into Primeaux's study.'

'Why the hurry to leave?' asked Jamie.

'After you raid Primeaux's mansion; make no mistake, they will be hunting for you,' Armstrong said. 'You will stay here the night before the operation with your dark clothes and tool satchels. You will change your clothes in the carriage taking you to your drop-off point. I will be in London for a while but I will be back here when you carry out the operation; you know the drill; be careful; use whatever force you need to and once you are finished, split up and head for the rendezvous. Good luck.' Armstrong turned and left the room without another word.

Chapter Nine

Cape Town

I would rather fall to my death than be chopped up by that mad white man, she thought as she grabbed the linen nightshirt and jumped through the trapdoor. It was dark and she was terrified as she plummeted through the air, but then suddenly it was daylight. The sun had not gone down yet. Within the few seconds of jumping, her feet and bottom hit the angled rock face below the house and she tried to keep her balance as she slid on the wet moss covering parts of the rock.

She looked down and could see thicker bushes below her and spread her arms to slow her fall, which it did to a degree. Parts of the rock face which were bare of moss stripped the skin from parts of her feet and buttocks. Her arms were lashed by small branches as she tried to keep them horizontal to her body to slow the speed at which she was falling. She fell into a thicker bush which almost stopped her fall. The pain on crashing through the branches was unbearable. She tried to grab hold of one but could not, then she fell into a void and landed hard on something fairly soft but her head bounced off something harder and she lost the light into the darkness.

She was definitely blinking her eyes but she could not see. She was surely dead and in hell, as the missionaries had promised for being a bad girl. Then she felt pain as the rest of her body started to wake up. She opened her eyes again and tried to turn her head. Looking up she could see stars and the partial moon when the clouds went past. As she tried to move the moon came out from behind a cloud and she looked into someone else's face, the lips curled back, teeth bared, lifeless eyes staring back at her.

She screamed and scrabbled backwards, her brain and her body shocked into moving away from this horrendous apparition. Turning to find a way out of this hell, she screamed again when she saw a ghostly figure, with its arms outstretched to wrap her into its deadly embrace. She lashed out to ward off the demon but it fell down on her. She was still screaming as she tried to fight it off, grabbing and scratching and kicking, when she realised there was nothing to fight but a piece of cloth. It was her nightshirt, which had somehow found its way down and caught on the bush above her.

She was panting and crying; she looked around, trying to make sense of what was happening. When she eventually regained her wits she could see in the flashes of moonlight that she was in a ravine. The house was nowhere to be seen above her but she could see a mountain looming above.

Then she remembered the eyes looking at her.

'Where am I?' she said to herself.

She put on the nightshirt to cover her nakedness, the feeling of the garment around her immediately making her feel better and more confident. She stared into the darkness waiting for the moon to shine and when it did, she could see what must be the body of the young girl who had been thrown through the trapdoor before she jumped. She had landed on top of her, which had saved her life.

She could see bones scattered all over this part of the ravine. There was water running through it; a stream no wider than an arm's length. Under a bush growing over the stream, the water trickled through the eyes and mouth of a dull white skull staring out with sightless eyes, then faded back into the darkness when clouds obscured the moonlight.

She started crying and speaking in Afrikaans she said to the dead girl. 'Jy het my lewe gered, ek is so jammer dat ek nie kon red joune. As ek leef ek belowe om terug te kom en jy gaan haal en vir jou 'n Christelike begrafnis'. *You saved my life. I am so sorry I could not save yours. If I live, I promise to come back and fetch you and give you a Christian burial.*

Somehow she knew leopards and wild dogs roamed these mountains. She had to get out of the ravine. She went to the stream and scooped up the cold water to her face with her right hand as her left arm was so painful she could hardly move it.

She felt her arm and winced when she touched the elbow. *It must be broken,* she thought.

She drank some of the brackish brown water then went back to the body to cover it with rocks but stopped, *they're bound to come looking for me,* she thought *any rocks I cover this poor girl with will surely be removed for the animals to devour the body; they would know with certainty I was still alive.*

Her whole body was so sore, her head hurt so badly she could barely think and she could not move her arm now because of the pain but she had to go on.

'Ek is so jammer' – *I am so sorry* – she said to the body. 'Ek weet jy sal verstaan dat ek het te verlaat voordat hulle hier kom. Vergewe my asseblief. Mag God met julle wees, en jy vind vrede met jou siel.' *I know you will understand that I have to leave before they come here. Please forgive me. May God be with you and you find peace with your soul.*

She walked along the side of the stream but was finding it difficult to see in the dark. It was painful going trying to negotiate around shrubs and small trees and the odd large rock, then suddenly she realised the stream was running louder than before. Stopping, she waited for the moon to appear again and saw the stream diverted by a huge boulder and then disappear. At this point the stream was deeper and much wider, the rushing water stronger. She gingerly walked along the bank and looked past the boulder and saw the stream cascading down a short, steep gradient, had she not stopped she would surely have fallen down the slope.

In the flashes of moonlight she could not see any safe way down but then saw that the water had thinned out over a wider area with rock fragments protruding above the water giving her a stairway down. Holding on to a small branch she slid on her bottom to step on the nearest rock, the rushing water pulling at her flimsy clothing, then using her good arm she managed descend the slope until the stream narrowed, the water rushing stronger the further down she went; she had no choice but to keep going.

She stepped onto a small rock and tried to stay there, she couldn't see what was further down the slope; hanging on she hoped the moonlight would appear again but her foot slipped and she slid the last few feet, thankfully there were no obstructions and she plunged into a small pool. Exhausted, sore and cold she managed to drag herself from the water on to her feet and continued to follow the stream.

I am so sore and tired, she thought and started to weep, *I fear I will die on this mountain… no; I will not; I will find a way to survive and tell the people about those cruel men.* Wiping away her tears she continued walking, trying to stay strong.

Closing her eyes she stopped, knowing she had to rest, she thought she was far enough away from the where she had fallen and decided to wait until dawn. She climbed in behind a bush and lay down to sleep.

Chapter Ten

Kroomie Heights, Eastern Cape

'We will give the heathens a surprise tonight, Mitchell,' said Sommerville. 'Especially after that fool Forsyth's disastrous campaign.'

General Sommerville was with Colonel John Mitchell's division of the 2nd Queen's Regiment and the 91st on the high plateau, whilst Colonel Forsyth was at the foot of the Kroomie Range with the 74th Highlanders, ready to march up to the ridge where he had been defeated not so long ago.

That evening it began to rain heavily and the soldiers shivered under their blankets, tents and other essential equipment had, somehow, not arrived from England. Up on the plateau it was colder and even more miserable.

At midnight both divisions were on the march to join up at the agreed location. The rain had stopped but a heavy mist was rolling over the ground creating an eerie feeling among the sodden soldiers. The going was tough as the wet ground was slippery and turning to mud. The mist made it difficult to make good time.

As dawn began to break, Mitchell's division approached the head of the Waterkloof Valley. Vision was limited. Nothing stirred. The silence was unnatural. Uncertainty and trepidation began to set in.

Mzingisi had been watching Mitchell's division since they had arrived at the plateau and had followed them to the Waterkloof. Earlier, he had seen Forsyth and his troops marching on the plain below and then rushed back up over the ridge and through the pass to the edge of Fuller's Hoek and joined up with Sandla. He was ready to do battle.

'Sandla, the mist has been sent by the spirits of our ancestors to cover us in battle. Are the dogs you brought from the camp in position at the edge of the forest?'

'They are there with the women as you ordered my brother,' replied Sandla.

'Take some of your warriors and let the soldiers see you as spirits running in the mist and tell the women to kick the dogs to get them barking and howling.'

'Brother, we can get close to them in this mist and take them by surprise. My spear wants the taste of the enemy blood. We can cut them down instead of this shooting and running. We are warriors, not cowards in the mist.'

'Have you not heard anything I have taught you? That is what the British want us to do. They are trained to form a line and they fire their guns at the same time. Even in the mist we will be the ones to be cut down. Go. Do as I ask until the sun tries to break through the mist, and then return.'

'Colonel Mitchell!' shouted Sommerville.

'Sir!'

'Order the men to stop here for now, set up skirmish lines. The enemy will know we are here so be on the alert.

Forsyth should be coming up through the ridge in the next hour or so. Tell the men to be aware of this because of the mist and not to open fire on them.'

'Very good, sir,' said Mitchell marching off and barking orders.

The troops could see figures darting around in the swirling mist. The howling of the dogs began to unsettle them. One or two shots were fired in fright and sergeants shouted for them to hold fire.

Mzingisi could hear the dogs and the odd bit of gunfire. He waited until Sandla returned and said. 'Take all your warriors out of the forest to the other side of the plateau and start firing towards the Waterkloof. Make sure they lie in the grass because the British will fire back.'

Mzingisi was aware of the other force coming up from the Kroomie, but they had not appeared yet. He sent some men to find out where they were and decided to wait a while longer.

Meanwhile Colonel Forsyth and his soldiers marched up on to the Kroomie and as he neared the ridge he halted his men. 'Captain, order the men stop here and to be on guard. We will wait to see if this mist clears before we go across the ridge.'

'Begging the Colonel's pardon, sir, but the General will be waiting for us to join up with him,' said the captain.

'I am aware of that, Captain, but in this mist, Colonel Mitchell's men could open fire, mistaking us for the enemy. We will wait.'

'Yes, sir,' *you week-kneed arse.*

Mzingisi's warriors reported back that the force from the south was still on the other side of the ridge. He acted at once.

Mzingisi ordered his warriors to run on to the plateau and open fire.

Hundreds of warriors poured from the bush on the edge of Fullers Hoek, Sandla from the north side and Mzingisi's men from the south; some of the warriors with their new guns with plenty of shot and powder.

The British skirmish lines fired into the mist with nothing to aim at. The Ngqika warriors rushed in and fired randomly in the direction of the skirmish lines and then fell back, both sides taking light casualties.

'Colonel Mitchell, is there any sign of Forsyth yet?' asked Sommerville.

'No, sir! Not yet.'

'Damn the man! Colonel, tell the bugler to sound a recall for Colonel Forsyth and be sure to pass the word to the troops that any signals from the bugler are to be ignored until further orders,'

Colonel Mitchell passed his order to his lieutenant. After a few minutes the lieutenant returned with the bugler in tow.

'Colonel, sir. The bugler, does not know any of the calls for the 74th Highlanders.'

Mitchell looked at the bugler. 'Private, blow the calls of the 2nd Queens. We need to signal Colonel Forsyth to cross the ridge and engage the enemy with us.'

The bugler went off and started with recall and waited for a response, but heard nothing. This went on for some time, playing different calls and eventually reporting that he did not have anything left to use.

Mzingisi heard the bugle sound more than once, which was unusual, and wondered what the British were doing. The only reason for this, he realised, was to signal the other division below to advance up through the ridge and join the battle.

'Xolaxola, the soldiers on the Kroomie will be crossing the ridge soon, take your warriors and lie in wait for them to march over the ridge. Like the time before they will be forced to walk in a line. Wait until they spread out and then fire on them. The mist will cover you, but stay under the cover of the forest.'

Xolaxola ran off, eager to be part of another great victory over the white men.

Mzingisi then poured more warriors into the melee shouting, 'My brothers, with me. Kill the white men who steal our lands.'

The mist was lifting and the enemy were attacking in force, Sommerville was now exasperated with Forsyth's lack of commitment. 'Colonel, send a detachment from the 91st Regiment and what is left of the Cape Mounted Rifles over the ridge and find the 74th and lead them back up here at the double before we are overrun.'

The 91st and the Cape Rifles rode for the entrance to the ridge and found it unguarded and the path clear. As they emerged on the south side to meet up with Forsyth, Xolaxola and his warriors infiltrated the bush along the ridge and waited for the troops to start their ascent over the ridge, unaware that Forsyth's force had been strengthened.

The lieutenant with the 91st ordered his bugler to blow a warning as he led the detachment into Forsyth's camp and gave the Colonel his orders from General Sommerville.

'The general's forces are under heavy fire, sir. He needs you and your men to join up with them as soon as possible.'

'Is the ridge clear to go through, lieutenant?' asked Forsyth.

'It is, sir, but I am sure we were seen coming down here. The General said to tell you that your division has to leave *right now* and join up with him on the plateau,' said the lieutenant getting irritated.

'Watch your tone of voice, lieutenant,' said Forsyth turning to his officer. 'Captain! Get the men ready to move. Lead on.' He said to the officer of the 91st.

Halfway up the ridge Xolaxola watched with alarm at the re-enforced column snaking over the ridge and signalled his men to open fire.

The troops were ready for them and fired volley after volley into the bush. The mounted troops crashed into the edge of the bush firing as they went ahead of the column.

There was some heavy skirmishing with Xolaxola's force as they advanced across the ridge but as the main Ngqika force was fighting with Mzingisi on the plateau plain Xolaxola's warriors were soon driven back and forced to re-join Mzingizi; Forsyth's division eventually joined up with Sommerville.

The mist was almost gone and Mzingisi cursed at seeing Forsyth's column emerge from the pass. He ordered his men to fall back into the bush at the edge of Fuller's Hoek.

Mzingisi called for his two brothers. 'Sandla, take all your warriors and watch over the pass to the ridge. Xolaxola, you take your warriors to the edge of Fuller's Hoek and be ready to fight at a moment's notice. The white General will send troops into the forest to clear us away from the edge of the valleys.'

'How do you know this, my brother?' asked Sandla.'

'I know this because after all the years of fighting

them, the British never change their tactics. Now go and wait for my signal,' said Mzingisi.

General Sommerville signalled the ceasefire when the enemy melted back to the forest. 'Colonel Mitchell, sound the recall back up to the north side of the plateau. Set up camp and regroup.'

'Yes, sir.'

'And, Colonel, tell Forsyth to see me in my tent when we make camp.'

'Yes, sir,' said Mitchell.

As the British columns marched off to set up camp hundreds of Xhosa warriors suddenly appeared from the forest and attacked the rear of the column.

'Colonel Mitchell, order the Cape Mounted Rifles Cavalry to take up position and charge that attack.'

'Sir, the Cape Rifles do not have sabres. They were relieved of them when they started deserting.'

'Then tell them to go in shooting and ride over them, use their guns as clubs. We just need some time to disengage and get to the plain to the north of the plateau,' said Sommerville.

Mzingisi saw the mounted charge without sabres. The Hottentot riders fired as they rode into the Ngqika warriors and scattered them, both sides taking one or two casualties but enabling the troops to retire and regroup. Once the columns were away the cavalry retreated and brought up the rear.

The camp was established and skirmish lines deployed to watch for any attacks. Fires were lit and food was cooked and the troops relaxed.

Forsyth went to report to General Sommerville.

'What the devil were you doing sitting down there? Were you waiting for a nice sunny day?' said

Sommerville angrily.

'Sir, because of the mist, I did not want to approach your position and start firing at each other,' stuttered Forsyth.'

'My god, man! You have a bugler, you have a voice. We could have been overrun by these bloody savages if I had not sent word for you to join up with us. Be aware, sir, your actions will be reported and you may face disciplinary charges.'

'I understand, sir,' said Forsyth looking at the ground.

Sommerville went to the entrance of the tent and pushed back the flap. 'Colonel Mitchell, would you join us.'

The General sat in his fold-up stool and spread a map of the Kroomie Range on his small table.

'From tomorrow, we will start sweeping the valleys and the kloofs in Fuller's Hoek and the Waterkloof, until we force the enemy away from the area. Then we will execute a concerted attack on both valleys and weed them out. Is there anything you would like to add, Colonel Mitchell?'

Mitchell placed his finger on the map and said. 'Well, General, this area here, which the men have named Mount Misery, borders the Waterkoof and Fuller's Hoek: the ridge is U-shaped, I would suggest we leave a force to hold Mount Misery.'

Sommerville looked at the map and nodded. 'Yes, I see what you mean. Colonel Forsyth, you will hold Mount Misery with the Highlanders to cover the columns going down into the Waterkloof to the west and Fuller's Hoek to the east, which will be led by me and Colonel Mitchell, respectively.'

'Yes, sir,' confirmed Forsyth. It had not gone unnoticed that he had not been asked for his input.

For the next few days the soldiers hacked their way around the forests bordering the plain. Their uniforms became tattered and torn from the dense bush and acacia thorns, the humid hot weather during the day taking its toll on the health of every one of them, whilst the Xhosa warriors slipped through the jungle of vegetation taking pot-shots, and avoiding the noisy, plodding soldiers with ease.

At night it was cold and rain would fall, occasionally turning to sleet. The men started to get sick with dysentery and fever and, eventually, Sommerville made the decision to attack in force.

'Gentlemen, these heathens will neither come out and fight nor surrender, so we will attack and secure the ridge. Then, as planned, we will send a column into each of the valleys with the Highlanders covering us. Order the men to pack up and start moving.'

Mzingisi's spies alerted him to the movement of the soldiers and he watched from Fuller's Hoek. He knew the familiar pattern of the troops. He sent word to Sandla and Xolaxola to have weapons loaded and ready the warriors for the forthcoming battle.

The columns marched down the plateau toward the ridge, the Highlanders out in front. Colonel Forsyth was leading them. He split his column in two to form a pincer movement coming into the entrance of the ridge, with the Cape Mounted Rifles riding through the centre, firing as they rode. There was light resistance from Xolaxola's warriors as the main bulk of the Ngqika were in Fuller's Hoek.

Once the ridge was secured Sommerville directed his

two columns into the Waterkloof and Fuller's Hoek, with the Highlanders covering them and holding Mount Misery.

Mzingisi watched all this unfold and worried that he would not hold his stronghold. Then he saw hundreds of Hottentot warriors appear, all with guns. These were the rebels of the Kat River settlement and were all fine shots. Their leader popped up and greeted him then dispersed his men along the edge of the forest.

At Mzingisi's order the Xhosa and the Hottentot warriors fired upon the British with devastating effect, the weary troops desperately trying to form skirmish lines to ward off the barrage.

Colonel Forsyth was trying to signal some of his men into a better position but they could not see him. *I have to hold this position or my career is over. The shame would never be forgotten,* he thought. 'Captain, can you signal the left flank to circle around to cover the north side of Fuller's Hoek?'

'I tried, sir, but they can't see me.'

'Damn!' shouted Forsyth and he ran out from cover across the plain, bullets flying in all directions waving his cap to attract his men's attention.

'Colonel, come back, sir!' shouted the captain.

Mzingisi saw Forsyth run from cover and recognised him. He ran to one of the Hottentot marksmen and said. 'You see the British officer waving his arm?'

The marksman nodded.

'Shoot him! Kill him in front of my warriors.'

The Hottentot rebel took aim and fired. The bullet hit Forsyth square in the chest and he fell.

The Highlanders saw him fall and under heavy fire they ran as one to him. The captain and a sergeant pulled him back to the skirmish line but the men kept running toward the enemy lines. They were being cut down rapidly, as they charged onwards; an officer fell, shot through head; then another was killed with a shot to the heart. The Xhosa and Hottentot warriors kept up the barrage, and finally, the Highlanders broke and retreated, losing more men and another officer as they turned to go back.

Sommerville's two columns had taken heavy casualties as well and the General ordered the retreat.

Mzingisi watched them retreat back to the camp further north and signalled his men to stand down. It had been many days since the British had arrived to drive them from their home. They had lost many men in this fight and many would never fight again, their wounds were so horrific. They collected the dead for burial and carried the wounded to Mzingisi's den.

That night as the rain poured down and, unlike the British Army, the Ngqika clan slept warmly in their huts exhausted after days of fighting, but the next day the sun was shining, the fires were lit and oxen were slaughtered. Traditional sorghum beer flowed to reassure their ancestors of participating in the celebrations. The Xhosa people considered their ancestors to be their guardians and the bringers of good fortune, who brought prosperity to the people and helped them celebrate the victory over the British.

'My brothers, the Dutch and then the British invaded our land, yet this is our land. They come and drive us off to place their own white people on our land and then they kill us when we fight to take it back,' said Mzingisi passionately. 'We have proved that we can fight them and defeat them, my brothers. We will never be driven from our homes again.'

The British troops had regrouped back at the camp on the north side of the plateau. The general ordered the skirmish lines out and he sat down heavily at his desk in his tent. He sat there until night fell, listening to the cries of the wounded and the death coughs from the hospital tent.

That night a thunderstorm swept the land, lightning flashing over their miserable camp. The troops huddled under their blankets, cold and wet, and prayed to be gone from this place of death.

The next day the dead were buried and General Sommerville marched his troops away from the Kroomie Heights, dejected, demoralised and exhausted. The loin-clothed heathens had inflicted yet another defeat on the British army.

From where did the chiefs get enough money to buy so much firepower? Sommerville wondered to himself.

He was glad to be away from Mount Misery.

Chapter Eleven

King William's Town, Eastern Cape

The Governor of the Cape Colony Sir Garry Smyth was an old campaigner for the British Empire. He had been fighting the Xhosa for more years than he cared to remember, especially his old nemesis, Mzingisi, the war chief of the Ngqika tribe. He had banished Mzingisi from the Kroomie Heights and the Amatola Mountains years before.

But Mzingisi was still alive and back in his den.

Sir Garry had been trapped in King William's Town as marauders and bandits roamed the countryside at will. All able-bodied men were with Sommerville in the Amatolas. He was desperately short of men and fire power, having lost as many as 1,800 deserters and the levies, whose period of served time was up. They would not re-enlist, as they believed his treatment of the Xhosa had started this war, so now it was Smyth's war.

The biggest blow was the Cape Mounted Rifles rebelling against him. Most of the nimble footed Hottentots had gone; only a few remained with the unit. Sommerville's destruction of the Kat River settlement and the burning of homes and schools had turned the

Hottentots against them for good. They had been hunted and killed, deserters court-martialled and given death sentences, which had been commuted by Sir Garry to life sentences, but for these people that was worse than the death sentence.

The whole situation was out of control.

Smyth watched with dismay as General Sommerville and his defeated army returned to King William's Town and thought, *Sommerville had sent the inexperienced Colonel Forsyth to flush out Mzingisi and had failed miserably. And so they went back with two divisions and it was a bigger disaster than the first campaign with huge losses. This time Colonel Forsyth did not come back and the white mans' superior thinking on bush warfare was proved to be seriously inferior to the native way of thinking.*

Smyth was reading the *Eastern Province News* when Sommerville knocked on the door and entered the small office.

'The newspaper says; *'Mzingisi remains proud master of the field, he has out-generalled, General Sommerville, cut down his divisions' soldiers and shows something approaching contempt for the rest.'*

Smyth slammed the newspaper down on his desk. 'I have to send this report to Earl Greyson in Whitehall. What do you think his response will be, General?'

'Governor Smyth, first of all let me tell you that the firepower of the enemy was quite substantial. Where are they getting the guns from? They seem to have a never-ending supply of guns, ammunition and powder. If we can stop the supply of guns then this war will be considerably shorter. Also, the conditions were atrocious up there, sir,' Sommerville said defensively. 'First there was rain, which turned everything underfoot to mud. Then there was so much mist we could not see a blessed thing. We did not receive the equipment from England I requested before we left; we had no tents or tarpaulins, and so when the hail came down, followed by the cold sleet, the moral and the health of the men was sapped trying to chase the kaffirs. They are like ghosts, the way they move through the bush. They will not stand and fight and they will not surrender. They ambush us and disappear back into the bush. We will need more men and heavy artillery to flush them out.'

'I, in the past, have cleared out Mzingisi and his tribe from that bush so do not tell me it cannot be done, general. I need to send some good news to Earl Greyson or my head is on the block,' said Smyth pausing for a moment. 'We may have been given that good news in the form of a report sent by the British Resident in Gcalekaland, accusing the Xhosa paramount chief, Samkelo, of receiving stolen cattle from the Ngqika and of harbouring Hottentot rebels. I have also received a report of white traders living in the same area who have been robbed of livestock. This gives us enough leverage to attack Samkelo and plunder his livestock.'

'Samkelo has always claimed neutrality throughout this conflict,' said Sommerville.

'So he says. But my spies have informed me that he travelled by night to a secret meeting of all the chiefs to incite rebellion among the Xhosa tribes, which, as you have probably noticed, is happening now, General. I need a victory to raise morale and send the powers that be in Whitehall a positive report.'

'The accusations against Samkelo do seem a bit flimsy, sir.'

'They are, but it is enough. So you are relieved of your campaign in Kroomie Range for now. You will take a force to Gcalekaland and round up the chief and his followers. They will not have the stomach to resist a well-organised and heavily armed assault. Capture any rebels for treason if you can. Take all the livestock and burn a few huts. Even you cannot botch this operation, General. The chiefs will then cry to the missionaries that they are starving and destitute, then the missionaries will come to me. That's what normally happens. Then I will give them my terms for cooperation and they will refuse, and so it will go on.' Said Smyth wearily.

'When do we march, sir?' asked Sommerville bristling at Smyth's comment.

'As soon as the men are ready. This campaign will not take very long. When you arrive back in triumph I will then plan a strategy to attack the Amatolas and the Kroomie with every man we have and with heavy artillery and blow them to hell. We will also take their livestock and burn everything in our path, and this time it will be finished, as I will be leading the attack on the Xhosa myself.'

'You will be leading the Campaign to the Amatolas, sir?'

'I will. It seems I am the only one with enough experience in bush warfare to put an end to this war and I have fought old Mzingisi before. I will have to get my old bones back into the action again and destroy Mzingisi and Sandla as no one else here can do it... apparently.'

Chapter Twelve

Cape Town

She awoke with a start. A noise had penetrated her subconscious and alerted her, the birds were singing their morning calls to each other; she heard the faint roar of a large cat far up on the mountain. It was still dark but there was a trace of grey in the sky to the east. She had to get off the mountain as soon as possible and get away from the animal and human predators.

She was so cold and her feet were bare and bleeding. She followed the stream as far as she could until it fell over a small waterfall. It was too steep to climb down so she went back to find a way down past the fall and walked with the stream again. The terrain was now less rocky, becoming more earth and grass which felt better underfoot. She drank more water and staggered on.

Williams was worried. Banbury explained that one of the girls had jumped, hopefully to her death, through the trapdoor and now they had to make sure she was in fact dead, because if she escaped and identified him as her kidnapper the locals would skin him alive.

They had ridden out of the grounds before dawn to

avoid any scrutiny and were now following a stream up to the ravine below the north side of the house.

'Are you sure we going in the right direction?' asked Banbury.

'I am very sure sir.'

'We must find the girl if she is still alive and kill her. If she identifies me I'm a dead man,' said Banbury.

These two Englishmen must be insane to do what they do. Thought Williams. *They pay me well but not well enough to kill young girls or anyone, but we have to find out if the girl is dead or alive.*

When the sun rose she felt the warmth of its rays flowing into her as she found her way through the undergrowth. She was very weak, the pain numbing as her brain gradually closed down. She carried on, on instinct alone. Eventually she sat down, desperately wanting to sleep. Then she heard a horse snorting.

Her need to survive made her immediately alert. She sat and listened. She heard the faint sound of voices.

Looking around she rose and stepped carefully on rocks, so as not to leave any tracks to follow. Making her way up the gentler slope of the lower part of the ravine she noticed some thick bush a few feet away and crawled behind the foliage startling some roosting birds, they squawked so loudly the riders must surely have been alerted. She sat and listened.

When the startled birds burst out of the bushes, Williams put up his hand for Banbury to stop.

'What scared those birds? Do you think it was her?' asked Banbury anxiously.

'More likely an animal; she must have been killed

falling into the ravine,' said Williams.

'You don't know that for sure. Did you see where the birds flew out of?'

'From that thicket about sixty feet up and over to the left,' said Williams pointing.

'Then let us go and take a look, said Banbury spurring his horse.

'Be careful it's not a leopard, they roam the mountain at this height.'

Banbury stopped and drew his pistol.

They rode further up to a point where they dismounted and continued on foot to the thicket.

The girl saw them struggling through the bush and turned to try and find a way along the slope without making any more noise. She made her way up and over a rock fall and saw a troop of baboons further up the slope. They hadn't seen her yet so she looked around for a hiding place and saw a gap between the fallen rocks. She made her way to it and squeezed herself into the narrow space and waited.

Before long she heard a scuffling sound close to where she was hiding and closed her eyes in dread of being discovered, for they would surely kill her. She opened her eyes and chanced a look through the entrance of her hiding place and saw a huge baboon perched on a rock looking agitated and making guttural noises, but not at her.

Williams led the way to the thicket and noticed a dried spot of blood on a rock, he stopped to look into the dense bush as Banbury went passed him and on to a pile of fallen rocks. He almost died of shock when he rounded the rocks and saw the biggest baboon he had ever seen in his life and fired his pistol at it, missing the animal completely.

'Sir, stop shooting,' shouted Williams coming up behind Banbury. 'We don't want to attract any attention.'

'Did you see the size of that monkey?' said Banbury. 'Of course I'm going to shoot.'

Williams watched the troop of baboons fleeing up the slope and said. 'Well, we know what scared the birds. Let us carry on up the ravine.'

When the gun shot rang out and she nearly screamed but managed to suppress it. The baboon disappeared. She overheard the two men talking they were so close; staying perfectly still, she hardly breathed until they decided to go.

Crawling out of her hiding place and around the rocks she could just see the two men disappearing past the thicket. Eventually, she heard the riders talking again and the noise of the horses walking on. They would go as far as the waterfall and climb the last part to the ravine, where the body was, but she had heard a leopard. Maybe God would be kind to her and send the animal to kill her pursuers.

The ravine was now behind her but she could not follow the stream any more as the bush was too dense, so she started on a more northerly route cutting horizontally across the side of the mountain, which was on her left, knowing instinctively that she would find help if she went in that direction.

She pushed through yet another bush and suddenly came across a very narrow animal path. Gratefully, she walked along the path but she was so tired she decided to climb up into the undergrowth to rest for a short while and then she would carry on. Lying down on some long grass she fell instantly asleep.

When she woke up she could hardly move she was so stiff and sore. The sun had set and it was almost dark. She must have slept for hours. Going back to the path she stopped and listened, then looked into the encroaching darkness in both directions. Hearing nothing and seeing no movement she tried to loosen her limbs and walk to find help. She prayed it must be close.

The path started to curve around the mountain and in the darkness she could make out some lights further down the slopes. She walked faster, peering through the darkness for a space to go down, it was difficult to see now as the cloud cover obscured the moonlight.

She noticed a change on both sides of the path, a landslide had fallen recently, there was enough light to make out a line of debris stretching down the mountain, pointing at the twinkling lights far away at the bottom of the slopes.

She decided to go down the slope but as she went down she found that the debris and shale under her was very unstable and it started to slide under her weight. She tried to move across and hold on to a branch or a rock but she just made things worse as her weight pushed the momentum of the loose shale and pebbles. The girl lost her balance and fell into the landslide turning over and over until she suddenly crashed into something solid. She fell into darkness again and did not move.

Slowly she became aware of noises; children laughing and talking and an adult scolding them to keep the noise down.

She felt warm but confused. What was happening to her? Where was she? What was she doing here? Her eye lids flickered and stayed still, then flickered again. She struggled to open them.

She was aware of someone touching her and saying, 'Mamma, she moved her eyes, mamma come quickly.'

'Are you sure, my lamb?' said the adult.

'Yes I'm sure, Mamma.'

Her hand that was being held and then she felt the sensation of a wet cloth dabbing her face gently. She tried to open her eyes. The lids parted slightly but things were moving in a haze. Slowly her blurred vision started to come in to focus.

'Oh my, she's awake. At last she's awake. Go next door and fetch Auntie Fatima, my lamb,' said the adult speaking in Afrikaans.

Her vision cleared and she could see a coloured woman sitting next to the bed in which she lay. A child darted through a doorway.

'What happened? Where am I?' she asked, panic rising in her.

'You are safe here, my girl. Do not be afraid. You are one of us, but I do not recognise you. You are not from around here. Where do you live and why were you up on the mountain?'

'Where am I?' she asked again.

The child returned with an older woman, her white hair wrapped in a head scarf. She had a round face and a wide smile that showed no teeth in her mouth.

'This is our house in the Bo Kaap, in Cape Town,' said the woman beside her, clearly a younger version of the older lady.

'Cape Town? What am I doing in Cape Town?' she asked sitting up and clearly confused. She knew of the city, but did not know why she was there.

The older woman said. 'I am Aunty Fatima. I will make some tea and I have soup. You need to eat something.'

'My husband and my son found you on the mountain. They were looking for rocks for building and saw you at the bottom of a landslide and carried you here. You are very lucky to be alive,' said the younger woman.

'How long have I been here?'

'You have been unconscious for many days. We managed to get you to drink some soup when you were delirious with fever, but the fever has nearly gone. You are a very strong young lady. My name is Salomé. Where do you come from and can you tell me your name?'

'My name is… my name… Where do I live?' she said, looking at Salomé. 'I don't know where I live. I don't know my name.'

Chapter Thirteen

September 1855

Liverpool

The boys continued training for another four weeks before they got the confirmation of Primeaux's party and the go ahead to break into his mansion.

They were running easily through a field of long grass after being dropped half a mile from the target. It was dark and they were concentrating on the wet, soft terrain so as not to stumble along the way. They were extremely fit and ate up the distance to the target in no time. The lights ahead were getting closer and eventually they came to a road which bordered the mansion belonging to Chester Primeaux.

The high wall surrounding the estate was easily breached as Jamie crouched on bended knees with his back to the wall, hands cupped in front of him. Iain stepped into his hands and then on to his shoulders. Carefully looking over the top and seeing no one around, he slid up on to the wall, bent over to grasp Jamie's wrists and then leant back to take his weight and assist him up.

Landing lightly on the other side they ran to the

nearest bushes and waited. Nothing moved except the slight rustle of leaves in a light breeze. They watched the mansion, which was well lit up, with wrought-iron fire baskets on the pathways around the house and along the roadways. Jamie elbowed Iain and they ran crouched over as close as they dared to the house, taking cover in some dense bushes.

They were at the rear corner of the house and, from memory of the house plans, they knew the French doors ahead of them were the way in to Primeaux's study. There were two other sets of French doors to the left towards the front of the house and they were open. The noise of people and music could be heard clearly now and they could see half-clad, naked people milling around through the ground and first-floor windows. The second floor was in darkness except for one dimly lit room, obviously out of bounds to the party guests.

As the boys watched they could see guards walking a perimeter about thirty feet from the house, passing one another and then turning to repeat the same exercise.

Jamie said. 'The guards stop for a chat but once in a while they have a smoke for about ten minutes.'

'I've timed them stopping to smoke every thirty to forty minutes,' said Iain.

'Right. The next smoke break we'll run over to that low wall in front of the ground floor windows and take cover there. The smoke break after that we'll break in through the French windows; agreed? Said Jamie.

'Sounds good to me; sooner the better,' said Iain.

Iain grabbed Jamie's arm and pointed at a couple coming out of the house through the open French doors nearest to them. They were kissing and giggling as they staggered out and into the garden and started to stray towards the boys' hiding place.

Iain leaned in to Jamie and whispered. 'Ye realise that our hidey-hole here is a great place tae get shagged.'

'Aye, I had realised that,' Jamie whispered back. 'A garden the size of Scotland and they have to come this way, for fuck's sake!' he said. 'Right, you take him down and I will deal with the woman.'

'How come you get tae take the woman?' Iain said.

Jamie knew he was having a dig and said softly. 'Get ready.'

The guards had seen the couple and turned a blind eye and let them go their way.

As the couple walked closer to them, the boys unsheathed their knives.

The man was pulling the young lady by the hand as they entered the bushes. Iain reached up and pulled the man down from behind and hit him on the temple with the butt of the knife handle. He fell, limp, to the ground. At the same time Jamie reached for the woman but she was a bit more aware and let out a squeal before he tapped her on the head and she sagged into his arms.

The guards heard the woman squeal and knew that the sounds of passion would be heard all night, so carried on with their rounds.

The boys watched the guards, then used their knives to cut strips of clothing from the woman to gag and bind the unconscious couple. Then they waited for the guards to have their next smoke break.

When the guards lit up their cigarettes the boys ran to a large tree and then on to a hedgerow and finally dived behind the low wall that bordered the enormous patio.

They waited for the guards to walk their rounds again and lay on the cold granite slabs for twenty-five minutes before the guards lit up another smoke whereupon they crawled to the French doors and stood up, hidden by the door recess. Moving quickly, Jamie looked inside to make sure it was quiet and opened the bag with the tools. As the noise level was high he decided to break the small pane of glass next to the door lock, put his arm through and unlock the door from the inside. They entered the dark room and closed the door, removing the broken glass from the frame so as not to be seen by the guard.

Drawing the curtains, Iain opened the tool satchel, removed and lit a small lantern; it was completely closed in apart from a two-inch-wide slit to direct the candlelight in one direction. They walked silently to the large desk at the end of the room and set to work on the drawers. They were trained to look for secret compartments but after ten minutes they had not found anything to interest them.

'There has to be something else,' Jamie said softly.

'Maybe he keeps his paperwork elsewhere. Another room perhaps,' Iain said sitting on the floor with his back leaning against the desk. On a whim he shone the small light along the underside of the desk where the legroom stretched to the other side. 'Jamie. Look there.'

There was a small recess in the corner under the desk top within reach of anyone sitting at the desk. Jamie poked his finger in and felt something loose. He curled his finger and pulled slightly. 'It's a lever,' he whispered.

Iain was on his knees now peering under. 'Pull it then,' he said.

Jamie pulled and they heard a click. Iain shone the lamp around; nothing.

'For fuck's sake! Where is it,' Iain said, getting frustrated.

'Shine the lamp on the front side of the desk.'

'Nothing there.'

'Try the side where the lever is closest to.'

'Jesus, there it is!'

One of the engraved panels on the side of the desk had sprung open. Inside there were three thin flat drawers. Jamie pulled the drawers out one by one and removed some documents while Iain held the lamp. 'There are some in English but there're clearly two other languages here.'

'Dae ye recognise them?'

'How would I? I only speak Scottish and English.'

Suddenly they heard a woman scream in what sounded like anguish.

'Right, we've been here long enough. Let's take the lot and fuck off out of here!'

'Aye, close it all up and dowse the lamp,' Jamie said packing the papers in the satchel.

Iain was careful not to disturb the curtain as he looked through the split and what he saw did not fill him with happiness. 'Aw shite!'

'What is it?' Jamie asked peering over his shoulder.

'That bloody woman we tied up must have woken up and rolled herself over the bushes. Can you believe it? She's lying in the pathway.'

'Can you see the guards?'

'No, not yet. Wait. Here comes one of them now.'

The guard ran up to the woman took one look and asked, 'What happened to you, ma'am?'

He removed her gag but she did not know anything. The guard stood up and turned to call to his colleague. 'Frank, go into the house and find Primeaux.' He turned back to the woman and started to untie her.

'Pull yer bunnet down because we need to get out of

here right now,' Jamie said.

Jamie slid through the curtain and quietly opened the door, closely followed by Iain. They drew their pistols and ran for the garden. As they ran, Iain shot Frank's partner through his left eye. The woman screamed and Jamie punched her as he ran past, knocking her out. Thank goodness the noise from the party was still going strong.

'Head for the east wall. They will think we're going for the main road,' shouted Jamie over his shoulder. 'Then we can use the trees to hide our run south to the field where we came in.'

They had no sooner reached the wall, when they heard the yelping of the dogs.

'Aw fuckin' great! We're never going to outrun dogs,' said Iain.

Jamie was looking toward the mansion at two figures on the third-floor balcony. A tall dark-haired man and a shorter thickset man. It was difficult to see them in the flickering firelight.

'There they are!' a distant voice from the balcony shouted.

'Fire into the trees,' the voice shouted again.

'Stop moaning and run,' Jamie said, grabbing Iain by the arm.

Musket fire started to *thunk* into the trees as they ran. Iain felt a tug at his jacket as a round came too close. The dogs were gaining ground fast as they now had the scent. More voices were shouting and more rounds were flying around them.

They reached the south wall as the fastest dog caught up with them.

'You're up on the wall first, Iain.'

Jamie boosted him up, drew his pistol and shot the snarling dog then reached up to the waiting hands of his friend and they were over, leaving the other dogs yelping at stone and ricochets.

They could hear horses being urged on as they split up and ran in different directions to hopefully meet at the rendezvous half a mile away.

Chapter Fourteen

London, Liverpool

James Storer had had enough of the puffed-up, pompous, upper-class idiots of Westminster and the Royal Court. Most of them had never left the shores of England but they were experts, one and all, about the problems in the territories and colonies.

The buffoons know nothing, but they will get their come-uppance when we are in control, he thought happily.

Since arriving back in England from Cape Town, he had made his reports, especially to Earl Greyson on an official level, and then met with him for lunch on an unofficial level. He had attended the luncheons and the dinners, smiled and been nice and courteous to colleague's wives and fiancées. Enough was enough.

His meeting with Earl Harold Greyson at his exclusive gentleman's club had gone extremely well, he recollected:

He had arrived at Greyson's club at the appointed time. The concierge had relieved him of his coat and hat and showed him into a grand room with thick leather chairs and sofas, thick carpets and stained oak-panelled walls with enough books to start a library.

Some of the members were sitting in their favourite comfortable chairs reading newspapers, sipping drinks, smoking cigars or pipes, and one or two older gentlemen were snoozing.

'James! Good to see you again. Let's sit down to lunch then we can chat,' said Harold Greyson.

'Thank you Harold. We have a lot to catch up on,' replied Storer shaking hands.

They finished lunch and retired to a private room sitting comfortably with cigars and brandies.

'So, Harold, what news do you have for me?'

Greyson opened a drawer in the small table next to him and extracted a flat stiff leather pouch which he handed to Storer.

Storer looked in the pouch to see sealed documents and closed it again.

'All the plans and arrangements in London are ready. Whatever signal you send will be executed to your timing,' said Greyson. 'And there is something else you will need to look into when you return to Cape Town.'

Greyson outlined the discovery of the clue and the buried treasure of the Knights Templar.

'All the details are in the pouch,' he said.

'That is good news, Harold. Is the second clue to this Templars treasure in here as well? And has it been deciphered?'

'It is in there but nobody knows what it means. The elder I spoke with agrees that it should go with you to Cape Town, and see if you can unravel this riddle and find the treasure. I have to tell you that we are not convinced about the existence of any treasure. What is important is our plans for the natives in the Cape.'

Storer reached into his inside coat pocket and extracted a buff envelope acquired in Westminster and handed it to Greyson.

'Please give my regards to the elders when you deliver these documents. Tell them all preparations are proceeding to plan. All the details are in the sealed documents in that envelope. Also, before I left Cape Town, I received word from my contact with the Xhosa chiefs that they have accepted our offer of supplying weapons, ammunition and powder; they will want more. The fighting has already started. Governor Smyth has sent in troops to clear out the Xhosa strongholds in the Amatola Mountains, but they were defeated. After this humiliation he had to restore the prestige of the ruling white man and launched an attack on the paramount chief of the Xhosa, Samkelo in Gcalekaland, who offered no resistance at all, Smyth of course, gloated on his triumph.'

'I did receive a report from Smyth, singing his own praises about how he restored morale and conquered the mighty Samkelo with the capture of thousands of beasts and rebels. Was our intervention of delaying the equipment and holding back the troops they needed a factor in his army being defeated?' asked Greyson.

'That and because Governor Smyth's an idiot and he appointed another idiot, a General Sommerville, to clean out the natives, but the old war chief of the Ngqika, Mzingisi, was too clever for them. Their defeat only strengthens our plan because now Smyth will pour in reinforcements totally inexperienced in bush warfare, and mount another campaign and fail again. Then, as we know, he will be removed and replaced by one us. Do you know who it will be, Harold?'

'Yes, Smyth's replacement will be General, Sir

Gerald Cuthbert.'

'Well done, Harold. With Gerald Cuthbert commanding, the Xhosa barbarians will be defeated. I will put my final plan into action and then… well, then we march north and nothing will stop us,' said Storer lifting his glass.

Greyson lifted his glass and said. 'Congratulations, James. I will pass on your good news to the elder.'

Yes, the future was taking shape, thought Storer.

But now he had arrived in Liverpool.

He informed his colleagues in London he would be visiting family and friends before departing for the Cape on a ship belonging to one of those old family friends, who, because of bad health, was going to live with his family in Cape Town.

Storer had no family and no close friends, only acquaintances of his choosing. One of those was his American acquaintance, Chester Primeaux. Chester, like himself, had a passion for young ladies.

The anticipation of meeting with Chester was growing, as was his need to satisfy his hunger to kill helpless young girls. Although, Chester tended to abuse them then let one of his henchmen kill them and dispose of the bodies.

Storer arrived at Primeaux's mansion after dark to avoid prying eyes. The butler let him in and ordered the servants to take his luggage to his suite, up the grand stairway.

Primeaux greeted him in the magnificent entrance hall, dominated by a huge chandelier of candles suspended above, reflecting off the marble floor.

'James, how are you? I hope you had a pleasant journey?'

'Good evening, Chester. As pleasant as one can expect, I suppose.'

They went straight to Primeaux's office in the study where the butler poured two glasses of cognac and left.

'It's so good to see you after all this time my good friend,' Primeaux said, his southern American twang sounding raw to Storer's ear. 'How are things down in the colonies?' He handed Storer a glass.

'Well, now that you ask, I can say things are rather good,' Storer said, pausing to sip his brandy. 'Is the next shipment of guns ready to go?'

'They're being taken to your ship as we speak, under the guise of ploughs and other agricultural implements. My best man will be there to make sure the gunpowder is stowed safely and securely. We wouldn't want you to be blown all over the Atlantic Ocean would we now.'

'No, indeed not. When will I receive my down payment in gold, and when will the rest of the shipment be delivered?'

'Your down payment will be delivered to the ship before you sail and, as long as you maintain safe passage for my ships past the Royal Navy, you will have the other shipments over the next few months. Then by the middle of next year, I'll be looking for delivery of my slaves to bolster production in the Southern States of America, because war with the Union is inevitable and we need to be ready.'

'We shall monitor the escalation of both of our pending conflicts and make sure we set the timing right.'

'We have to get it right, sir. There is a country's destiny riding on this venture and it has to tie in with other operations, so the timing is everything.'

'Chester, don't worry, we have our arrangements in

place and all is going to plan. We will both achieve our goals. We have our people in place and my political party is moving to be in control of the Government around the same time frame,' said Storer.

He told Primeaux his party would win the next election. *God, the Americans were totally ignorant of British politics,* he thought.

'When the Confederates overrun the Union and we win the confidence of the American people we will build an alliance with the British that will be unbreakable,' Primeaux said with gusto.

So you think, you stupid cotton farmer, Storer thought. 'I came here to reassure you and to pass on the compliments of my colleagues and partners in this venture. We are all behind you,' Storer said lifting his glass.

Primeaux lifted his glass as well and said. 'Well now that business is out of the way let's talk about our fund-raising party.'

'You are aware I cannot be seen to be participating in your fund-raising?'

'I am aware of this, sir. However, I'll have an open fund-raiser and then there will be a private party with invited guests only and all will be wearing masks. We'll also have some young invited guests who don't know they are invited yet,' he cackled.

'I've brought you a very special gift,' Storer said removing a small bottle from his coat pocket. 'This is an elixir, the ingredients of which are made up of pulped leaves and the juices from the rarest herbs and plants of tropical Africa. The locals in the Cape call it *muti,* simply because they would think of it as medicine.'

'And if it's not medicine, then what is it, this *muti*?'

Primeaux asked suspiciously.

'If you feed a few drops to your next victim you will see a transformation in them that will make them more compliant. It also calms them down and they will basically do anything for you. If you take a drop yourself, and mind you, only a drop, for this is a very powerful mixture, it will enhance your manhood and your pleasure because, when the victim comes out of her stupor and starts to panic, your own senses are heightened to a degree that it takes you to a new level of pleasure altogether.'

'So you have obviously used this muti?'

'With great effect, Chester.'

'Well, we'll have to use it to great effect on the night of our party. Your luggage has by now been taken to your rooms. Tomorrow morning after breakfast we'll go riding for an hour or so on an American saddle, and not those little English ones I slide around on, and we can finish up the details of our business.'

'Learn to ride properly and you will not slide around,' Storer said and finished his drink.

'Until tomorrow then. Goodnight.'

'Goodnight.' *Stuck up English idiot,* Primeaux thought when Storer left. *You'll get what's coming to you if you don't deliver, but I will use you for now.*

'I need to get home to Louisiana away from these prigs,' he said to his empty glass.

The fund-raiser had a fair turnout but the party was going very well. The guests had eaten lavishly and were consuming copious amounts of drink.

Storer was keen to go up to the second floor and meet his young victim. It was a need that consumed him. *I do not understand why I am the way I am. This need for violence whilst having sex was getting worse. Or was it getting better?* He wondered to himself. *It is getting better,* he preferred. *This is getting so much better.*

As he sauntered through the house, the party was in full tilt; screeched laughing; boring conversation; rich socialites looking to brighten up their dull lives.

The *'hello dahlings'* and cheek kissing had stopped, couples were brazenly touching each other's private parts, one woman was sitting on a man's lap with her back to him, her dress spread over the two of them with her clearly pumping herself up and down on him.

But that was what these parties were about.

Primeaux suddenly appeared beside him. 'The ladies are ready for us upstairs. I'll go on ahead and you follow in about five minutes. The guards will make sure we are not disturbed.'

When Storer was admitted to the large suite, two peasant girls in their early teens were already tipsy and awed that they had been invited to such a grand house.

They had been recruited far away from Liverpool with the promise of work in a fine mansion, with lodgings and a weekly wage. They had been given a room with a bathroom and some fine new clothes to try on. Then they were to serve drinks at a private party and allowed to sip on the wine.

Storer sat down on a long, wide settee as did Primeaux on the other side of a low table. The girls served their brandy and giggled. 'Would sir like anything else?' one said brazenly bending over to show her cleavage, the effects of the alcohol giving her false courage.

'Yes, there is something else,' Storer stood up now, starting to play the game. He took the serving tray from her and said. 'Let's pretend you are the ladies of the house and we will serve you some drinks.'

They took the girls by the hand and sat them down, then went to the drinks cabinet.

Primeaux watched Storer take a small bottle from his pocket and said. 'What is that? Is that your *muti*?'

'Yes, I promise, you will enjoy this immensely,' said Storer.

He poured a few drops into each wine glass, then topped them up with wine. He then dripped one drop each into two brandy goblets, poured in the cognac and gave one to Primeaux. He took the wine glasses on a silver tray to the doomed young girls who bowed, giggling and began to drink the wine.

'Ooo, is that a different one? It don't 'alf taste 'orrible,' said Storer's victim, screwing her nose up.

'I can assure you this is the best wine from France. It is an acquired taste,' said Storer, thinking, *just drink it, you bloody peasant.*

She was coarse and illiterate but beautiful, just as he liked them. *I'll have to teach her some manners,* he thought, his demented hunger taking over now as he sipped on his brandy and the girls finished off the wine.

'What are you doing?' shouted the other girl suddenly.

Storer looked across at Primeaux whose demeanour had changed dramatically. He threw off his jacket and roughly grabbed the girl's breasts. She pushed him off but Primeaux slapped her hard and she screamed, falling back suddenly stunned.

The girl with Storer tried to get up and he grabbed around the neck with a one-handed grip, pushing her back on to the cushion. He could see in her eyes that the muti was taking hold of her senses and he relaxed his grip.

She looked at him strangely and put her hand on his face and then tried to kiss him. He pushed her away and glanced over at Primeaux who was now shirtless, his breeches at his knees, his hard manhood pumping the other girl's mouth. She was gagging and choking but he held her by the hair and forced her to stay there.

Storer looked down and got rid of his clothes then grabbed a handful of his girl's hair and using his other hand forced his erection into her mouth. She responded immediately and seemed to like the idea, which did not please Storer at all. He pulled her head back and was about to strike her when there was an almighty banging at the door.

'I thought we wouldn't be interrupted,' he said angrily.

'My men wouldn't interrupt unless there was something seriously wrong. Get dressed,' Primeaux said pulling on his clothes.

A gunshot rang out. The two men looked at each other then ran to the huge French doors leading to the balcony.

They looked down to see two bodies, a male and a half-dressed female lying on the pathway. On hearing more shots they looked up and across the huge manicured lawns and could just see two dark figures running for the boundary wall.

'There they are!' shouted Primeaux to his men and pointing.

'Fire into the trees,' he shouted, then turned and went to the door and let his men in. 'I just saw two men running away. What is going on?'

'Sir, they were running from the back of the house, from the study.

A cold shiver ran down Primeaux's spine. He signalled his men to take the girls away. 'James!' he called and Storer followed him down the huge stairway to the ground floor. He produced a key and opened the door to his study going straight to his desk. He opened the secret panel and realised his worst fears, discovering the drawers were empty.

He sat in his chair and his face paled.

Storer went to the glass door with the broken glass and went outside. Men were running around, some on horses riding to the main gates.

'What did they take, Chester?' said Storer walking back into the study.

'All the plans and some names for the slave ships from the Arab and the French slavers were in the desk: the number of vessels and the rendezvous points. There was nothing there with your name or of my plans with you, thank the Lord, although there was mention of the delivery of guns to the ship you are sailing on. But how could they have known where to look? I'm the only person who knows of that secret panel in my desk. There has to be a traitor in my organisation.'

Storer heaved a sigh of relief. 'No, there's no traitor. This robbery was too well executed and too well planned. This could only have been committed by Government men.'

'Government men, you say?'

'Yes, but which Government? British or American? Apart from your men are there any other Americans in Liverpool that you know of?'

'Yes, there are, but they're here purely on business, I know of them, they are profiteers with no affiliation to the north or south.'

'Then the burglars must be from London. I have heard whispers in the corridors of power that there's a secret service in Westminster, but nobody knows them, which is why, I suppose it is secret. I'll make enquiries through some powerful friends of mine.'

'The papers taken from my desk are in English, Dutch, Arabic and French. There is no information on the English papers, but there is on the others and the delivery of the guns are recorded in the French documents. It's just as well you're sailing the day after tomorrow. It will take them some time to translate all those papers so you'll be well on your way and I'll have to change some arrangements. I'm also going to make it known there will be a substantial reward for turning these thieves over to me. I'll put the word out. If they are in this city I will have them.'

Chapter Fifteen

Liverpool

Avoiding the roaming horsemen looking for them, Jamie and Iain boarded the carriage waiting for them at the rendezvous point. The driver took them on a precautionary route through the suburb of Childwell, then south to the road that ran along the northern bank of the Mersey River through Toxteth Park, dropping them a street away from Rigby's tavern. They had changed in the cab back into their normal clothes.

When they entered Armstrong's office from the back of the building, the man himself was pacing the floor.

He looked up as they entered the room. 'Thank god! What the hell happened?'

'Why, what have you heard?' Jamie asked.

'Bad news travels fast. We heard that there were gunshots, horses galloping up and down the roads around Primeaux's property and his thugs searching high and low for thieves who broke into his house, and there's a body.'

The boys related their night's work and emptied the contents of the satchel on to Armstrong's desk.

'Are these all the papers from Primeaux's desk?' asked Armstrong.

'Yes. We took the whole lot,' said Iain.

'Did anyone see you?'

'I'm sure one or two people did see us but they would have been too far away to make out our features,' Jamie replied.

Armstrong was about to say 'Are you sure?' but stopped, knowing what Jamie said was an accurate account.

He looked at the papers before him. 'That, I am sure, is Arabic, these are French, those are definitely Dutch,' he said pointing at three piles of pages. He picked up the remainder written in English and read through them, passing each page to Jamie and Iain as he read them. 'Well, there is nothing much to interest us except for this last paragraph here,' he said holding up the page. 'I will read it out.

'The Englishman has been made aware that it is his responsibility to have the cargo in place for pick up at a designated departure point yet to be decided. This is a straight transaction: a down payment of gold, and the supply of guns, ammunition and powder in exchange for the cargo. The rest of the shipment of guns will be delivered as per instruction from the recipient, the last shipment two months before delivery of the cargo. We will be responsible for the ships to take the cargo.'

'There are no names or dates here,' said Armstrong. 'I'll have the other papers sent to London to be translated. Maybe there is something we can use.'

'We know now at least that this terrible deed is going to happen,' Iain said. 'And the only way we're going to find who, how and when is to be there in Cape Town and put it down.'

'This is precisely why you are leaving on the

morning tide in two days' time for the Cape of Good Hope,' said Armstrong.

'That's a bit sudden, is it not?' Iain asked.

'I did warn you, besides, in this business, Iain, you only need to know *what* you need to know *when* you need to know it.'

'Aye, right. Whatever you say,' said Iain smiling.

'As luck would have it, the ship you are sailing on is *The Flying Fish;* the same ship James Storer will be sailing on to Cape Town. I was alerted by our informants in London about this ship and Storer.'

'So we'll be keeping an eye on him as well as watching our back?' said Jamie.

'Yes, and you will search the ship for guns and, according to this letter, perhaps gold as well. He'll probably have some henchmen on board so don't trust anyone. Your bags and personal belongings have been taken from your hotel and are now in the back room there. Get a few hours' sleep and then go and book into Monaghan's in the morning, I know they ask for a week in advance so pay that to avert any suspicion. I'll have the bulk of your luggage and two large toolboxes, which will have concealed compartments built in to store your weapons, currency and gold, put on board the ship, and there will be one or two cases of malt whisky for you as well.

'Well, thank you for that. What about our tickets?' Asked Iain.

'Rosemary will have your travel papers and money for you on the morning you sail. Also with your papers will be a document with a code phrase for your contact in Cape Town, along with the clues for the so-called treasure. Your contact is Bill Hutchison. He will help you get acquainted with the local people and you will just have to decipher the clues as best you can. It has been a long time since these clues were written, so there might not be anything left to find. Rosemary will meet you outside Monaghan's early in the morning of your departure so for god's sake don't be late. I won't see you before you sail. I don't want you to come back here as I think we may have been compromised. You boys have been given a huge responsibility and we are relying on you to get the job done.'

Armstrong stood and shook hands.

'You can rely on us, sir,' Jamie said earnestly.

'Don't worry, Mr Armstrong. We'll take the fight to them,' said Iain.

'Yes, that's what I am afraid of,' said Armstrong laughing. 'God be with you and take care,' he said seriously, then turned and left.

It was late morning when the boys went to Monaghan's and paid a week in advance for a room with two single beds. They stowed their bags and went down to the pub.

'So you came back to for me then, Jamie?' Maggie Monaghan asked with a smirk as she served up the beers.

Jamie was trying to stick with the cover story but he was having a hard time lying to Maggie even though she was basically a stranger. 'We're staying here now so let's see how we get along.'

'There's a party tonight and Brendan's in charge, my mother has gone to my aunt's for a couple of days so we can have a good time tonight,' Maggie said stroking his cheek with her forefinger, then moved off to serve another customer.

'It looks like we're having a going away party,' Iain

said waving at Marie.

'Keep your voice down, Iain, ye might get castrated.'

Maggie and Marie joined the boys when they finished work, bringing food and more drink and four young men and women happily danced the night away.

At the end of the night, Brendan called time for drinking up and started the process of getting everyone out of the tavern.

Maggie said. 'Me and Marie will help Brendan clean up. We won't be long. Go to room nine on the second floor and tell Iain to go to room twelve. They are empty tonight but we'll only be there for a little while. Brendan is fine with that because he thinks we are all together in one room as long as it is not all night. He doesn't know about room twelve.'

Iain went to room twelve to wait for Marie. Jamie lit the lamp in room nine and made himself comfortable lying on the bed until Maggie came into the room with a flagon of cider.

'Now don't be gettin' get the wrong idea, Jamie Fyvie, we're just going to get to know each other and have some fun, alright?'

'Of course,' Jamie said innocently, holding his hand out for hers.

She slid down beside him and they started swigging on the cider, they were very comfortable with each other and kissed lustily. Maggie took another swig and kissed Jamie passing the cider into his mouth. He responded, using his tongue in her mouth. The cider went back and forth until they both swallowed and broke off to take a breath.

Jamie was aware of his very hard erection and he hugged Maggie, pressing his hardness against her thighs.

'Whatever is that, Jamie Fyvie?' she said reaching down to touch him through the fabric of his breeches. 'You just be leaving that thing where it is,' she said, kissing him hungrily.

Jamie kissed his way down to her neck and then used his teeth on her neck on to her shoulder. She moaned at the sensation and felt her nipples stiffen almost painfully as Jamie pulled the loose fabric down over her plump breasts. He moved his mouth down and sucked her nipple into his mouth, moving his tongue around and teasing it with his teeth.

Their passion intensified as they lost themselves in their own world. She pulled her top off as did he. Holding her breasts in both hands he used the wetness of his mouth to slip between and around them, kneading her nipples with his teeth.

He put his hand up into her skirts between her thighs. She had nothing on underneath. His finger went into the soft hair, finding the opening to her sex as she parted her legs. She sighed as he pushed gently into the wetness.

She suddenly pushed his face away from her and he said. 'What's wrong?'

'You are the devil himself,' she said pulling off the rest of her clothes.

They were breathing heavily as Jamie threw his breeches on the floor. She took his hardness in her hand and moved it up and down, his juices also leaking freely. The passion was overtaking them now as they enjoyed their hands on each other.

Jamie rolled over her, she opened her legs wide and brought her knees up, feeling the head of his erection part the lips to her vagina, sliding up and down outside on her clitoris to heighten the pleasure. Their body fluids were running freely now, lost in lust.

Then Maggie suddenly came to her senses. 'Jamie don't; please don't,' she sighed in his ear.

He seemed to realise where he was as well, but he knew if he pushed himself into her she would let him do it. He wanted it so badly, the sweat, the heavy breathing, and oh the passion. But he heard her plea and he slid over on to his side putting his finger back into her vagina and massaged her clitoris, gently building her up to a climax. She put her hand on his, guiding him to rub on the pelvic bone and her breathing started to expel in short bursts as she began her orgasm. Her mouth was kissing his neck. She could taste the salty sweat as she moaned a guttural sound. Her body shuddered at the intensity of the orgasm and she wished he was inside her, coming into her body at the same time. *Why did I not let him?* She thought despairingly.

As she climbed down from the euphoria, she took his hard penis in her hand and masturbated him, the wetness making it much more pleasurable, cupping his testicles with her other hand. He had almost come by himself at seeing her orgasm and it was not long before his started.

He was looking at her and she was looking at his face as it seemed to contort as though he was in pain. He let out a gasp and she felt the head swell as he ejaculated all over her flat belly.

'Don't stop,' he gasped as the pleasure flowed through him.

He kept spurting all over her and she looked in wonderment at the amount of fluid coming from his body.

Eventually the flow stopped, she rubbed her hand over the wetness on his genitals; he rubbed his hand over the wetness on her belly and over her breasts and between her legs catching her breath at the tenderness of her clitoris.

They lay entwined in slippery arms and legs in silence as they let the passion subside.

'That is the most wonderful thing I have ever experienced,' she whispered. 'I can't imagine what it would feel like if we made love. I'm sorry I stopped you, Jamie.'

'No, don't be sorry,' he said pushing her hair back and caressing her face. 'There's nothing to be sorry about. You did the right thing bringing me to my senses. It was so intense.'

She felt so much for him for saying that.

'When we do make love it will be such a warm and wonderful thing to behold,' she said cuddling closer to him.

'Yes, it will be,' said Jamie.

She's falling in love, he thought, the guilt taking over. *How naive to think she just wanted some fun when in fact she was seeking a relationship.*

They pulled the bed covers over and fell asleep.

They awoke before dawn, Maggie got up, dressed and then she kissed Jamie passionately, her eyes alive with happiness. 'I'll see you later when you get back from work,' she said and walked to the door. She opened it and gave him a twirl of her fingers and softly closed the door.

I should have told her the truth, he thought sitting up and pulling on his clothes. *No, better to just leave. She'll get over it. Problem is, will I? I really like her, or is it just that we had good sex? But we did not have sex. Oh, but it was good. Just run away, ye fuckin' coward'* he castigated himself.

He opened the thick curtains and realised the sun was

almost up.

'Shite! We're sailing on the morning tide,' he said to no one.

He looked out the door and seeing the coast was clear ran down the stairway to his room where he found Iain snoring his head off.

'Ye see, you are the one that snores the loudest,' Jamie said shaking his shoulder. 'Come on, Iain, wake up. That bloody ship is going to sail without us.'

'What? What's going on?' Iain said bleary-eyed.

'Move yourself. Get your stuff in your bag. We'll need to run like hell.'

Jamie looked out of the window and saw the carriage with Rosemary in it waiting just past the Monaghan's building.

The window was open slightly. He looked out carefully, but as he glanced to his right he could see Maggie looking out of her window down at the carriage. He ducked back in at once and turned to Iain. 'We need to get out of here without Maggie seeing us. She'll cut my balls off if she catches me running out of here after last night. I think she wants to get serious.'

'Oh, so you got shagged last night, did you? Well at least one of us did. What a waste of time. All I got was a feel of a left tit and told to behave myself.'

'No, I did not get shagged – everything but that, but let's go… quietly.'

Iain opened the room door a crack and listened. There were only the sounds of people getting ready for the day.

They moved quickly along the corridor to the head of the stairs. They heard a door slam and Marie's voice saying. 'I'm making some tea, shall I take some up to the lads?'

'You might as well,' they heard Maggie say faintly.

Jamie looked at Iain and they ran down the stairs as silently as possible, which was not silent at all. At the bottom of the stairs they went through the hall to the front door, it was bolted top and bottom and locked... there was no key in the lock.

'Shite! Where's the fuckin' key?' Iain said his voice slightly panicky.

Then they heard a voice from upstairs. 'They're not there,' shouted Marie to Maggie.'

The boys searched a small table with drawers at the side of the door. Nothing. There was a cupboard on the other side of the hallway and Jamie opened it but could see no sign of a key.

'Are you sure you're at the right room?' they heard Maggie shout down from the top landing.

Jamie felt up and down the inside of the door posts on both sides, nothing.

'Of course I am,' they heard Marie shout back.

'Jamie, for fuck's sake, hurry up!'

Then a realisation came over Jamie. He stood inside the cupboard and looked at the back of the door and there, hanging on a nail was the key. 'Got it.'

Iain pulled the bolts back, making two loud cracking noises and Jamie unlocked the door. They ran over the wet, slippery cobbled stones to the carriage and opened the door to find a grumpy-looking Rosemary.

'Where have you been?' she scolded them.

'You bastard, Jamie Fyvie! Where are you going?' the voice of Maggie screamed from the window above.

They jumped in the carriage and Iain pounded the roof shouting to the driver. 'Get going fast. Move!'

'Iain McColl, I'll get you,' they heard Marie scream.

The driver got the message and flayed the horses with his whip and they took off down the street.

'Sorry ma'am,' said Jamie. 'We overslept and had a bit of trouble getting out.'

'So it would seem,' Rosemary said disapprovingly.

She had two leather satchels with her and gave one each to the boys.

'These are your travel documents, some money and instructions to be read whilst you are en-route. That includes the clues of the Knights, whatever that means,' she said misunderstanding. 'In those satchels is your life so make sure you look after them. There is a money belt in each one and keys for the padlocks to your boxes in the hold. The password for your contact in Cape Town is there as well. Memorise it and destroy it. I suggest you lock up anything you don't need in the boxes for the voyage once you are aboard.'

The docks were busy with people finishing off the loading of ships ready to sail on the morning tide. There were one or two ships already moving off from the dock.

The carriage stopped next to a clipper ship, the name on the prow declaring, *The Flying Fish*. The boys jumped out and turned to Rosemary.

'Goodbye, ma'am. Thanks for everything,' Jamie said.

'Goodbye. You both have a safe journey and for goodness sake, behave yourselves,' Rosemary said smiling.

'Come on. Let's get on board,' said Iain, whilst watching for the arrival of any familiar faces.

They walked up the gangway and Jamie noticed a tall dark-haired man entering a doorway to the rear end of the ship.

At the top of the gangway a huge man in the form of the first mate did not look too happy to see them.

'We should have slipped our moorings ten minutes ago. CAST OFF!' he shouted waving to the bosun who informed the crew.

'CAST OFF!'

The deckhands pulled in the mooring ropes aft and stern as the dock workers untied them and dropped them in the water.

'I'm Bill Wilson the first mate. Can I see your travelling documents, if you please?'

Jamie and Iain noticed that their documents had their real names on them as opposed to Rattery and Black. They handed them over to the first mate.

Bill Wilson looked fat but he wasn't. He was all natural muscle with a baby kind of face, a thick neck, long blond hair plaited and tied halfway down his back. He had bulging biceps and huge hands, but looked likeable and trusting for his size, but Jamie felt he had a definite hostility towards the boys.

'Sorry about that,' Iain said holding out his hand to shake. 'There was some trouble with the carriage.'

Wilson ignored him. He looked at their tickets and appeared to see nothing amiss. He handed them back, then waved over a steward to show them where to go and he wandered off.

'Well, that's nice, isn't it,' said Ian sarcastically. *'Welcome aboard, nice to see you.* Fuckin' arsehole.'

Jamie said. 'I don't think they were expecting us, Iain, We had better watch our back. The tickets are in our real names. I wonder if the passenger manifest has the same names.'

'I think Armstrong would have logged Rattery and Black at the booking office to throw off anyone looking for us and our real names on the tickets to enter Cape Town,' said Iain.

Their cabin had a bunk on opposite bulkheads, with a wash-hand basin and a pitcher of water in recesses on top of a small cupboard between the bunks. There was a mirror above the basin with oil lamps on either side. Just inside the door on the left was a fair-sized cupboard with secure doors; to the right was a built-in desk with a small stool. There was space built in above the bunks for personal items and clothing.

They unpacked, making their private living space as comfortable and cosy as possible, settling in for the long voyage south.

On the dockside two broken-hearted young Irish girls, tears streaming down their faces, watched as vessels sailed away, not knowing which ship their lads were on.

Further along the dock a man watched the Flying Fish head out towards the river Mersey. He was fairly well dressed and wore a woollen cap.

Chapter Sixteen

Liverpool Docks

Two hours before Maggie left Jamie in bed, James Storer was making his way from Chester Primeaux's Mansion to the docks in Liverpool, the break-in at the mansion the previous night still preying on his mind. It was cold and a slight breeze chilled him as he boarded the ship.

He was greeted on board the Flying Fish by the first mate, Bill Wilson. 'Morning, Mr Storer. I'll get the stewards to stow your belongings.'

'Is everything on the cargo manifest loaded and secured properly?' Storer asked.

'Yes, sir. All cargo is aboard and stowed safely. The Captain is secured in his cabin.'

'So, we can get underway. Are all the passengers on board?'

'All the passengers are aboard but two; a Mr Fyvie and Mr McColl.'

'Who the hell are they? I was not aware there would be anyone except Mr and Mrs Knowles, their daughters, the doctor and me sailing for Cape Town.'

'I know, but Mr Knowles gave me instructions when he came on board this morning. It seems the immigration people asked him to give passage to these two as they were needed in the Cape to do some kind of survey. Their stuff was loaded yesterday with everybody else's and apparently all paid for by the Government's Immigration Department.'

'This is very odd even for the Government,' Storer said worriedly. *Especially after the events of last night,* he thought. 'Wait ten minutes. If they have not arrived, unload their belongings and leave them on the dock, then cast off.'

Just then a carriage came careening along the dock clearly in a big hurry. It stopped at the gangway and two young men got out. They said goodbye to someone in the carriage but Storer could not see who it was.

'It seems our two new passengers have arrived. There is something wrong here, Bill. Keep an eye on those two and report to me if you think there is anything unusual,' Storer said turning away.

'I will, sir,' said Wilson, watching the two come up the gangway.

Storer turned and walked to a doorway aft of the mizzen mast into a small stairwell which led to the officer's quarters and saloon. There was a stairway to the cargo deck below and one up to the charthouse on the quarterdeck.

Storer locked the door and went up to the charthouse. He watched through the porthole as Wilson shouted his orders, talked to the two young men and checked their tickets. It was time to talk to the captain; he was not a happy man.

Wilson left the boys with the steward and went to look for Storer in the officer's quarters and found him in the saloon with Captain Roger Willard.

'You will be going to meet your passengers, as captains do,' Storer was saying to Willard. 'We have two added passengers on our guest list who were given passage by Knowles, who is after all the owner of the ship so we cannot really object. However, he was approached by a Government department to let these two young men sail with him and I think they are here to keep a watch on us.'

'So why are you telling me this? I know nothing of any other passengers.' Willard said angrily. 'You and your henchmen are in control of the ship and Knowles seems to have put his trust in you. Lord knows why. So you deal with them.'

'When you introduce yourself do not give anything away. I will be listening. Make it short, then feign illness and retire. Do not forget our arrangement. I would hate for anything to befall our two new guests if they became suspicious and discovered something they should not know,' Storer said, the intent clear.

'I will not have to feign illness, that potion you force me to drink is making me so ill, anyone can see I'm not well.'

Storer motioned Wilson to take the captain back to his cabin. 'I will let you know when to give him another dose for his meeting. Secure him in his cabin and make sure we are safely underway.'

Storer went up to the charthouse to think on the two young men who had joined the ship. *They seem to be too young to be Government men,* he thought; *maybe they are just entrepreneurs taking advantage of an offer from the Government by doing some work for them.* He looked at some charts on his table and said out loud, 'I do not trust this situation'.

He traced his finger along the path of the trade winds on the chart thinking, *south of the equator, when we turn east for the coast of Africa, those two spies can join George Knowles when he is washed overboard in a terrible storm... with a helping hand, of course.* He smiled rolling up the charts. *Maybe I can have some fun with Knowles' two offspring once they are under the guardianship of their stepmother.* He shuddered at the thought.

Chapter Seventeen

River Mersey, Liverpool

'Let's go up on deck and say cheerio,' said Jamie.

'Aye, alright,' Iain said with a heavy heart.

The dull, wan tufts of autumn grass poking out from the harbour wall looked like they were waving them an erratic goodbye in the morning wind as the ship passed through the lock into the River Mersey, which flowed into the Irish Sea.

It was a dreary day, cloudy, cold and damp. They propped their elbows on the gunwales and watched England drift away.

The Flying Fish was a clipper refitted to take passengers as well as cargo. In their day they had been the fastest ships to transport cargo to Europe from the Far East.

Jamie looked around for any eavesdroppers and said, 'When we boarded the ship, did you see the man going through the door into that cabin thing at the arse end of the boat?'

Iain started laughing. 'The arse end of the boat?' he said incredulously. 'I think we better get your seafaring terminology sorted out. The boat is a ship and the arse end of the ship is the stern or aft. And no, I didn't see him.'

'I'm sure I've seen him somewhere before,' Jamie said thoughtfully. 'He could be Storer.'

'Well, I'm sure we'll know soon enough. So what dae ye think?' said Iain, changing the subject.

'What dae I think about what?'

'Dae ye think we'll ever see Scotland again?'

'I don't know, Iain. Maybe we'll make our fortune and come back; maybe we won't. I don't have any family left in Scotland and neither dae you. I just feel glad to be going to something else, something different, like an adventure, ye know?'

'Aye, I think I know what ye mean,' said Iain sounding unsure. 'After the last few weeks with Hugh Armstrong I'm not surprised by the way you're thinking. I think I trust him but it is some story. I mean, it seems to me we're being told a lot which is supposed to be secret and can't be proved. Christ's sake, it's a hell of a lot to take in, don't ye think?'

'It's certainly a lot tae think about,' said Jamie. 'I read a lot, I look at newspapers as much as I can and I read about things that happen in other countries and why the army and the navy are fighting in wars in those countries. All for the empire I suppose.'

'I'm all for the empire,' said Iain. 'If we don't get in first then it will be the French, the Dutch or the Portuguese and it's all about money; wealth and power, Jamie. Britain is not about to let it go elsewhere.'

'Well, this quest that we are embarking on is just… it's just unbelievable. I mean, slavery and gun-running, plots to topple the Government? This is an enemy within our own people as opposed to charging headlong into battle with guns and swords, and fighting a foe you can see. But the reality is; it's happening and we have pledged to fight the enemy within our country and away from our country.'

They paused for reflection a while longer then Iain said, 'It's too cold and miserable out here. Let's go and find the saloon and get a drink.'

'Aye, that's a good idea,' Jamie agreed. 'I am actually looking forward to this, Iain. We have been given an opportunity, not only to help the country, but ourselves. You and I, we can really do something with our lives.'

Iain turned and looked him in the eye for a second, smirked and then turned toward the companionway down to the cabins and saloon.

At the bottom of the stairs they walked past the cabins on the port side of the ship and a small galley on the right in the middle of the deck which had access through to the passageway and cabins on the starboard side. There were three double cabins on each side for paying passengers and another cabin with a bathtub and a small stove in it.

Both passageways led to the spacious and very comfortable saloon furnished with a dining table fixed to the floor in the middle of the cabin, below a larger than usual skylight. The padded chairs around the table had an ingenious device in the shape of a thin linked chain fixed to the deck with the other end attached to the underside of the chair to stop them sliding too far or falling over in rough weather.

The oak-panelled walls had padded bench-like seats fitted all around, with a Welsh dresser and drinks cabinet built into the aft side wall. A small pot-bellied coal stove was fixed into the corner of the opposite wall.

'Well, this is fine and cosy,' said Iain, rubbing his hands together.

There was one person in the saloon before them.

'Good afternoon, gentlemen. Allow me to introduce myself, Doctor Derek Morgan.'

'I'm Jamie Fyvie, this is Iain McColl,' Jamie said nodding at his friend.

They shook hands and looked awkwardly at the drinks cabinet.

'Join me for a drink and let us get acquainted,' the Doctor said cheerily as he rose to his feet and lurched unsteadily to the drinks cabinet. 'After all, we have to share a confined space on a long journey so let us make a start to making the best of the voyage.'

'Well, I would hate to see you drinking by yourself, Doctor,' Iain said with enthusiasm. 'I'm sure Jamie would agree with me and raise a large whisky to toast our voyage into the partially unknown.'

The doctor poured two healthy drams of whisky and handed them over. 'To fair winds, I believe is the saying, and a safe voyage,' the doctor raised his glass.

'Cheers,' came the reply from Jamie and Iain together.

'So what has inspired you to leave England for Cape Town, Doctor?' Jamie asked.

'Well apart from being a general practitioner I am also a surgeon and the colonies desperately need doctors. So I am going to set up a practice in Cape Town and to help with the new hospital, which I am told, is in the planning stages and will be built in a suburb called Green Point.'

He sat down on a chair and placed his drink on the table and asked. 'And what of you two able looking lads?

Off to seek your fortune no doubt.'

Jamie responded first.

'We are taking up the Government's offer of some land. We want to erect a workshop to produce wagons and agricultural implements among other industrial tools. We have been offered the chance of more land if we write an independent report about the new settlers,' Jamie kept to the cover story.

The Doctor tipped a healthy drop of whisky into his mouth. 'That's very interesting. Why would the Government ask two young men such as you to write such a report? Not that I am saying there is anything wrong with you two. It just seems very unusual for non-Government people to compile something like that.'

'Oh, there is nothing unusual about it,' said Jamie. 'The man that runs the Department of Immigration to the colonies just wants an objective and honest view outside of the Government about how the settlers are faring, and how the process can be simplified, both in Britain and in the Cape, maybe to give them better equipment and more help in settling in. The exercise will also give Iain and me a chance to set up a network to supply traders and look at what the settlers needs are.'

'Yes, I see the wisdom in such a project,' the doctor agreed. 'In Cape Town and Kaffraria, which is the Eastern Cape region, the opportunities are wide open for young men such as you. The wine industry and agriculture are starting to have an impact on the local economy, so there is scope for fresh and innovative ideas, and I believe the sheep farmers are bringing in a new strain of sheep for wool production. There are also investments if you want to make money.' He paused and had another swig. 'The only drawback of course is the persistent fighting with the natives. The wars hold up growing the economy, expansion and getting produce to the market place, it also costs the Government a lot of money to put down, and I believe the sabre rattling is starting again with native chiefs.'

'So you think another war is starting, Doctor?' asked Jamie.

'I really don't know. It is possible, I suppose, if you look at the history of that part of the country.'

'Well, is that not just our luck, starting a new venture in the middle of a bloody war,' said the ever pessimistic Iain.'

'Oh, for goodness sake, shut up with the doom and gloom,' said Jamie.

Iain was about to reply when the saloon door opened and two young ladies entered, followed by a very striking and beautiful woman on the arm of a sickly looking gentleman.

The two ladies looked to be in their early twenties with long blond tresses, piercing blue eyes and white complexions. They were wearing gaily coloured cream frocks and black flat shoes.

'Welcome aboard, gentlemen,' said the sickly man. 'I am George Knowles, the owner and operator of this ship, among others, and this is my family.' Knowles shook hands with the three men. 'This is my wife Anne and my eldest daughter Lydia, and Clara, my baby.'

'Oh, Daddy, I am not a baby,' protested Clara Knowles as everybody said hello and introduced themselves.

George Knowles started coughing and held a hanky to his mouth. Lydia rushed over and helped him to a chair.

He had a tall thin frame and pasty coloured skin. Yet

he had a commanding presence and a resonance in his voice, with a worldly and knowing look about his sallow face. His eyes were sunken, his lips seemed slightly blue.

'You must forgive me. I have very bad lungs and that is why we are heading south to Africa. I need to get away from the English weather to a better climate. It has just taken a bit longer than I anticipated organising my business affairs to be transferred to Cape Town.'

Anne Knowles was a beauty.

She looked at Jamie and then at Iain, then back to Jamie and looked him up and down as though appraising the merchandise.

Jamie appraised right back.

Her auburn hair was neatly coiffured around her magnificent head. Her almond-shaped dark eyes were perfectly placed above a slightly upturned nose and full, red lips. Her porcelain skin was flawless.

She was tall for a woman, wearing a figure-hugging dress, which accentuated her narrow waist and ample breasts.

As the company started chatting and found seats and chairs, drinks were handed around.

Jamie and Iain were sitting at the end of the table. Iain leaned close and said softly. 'Down boy, would ye like a knife and fork? I saw the way you and her were looking at each other. You looked like you were going to eat her.'

'I don't know what ye mean. Besides she's a married woman with two children, in case ye haven't noticed.'

'I don't think they are her daughters, for god's sake. They are nothing like her,' Iain whispered.

'Hmm, you might be right,' Jamie said thoughtfully.

'And do you really think Knowles is keeping her

satisfied in the bed chamber? I don't think so.'

'You've a dirty mind, Iain McColl, but there again, ye could be right.'

Anne Knowles refilled her sherry glass and drifted over to them.

For a moment Jamie thought she had overheard them.

'Well, this voyage is not going to be as boring as I thought it might be. I hope you gentlemen will keep us entertained and amused,' and looking straight at Jamie she said almost in a whisper, 'or me, at least.'

Jamie's face reddened and he replied. 'We aim to please, ma'am.'

They looked across the cabin when George Knowles said. 'Ah there you are. Come in, come in.'

A tall dark-haired man entered the saloon.

'Gentlemen may I introduce you to the Government man through whom I will be investing in the Cape Colony. This is the Cape Colonial Secretary, Mr James Storer.'

James Storer moved in to the saloon to allow somebody else in.

'And this is our good Captain, Roger Willard,' Knowles said, struggling to his feet.

'Father, please sit down for a while and rest. You have been travelling all day,' Lydia said holding his elbow.

'Oh don't fuss. I will be fine. I will get a good night's sleep tonight after dinner.'

Behind the captain the giant first mate entered and made the saloon look a bit cramped.

'And this is Bill Wilson, our first mate. He is new to our company crew and has volunteered to mind after the

Captain as he has come down with a malady from which he is slowly recovering, but insisted on overseeing this voyage.'

The Captain seemed to be sedate, even docile. His weather-beaten face was vacant and yet aware.

He was wearing a neatly pressed uniform, his captain's cap tucked under his right arm.

He sat down and said. 'On behalf of the owners and the crew I welcome you all on *The Flying Fish* and I hope you have an uneventful and comfortable voyage to your final destination. I really must apologise for my short welcome. I hope to recover in a few days and then we can get to know each other a little better. But for now I will retire and rest for a while. Please excuse me.'

'I could look in on you later, Captain, if you wish,' the doctor offered.

The Captain looked confused and Storer said. 'Oh that won't be necessary, Doctor. The Captain just needs some sea air. He'll be fine.' He looked at Knowles as though for support.

An awkward silence ensued in the saloon.

'Yes, he will be fine. We will call if we need your services, Doctor,' said Knowles.

Without another word, the first mate escorted the captain out of the saloon and the conversation slowly rose to a jovial level again.

'Well, that was short and sweet,' said Iain.

The doctor wandered over to where the boys were sitting and occupying a chair next to them leaned in and said. 'The good Captain seems to be under a bit of strain.'

'What makes you think that?' asked Jamie.

'You would not notice it but his eyes were much dilated. I have only seen that in people who have been using opium, or extracts of opium.'

'Opium?' whispered Iain. 'Isn't that a Chinese thing? Smoking some kind of weed or something?'

'Something like that,' the doctor said. 'But he does not have the sleepy, vacant look of the opium smoker. It may be something else. Very unusually interesting.' He stood up suddenly. 'Another drink, lads?'

'Aye!' exclaimed Iain as though he had just heard the stupidest question in his life.

Drinks poured and the doctor visiting the heads, Jamie said. 'Armstrong was right. There is something going on here.'

'Storer seems to be the controller of whatever it is,' said Iain.

'He just looks at people and they jump.'

'We'll draw up a plan of action later. Right now we just have to stay alert and stay friendly.'

The doctor came back and noticing Storer's absence said sarcastically. 'Mr Storer looks like the friendly type.'

'Aye, about as friendly as a snake in a hole,' said Iain.

The saloon was warm and comfortable and dinner was a pleasant affair with Jamie, Iain, the doctor and the Knowles family. The captain and Storer were dining together in the officer's saloon.

George Knowles picked up his glass and said. 'I'm afraid this will be the sort of fare we can expect for most of the voyage as the cook has limited resources.'

Knowles' daughters were giggling and whispering to each other.

'My daughters seem to be very taken with you young men,' said Anne Knowles.

'Stepdaughters,' Lydia said sharply.

'Yes, stepdaughters,' Anne said slowly, glaring at Lydia.

'So have you known Mr Storer very long, George?' asked Jamie.

'About eighteen months. He was introduced to me at a gala dinner by an acquaintance of Anne's funnily enough.' He moved his hand across the table and squeezed his wife's, at which, Lydia and Clara looked away in disgust.

'He has been very helpful in dealing with lots of red tape to help me move my assets,' he said as though in way of an excuse.

'Yes, I'm sure he has been very helpful,' said Iain smiling at Anne.

The Knowles' left for bed leaving Jamie, Iain and the good doctor to have a couple more drinks before deciding to call it a night.

'It is going to be an interesting voyage, lads,' said the doctor. 'Sleep well. Goodnight.'

The boys were lying facing each other in their bunks. They were in the middle cabin on the port side of the ship, it was late and the ship was cutting along on a calm dark sea, the noise of the bow wave and the wind sounding strangely comforting.

They were sipping a dram from the stock of whisky supplied by Armstrong; Jamie was trying to read the label in the dimness of the lamplight. 'I think we should wait for a few days, then search the cargo holds thoroughly from stem to stern over a couple of weeks. What dae ye think Iain?'

'Aye, but we should do the searches every second or third night so that it's just a short search; in and out so as not to attract attention.'

'Right, one person to keep watch and one to dig around.'

'This will be our first real test, Jamie, but if we don't pass it we won't have to worry about it.'

'Why won't we have to worry?'

'Because we will be food for the fishes and all the other nasty beasties that swim and crawl around in the sea.'

'We need to find out who is with Storer and who is not,' said Jamie.

'We would have to assume Wilson, the first mate, is with him. I'm not sure about the Captain though. Knowles is sure to be in cahoots with Storer. I mean he is a business man and he won't be going to Cape Town just for his health. He'll be looking to make a lot of money.'

'Agreed, but is he going to use his businesses as a façade to hide darker dealings with Storer and his *enlightened* boys, such as selling slaves?'

'Enlightened boys? I like that, Jamie, what about *light boys?*'

'Aye, *light boys.* That's what we'll call them,' said Jamie, fading fast with the effects of the wine and whisky.

'If Knowles is in with him, he would need some kind of business to cover his earnings, imports and exports, I suppose.'

'That he would. Right, that's me,' said Jamie swallowing the remains of his whisky. 'I need to sleep. Goodnight.'

Chapter Eighteen

London

The carriage was travelling at speed at the insistence of the solitary passenger. The intelligence report received by Earl Greyson from Liverpool was not what he wanted to convey to his masters.

He had sent an emergency communique rather than the usual line of communication to arrange the meeting and was hanging on for dear life as his transport hurtled around the roadways on the outskirts of London.

Reaching his destination, he was led through another magnificent mansion and positioned behind the elder seated in front of him, again with his back to Grayson.

'I believe you have an urgent report,' the voice in front stated.

'I received this information late last night by hand from one of our couriers,' said Greyson.

'I trust you have not divulged this information to anyone else.' It was a statement, not a question.

'No, elder. As soon as it came into my possession I made arrangements to report to you.'

'Then tell me what the content of this information is.'

'Fairbrother was followed to Dale Street. He entered

a tavern by the name of Rigby's, which was difficult to infiltrate because it had a local patronage. Our men have established that this is a front to conceal a secret-service base of operations and there were indeed two other men. They were seen being invited to a *private card game* in a room at the rear of the premises. The two men in question were staying at the Royal Park Hotel under the names of Steven Rattery and Trevor Black. Three other men in our employ happened to be in Rigby's keeping an eye on the place when these two first appeared and could not resist picking a fight with them. Needless to say our men were soundly thrashed and got themselves barred from going back. We then instructed them to stage a mugging and severely injure or eliminate them but they were all killed. We think two were left in the street by Rattery and Black, the other two were shot by an unseen gunman according to the police report. I am waiting to find out what actually happened there. Rattery and Black then disappeared from the hotel right after the break-in and subsequent theft at the American's mansion. They booked passage at the last minute through the Government Immigration Agency, on a ship bound for Cape Town, which sailed two days later.'

'You are sure they were the same men from the hotel, with the same names on the ships passenger listing?' 'Absolutely, I double-checked the names myself, but there is no way to verify if they used the same names on their travel documents'

'Which ship did they sail on?'

'They sailed on *The Flying Fish;* the same ship as James Storer.'

To say the silence was deafening would have been ludicrous under the circumstances.

A taper was lit and a plume of blue smoke emerged

from the chair in front of Earl Greyson and the pungent whiff of cigar smoke filled the air.

'I know that Storer hired five seafaring henchmen, who believe they are doing a bit of gun-running. They are also to take over the ship with violence if it becomes necessary,' said the man in the chair calmly. 'The captain is under our control, as is the ship's owner because of Storer's manipulation, but if the strangers on board are Government men, then we must assume the worst in that Storer has been compromised and any paperwork he was carrying has been discovered and will be turned over to the authorities in Cape Town, which hopefully, will be to one of our elders.'

'But what if Storer has discovered the strangers and disposed of them?' said Greyson.

'We cannot take that chance. We must send a courier with instructions on the next available ship. After we make some changes you will get duplicates of Storer's letters and documents. The Templars' clue will be duplicated as well and sent to you. If these strangers have managed to take the ship then they will have to be found in Cape Town, what names they used to enter the colony and find out what their mission is. We need to find them and make sure they have a fatal accident.'

'Yes, sir. I will make all the arrangements and keep you informed,' said Greyson.

'These events have changed the timetable for our plans dramatically. We are now forced to bring our plans forward,' said the senior elder of the ELOS. 'You have proved yourself a worthy asset to us, Earl Greyson. Keep it up and let me know what becomes of Storer. He could become a liability simply because of his position in the Cape Colony Government. If he is not compromised then the operation can move on as planned. The whole idea and planning is his, but if he is lost it would be a disaster for us in terms of the timing of the whole campaign, and his position will pass to his assistant. What is his name?'

'Nicolas Banbury, sir.. A capable man who, like Storer, has a taste for young dark-skinned females, although he is not aware that we know this.'

'Ah yes, Banbury. He will be promoted should Storer fail. Write a letter to Banbury explaining in detail what has happened, and to be ready for implementation of the new plans should they go ahead. Also tell him to make sure the demise of Smyth is whispered to the general public, and especially to the Xhosa chiefs before there is a public announcement. That should stir up the hostilities until Cuthbert is in place. There is only one punishment for failure. We cannot allow our plans to fall any further behind schedule. Africa is the prize that awaits us.'

Earl Greyson was escorted to his windowless carriage to return to Whitehall and start a sequence of events that would not only change the political landscape but also devastate the eastern frontier of the Cape Colony.

Chapter Nineteen

October 1855

Flying Fish, North Atlantic Ocean

As *The Flying Fish* continued sailing south away from the on-coming winter of the northern hemisphere, so the air temperature grew steadily warmer and Jamie would often walk around the top deck to get some exercise.

In the early days of the voyage Iain had suffered from severe sea sickness. Jamie suffered as well, but had recovered more quickly as his body got used to the ship's motion.

On some days he walked aft to try and catch a glimpse into the skylight on the quarterdeck above the officer's saloon behind the charthouse and high up in front of the helm.

There was a single, central stairway behind the mizzen hatch leading up to the quarterdeck. Jamie would climb the stair to chat with the helmsman and crane to see in the skylight, but it was a bit too high and the interior was always dark so there was nothing to see. So one day he took a chance and jumped up on the roof of the saloon and steadied himself with a hand on the apex of the skylight as though to get a better view ahead.

'Sir, you are not supposed to go up there. Please come back on deck,' said the helmsman.

Jamie was looking intently in the skylight but could see nothing. 'I just wanted to get a better view from up here,' he said

'Sir, I must ask you to come back on the deck,' the helmsman said getting agitated.

Just then the door in the charthouse opened. Storer stepped out and came up next to the wheel.

'I insisted he come down, Mr Storer,' the helmsman said, genuinely scared.

'Your insistence is noted Mr Higgins,' Storer said sarcastically whilst looking at Jamie.

'You really should heed Higgins' advice. It is for your own safety. After all we would not want you to come to any harm, Mr Fyvie.'

'Oh, I'm fine, I'm just trying to get a better view of what is ahead of the ship,' Jamie said without looking back.

'I am now insisting that you get down on to the deck. Otherwise I'll have to have you taken down and escorted to your quarters,' said Storer.

Jamie swung around, still crouched, balancing on his toes. He looked slightly down at Storer and said. 'I didn't know you had been made Captain, Mr Storer.'

'Only until Captain Willard recovers. George Knowles asked me to take command as I have a Captain's ticket.'

'And how is the good Captain? Getting better?' Jamie asked as he jumped effortlessly down to the deck.

'He is recovering slowly, and you don't have to worry. We'll take care of him.'

'I am sure you will,' Jamie said looking straight into the eyes of Storer.

'This area,' Storer swept his left arm around the quarterdeck, 'this deck, is off-limits to passengers and that comes from Captain Willard.'

Jamie gave an exaggerated salute and turned to continue his walk. He went around the front of the charthouse and down the stair. He quickly tried to open the door from the main deck under the stairs into the officers' quarters but it was locked.

He walked on a bit past the mizzen hatch and turned to look at Storer. The vision of the two men on the balcony at the Primeaux mansion suddenly popped into his head; he was sure this was the same man. He turned and carried on forward knowing he was going to find a way to break in and find out what was happening with the captain.

He saw Lydia Knowles coming towards him. When she reached him she turned and walked at his side.

'Do you mind if I join you for a walk around the deck, Mr Fyvie?' she asked.

'You are most welcome, Miss Knowles, but only if you call me Jamie.'

'And if you call me Lydia.'

'Good, Lydia. Is this your first journey over the seas?'

They were now walking port side past the crew's quarters and main galley amidships.

'Good gracious no, I've sailed with my father many times on our ships, especially this clipper. He had *The Flying Fish* refitted to take passengers, mainly for family and friends. I can handle the helm as well. My father taught me,' Lydia said proudly.

'Well, that's very impressive.'

'Have you sailed anywhere before this, Jamie?'

'No, this is my first time. Iain has sailed before, but then he was involved in ship-building in Glasgow. He's trying to avoid being seasick at the moment, I seem to have a higher resistance to it. Do you know the captain well, Lydia?'

'Fairly well. I've met him on occasion with my father. He's a very nice man and my father's best skipper. It's very unusual that we have not seen him since we sailed.'

'And Mr Storer?'

'I do not know him and I certainly do not like him,' she said sternly. 'Maybe I should not talk out of turn.'

'That's alright. Anything you say to me stays with me, and that goes for Iain as well. So why don't you like Storer?'

'Well, for one thing he's a bit overfriendly with my stepmother, and I have caught him leering at me and my sister with a very strange look in his eyes. Even when I look right back at him he just smiles and licks his lips. He is lecherous and I do not trust him.'

Jamie stopped and looked at her. 'Well, you seem to be a strong-willed young lady and you speak your mind,' he said. 'I like that in a person. Don't ever change that. Another thing, if you have any trouble at all, even when we get to our destination, send word to me and I'll be there. Alright?'

'Thank you, Jamie that is very sweet of you. I'll remember that,' she said looking into his eyes.

They continued walking their circuit of the deck, all the while being observed by Storer who went below when he saw them coming back.

'So you must know the ship very well.'

'My father showed me the drawings for the refit. I think I'm the replacement for the son he never had before my mother died. He explained the need for good workmanship and ballast, and making sure the cargo is balanced and held in place for going to sea. He has taught me so much I just cannot bear to see him the way he is. It breaks my heart,' she said, tears welling in her eyes.

'Let's hope that the climate in Africa will make your father well again. Never give up hope,' said Jamie.

'Don't misinterpret my compassion or quiet demeanour for weakness of resolve. I'll defend my family, that is, my father and sister, to death. As you say; never give up.'

'I never doubted you for a single moment,' Jamie said, meaning every word, and right there he made a decision to trust this young woman for she had a mind much older than her years. 'Let's stop here and look out over the ocean so we cannot be heard.'

'Alright,' she gave him a worried look.

'I'm going to take you into my confidence. Do you think there is something amiss with Storer and the captain?'

'Oh god, most definitely yes,' she said looking suddenly relieved to be sharing a burden that had been weighing on her mind.

'Keep your voice down, Lydia. Nobody can be trusted,' Jamie said softly.

'I apologise, Jamie. I'm just so relieved that someone else has noticed this. I'll try to stay calm. I fear for my father and not just because of his malady. You see my fears started long before we boarded *The Flying Fish*. After my stepmother introduced Storer to my father she has been helping father to transfer his assets and his money, but I have seen her and Storer meeting at night at the house when my father was away in London, and I have seen them kissing. I told my father, but he passed this off as a young girl's fantasy, and said that if she was meeting Storer it was on his behalf. She was merely kissing him goodbye and because I was missing my mother, I was seeing something that was not there, but I know I was not.'

She was getting agitated and her voice getting louder again.

'Lydia, look at me and smile. Can you do that?'

'Yes, sorry, 'she smiled and looked calm.

'You said you know this ship and you have read the drawings of the refit. Correct?'

'Yes, I know every inch of this ship.'

'I want to get into the officers' quarters but the door off the deck is always locked and apart from the helmsman there is always a crewman on watch. Do you know of any keys to unlock that door?'

Her smile suddenly got wider. 'I can do better than that. When my father started the refit he had a concealed trapdoor built into the deck in his cabin, which leads to a narrow passage between the real bulkhead and a false bulkhead built in the first cargo deck. The passage goes all the way along the deck to the officers' quarters and opens into the captain's cabin in which there is also a concealed door, but in the wall of the cabin. My father built the passage simply because if there was bad weather above on the main deck the captain or my father could traverse the length of the ship unseen. It's not common knowledge that it's there. In truth, I think Captain Willard and father are the only people aboard who know of it, and me of course. It's very rarely used so it's been forgotten.'

'Well now, that is very interesting information,' Jamie said thoughtfully.

'The trapdoor is very narrow. You might just fit through it. You are a big man. Oh, there's also a concealed door leading into the first cargo hold a third of the way into the passage.'

'Is your stepmother aware of the passageway?'

'I don't know. It's possible, I suppose. This is only the second time she has been aboard so why would she need to know? I wouldn't think father would need to tell her.'

'Your father and his wife are in separate cabins, aren't they?'

'Yes, she says father keeps her awake at night. Selfish bitch!'

Jamie raised his eye brows and started laughing.

'Do not laugh at me, Mr Fyvie.'

'I am not laughing *at* you. I just find it stimulating to hear a young lady using such colourful language.'

'Well, that's alright then,' Lydia said smiling.

'Apart from the officers' quarters, I don't see any way to get into the cargo hold either, except through the three topside hatches,' said Jamie.

'The only way down to the hold is the companion way from inside the crew's quarters and the one inside the officers' quarters. There is no way down from the passengers' quarters.'

'Which is why your father built the passageway. I need to access that passage in the next few days, along with Iain. I'm going to need your help to keep your father out of his cabin for a while, so that we can get in and out without being seen. Can you do that for me?'

'I can try, but I will not lie to my father.'

'I appreciate that. You won't need to lie to him. We'll wait for a calm, warm night when the stars are clear and the wind is not too strong, then you can get your father and stepmother to come up on deck and take a stroll for an hour.'

'I could get father to come for a walk but I don't think she will. She'll be in her own cabin, as usual.'

'Well, we'll have to plan this when the opportunity arises. Lydia, it's very important that you don't share this with anyone, not even Clara.'

'Jamie, I think I have grasped this fact already, I may be young but I'm not an imbecile,' she said haughtily.

'I have realised this. I didn't try to demean you in any way. I just don't want anyone to get hurt, especially you and Clara.'

'Thank you, Jamie.'

They continued walking. Jamie felt a strong bond forming between them.

'Well, she is old enough. She must be at least twenty two years old.'

'Trust you tae bring sex into it! It's not like that.'

'Aye, famous last words. I've seen the way she lusts after you.'

The boys were relaxing in their cabin, Jamie relaying the conversation he just had with Lydia.

'She may be twenty something, but she has a thirty-year-old head on her and believe me when I say, she's nobody's fool. There's nothing going on between us. We have a good ally in her.'

'I believe ye; don't get excited, old son, I'm just having a go at you,' Iain said smiling.

'Aye, I know. Ye can't help it, can ye?'

'No.'

A few days later the perfect evening they wanted presented itself.

The wind dropped, the sea had hardly any swell and the stars seemed to fill the sky from one horizon to the other.

All the paying passengers were on deck except for Anne Knowles.

The doctor was sitting on one of the steps leading up to the fo'c'sle. The Knowles family were sitting comfortably on top.

Jamie and Iain were lying down on top of the forward hold hatch staring up at the night sky.

'This is unbelievable. I've never seen anything like this,' Jamie said, amazed at the night sky.

'I have to confess, I never ever thought about looking up at the sky at night with another man,' said Iain, looking around guiltily.

'What? You don't like doing this with me?' Jamie said grabbing hold of Iain's hand.

'Ye daft bastard. Don't do that! Somebody might be watching,' said Iain, pulling his hand away with fright.

Jamie was laughing still looking at the stars above.

'Very funny,' said Iain.

'Come on, let's go exploring,' Jamie said getting up.

They went over to the door leading to the cabins and looked casually up at the stars again. When everybody was looking away from them they slipped down the companion way into their cabin to get the leather satchel with the tools and the candle in the special lantern.

The stewards and the cook had gone off duty, so they went through the galley and silently to George Knowles' cabin and let themselves in. Closing the door quietly they lit the candle lantern with the special slit, observing that the owner's cabin had more space than the others, as it would do.

'Lydia said the trapdoor is under the rug on the right side of Knowles' desk,' whispered Jamie.

Iain shone the light from the candle on the rug and Jamie pulled it away revealing nothing.

'Oh great; no door. What now, great undercover agent,' Iain said sarcastically.

'There, big mouth,' said Jamie pointing at a large knot in the planking on the floor. 'Lydia said to push down on the side of the knot and it will swivel and if I poke my finger in the hole I should feel a piece of string.'

He pulled the string out and discovered it was attached to a thin link chain. He pulled the chain and the concealed trap door miraculously revealed itself swinging up on hinges screwed to the underside of the door.

'It's no' very wide, is it. You'll barely fit through,' said Iain.

'Hold this,' Jamie said as he passed the tool bag and sat on the edge of the hatch. Squeezing himself through the gap, he had to hold his arms straight above his head to get his shoulders in.

He stooped in the passageway as Iain passed the lantern and tool bag and followed him down. Closing the hatch they moved sideways along the narrow passage until they could see the door leading to the cargo hold.

Jamie said. 'Lydia said the two doors and the trapdoor into her father's cabin are fitted with a small round dowel protruding from the false bulkhead so that when the dowel is pulled out, a person could see if anyone was on the other side.'

Iain held up the lamp and said. 'There Jamie; is that it sticking out on the other side of the door?'

Up on deck, George Knowles was looking at the stars with his daughters.

'This sight never ceases to amaze me,' he said. His arms were around Lydia and Clara's shoulders. 'The good Lord has given us such a wonderful way of life,' All of a sudden he started coughing violently. He sat down on the stool brought up on deck for him and hacked into his hankie. 'I think I will retire to my cabin,' he said wheezing.

Lydia felt the panic rise and said. 'I think you should wait until this attack has passed, father,' she pulled a blanket over his shoulders. 'Besides, the fresh night air will help to clear your breathing.' She said hoping to keep him on deck.

'Well, just for my girls, I shall stay a little longer,' he said, the coughing attack subsiding.

Back in the passageway, Iain covered the light of the candle as Jamie pulled out the dowel and peered through into the hold. All was dark and quiet. He replaced the dowel and opened the door. He stepped through, closely followed by Iain and they made their way down to the lower cargo hold. They searched quickly and methodically for five minutes and then silently went back the way that they had come.

'Shite!' Iain said when they were back in their cabin. 'Nothing there. Mind you, we only searched a small section.'

As they made their way back up on deck, they found Lydia helping her father down the steps to his cabin. She glanced at the boys with look of relief on her face when she saw them.

'You boys are missing the night sky. It is truly a splendid sight,' Knowles said as he sat on the step for a moment.

'We were up on deck earlier,' Iain said. 'We just went down for a bit of refreshment and now we are going back.

'You girls go on back up on deck with the lads. I will be alright. Off you go.'

Clara said. 'We will, father, as soon as I get you to your door.'

Clara walked with her father to his cabin whilst Lydia and the boys went topside.

'Did you find anything unusual?' she asked to no one in particular.

'No, we didn't,' said Iain. 'But we only searched a very small area. We need more time to do a thorough search. I don't suppose you were around when the holds were being filled?'

'No, I wasn't, but I did go down to the docks on one occasion with father, as he had to sign some documents. Now that I think of it large nets were being hoisted aboard that were filled with boxes and some other cargo covered with tarpaulins, but I didn't think anything of it until now. What are you looking for anyway? You seem to know that there is some cargo on board that shouldn't be there.'

'We don't know,' Jamie lied easily. 'I think we are all agreed that there's something amiss here with Storer and the captain.'

'Maybe they're smuggling gold or something,' Lydia suggested.

'That could be,' said Jamie. 'Which hold did you see the covered boxes being loaded into?'

'The mizzen hold in front of the officers' quarters,'

said Lydia.

'Well, that would make sense. If they were hiding something under the tarpaulins then they would stow it right under their arses, excuse my language.'

'Oh that's alright. It is actually quite refreshing.'

Clara joined them on deck after seeing her father to his cabin. 'What are you talking about?' she asked.

'WOW!' exclaimed Iain looking up at the stars.

'What? What is it?' said Jamie looking around.

'It was like a streak of light. It was only a second and then it was gone.

'It was a shooting star. I saw it as well,' Clara said standing right next to Iain.

'A what?'

'A shooting star. It is supposed to be a star that has fallen from heaven to earth.' She turned to Lydia. 'Father is fine. He is going to write some letters and go to bed.'

Lydia nodded.

'A shooting star, that's amazing,' said Iain.

'It is very lucky to see one and even luckier for two people to see one at the same time. When you see a shooting star you are supposed to make a wish,' she said, making it up, and looking at Iain with a cheeky grin.

George Knowles finished writing and was about to retire when he noticed the rug on the right of his desk was slightly askew. He bent down to straighten it and decided to lift it up to check underneath. The knot was slightly out of place, so he pushed it flush with the floor board and replaced the rug. He sat and looked at the rug for a minute and then went to his bunk, wondering briefly how the rug had moved and then fell asleep.

Chapter Twenty

Eastern Cape frontier

After his disastrous campaigns on the Kroomie Heights, General Sommerville swept into Gcalekaland with virtually no resistance. He captured the Xhosa Paramount chief, Samkelo with his followers, Samkelo protesting his innocence saying. 'Tell his Excellency Governor Smyth I am not in this war, I am innocent'.

But Sommerville was not listening. He was under strict orders from Smyth to undermine Samkelo's authority and *repatriate* stolen cattle. Some Hottentot deserters and rebels were chased down and shot if they showed any resistance; others that surrendered were taken for trial.

When Sommerville arrived back in King William's Town he drove before him hundreds of horses, sheep, goats, even dogs and around 30,000 head of cattle, all taken from the now destitute Gcaleka clan of the Xhosa people.

Charles Blackwell was a missionary to the Xhosa people as his father had been before him, and he had dedicated his life to their social and religious upbringing.

He was in Governor Smyth's outside office pleading

his case for the destitute people in Gcalekaland.

'You don't understand, sir. The Gcaleka people will starve now that the army has taken all the cattle, all the animals,' said Blackwell.

'Oh, but I do understand, Mr Blackwell. You see, if you break the law you will be caught and punished. Samkelo was caught with stolen cattle. He was harbouring fugitives from the law and therefore forfeits all his possessions, as do the people involved in the aforementioned crimes. They are free to return to whatever remains.'

'But sir, show some leniency. They have no food.'

'They should have thought of that before they took to stealing cattle and harbouring criminals. I cannot afford leniency, otherwise I would have total rebellion all over the country. They must realise that they cannot, and will not, get away with theft and treason. Now Mr Blackwell, I am very busy. Thank you for calling but it is in the hands of the courts now. Goodbye,' said Smyth. He went into his office and closed the door.

Blackwell looked at the closed door and knew there was no point in pursuing the matter any further.

As they had done so many times in the past the British had used the slightest excuse to start hostilities with the Xhosa; taken what they wanted, killed them and stolen their assets to enhance their prestige, just to show how powerful they are.

Samkelo and the people of the Gcaleka clan were left with nothing to survive, the British army had taken or destroyed all the food. Samkelo wanted revenge so once again he summoned all the Xhosa chiefs and their pakati to discuss a plan of attack on the British troops and the white settlers.

'Once we have taken possession of more guns from the British traitors, we will hunt the British troops and the settlers all the way to Cape Town and drive them out,' said Samkelo, looking to Mzingisi for support.

'Inkosi, the white men, will be driven away, but first we must take back the land between the Amatola Mountains and the Kei River. Your country, Samkelo, needs to be free of the white settlers. All the clans need to be free of the settlers, and then we will take the fight westward and free our land,' said Mzingisi, knowing Samkelo would take this advice and act on it.

'So will it be,' said Samkelo to all the chiefs. 'Send out your warriors and bring back the cattle that were taken from us. Burn the homesteads and drive the white man into the sea.'

General Sommerville was sitting at Smyth's desk sipping a glass of brandy when Smyth closed the door.

'We need to keep up the momentum, General,' said Smyth. 'I have drafted in some reinforcements to attack the Amatolas and the Kroomie Heights in force. I will lead a force of seven columns.'

'Seven columns? That is a force to be reckoned with, sir. I will of course have the supply lines knocked into shape and packed with enough ammunition for the duration of the campaign,' said Sommerville making notes.

'I also want you to tell your quartermaster to acquire some scythes and sickles; enough for every man in all seven columns.'

'I doubt if there are that many of those implements in storage anywhere. I would have to order them and that will take some time. Are you planning to cut your way into that infernal jungle up there?'

'Something like that,' said Smyth. 'They will be used for the purpose of hacking the vegetation, but the main use for these will be to cut down and destroy all the crops we come across in every single village in Xhosaland.'

'So we carry on from where I left off in Gcalekaland?'

'Not quite. You were a bit lenient. You did not destroy *all* the food. I will lead this campaign and we will leave nothing. Anything left when we leave will be burned to the ground. I want the chiefs to come begging at my door, or starve to death. Make sure we have the appropriate number of agricultural implements to cut everything down. The Government suppliers will deliver the tools we need or have them made. Tell them time is of the essence.'

There was a knock on the door.

'Come,' commanded Smyth.

Smyth's aide came in to the room. 'Begging your pardon, sir: despatches from London. I thought you would want them immediately.'

Smyth took the package and the aide left.

'This must be from Earl Greyson, to give his blessing on our campaign,' said Smyth as he emptied the documents on his desk and, finding the one he wanted, broke the seal and began reading.

Sommerville watched Smyth's pallor turn to pale as he read.

'Sir, is there something wrong?' asked Sommerville.

'I cannot believe what I am reading,' Smyth said standing up from his chair. He ran his fingers through his hair and said. 'They cannot do this to me, after all I have sacrificed and endured for the British Empire to maintain a foot hold in Africa.'

He sat down heavily in his chair and handed the letter to Sommerville.

'I have been dismissed. I am to stand down as Governor and hand over to my replacement. He is on his way to the Cape as we speak,' said Smyth, visibly shaken.

Sommerville read the letter and was speechless, not knowing what to say or do. 'They need to give you more time, sir. Our next campaign will crush the Xhosa.'

Smyth took back the letter and read it again. His face changed from a man who was defeated to a man who knew exactly what he was going to do.

'General, organise your troops, the heavy guns and as many scythes as you can muster. We leave for the Amatolas within the next two weeks, and I will show them what bush warfare is about. I put down these bloody natives once and I can do it again. Mzingisi will fall again. Once he knows I am coming, he will run.'

When Mzingisi returned to his den in Fuller's Hoek he sent out bands of warriors to attack farms and steal cattle in retaliation for the cattle that had been stolen from his people. Sandla went back to the Amatola Mountains and sent his warriors to take back cattle and burn homesteads. He would also have his revenge. The chiefs were still delirious with their victories in battle over the British and now they really believed they would take back their land and drive the British out.

After many days of plundering the countryside and instilling the fear of death in the settlers, Mzingisi was with his great wife in his hut feeling very pleased with himself. His crops were growing and he had a fine herd of cattle, which was every Xhosa's dream; to have his eyes filled with his cattle.

He was just finishing a fine meal and drinking sorghum beer when he was told that one of his spies had returned from King William's Town with news of Inkosi Enkhulu Smyth. Mzingisi commanded his wife to leave him and summoned the messenger.

'Inkos,' said the messenger respectfully, using the Xhosa name for 'chief' and bending on his knee.

'What news do you have of Smyth?' asked Mzingisi.

I have heard that the white chief Smyth himself will be leading thousands of troops to the Amatolas.'

'The word that Smyth marches soon is reliable?'

'Yes, Inkos, overheard by one of the servants in the officers' eating place.'

'Is there any other news?' asked Mzingisi.

'Inkos, there is other news. The Inkosi Enkhulu Smyth is being sent away.'

Mzingisi stood up and said. 'What did you say?'

The messenger cowered before his chief. 'Inkos, it is true. I heard this from two different people from the military compound. There is to be a new governor soon.'

Mzingisi waved his informant away and summoned his pakati to inform them of another impending battle and the news of Smyth's departure.

After much discussion it was decided that if Smyth arrived in force they would move the cattle and take what they could and flee into the areas in the Amatolas, where the white man had never been. They would leave warriors behind to engage the troops and disappear into the bush. Mzingisi left his den and travelled into the Amatolas to warn Sandla.

All the chiefs were warned and the plans agreed. At

all cost they would avoid Smyth's forces until he was replaced, and then they would dictate terms with His Excellency's replacement.

Mzingisi knew Smyth would not drive him out. As he had told the other chiefs, Smyth was too old and Sommerville did not have a warrior's heart to fight him. He had a dream that the white man would fail again and this would surely be a sign from his ancestors that they would slay the enemy.

Thirteen days later, Governor Smyth led a force of seven columns out of King William's Town and marched on the Kroomie Heights. Knowing that this was to be his last campaign, he wanted to end this war with the Xhosa before his replacement arrived to take over and take the credit.

He set up his headquarters in the Blinkwater Post and sent three columns to the Kroomie Heights to find Mzingisi's den and destroy it. General Sommerville had his heavy guns bombard Fuller's Hoek, and then sent in his divisions to rout the Ngqika people at bayonet point.

The only problem was that when Sommerville's soldiers arrived to start the rout they discovered that Mzingisi, Sandla and all their warriors, along with their people and most of their cattle, had already fled from Fuller's Hoek, leaving very few women and children to be captured. The villages and crops were burned and cut down leaving nothing, and any livestock remaining was confiscated.

Two columns from the remainder of Smyth's forces stormed the Amatolas, meeting up with Sommerville's columns, chasing the Ngqika from the west.

For days the destruction went on, as they took the

few cattle they could find, burned huts and villages, then went back again to make sure the Ngqika were not re-establishing the villages. Smyth was convinced the chiefs would beg for mercy, until Charles Blackwell paid him a visit.

'The chiefs know you are to be replaced your Excellency,' said Blackwell. 'They will never surrender knowing you are leaving.'

'How can they know about my leaving? Nothing has been made public as I hold the only letter confirming this,' said Smyth.

'Sir, news of this nature always gets out. The chiefs will run and hide until you are gone. They are convinced they will dictate their terms to the new Governor to end the war.'

Smyth thanked Blackwell and retired to think on this news. Someone had leaked his impending demise, but who? It would not have been Sommerville, of that he was sure. So it had to be someone in London which meant they wanted him shamed into leaving without ending the war.

He recalled Sommerville and his troops and led them back to King William's Town. He started putting his papers in order and waited for his replacement.

The chief of the Ngqika clan, Sandla, was still in the Amatolas with over 2,000 warriors. His war chief, Mzingisi, was back in his den in Fuller's Hoek with 3,000 warriors, replanting his crops and rounding up stray cattle.

Smyth knew this was the end; it had all been for nothing.

Chapter Twenty One

King William's Town, Eastern Cape

The Honourable, General Sir Gerald Cuthbert, arrived in King William's Town with a swagger and a confidant air about him which did not go unnoticed by Smyth who was waiting to greet him.

'Governor Smyth, I am General Gerald Cuthbert, here to relieve you,' said Cuthbert, who was taken aback at Smyth's appearance; he was clearly suffering in mind and in body.

'I am relieved, Gerald, and please call me Garry,' said Smyth, saluting and then shaking his hand. 'I have to tell you right off that I have sent a scathing letter to Earl Greyson about my achievements here and the way that I was summarily dismissed.'

'That is of course your prerogative, Garry,' said Cuthbert, feeling uncomfortable about talking to each other on a first name basis. 'I am following orders, you understand.'

'Yes of course you are, Gerald. I will pour us a brandy and then I will formally hand over to you.'

They spent the rest of that day and the whole of the next discussing the state of the Cape Colony, with Smyth trying to tell the new governor how to handle the natives, and the new governor humouring him.

A week later just before dawn Sir Garry Smyth rode out of King William's Town, the town he had named with General D'Urban all those years ago. The troops that had been under his command cheered him as he went passed as did the townsfolk.

On the hills and from the surrounding bush thousands of Xhosa warriors emerged to salute this lion of a warrior of many conflicts with the cry, *inkosi enkhulu. The great chief.* Mzingisi, taking up the cry more than anyone, felt honoured to be part of this rich vocal tribute that filled the air for miles around.

Mzingisi watched Smyth ride away and was gripped with a dark feeling of foreboding.

When Smyth reached the harbour in East London, he boarded *HMS Styx* and sailed for Cape Town to be reunited with his wife. He sailed from there to England aboard the aptly named *HMS Gladiator* never to return to his beloved Cape.

The plans of the ELOS to discredit Smyth and replace him with one of their own was now complete.

The unrest along the frontier continued, with bands of Xhosa warriors roaming the countryside virtually unopposed, as they looted and plundered at will, convinced of their invulnerability.

Chapter Twenty Two

Flying Fish, North Atlantic Ocean

A light, warm breeze wafted across the top deck of *The Flying Fish.*

Jamie and Iain had been watching the crew and chatting to them when they got the chance without raising suspicion, trying to find out who was with the captain and who was with Storer.

'The way I see the situation is this,' said Iain. 'The crew are company men, loyal to the captain. Some of them have been working on Knowles' vessels for years as he treats them well. They have a high respect for the captain and have sailed with him off and on for a long time except, that is, for two seamen, Higgins and Slater and the first mate, Bill Wilson who they don't know and have never worked with before.'

'That's about the same information as I have. Those three only joined the crew with Storer for this voyage and the company boys don't like them one little bit,' said Jamie. They were at the usual place on deck so as not be overheard. 'I don't know what Storer is up to yet, but I'm sure George Knowles is not with him. I think it may be Anne Knowles.'

'Anne Knowles? What makes you think that?' asked Iain.

Jamie related to Iain what Lydia had told him about the goings on at her home before coming on this voyage. 'But I can't see how it all fits together,' said Jamie.

One of the stewards came on deck and came up to them. 'Your hot water is ready for the bath, Mr Fyvie and there are towels in the cabin as well.'

'Thanks, I'll be right there.'

'Bath time?' Said Iain.

'Aye, I asked the cook after breakfast to get it ready.'

'Watch ye don't get murdered in your bath,' Iain said smiling. 'Take your dirk in the tub with ye, just in case.'

'Och shut up!' Jamie said and went below looking forward to relaxing in some hot water.

Jamie was luxuriating in the bath, smoking a cheroot and sipping on a large whisky, when he heard a tapping on the door.

'Aye, I'm taking a bath. Who is it?'

After a pause there was a tapping on the door again.

Curious, but irritated, Jamie put down the smoke and the drink on the floor and got out of the bath. Wrapping the towel around himself he unlatched the door to look out when Anne Knowles pushed her way in, almost knocking Jamie over.

'What the hell are you doing?'

She closed the door and locked it. She was wearing a dark-green satin cape with a large hood.

'I asked the cook for hot water for bathing,' she said. 'He told me you had ordered before me, so I waited for you to come in here and gave you time to undress.'

She flung off the cape, revealing what looked like a nightgown. Stepping back she pulled it up by the skirt and over her head not in the least bit shy at revealing her flawless body; smooth, white skin, perfect hips and long legs, a dark triangular patch of hair at the top of her thighs and those magnificent breasts.

'I have seen the way you look at me,' she said stepping toward him.

He couldn't take his eyes of her breasts; the areolas covered almost the foremost part of her breasts. He had never seen nipples so perfectly formed and so long. He just wanted to take them in his mouth.

'You want to feel them, Jamie?' she said, her voice sounding so erotic. She took his hands and placed them on her breasts. 'Squeeze my nipples, Jamie.'

He took each nipple between his forefinger and thumb and squeezed gently.

'Harder, Jamie: Hurt me, squeeze harder.'

He instinctively took her nipples between his thumb and the side of his finger and pulled as he pinched them hard.

'Oh, that's it. Keep doing that, I like some pain, Jamie,' she said, as she pulled away his towel and grabbed his testicles with one hand and his penis with the other, 'My, that *is* big and hard, Jamie.'

She squeezed his balls just enough to hear him take a deep breath. She started to masturbate him as he kept pinching her nipples and she licked his still-wet body all the way down to his hardness and took him in her mouth, clearly savouring the moment when she took it out and looked at it, admiring it as though comparing it with something in her memory. She then sucked in one of his testicles and teased it with her tongue, licking all around it in her mouth, then she did the same with the other, biting with just enough pressure to make him wince with pleasure.

She suddenly stopped what she was doing and stood up encircling her arms around his neck. Knowing he could hold her weight she pulled herself up his body, her legs clasping around his waist. He pushed his hands down between his body and her thighs and held her firmly with his hands on her buttocks and then she lowered herself slowly onto him, gasping as he filled her to the hilt.

She started to pump up and down slowly at first and then getting faster and harder until their skin and muscles were slapping against one another. Looking into his eyes she said. 'Fuck me hard! Fuck me good and hard!'

He responded. They stood in the middle of the cabin and battered their bodies against the other. He walked with her still impaled on him and put her back to the bulkhead and pounded in and out of her until he felt a change in her muscles as she started her orgasm.

Her arms straightened out over his shoulders and she let out a low moan, grinding her pelvis against his, tightening her legs around him making him gasp. She let go of him and slid down to her knees and took him in her mouth once more and sucked greedily at it until he ejaculated into her mouth, trying to swallowing his semen. Some spilled out of her mouth and ran down her chin and on to her breasts. She kept massaging his penis as the hardness faded and his majestic erection started to go limp.

'Now that's what I call spontaneous fucking,' she said, stepping into the bath to wash herself. Stepping out, she towelled herself down and, putting on her nightgown and cape, she cupped his balls in her hand and said, 'I want more of that, Jamie Fyvie.'

She opened the cabin door, made sure the

passageway was clear and was gone.

'What the hell was that?' said Jamie, talking to himself. 'That couldn't have lasted more than fifteen minutes.'

He slid back into the bath and relit his cheroot, feeling mighty satisfied.

He rinsed himself off and got dressed, all the while thinking of what had just happened. *I've just had great sex with a married woman, whose husband is lying ill a couple of cabins away* he thought, *the problem is; I really like her stepdaughter. Shite!*

Gulping down the remains of the whisky, he went back to his cabin and told Iain what had just taken place.

'I knew it, I knew it!' said Iain punching his fist into his palm. 'She was gagging for it, but how come it's always you that gets shagged? What about your pal here?'

Jamie ignored the question. 'What a body, Iain. She's got nipples like organ stops.'

'Organ stops? What dae ye mean… organ stops?'

The Flying Fish sailed on encountering only fair weather and scorching sunshine. The crew had taken a piece of sail material and made a sun shade for George Knowles, who was settled underneath with a book, Lydia and Clara in attendance. He was clearly looking better and had some colour in his face. The fact that his girls were with him made it obvious he was a happy man.

As usual, Anne was nowhere to be seen.

Lydia wandered over to Jamie and said. 'I just thought I would let you know that father is going to be up here for a while. Where is Iain?'

'He's below,' Jamie said 'The sun is not good to him with his fair skin. I won't stay out too long myself. So you're saying we have some time to use the passageway from his cabin?'

'Yes. I thought it would be ideal.'

'The problem is getting into his cabin without being seen.'

'I have thought about this. I will go and call the cook and the stewards to discuss food or cleaning or something, and you can slip into father's cabin. After an hour I will go to father's cabin as though to look for something. If you have not returned I will go back ten minutes later and every ten minutes until you emerge, and I will call the crew for another meeting so as you can get out. What do you think?'

'That sounds great,' Jamie said clearly impressed. 'That should give us time to have a good look below, as long as there is not too much activity with the crew.'

'You should not have too much trouble as the crew is usually busy with repairs and cleaning. I am going back to my father. When I see you going below I will wait a while and then you will hear me calling the crew. Good luck.'

Jamie waited for a while and then went to go below when Anne Knowles stepped on to the deck. God, she was beautiful and Jamie felt a twinge in his groin.

'Good morning, Jamie,' she said, waving to her husband and stepdaughters. 'Enjoying the voyage? If George would spend the money we could buy one of those new steamships and travel a bit faster and with a bit more comfort.'

'Is it not more romantic to travel under sail and enjoy the wind in your hair?'

'Maybe for some, but definitely not for me. I am so bored,' she said lowering her voice. 'Why don't you come to my cabin and play cards with me tonight when everyone is asleep?' She winked.

Jamie was once again taken aback by her forwardness. 'Your cabin is between your husband's and the girls' cabins. It would not be a good thing to get caught sneaking in or out of yours,' said Jamie.

'Oh, don't be such a prude. We are both adults and my husband is not physical enough to take care of my needs. You will have your eyes opened in Cape Town; there are lots of bored, married women. The men have a liking for dark skin and believe me when I tell you they make the best of the servants, being the master of the house.

'You are in a different world now; Jamie. Best you get used to it and make the best of it. Well, the offer is still open,' she said as she walked over and sat with her husband.

Jamie nodded at Lydia and went below to find Iain. He was sitting in the saloon reading a book.

'Come on, Iain. Knowles is going to be up there a while. Let's get the tools and go exploring again.'

'What, in broad daylight? I'm really looking forward to completing this voyage, not being thrown overboard if we do find something.'

'Lydia's going to help us. Move your arse.'

They went to their cabin and a few minutes later Lydia called the galley crew into the saloon.

Crossing through the galley to starboard, Jamie checked the passageway and opened Knowles' cabin door.

They went into the hidden passageway and seeing no one in the top hold went through the concealed door and hid themselves where they could see the stern stairway under the officers' saloon. Below that was the ladder to the deck below.

'You go first, Iain. I'll be right behind you.'

'Fuck off! You go first and I'll follow you. You can get yer balls blown off before me.'

'Oh for god's sake, yer a big jessie.'

Jamie moved off and swiftly went down the ladder. Iain came down seconds after. Lighting the candle they went as far to the stern as they could and removed some bags of grain until they found a tarpaulin covering what felt like wooden boxes. After some effort they pulled back the cover and jimmied open one of the crates. It was full of muskets.

'Jesus, Jamie, with this amount of guns these people are really going to start a revolution.'

'I'm assuming the shot and powder are here as well. Let's go further up and see if we can find them. For god's sake don't drop the candle or you'll blow us all to hell.'

They found the shot and the powder, then put everything back as they had found it. They were recovering the guns with the tarpaulin when they heard voices drifting down from amidships.

They saw the glow from a lamp and dancing shadows as someone descended the ladder from the deck above down on to the same deck as the boys.

Iain covered the small candle and watched with Jamie as two crewmen moved forward and started checking the cargo was lashed down safely. The boys quickly and quietly replaced the sacks as best they could and extinguished the candle. They crawled stealthily over the cargo to where the ladder was and waited for the crew to move further forward before they went up.

Checking there was no one else around they went to

the concealed door, opened it and slipped through, securing the door back in place.

Iain relit the lamp and looked up. Jamie held his index finger vertically across his lips and motioned to Iain to follow him. Iain screwed up his eyes and shook his head mouthing, 'What?'

Jamie moved on aft and the passage angled up to the same level as the officers' quarters. He moved up behind the hidden door and slowly pulled out the dowel to see into the captain's cabin. He could see Captain Willard lying in his bunk with James Storer standing over him and Bill Wilson standing by the door.

'You will never get away with this,' the captain was mumbling. 'You're mad.' He tried to sit up but Storer pushed him back down.

'I am tired of hearing you say that, captain. You will stick to the plan. When we get to the Cape you will report a terrible storm and say that some people were lost overboard. We will then sail to a deserted beach just past Algoa Bay and deliver the guns. Are we clear?' he said a bit louder.

Iain pulled on Jamie's sleeve and gestured to let him see. Jamie waved him back and he continued to listen.

'Very clear,' croaked the captain.

'Bill, give the captain his medicine.'

'No! No more of that infernal potion.

Storer held the captain's wrists as Bill poured something into his mouth.

Jamie could not believe what he was seeing. The captain was shackled to a metal ring on the bulkhead. He leaned back to let Iain peer through the hole and see what was happening to the Captain, then replaced the dowel and indicated to Iain to move back. They shuffled their way back to Knowles' cabin and Iain peered through the dowel hole. 'I can't see much from this angle but I think the cabin is empty.'

They went into Knowles' cabin and replaced everything as normal. As they waited for Lydia, Jamie and Iain discussed what they had witnessed in the Captain's cabin.

'I think we should insist that the doctor take a look at the captain,' said Iain.

'You're right, but that will only arouse their suspicions and they might clap us in irons before we can take the initiative. What do you say we alert the doctor to what we have discovered? I don't think he's in cahoots with them.'

'Aye, we'll have a quiet word with him in the saloon when nobody's around.'

They sat for about another ten minutes when the door suddenly opened making the two of them jump at the same time; Lydia stuck her head in.

'Jesus Christ, my nerves!' said Iain.

'What happened?' asked Lydia.

'Not now. We need to get out of here.

'I will go to the galley and when you hear me shout for the cook the way should be clear. Then I will meet you on deck, Jamie Fyvie.'

'Indeed you will, Lydia Knowles.'

'Jesus, what is it with you and women?' Iain said shaking his head.

Jamie ignored him and on hearing: *Cook!* He made sure the passageway was clear and went straight topside whilst Iain went to their cabin.

Chapter Twenty Three

Flying Fish, North Atlantic Ocean

Bill Wilson knocked heavily on Storer's cabin door.

'Come in!' he shouted.

As Wilson entered Storer said. 'My god, man! Why are you trying break my door down?'

'Sorry sir, but I think you need to come below.'

'Why, what's wrong?' he asked suddenly alert.

'Higgins and Slater say the cargo above the guns has been disturbed.'

Higgins and Slater were the only crew allowed to check and secure the holds, as ordered by Storer.

They went below and Dan Slater, the bosun, who was not popular with the regular crew, showed them where the disturbance was.

'Higgie and me, we stowed them grain sacks ourselves, as was your orders, sir,' said Slater. 'You can see they've been moved and put back because they're a bit loose and the net isn't secured properly.'

'Did you search to see if anyone was down here?'

'We did, sir, but there was nothing and nobody. That's when we called the first mate.'

'Whoever came down here did not enter through the

aft saloon, so, as there are only two ways down here, they must have entered through the crew's quarters.'

'That's not possible, sir. Someone would have seen them as there is always a watch on duty.'

'So either somebody on watch was bribed, or one of the crew is snooping, or there is another entrance that we do not know about,' Storer said, looking around the packed hold. 'Slater, I want you and Higgins to go forward and search below the passengers' cabin area and look for a concealed door. Look closely mind and do a thorough search. If you see anything you are not sure of come and fetch me or the first mate.'

Storer and Wilson went topside through the crew's quarters and looked around. The sailmaker was sitting aft doing some repairs; the carpenter was checking the deck planking for any leaks; other crew members were climbing about on the rigging, going about their business.

Jamie Fyvie was looking in their direction as he talked to Lydia Knowles sitting at the fo'c'sle head.

'They are up to something, I will find out what and it will be dealt with harshly,' said Storer.

He walked off and left Wilson wondering what he meant by harshly. *This voyage is getting more uncomfortable by the day,* he thought. *I only signed up with Mr Knowles because of the offer from Storer to keep the guns from scrutiny. After all, what harm was there in selling a few hundred guns to some bloody natives*? He walked aft toward the quarterdeck wishing he had not got involved with gun-running.

Chapter Twenty Four

Flying Fish, South Atlantic Ocean

Jamie and Lydia were sitting, cross-legged on the fo'c'sle and Jamie was in a quandary.

Lydia is totally faithful to her father and would never lie to him, he thought. *The problem is I don't know where Knowles' priorities lie. Is he with Storer or is he a pawn? Should he go against everything he learned from Armstrong and tell her everything he had discovered in the hold today? And if he did, would she go to her father with it and unwittingly help her father to carry out this madness, or would he, or could he, turn the ship around and end it?*

'So tell me what you found out?' she whispered excitedly.

Jamie was looking over Lydia's shoulder at Storer and Wilson as they alighted from the crew's quarters. Without moving his head he met Lydia's eyes and said. 'Don't turn around until I tell you. Understand?'

'Is someone watching us?' She immediately caught on.

'Yes,' he said, looking back at Storer.

Storer looked at him for a few seconds and muttered

something to Bill Wilson and then went back towards the quarterdeck. Wilson did not look happy in his world.

'Who is it?' she asked still looking at him.

'Wilson and Storer, and I think they might have discovered what part of the cargo we were searching. Wilson doesn't look very happy.'

'So what did you find, Jamie?' she said earnestly.

'Lydia, you cannot react to what I am about to tell you. Wilson is still on deck watching us.'

'What is going on, Jamie? I will be still, don't worry.'

'We found guns, gun powder and shot in the hold.'

'Guns? How many?'

'Hundreds. Not only that, Storer and Wilson have the captain subdued with some kind of drug,' said Jamie.

'Oh my good god,' said Lydia, putting her hand to her mouth and going slightly pale.

'If you tell your father and he is in league with Storer, then…'

'Never! My father would *never* smuggle guns.'

'Please let me finish what I need to tell you, Lydia. Please listen.'

She nodded. 'Alright, I'm listening.'

'If you tell your father about this and he is in league with Storer, Iain and I will not see the end of this voyage in Cape Town. We will be at the bottom of the Atlantic Ocean. If he is not with Storer and he confronts him then we could all be in danger of being fish food, because Storer is already in control of this ship.'

'What are we to do?' She said starting to quiver.

'We mustn't panic, Lydia. Together, we will find a way out of this. Here comes the doctor.'

The doctor wandered out on to the deck and walked

up to meet them.

'Good day. Looks like the weather is going to change for the worse, I fear.'

Jamie and Lydia had been so engrossed in their conversation they hadn't noticed the swell getting bigger.

'Oh my, I think you're right, doctor,' said Lydia, looking to the horizon. 'That looks like heavy rain we're sailing towards.'

'Yes, it does,' the doctor concurred. 'Well, it will not be the first time I have weathered a storm and, hopefully, it will not be the last. We will just have to pass the time in the saloon with a couple of drams of whisky until it passes. What do you say, Jamie, my boy?' Not waiting for an answer he wandered off to claim his chair in the saloon.

Jamie was looking in the same direction as Lydia and said. 'You said heavy rain and the doctor said a storm. So which is it?'

'I think it will be a storm, seeing as we're out in the ocean,' said Lydia.

'Oh god! I don't want to be sea sick again.'

'I don't think you will, after your first bout you should have your sea legs by now.'

The bosun was shouting orders to the crew to secure the rigging and batten down the hatches.

Bill Wilson emerged on deck to do a quick inspection and barked some orders as he approached the fo'c'sle.

'Miss Knowles, I would advise you and the gentleman to go below in a few minutes. We're sailing into some rough weather. It'll be getting dark in an hour or so and it wouldn't be advisable to be exposed on deck.'

'Thank you, Mr Wilson,' replied Lydia.

Big drops of rain started falling and they scurried

below. Lydia went to check on her father. Jamie went to the saloon where the doctor, Iain and Clara were sitting chatting.

'Where did Lydia go to, Jamie?' asked Clara.

'She went to look in on your father.'

'Thank you. Please excuse me.'

'The Knowles' girls are so well-mannered and always courteous,' remarked Doctor Morgan, refilling his glass with whisky and pouring another two for the boys.

'We need to talk to you, doctor,' said Jamie.

'What seems to be the problem?'

A steward came in to check that everything was locked away and secured. He turned to the three men and said. 'Please make sure the drinks cabinet is closed when you have a refill, otherwise if we hit heavy seas the bottles will fall out. The galley crew will be going to their quarters now till the storm is over.'

The doctor watched the steward leave the saloon. 'Now what do you need to tell me?'

Jamie and Iain took it in turn to tell Doctor Morgan what their suspicions were and what they had found in the hold without divulging their true mission.

'Well, now that you have told me, I'm implicated as well.'

'Lydia knows, but Clara does not,' said Jamie.

They could feel the ship's movement becoming more erratic as the storm grew.

'We must assume the worst,' said Jamie. 'They can't take a chance on letting us arrive in Cape Town with this knowledge.'

'But what on earth would they want with all those guns?' asked the Doctor.

'You mentioned a war brewing with the natives on

the eastern frontier,' said Iain.

'Oh, you think they are selling the guns to the natives? I cannot believe it,' the doctor said, realising what they were implying.

Lydia opened the saloon door and looked at the doctor. 'Please could you come and look at my father again, doctor. He is so lethargic, I don't know what to do.'

'He was fine when I looked at him this morning. Let me have a look. I'll just get my bag from the cabin and I will see you there.' He turned to Jamie and Iain and said. 'We will talk later.'

'I'll come with you, Lydia,' said Jamie.

George Knowles was lying in his bunk. He opened his eyes and looked at his daughter. 'I must have dozed off, Lydia.'

'The doctor is here to find out what is wrong with you, father.'

'I'm just very tired, my dear.'

'Hello, George. You are not doing so well, are you?' said the doctor clamping his stethoscope in his ears.

'I was feeling fine up until a few days ago, I don't know what is wrong with me, Doctor. I have no fire in my belly.'

'Have you been drinking lots of water and eating regularly? I have not seen you at the dinner table?'

'Yes, I have been eating and drinking. Anne brings me my food and she brings me tea three or four times a day. The tea is bloody awful. We must change it.'

The doctor saw the tea cup, lifted up and sniffed the dregs. He handed it to Jamie. 'Keep this for me,'

Jamie nodded.

'No more tea. From now on just water and I will see to your diet,' said the doctor.

'Nonsense! George loves his tea, don't you George?' said Anne Knowles.

Nobody had seen her enter Knowles' cabin.

'Mrs Knowles, I must insist. There is obviously something about the tea that is reacting with him.'

'Well, if you insist I suppose it will have to be water only,' she said icily.

The ship was rolling and heaving quite violently now. Outside the dark sea was raging. It would be a long night.

Knowles could feel his ship beneath him and suddenly took command. 'Everyone to their cabins, please. You too, Anne. Make sure there's nothing loose lying around.'

'I'll come back in the morning, George,' said the doctor. 'I'll get some whisky from the saloon and then go to my bunk. Try and get a good night's sleep. Goodnight.'

'Lydia, Clara, go and get to your bunks. I'll be alright. I've been through this before.' He sagged back on to his pillow. 'Go!' he said.

'Jamie, do you have the cup?' the doctor asked.

He showed him the cup.

'Off to the saloon then.'

Iain was still there and poured drinks as best he could by trying to anticipate the roll of the ship. He brought the drinks to the table.

The doctor lifted the tea cup and sniffed at remains again and then let Jamie and Iain smell it. 'There's something odd about the residue in there.'

'It smells terrible,' said Iain, taking the cup and sniffing.

The doctor poked the tip of his finger in the residue and tasted it. 'It's very bitter and tastes awful. Something has been mixed in with the tea.'

'Maybe Anne mixed in some medicine,' said Jamie.

'Nonsense, there is no medicine in here, I can assure you. Did you see George's eyes?'

'I'm not in the habit of looking into men's eyes,' said Jamie.

'Seriously, it was the same dilated look the captain had when he introduced himself.'

'Yes, I remember you saying that.'

'When you related your story of the goings on aboard this ship, you said Storer and Wilson were forcing the captain to swallow some kind of medicine or potion, is that not so?' asked the doctor.

'Yes, he said something like: *no more of that infernal stuff,*' replied Jamie.

'My god,' Iain said, 'George Knowles is being drugged as well as the captain. How do we know it is not a slow-acting poison?'

'But who would give it to him? Certainly not the girls, not us, which leaves the galley crew and–'

'Anne Knowles!' they all said in unison.

'But why would she do that to her husband, unless she is in with Storer?' Jamie said almost in a whisper.

The three of them sat and looked at each other. Iain tossed his drink back and went for a refill.

'We can't confront her right now in case she is party to this plot. As long as she does not suspect that we know – if it is her – then everybody should be safe for now. We need to be ready to deal with whatever comes when the storm blows over,' Jamie suggested.

'Let us all retire, and lock your door,' said the doctor. 'We will convene again tomorrow.'

Chapter Twenty Five

Flying Fish, South Atlantic Ocean

Storer was enjoying his brandy and smoking a cigar. The rolling of the ship did not bother him at all. His plans were moving forward, that was the main thing. *Who booked passage for those two Scotsmen?* He wondered. *They are not aboard this ship by chance, of that I am sure. It had to have been Fyvie and McColl who found the guns!* But no matter, the storm will give us the excuse to dispose of them along with Knowles. *How did they get in to the hold?* He wondered. Slater had searched high and low but had found no other entrance. The ship would be stripped when it reached Cape Town.

His thoughts were interrupted by knocking on the cabin door.

'What?'

Bill Wilson opened the door and stuck his head in. 'There's something happening on deck. I think you should see.'

'Well, what is it? Can you not deal with it? I do not really want to go out there and get wet.'

'It's really strange. It looks like Fyvie out on deck with a rope around him.'

'What?'

Donning his waterproof sou'wester, Storer joined Wilson and Higgins at the helm. They had been taking it in turns to keep the ship heading into the waves.

Storer was trying to see through the driving rain and water cascading over the deck and then suddenly he saw Fyvie, clutching someone else. Storer realised he was hanging on to George Knowles, trying to save him.

Anne Knowles must have taken advantage of the storm, he thought. *Clever woman, she does not miss a chance! She must have been adding the muti to his drinks and managed to get him on deck.*

He could see Fyvie being hauled in by the rope around him. He could not let that happen.

'You two go below. I'll take the wheel for now,' Storer shouted.

Wilson pointed to Fyvie. 'What about–?'

'Never mind them. It's their own fault going on deck in this weather. Now go below!' Storer shouted.

Higgins did not have to be told again. Wilson looked at Storer and reluctantly went below.

Storer spun the wheel and sent the ship sharply to starboard and the two men on the rope rolled into the gunwales. Seeing Fyvie still holding Knowles he turned the wheel in the opposite direction, and they rolled back across the deck into the hatch cover. He then repeated the manoeuvre and, straining to see through the deluge, he saw only Fyvie. Knowles must have slipped from his grasp and been washed overboard.

How can Fyvie still be there? He thought. *The bastard should be over the side, being dragged along the side of the ship.*

Fyvie looked in his direction and pointed straight at

him, sending a shiver down Storer's spine. He watched Fyvie being pulled through the door to the forward saloon by McColl and knew there would be a fight for the ship when the storm abated. But he had the men and the guns.

He called on Higgins to take the wheel.

'Keep a sharp eye and inform me at once if anybody tries to move on deck.'

'Yes, sir, Mr Storer.'

He went below, shed his sou'wester and found Wilson in the officers' saloon. He poured himself some brandy and said. 'When the storm starts to ease get Slater and load the guns. Fyvie and McColl have to be dealt with. Be ready to go forward. Get the two stewards, Baily and Harkness. I've paid them half of their bribe money so they can join the fight as well. We will deal with those meddlesome Scotsmen once and for all.'

'You never said anything about killing anybody,' said Wilson.

'Oh, really? So what did you think? We would have a nice quiet cruise down to Africa, dump the guns, take the payment and sail back to jolly old England?' asked Storer sarcastically.

'Of course not, but killing people... that's murder. I'm not a murderer.'

'This is not a game, Wilson. People get killed when the stakes are high. You're already up to your neck in it so just stick with the plan and you will go home a richer man than when you left. Now, please go and fetch the captain. We have things to discuss.'

Wilson brought the captain and sat him next to Storer, then went to fetch the pistols and load them.

A long while later the storm started to ease and the ship's motion was a lot calmer.

'We'll be making the ship a little lighter shortly, Captain. The two passengers Knowles signed up at the last minute will be leaving us. Oh, and George had an accident,' said Storer.

'What do you mean… an accident?'

'The silly old duffer went out on deck during the storm and I'm afraid he was washed overboard.'

The Captain looked at Wilson for confirmation but when none was forthcoming he looked back at Storer and shouted. 'You are lying. You could not have killed that poor man.'

'He killed himself,' Storer said angrily.

'You fed him that disgusting concoction so he would not know what he was doing, didn't you? You killed him.'

Storer was about to reply when the roof caved in.

Chapter Twenty Six

Flying Fish, South Atlantic Ocean

A short while before Bill Wilson interrupted Storer's brandy and cigar, the boys were dozing in their bunks when the banging on the cabin door and Lydia shouting Jamie's name roused them.

Iain got to the door and opened it admitting Lydia and Clara in a tearful state. 'Oh, Jamie, my father's not in his cabin,' Lydia blurted out.

'I went to him an hour ago and he was asleep in his bed,' said Clara.

'Then I went to look in on him just now and he was gone,' said Lydia.

'He can't have gone outside; it's too wild by far. Besides, he's not fit enough,' Iain said, struggling into a shirt.

'Iain, you and Clara search the saloon, the galley and the doctor's cabin. Lydia, you and I will search the other cabins.'

They staggered out, trying to keep their balance in the roll of the ship, the noise from the storm still deafening. Jamie and Lydia went immediately to Knowles' cabin and went straight to the trapdoor, thinking the same thing. The carpet had not been disturbed so he could not have gone down there.

'Let's wake up your stepmother.'

Jamie hammered on the door, and eventually she unlocked the door, saw Jamie and smiled. She then saw Lydia and the smile vanished.

'What do you want?' she asked indignantly.

'Is George with you?' Jamie asked.

'No, he is not. What is going on?'

Iain, Clara and the doctor came along the passage. 'We haven't found him,' said Iain. 'What about you?'

Jamie pushed his way past Anne Knowles and looked around the cabin. 'Your husband is not in his cabin, and now we don't know where he is.'

'How dare you push…,' she began. 'What did you say?'

She pushed past everyone and went into Knowles' cabin. 'This cannot be possible. He is in no condition to get about by himself.'

Jamie thought, *she doesn't seem to be too concerned.* The girls were distraught but Anne Knowles was not really disturbed.

'Doctor, escort the ladies to the saloon and wait for us there,' Jamie said.

'Of course,' said the doctor, leading the way.

Lydia turned and asked. 'Where are you going Jamie, where do you think father is?'

'Just go with the doctor. I promise I won't be long.'

'I am going to my cabin,' said Anne Knowles.

Jamie grasped her arm and said forcefully. 'You will go to the saloon and wait there.'

He propelled her along the passage.

'How dare you!'

'Get your fucking arse into that saloon and stay there until I come back, otherwise I will tie you to a chair. Do not test me on this,' Jamie shouted angrily.

She cringed visibly at this verbal onslaught and went to the saloon.

Iain looked in the saloon and said to the doctor. 'Keep an eye on her,' and pointed at Anne.

'What is going on, Iain? Is there something going on that we do not know about?' Clara said, tears streaming down her face.

'Let us go and find your father and all will be revealed.'

Clara nodded and Iain went to find Jamie.

He was at the top of the companionway at the door to the top deck.

'Iain, come and help me to hold this door when I open it because if the wind catches it, it might tear it off. I'll look out and see if Knowles is anywhere to be seen.'

'Jamie, if Knowles went through this door then he is overboard.'

As Jamie opened the door a huge wave came over the bows and swept down the ship slamming the door closed.

'Jesus, we could have had our fingers broken there,' Iain shouted. 'When you open it again we'll lean into it and you take a quick look.'

They pushed the door open and both of them leaned into it. Jamie strained to see along the deck through the driving rain and the waves breaking over the ship. He stepped out with his right leg on the deck and drew himself up to his full height just as a wave disappeared through the scuppers. There was a lull for a brief moment.

He saw Knowles' body up against the bulkhead of the main galley in front of the crew's quarters, on the other side of the forward hatch.

'I see him,' shouted Jamie as he nodded to Iain to go back in. 'He's lying against the bulkhead on the other side of the hatch.'

'*Father!*' screamed Lydia coming halfway up the stair. The boys hadn't noticed her because of the noise. 'I must get to him.'

Jamie and Iain blocked her way, Jamie said. 'If you go on deck you will be washed overboard, so what good will that do?' he shouted over the noise. 'We'll get him but I need you to go back down and stay calm.'

'Please bring my father back, Jamie.'

'Ask the doctor to lock your stepmother in her cabin and then to come here, we'll need his help.'

She nodded and reluctantly went down stairs.

Jamie had to shout above the din of the crashing waves. 'Iain, the locker under the stair… I saw a rope in it when I was being nosey a few days ago. Can you bring it here?'

Iain brought the rope and a big wooden mallet to jam the door open. Jamie looped one end around his waist and knotted it.

'You're not serious?' said Iain. 'You'll never make it. He's a goner Jamie, and so will you be if you try this.'

'Tell that to those two girls.'

Iain looked at him and said. 'Aye, I suppose.'

The doctor appeared and Jamie told him about Knowles. 'I need you to help Iain on the end of this rope to pull me in once I get a hold of George and stop me from being swept away.'

The two girls came up behind the doctor. 'We will help too, Jamie,' Clara shouted.

Jamie went to go through the door and turned to Iain.

'Let the rope out slowly. If it goes slack, stop. I'll give three sharp tugs to stop letting the rope out, two to pull me in and one to play it out. I know you'll be watching but just in case.'

'We won't let go, my friend, so don't worry.'

Jamie slipped out of the door and decided to crawl backwards on all fours and close to the bulkhead. A wave broke over the bow and the ship tilted to port. He started to slide across the deck but was checked by the rope.

The ship then righted and then tilted in the opposite direction when another wave swept into him and he crashed back on to the bulkhead, the rope chafing him through his shirt.

Iain was watching all the time shouting, 'Hold tight!' Then. 'Let out the rope.'

Jamie waved to Iain to play out the line quicker.

'Let go the rope slightly, but be ready to grab it,' shouted Iain to the others and gave Jamie some slack.

Jamie felt the slack and moved to leave the comparative safety of the bulkhead to get to the forward hatch. A monster wave broke and hit Jamie with such a force that it picked him up and dashed him into the side of the hatch cover.

'Hold tight!' screamed Iain, the rope slipping through his hands, taking the skin off. The others grabbed hold as well. He could just see Jamie hard up against the hatch cover.

'Pull in, pull in,' he shouted to the others.

When the slack was taken up he shouted for them to stop and hold.

The sea water was stinging Jamie's eyes and he had swallowed a lot of water. The last wave had winded him when he struck the hatch. He was choking, trying to get a breath, but the water just kept on rushing over him, not giving him a chance to draw a breath.

He felt the slack being taken up on the rope and then there was a lull in the constant rush of water.

Looking over the hatch he thought. *Going over it would be quicker, but going around it would be a helluva lot safer. Fuck this! I am not drowning today. Let's get this done.* He was getting angry now.

He gave the rope a sharp pull and scurried on all fours around the edge of the hatch, along the side and around to the aft end so he was now slightly sheltered from the waves of water washing over the hatch.

Knowles was still in the same place, which was a minor miracle in itself. Another huge wave crashed over the deck and lifted Knowles slightly to the right of Jamie.

Another one like that might take him away, he thought. He noticed that after every six or seven waves there would come a really powerful one, then a slight lull and the process would start again.

He pulled sharply on the rope every couple of minutes, keeping it taught whilst he did this and once he had enough slack he waited for the big wave and then the lull, then he jumped up and dived across the deck and grabbed hold of George Knowles.

He wrapped his legs and arms around him, then used one hand to give two sharp pulls.

'Everybody start pulling!' shouted Iain to his rope team.

Jamie hadn't noticed how cold he had become. He put his hand under Knowles' chin and turned his head.

'George! George!' He shook his head slightly.

Knowles' eyes fluttered briefly. He tried to talk but it was impossible with the waves crashing over and the noise was deafening.

Jamie held on to Knowles with one arm, trying to crawl along with the other, to help Iain pull in the rope.

Suddenly the ship turned sharply to starboard. Jamie, clinging to Knowles, rolled over and over and battered against the gunwales. Another wave crashed along the deck. The ship was at a steep angle and sea water washed over them, the pull of the water like invisible hands trying to drag them over the gunwales and into the sea.

Jamie was hanging on desperately to Knowles but he was getting tired and the rope felt like it was cutting him in two.

The ship suddenly turned in the opposite direction and they rolled back across the deck and crashed into the hatch cover. The waves kept up the onslaught of water; there was no respite, the noise deafening.

Jamie realised that this was not the sea nor the waves doing this; someone was at the wheel, deliberately trying to get them overboard.

The ship turned sharply to starboard again and they dashed against the gunwales, the next wave lifting them almost up and over.

Jamie was hanging on for dear life to the rope with one hand but Knowles was slipping out of his grasp. He tried to pull him up but another huge wave crashed into them and he felt Knowles slipping away.

The ship righted again. Jamie could no longer feel Knowles. When his eyes cleared he could not see him. He was gone. 'Nooooooo,' he screamed.

He felt the pull on the rope and hung on. As he slipped backwards along the deck he looked towards the quarterdeck and behind the charthouse he saw Storer standing with his hands on the wheel.

Jamie half sat up and pointed at him to tell him *I see you*. But then, as he was pulled along the deck, the crew's quarters obscured his line of sight.

Iain had witnessed the whole thing and was telling the others to pull and don't stop.

Jamie came alongside the companionway bulkhead and thumped the side of his fist against it shouting. 'Fuck… fuck… fuck!'

Iain grabbed Jamie under his armpits and hauled him through the door, nearly falling down the stairs as he managed to pull the mallet free and the door slammed closed.

Jamie was completely exhausted and he was crying, 'Iain, I had him! Then that bastard Storer turned the ship.'

'I know, I felt it. So it was Storer at the helm? You saw him?'

'I did. He was trying to kill us, and succeeded in killing one of us.'

Jamie realised what he had said and turned to see Lydia standing at the bottom of the stairs with Clara, looking up at him, tears streaming down their faces at the reality they now faced.

'You said you would save him,' she said accusingly.

'I… I had him... I am so sorry, Lydia… It was…'

'You said you would bring my father back to me. You did!' she cried.

Doctor Morgan put his arms around the two girls and led them away to their cabin.

'It was Storer, Lydia. I tried… I… really… tried.'

Iain put his arms around his friend's shoulders and said. 'I know you tried, big man, I know you did, come on, you're bloody frozen, let's get a dram down your throat and get some dry clothes.'

Jamie turned and took hold of Iain's lapel. 'As soon as this storm calms down they will be coming for us. But we will get to them first, Iain. Storer is mine. He's a fucking dead man!'

They had a couple of drams of whisky, changed into dry clothes and ate some cold meat with bread then went to the saloon to find Dr Morgan.

'How are the girls doing?' asked Jamie.

'They are inconsolable, I'm afraid. They are so young to lose their father as well as their mother.'

'What about their stepmother?'

'They do not want her near them. Mrs Knowles has not left her cabin since I locked her in,' said the doctor.

'I need you to come with me as a witness to what I am about to do, Doctor,' Jamie said.

'What are you about to do?' he asked, looking a bit worried.

'We – that is to say Iain and me – are going to search Mrs Knowles cabin for that potion. If she has it then she has been poisoning old Knowles. We don't know if she got him out on deck because nobody is a witness to it.'

All three went to Anne Knowles' cabin and Iain unlocked the door but it would not open, it was bolted on the inside. 'I will ask you only once to open this door, otherwise I will smash it down with an axe,' shouted Jamie thumping the door with his fist.

They heard the door unlock and Jamie barged in, pushing Anne Knowles on to her bunk.

'How dare you!'

'Shut up and sit on that bunk!' Iain said.

They looked around and Jamie said. 'Where is it?'

'I don't know what you are talking about. What

exactly are you looking for?' she said calmly.

'The potion. The poison you fed your husband in his tea. Where is it?'

'You're insane. I haven't been giving my husband anything in his tea. Now I insist you all get out of my cabin.'

'Search every inch of this place,' said Jamie.

'You will certainly not...'

'Do not try my patience, woman!' said Jamie with such force she just stopped talking.

They searched every single space, her personal belongings; they stripped the bed, and rifled her clothes but found nothing.

'I told you there is nothing to find. These accusations are preposterous.'

Jamie looked at her and fell silent. He sat on the bunk and looked around. After a minute he got up and closed the door. On the coat hook behind the door hung the velvet cloak with the hood. He searched it and found a pocket; it was empty. He was just about to give up when he put his hand into the hood and brought out a small green bottle. Shaking it he could see some liquid in it. He handed it to the doctor.

'Would you care to check the contents of this bottle, Doctor?'

Anne Knowles' face paled as she watched the doctor leave her cabin and come back with the teacup that George Knowles had drunk from. He smelled the contents and turned up his nose, then pulled the cork out of the bottle and putting his finger over the opening to pour some on it, smelled and tasted it.

'This is what was in George's teacup,' the doctor confirmed.

'And I'll wager it's the same potion being used on the captain,' said Jamie looking at Anne.

'How could you possibly know something like that?' she blurted out before realising what she had said.

'Something like what, Mrs Knowles? This potion in your possession implicates you in the death of George Knowles.' Jamie was right in her face. 'A father to those two girls. He was all they had. You are confined to this cabin under lock and key until we get to Cape Town. If you need to go the heads you will be accompanied. If you take one step out of this cabin you will be tied up. I hope this is clear because I will not tell you a second time.'

'You are the one who will be tied up when James and his men come to get you when the storm blows over,' she said.

'I advise you to heed my warning, Mrs Knowles.'

'You do not have the authority to keep me prisoner, especially on my own ship, Mr Fyvie,' she said with venom.

Jamie took a step toward her and said. 'Oh, so it is your ship and your business now that you have managed to kill your husband? Even if you do inherit everything it will all be taken from you, and the girls will get everything when you are convicted.'

She went to strike him but he caught her wrist and twisted it away. She winced and looked up at him.

'When we liberate the crew you will be put under guard, you have been warned,' said Jamie.

Back in the saloon Iain poured a stiff whisky for each of them. They all quaffed their drinks and sat in silence for a while.

'Doctor, the next two or three hours will be crucial.

It is imperative you stay with the girls in their cabin,' said Jamie. 'Iain, tell the doctor what is going to happen next, I am going to have another whisky.'

'Jamie and I will go to the cargo hold via a secret passageway from Knowles' cabin and retrieve our weapons from our boxes in the hold. Then we will break in to the crew's quarters to find out who's with who, surely most of them will be behind the captain. We will need to identify any crewman in league with Storer. Any enemies will be subdued, tied up and put under guard. Then we will send the rest back through the passageway to watch over you,' Iain took a sip of his whisky. 'You need to be prepared for bloodshed doctor.'

'So you are going to attack them before they come here? Just the two of you?'

'If we don't come back you will have to take your chances and just deny everything and anything we have talked about. Of course I don't know about Anne Knowles. As far as she is concerned you only identified the potion and did what we asked you to do, so you should be alright.'

'Good luck, Doctor,' said Jamie.

The boys were at the door to the hold in the secret passageway. Jamie peered through the spyhole but could see nothing in the darkness. It was difficult because of the motion of the ship to see if anything was moving.

'Did you ever think we would be in a situation like this a few weeks ago, Iain; making a decision of life or death for them or us?' said Jamie.

'No, but then after what has happened to us up until now it doesn't surprise me. But you know, Jamie, it will have to end in the next couple of hours, one way or the other.'

'Yes, it will, and I could not think of a better man to end it with.'

'Jesus, I was talking about you and me coming out alive.'

'So was I. I have a feeling there is a man hidden in the hold waiting for us to appear.'

'And I have a feeling you're right,' said Iain. They were talking in each other's ear below the noise.

'Would you like me to go first again to get my balls blown off, or would you like to go first and I will follow and ambush the man who wants to blow your balls off?'

Iain held the covered lamp up and looked Jamie in the eye. 'Aye, I will go out first but you'd better be looking after my balls.'

Iain went through the door with the lamp extinguished and moved quietly along the deck to approximately amidships and relit the lamp. As he made his way to the passenger storage area Jamie slipped out and followed him.

Iain found the boxes he was looking for and was about to secure the lamp when a voice behind him said. 'I have a pistol aimed at your head, Mr McColl. I have been instructed to kill you if you try anything stupid, so lie down with your arms and legs out wide and let me shackle you and take you to your fate.'

Iain turned around slowly and looked at the steward who had served them throughout the voyage so far.

'You! Ye treacherous bastard.'

'I told you to get on your belly.'

'No, you told me to lie down. If you pull that trigger there is enough gun powder below you to blow us all to kingdom fuckin' come,' said Iain, hoping the steward did not know the powder was aft.

The steward looked down. 'I don't believe you.'

'Do you want to take that chance? You should take your finger off the trigger and lay your finger across the trigger guard. That's the safe way to hold a gun.'

The steward moved his finger involuntarily and Iain said loudly. 'There you go. That's safer.'

Jamie heard the signal and leapt over the packing cases. He clamped his left hand over the steward's mouth and stabbed him through the neck before he could fire a shot.

The steward's body convulsed with shock and the gun slipped out of his fingers, Iain grabbed it before it hit the deck. Jamie caught the steward as he fell. Both men paused for a reaction above.

Nothing moved.

'What was his name? I can't remember,' said Iain.

'I don't know and I don't care. Fuck him! He's part of them. They killed an innocent man and they want to kill us. We're all in a fight for our lives now, so fuck him and fuck them,' said Jamie with venom.

Iain could see there was vengeance in Jamie's heart and a ruthlessness he had never displayed before.

They hid the body and opened up their respective tool boxes and the hidden compartments within. Jamie removed his two over and under percussion pistols. Iain took out his blunderbuss rifle and blunderbuss pistol, fitting the specially made bayonets to both guns.

They were both already carrying their other weapons of choice: two daggers, a dirk and a sgian dubh; the dirk being the longer dagger of the two; the short one only six inches long could be easily concealed. They fastened the weapons to their person and started up the stairway leading to the crew's quarters.

'How do you want to do this, Iain?'

'I think we go up and just walk in very casually, because somebody will be expecting our dead pal down in the hold here. You cover the left side and I'll cover the right and if anybody moves for a weapon we shoot them.'

'Good plan. Let's go.'

At the top of the stairs they simply walked straight in with guns levelled covering the whole cabin. Most of the crew were lying on their bunks and stayed perfectly still when they saw the two armed men enter. Only one person sat at the communal table in the centre of the cabin, a pistol next to his hand.

It was the other steward. He looked up expecting his friend and flinched when he saw the boys with their guns aimed at him. He looked at the pistol on the table and then back at the door.

Jamie said. 'Looking for your friend? He's in the hold with a hole through his neck.'

The steward looked at the pistol again.

'Don't be stupid, 'cause you'll join your friend. Jamie here just needs one tiny excuse and he'll kill you,' said Iain.

The cook got out of his bunk, lifted the pistol up by the barrel and clubbed the steward on the side of the head with it, he fell like a stone off the bench and lay still.

'You'll not be getting any more trouble from him,' said the cook looking at the boys with their guns still ready. 'I have been with Mr Knowles and his family, when his first wife was alive, since he bought his first ship. I am still with him and the captain.'

'Who else is with Storer and Wilson, and who stands with the captain?' asked Jamie.

'I can speak for all the lads,' said the cook. 'Those two stewards, Bailey and Harkness were bribed. Higgins, Slater and Wilson are the only crew members that the rest of us did not know. They are Storer's men. We are all with the captain and, by the looks of it so are you two, thank god. We did not know what the hell was going on.'

The boys lowered their weapons and Jamie said. 'Look, we cannot explain the whole story at the moment. As you probably know, Storer has command of the ship.'

'But surely Mr Knowles would be in command while the captain recovers,' interrupted the cook.

'A lot has happened tonight. The captain is being held captive and I am sorry to tell you that Mr Knowles was washed overboard. He's dead.'

The remaining crewmen were visibly shocked by this news and were silent. The noise of the storm seemed to grow louder.

'We cannot dawdle here. Iain and I have a plan to take back the ship tonight. Is there a helmsman among you?'

'Aye, sir. I am the relief steersman.' It was the sailmaker.

'Reynolds is a good man, Mr Fyvie. You can rely on him,' said the cook.

'What is your name?' asked Iain.

'Tom Watson sir but everybody just calls me Cookie.'

'Do any of you have a weapon?' asked Jamie.

They all revealed some kind of knife or blade from nowhere.

'Apart from these we never had a need of weapons here. The guns are all locked up in a cupboard in the officers' quarters, next to the bosuns' cabin.'

'Oh great,' said Jamie. 'Reynolds, you stay behind and get your sou'wester on, get one for me. The rest of you follow Iain below and he will show you where to go. Take this piece of shite with you and shackle him to something,' he said nodding at the unconscious steward.

'You will go forward to the passengers' quarters and guard the doctor and Knowles' daughters with your lives.'

'Don't worry, sir, there are plenty of weapons in a kitchen. But how will we get there going below?' asked Cookie.

'Iain will show you. Come, it's time to go,' said Jamie.

He pulled Iain to the side. 'After you show them the way, go aft along the passage and see if the captain is in his cabin, I will come down and wait for you.'

Iain showed the crew the secret passage then went back along to the captain's hidden door and pulled the dowel from the hole. He looked in. The cabin was empty. He shuffled back to Jamie.

'He's not there, Jamie.'

'Good, I was hoping for some luck. Go into the captain's cabin in about fifteen minutes. Wait for my signal followed by a pistol shot, then rush the saloon and shoot anything that moves, except me and the captain of course.'

'What's the signal?'

'I don't know yet, but you'll know it when you hear it.'

'Aye, right enough. Stupid question,' said Iain rolling his eyes up.

Iain waited in the hold and Jamie went back to the crew's quarters to find Reynolds nervously waiting for him.

'Reynolds, I'm going to relieve Higgins at the wheel permanently. You will take over. That's all I want you to do.'

Jamie and Reynolds moved through the doorway on to the deck. The ship's movement had noticeably changed for the better and the swells were decreasing in size, although the rain was still hammering down.

Reynolds went aft on the starboard side to the quarterdeck stairs and went up past the charthouse to the helm, making himself as visible as possible to Higgins, while Jamie did the same, but unseen, on the port side.

Jamie touched his guns, kept dry under the sou'wester, as he stepped onto the quarterdeck at the top of the stairs. He peered around the charthouse and could see the wheel and Higgins with his back to him talking with Reynolds, as planned. He did not hesitate.

He walked swiftly along the side of the charthouse, drew the dirk and came up behind Higgins; his left arm went around his neck and pulled him backwards as his right hand came around plunging the long bladed dagger at an angle up into his chest.

Reynolds stood petrified.

'Reynolds! Take the helm! Reynolds.' shouted Jamie.

Reynolds snapped out of temporary shock and caught the erratically turning wheel and righted the ship.

Jamie dragged Higgins backwards. Turning him around to face him, he pulled the dagger out and let him stumble back with the look of disbelief in his eyes. Jamie kicked him on the chest and he went flying over the side into the cold depths of the Atlantic Ocean.

With Reynolds at the wheel, keeping the ship under

control, Jamie quietly climbed up on to the skylight above the officers' saloon. He looked down cautiously through the skylight.

The captain was sitting slumped in a chair at the table, Storer was sitting next to him brandishing a pistol in one hand and pointing his finger in his face with the other, clearly shouting at him. Jamie slid over to get a better view on the other side of the window and could just see Wilson sitting on the other side of the cabin. There was a pistol on the bench and another on the table.

But where's Slater? Thought Jamie. *In his cabin most likely. It's now or never.* 'And fuck them anyway!' he said out loud.

Reynolds looked at him wondering what he was on about.

Jamie felt the pitch and sway of the ship and waited until the timing was right, then he stepped back, slipped off the sou'wester and leapt at the skylight, going through feet first.

As his feet hit the table he drew one of his pistols, firing a shot at Storer who jumped up and fired his pistol, but the shot went wild as Jamie's shot found its mark in Storer's rib cage above his left hip and he went down.

The captain was lucid enough to dive for cover under the table but Jamie landed awkwardly and fell off the table.

Bill Wilson got such a shock he did not respond immediately. As Jamie fell of the table, Wilson lifted the pistol from the bench beside him to take a shot at Jamie. Right then, Iain burst through the saloon door at almost the same time, confusing Wilson as to who to shoot first.

His hesitation cost him dearly as Iain fired the blunderbuss point-blank from the hip, but the roll of the ship spoilt his aim and he hit Wilson on the top right arm and shoulder, the blast almost severing his arm from his body.

Wilson looked at the damage in disbelief. He looked at Iain with rage in his eyes raising his pistol. Iain let him have baby blunderbuss in the face leaving it looking like a pound of mince. The great body swayed and fell near Jamie, who was getting to his feet.

Storer was also getting to his feet, bellowing like a madman and raising another pistol which must have been stuck in his waistband. Jamie saw him rising, pulling out the gun. He instinctively drew his dirk and threw it with all the strength he could muster. The captain under the table stuck out his leg tripping Storer as he fired.

The shot hit Jamie in the left shoulder as the dagger buried itself up to the hilt in Storer's jaw, entering through his cheek, between his teeth and through the roof of his mouth, the point exiting next to his right ear.

Storer went down, utterly stunned.

Another shot rang out, causing Jamie and Iain to duck as they turned to see Slater fall through the door face first on to the deck with a nasty hole in the back of his head.

Suddenly the noise of the weather and the ocean was deafening; nothing moved. The smell and smoke of cordite dissipated quickly through the broken skylight, sea water and rain dripping into the saloon.

'Is it safe to come in?' shouted the doctor.

Iain looked around the open door at the doctor standing in the passage with a pistol in his hand.

'Come on, doctor, we need you in here,' said Iain waving him into the saloon.

The captain, clearly still under the influence of the

potion, came out from under the table and looked at Storer.

'Oh fuck, that is sore!' said Jamie, looking at his bullet wound. 'I've never been shot before.'

Iain went and lifted him on to a chair. He helped him take his shirt off to inspect the wound as the doctor came in to the saloon and looked around.

He shook his head and went over to Jamie to look at his wound. 'You're lucky the bullet missed the bone and came out again. Hold your shirt against it to stem the bleeding. I brought my bag. It's in the captain's cabin, I had a feeling I might need it.'

'But where did you come from, doc?' asked Iain.

The doctor did not answer right away. He had seen Wilson and did not need to check for life and so went over to the captain.

'Are you alright, captain? Any injuries?'

'No, Doctor. Thanks to these two young men, only my dignity and my pride.'

The doctor went over to Storer and checked for any sign of life.

'Storer's still alive,' he pronounced.

Jamie looked up and saw the unfired pistol on the table; he stood, picked it up and said. 'Move away, doctor.'

'Do not be hasty, Jamie, I don't think he will survive his wounds, but if he does, he must stand trial and be made an example of.'

Jamie looked confused.

'You need to sit down. The shock to your body from a bullet is severe and the body needs to adjust itself and heal. You didn't think Hugh Armstrong would send you on your first mission without someone to watch over you, did you?'

Iain and Jamie sat and digested this news for a moment.

'You were sent by Armstrong to watch over us then?' asked Iain.

'It's not that he didn't trust you. He would never have sent you if he didn't think you were capable. I was a doctor with the army so I have seen some action, but I was injured, hence the limp, and so was recruited by Hugh. He sent me along on this mission as insurance because he was not sure what and who you were up against, and believe me, it's fine to have a back-up team.'

'The old bastard!' said Iain. 'So he had our back covered. I like that, I do. I like that.'

Jamie still had the pistol in his hand.

Iain said. 'Jamie, come on, put the pistol down. There's been enough killing today. Let's get to somewhere dry and tend to your wound.'

'He killed Lydia and Clara's father. He wanted to kill us as well,' said Jamie visibly shaking now.

'I know, so let the bastard suffer until he kicks the bucket. We'll shackle him below and see what's to be done,' Iain said as he took the pistol from Jamie's hand. 'I don't know about you, but I need a fuckin' whisky.'

Chapter Twenty Seven

November 1855

Flying Fish, South Atlantic Ocean

It was still raining but the sea was calm. Jamie was bandaged up in Storer's cabin and he stayed there, sleeping.

Storer was taken to the bosun's cabin where the doctor removed Jamie's knife from his face and dug out the bullet from his ribs. He was in bad shape but the doctor patched him up as best he could, then Iain and two crewmen took him below and shackled him in the chain locker on a makeshift cot.

The captain was recuperating in his cabin and writing up his log about all that had happened.

Iain supervised the disposal of the mutineers' bodies with a burial at sea. The crew held the corpses by the wrists and ankles.

Iain said. 'And may God have mercy on their souls. Right, throw the fuckers overboard!' The crew swung the bodies once and dumped them unceremoniously over the side and walked off without a second glance.

The crew started a clean-up. The carpenter covered

the damaged skylight whilst Iain, with the help of the cook, got the ship back to some normality.

Jamie slept while all this was going on and the following morning he ate breakfast then went out on deck to a warm sunny day.

His arm was in a sling and he was stiff and sore from the deep cuts and grazes he had collected when he'd jumped through the skylight. He looked around and was surprised to see the captain at the wheel.

'Morning, captain. You seem to have regained your strength quickly.'

'I have, Jamie. I have eaten well and slept well and I don't have that infernal potion in my system anymore. The doctor does not think there will be any lasting effects. How is the shoulder?'

'It's bloody sore, but it will get better. Where is the doctor?'

'He is either in the for'ard saloon or tending to the patient below.'

Jamie turned and winced at a stab of pain. He walked forward, feeling a different mood on the ship. All the crewmen he saw greeted him with reverence as he walked by.

'Mornin', sir. Feeling better today?' cried one.

'Mornin', sir. Anything you need, just call out we'll sort you out,' cried another.

'Morning, lads. I'm feeling much better, thank you.'

He went below and asked for some hot water in the bath. The hot water soothed his damaged body for an hour and then he changed into a fresh set of clothes and decided to go to the saloon and have a drink. He found Iain and the doctor sitting there, as usual.

'You look really shite,' said Iain. 'Jumping through

the skylight? Yer a daft bastard! Only you could have thought of that one.'

'Ah shut up and get me a drink,' said Jamie.

They were all in good humour.

Jamie took his shirt off so the doctor could change his dressings.

'I advise you to sit in the sun as often as possible and rest, because you are going to be very sore,' the doctor said.

'I'm already sore. How are the girls faring, Doctor?' asked Jamie.

'As you can imagine, they are still very upset. I was talking to them earlier and told them what happened and who was responsible for their father's death.'

'What was their reaction?'

'They were shocked at the chance you two took in regaining control of the ship and, of course, at the deaths, but they will need time to get over their father. They must be very worried what will become of them.'

'I feel really sorry for them,' said Jamie thoughtfully. 'What about that bastard Storer, Doctor?'

'I was just telling Iain, that there is a bit of redness around his facial injuries and inside his mouth. If that is the start of an infection then I doubt he will make it,' the doctor replied.

'Good enough for the bastard!' said Jamie taking his drink from Iain. 'We should put him out of his misery and put a bullet in his head.'

'And sink to the same depths of monstrosity as him? No, Jamie, let us hope he lives to be humiliated in public and face the gallows.'

They heard someone approaching and looked up to see the captain enter the saloon.

'Captain, good to see you. Can I pour you a drink?' inquired Iain.

'No, thank you, I'm fine, I do not drink on duty. I'm glad I have got you all together as I would like to explain my involvement in this whole sorry mess.'

'You do not owe us any explanation, Captain. You were drugged,' said the doctor.

'Yes, I was, but I did not know how long I had been drugged until I came aboard the ship. You see this started before Storer took up his new post in Cape Town. I first met Storer and one of his friends with the Knowles' family. We were invited to dinner with George, Anne and the two girls, after which Storer, his friend and I squeezed into a hansom cab and went to a house in London for a nightcap. There we had cigars and drinks but after a while I started to feel very light-headed and thought I must be drunk. The other two, Storer and his friend, whose name escapes me, kept telling me I was fine and I believed them. That was the strangest thing; I did not realise they had started dosing me with that concoction then. However, I blacked out and woke up the next morning in a strange bedroom. It was dark, so I got up to draw the curtains. I felt something in my hand and dropped it, I felt wet bed sheets and my skin was wet. I could not understand how I would come to be wet. I opened the curtains and nearly died of shock.' He suddenly looked shocked at reliving the story. 'Maybe I will have a small whisky.'

Iain gave him a small whisky, about three fingers, and he continued.

'There was a dead girl – not a woman – but a girl on the bed. She had obviously been stabbed to death, but violently, for there were many stab wounds, I was covered in blood and there was blood everywhere. The thing I had dropped was a knife that was covered in blood as well. I ran for the door and shouted for help and Storer appeared from nowhere, along with his friend. Bearing in mind I was still under the influence of that potion, they basically took control and said they would fix it, that she was just a local whore, but someone would have to dump the body. Storer kept asking me, *why did you kill her*? That's when the blackmail started and the drug kept me believing I had to go along with their demands. Now that I am free of it I can remember everything that happened. I did not kill that girl. They brought her limp body into the bedroom and dumped her next to me and stabbed her to death right next to me.'

'So what did they tell you to do?' asked the doctor.

'They told me to play along with their plans, of which I had no knowledge, but I know now that they wanted to ship guns and kill Knowles to take control of all the ships in his fleet through his widow Anne Knowles. I had to keep George happy with lies and deceit, telling him that everything was normal. You must understand that I was so far gone I just agreed to everything, otherwise they would have ruined me. But it was all a dream; that drug had total control over me. It has to be destroyed forever.'

'We have found bottles of it on board,' said Iain. 'I searched the whole ship, apart from the cargo decks, but the bottles we did find have been emptied overboard along with the bottles, except for a sample which the doctor will take to his colleagues in Cape Town.'

'I have written an account of everything I can remember since meeting Storer and I have written up the ship's log, which I will submit to the authorities in Cape

Town. It is going to take a lot of explaining to convince them that the Secretary to the Colonial Government was smuggling guns with the possibility of plotting to overthrow the Government.'

'They will probably try and keep the whole affair quiet,' said the doctor. 'The Government does not hang out its dirty washing.'

'I am not a politician. I can only submit my report and, if I am free to go, I will submit the same account in England when I return,' said the captain.

'You will have our full support,' said Jamie. 'Storer and his henchmen obviously staged the murder of the girl in your bedroom in order to lay the blame with you, I don't foresee any problems.'

'I spoke with Lydia and Clara and reassured them that they will be under my wing, as it were, whilst in Cape Town. George's solicitor and business partner there is Godfrey Butler. He and his wife will take care of them and me until I sort out this business with the authorities. I will extend my stay indefinitely and then I shall take the girls back to England. I think they have family in London somewhere. What a bloody mess!' the captain said wearily.

'Iain, what do you say to bringing Mrs Knowles in here for a wee chat? Quietly though. Don't disturb Lydia or Clara,' said Jamie.

'I think a wee chat might clear up a few missing details,' Iain said, walking off.

He walked straight in to Anne Knowles' cabin.

'What do you want?' she said tonelessly.

'You're coming for a wee chat.'

'No, I am not, I am staying right here.'

'I beg your pardon?' Iain said a bit louder. 'Get up

off your arse and come with me, *now*!'

Iain walked her into the saloon and closed the door; she sat at one of the chairs at the table.

'This is preposterous, I have not done anything.'

'You never give up, do you?' said Jamie.

'You cannot keep me–'

'Shut up!' Jamie said quietly, not looking at her.

'I don't know how long ago this plot started but I think it started with you being told by Storer or his colleagues to get to know George Knowles and then marry him because of his wealth, but most importantly, because he owns a shipping company. You then introduced him to Storer, who just happened to be in a position to help him cut through the red tape in moving his assets and money to Cape Town. You then planned to get rid of your husband and inherit his wealth and his shipping company, in order to smuggle guns to South Africa to escalate a war with the natives. While all this mayhem was unfolding, Storer and his henchmen would infiltrate the Cape Government at all levels from the top, down.'

Jamie sipped his whisky and looked at Iain.

'What were you going to do with Lydia and Clara, Anne?' asked Iain. 'Throw them overboard as well?'

'Guns… war… infiltrate governments… what are you talking about? You cannot prove I had anything to do with the death of my husband and whatever other nonsense you are talking about.'

'One steward is dead; the other is in chains. He will be a witness. Higgins and Slater are dead, and so is Bill Wilson. They are all feeding the residents of the Atlantic.'

'You killed *all* of them?' she said with disbelief.

'It was them or us, and it wasn't going to be us.'

Iain gave her some time to digest the information. She was a bit confused and did not look too comfortable.

'Storer is shackled in the hold with serious injuries. He probably will not survive, but if he does he will be arrested and may ask for clemency by testifying against you. If not, you are both going to swing together.'

She looked at him with a puzzled expression.

'Swing means hanging,' explained Iain.

Jamie rubbed his sore arm. 'I think Mrs Knowles should be secured in her cabin, Iain.'

'I think you're right.'

Anne Knowles stood up and looked at Jamie. 'You were not so moralistic when you were fucking me against the bulkhead at bath time,' she turned and went to the confinement of her cabin.

The doctor and the captain looked at each other, then at Jamie, but did not question him. The doctor poured a drink instead.

'I am going up on deck to rest,' said Jamie.

'I will accompany you,' said the captain. 'I want to take this opportunity to thank all of you for saving us and the ship from those pirates and I will make a full report on you as well when we arrive.'

Up on deck the captain headed aft and Jamie was going to the fo'c'sle when he looked back and noticed Lydia at the helm with Reynolds, keeping watch.

Jamie walked back and took the stairs up on to the quarterdeck and approached Lydia.

'I see you're keeping your skills polished at the wheel, Lydia,' he said, leaning against the roof of the repaired skylight.

'I am, Jamie. Will you come and hold the wheel with me, please?' she asked looking straight ahead.

He went over to her and saw Clara sitting beside a rope locker behind her sister.

'Hello, Clara. It's really nice to see you.'

She looked up and smiled. 'It is good to see you too, Jamie.'

He looked at Lydia and said. 'Lydia, I am—'

'Please, Jamie, you do not have to say anything. The captain told us what happened. Clara and I are so grateful to you and Iain for saving the ship, and us, from that woman and that dreadful man. I want to apologise to you for the terrible things I said to you,' she said starting to get misty eyed.

'You were upset and shocked. You do not have to apologise.'

'Yes, I do. I know you tried your best to save our father. You would have, except for that awful man Storer, who will hang for the murder of our father. So let us leave it at that and we shall carry on. Agreed?'

'Agreed,' said Jamie.

Jamie was relieved that Lydia was speaking to him and he felt exhilarated that she did not hold him responsible for her father's death. He excused himself and went below to Storer's cabin. He sat on the bunk and thought, *Christ, I am really fond of Lydia and I think she is fond of me too, she is so tough and wise for her age. But what can I do, if she finds out I had sex with her stepmother she will never talk to me again. She must never find out.* He pushed the thoughts out of his mind and started to search through Storer's belongings.

The cabin was slightly larger than the others, except for the captain's, but he did not find anything interesting in the small desk or any of the cupboards. He wondered if maybe there was anything incriminating stored in his baggage in the hold. *I will do a search down there when I am fitter, or Iain can do a search,* he thought.

He stood at the door and looked around the cabin for any likely hiding place. He looked everywhere, pressed, prodded and knocked on the walls and cupboards, but nothing could be found. *Unless… It could not be that obvious, surely!* He thought.

He went to the bunk and lifted the bedding and mattress. He felt the slats underneath and found two to be slightly loose. He prised them up and removed them. There was a leather pouch full of documents hidden beneath, and he knew he had found the prize. He would take them to Iain in their own cabin and go through everything without telling anyone at this stage.

He went topside not bothering to hide the pouch and walked along the deck waving to Lydia who was still guiding the ship southwards.

He laboured up the stairway to the fo'c'sle and sat down to think through the events of the last few days again to see if he had missed anything.

Fairbrother and Armstrong had drilled it into them to stop and go over any incidents, remember who was involved, what they were doing then ask themselves was there anything unusual, anything missing, before assessing the next move.

Jamie knew Iain would be doing the same thing. Then they would compare notes, discuss and agree on a strategy to carry on.

Jamie looked through the documents in the pouch and saw a sealed letter. He went below to find Iain.

On the way to the saloon he decided to conceal the pouch in his cabin. He would go through the documents with Iain in private. The doctor would be told only what they thought he should know.

He found Iain alone in the saloon. 'I found some documents hidden in Storer's cabin, I think we should go and read them in private. Someone may walk in on us here.'

They emptied the contents of the pouch on to the bunk in their cabin and started sifting through them.

'There's a reference here to "C", about sending dates for transport to pick up cargo,' said Iain.

'Aye there's something here about "B" sending transport down from Portuguese East Africa to pick up cargo, and "N" keeping "B" informed of our progress. These are obviously the initials of people working for them or with them,' Jamie said sifting through the other pages for more information.

'It says here, "Meet with EG in London and receive instructions for the meeting in Liverpool", and Bradley Fairbrother's name is on here.'

'What? Let me see that,' said Jamie.

He read the page and looked at another two pages while Iain was reading another.

'Fairbrother was followed to Liverpool, Jamie, and here, it mentions two unknown probable recruits. That's why we had to fight our way back to the hotel that night. 'Aye, it looks like it. It's just as well we moved to Molly's place when we did. There's no mention of Armstrong's name, only that the head of the secret field police maybe in Liverpool. But they may have found his office behind the pub.'

'This is bad,' said Iain.

'Damn right it's bad. I just hope Armstrong has been warned that his suspicions were correct that he has been compromised.'

'There's nothing we can do until we reach Cape Town.'

Jamie opened the only red wax-sealed document and said. 'Shite, it gets worse!'

He handed the paper to Iain. 'It's the clue to the treasure; the same one we have, which means they won't be looking for the treasure and we won't have anybody to identify and follow.'

'I doubt that, Iain. This is a copy. They will send someone else. Besides, if these people are as good as Armstrong says they are, it won't take them long to figure out that two passengers were added to Knowles' passenger list at the last minute. I think we need to have a chat with Mr Storer.'

They went below to the chain locker where Storer was being held. The crewman standing guard opened up for them.

Storer was lying on a cot with a cover over him, his wrists manacled to the bulkhead. His head was heavily bandaged and he did not smell too good. He tried to pull his arms up when he saw the boys enter.

'I will have no compunction at all punching your fucking sore face, Storer, so lie there and be a good boy, and don't give me any excuse to throw your arse overboard,' said Jamie.

Storer lay back and barely audible said. 'Come to gloat?'

'That just shows you up for what you really are, Storer. Only a coward and a cretin like you would ask a question like that. Just tell us who the initials are referring to in the documents we found in your cabin.'

'You fools think I would just tell you?' he said lifting his head, his voice raspy and quiet.

'We will find out eventually.'

'You may have finished me but our cause will continue. You do not know what you are dealing with,' he said laying his head down. 'You are both dead men.'

The boys left him to his pain.

'The ELOS are after us,' said Iain.

They had been at sea for just over five weeks and *The Flying Fish* was making good time with fair winds pushing her along. Jamie, Iain, the doctor and the captain were having dinner, along with Lydia and Clara.

'Storer is in a bad way. His wounds are badly infected. His lower jaw will turn to gangrene before long and I do not have the proper facilities here to perform surgery on him,' said the doctor.

'If the weather holds we should be arriving in Cape Town in two days, Doctor,' the captain said.

'He should be brought up from the hold and placed in a cabin so that I can tend to his wounds in cleaner surroundings.'

'There's only two ways Storer will be allowed up here; for his burial at sea or disembarking in Cape Town,' said Jamie. 'I don't mean to undermine your authority, captain, but Storer is our prisoner and he will stay locked up below.'

'That is quite fine with me, Jamie,' the captain replied.

'The owners are fine with that decision as well,' said Lydia seriously.

On the morning of the expected arrival day in Cape Town the mood on board was infectious as everybody, including the crew, talked about what they would do when they stepped on dry land and where they would go.

Breakfast was a very cheerful event with the boys and the doctor washing it down with wine and the girls coming and going, sorting clothing and packing.

Cookie came in to the saloon and said. 'Captain Willard wants everybody topside, please.'

All the passengers joined the captain up on the fo'c'sle head and looked ahead at the spectacular sight. To the left they could see miles of golden beaches and off to the right was an island as they were heading into Cape Town.

'You will see Saldanha Bay to port,' said the Captain pointing to the beaches. 'And as we sail closer to our destination you will see the infamous Robben Island, which is used as a prison. If you go further around the coast you will see the Cape of Good Hope, but now we are sailing into Table Bay, so called after the flat mountain that overlooks the town.'

The sky was blue with a few puffy clouds pushed along by a light south-easterly wind. As the ship sailed closer they could see the town nestled below the majestic Table Mountain, named by the Portuguese who had first discovered it, flanked by a sharp peak on the left and a rounded peak on the right.

The captain turned and said.

'Welcome to Cape Town.'

Chapter Twenty Eight

Table Bay, Cape Town

The Flying Fish sailed into Table Bay and dropped anchor. The crew, having furled the sails, were now preparing for the departure of passengers and unloading the cargo.

The feeling around the ship was that of excitement, relief and apprehension.

Captain Willard had prepared his log and the paperwork he would require when he made his report to the authorities in Cape Town.

The Captain was looking a little pensive standing on the deck with Jamie and Iain, waiting for the lighter to come alongside. They were gazing up at the magnificent mountain watching over Cape Town.

'It's going to be fine, Roger. You have Iain and me as witnesses. We are technically working for the Government, although we haven't made a report yet on the settlers,' said Jamie, not giving away their cover.

'The doctor's word as a witness will clear you of any wrong doing, captain,' added Iain.

'Does that peak on the left have a name Roger?' asked Jamie pointing up at the mountain, trying to lighten the mood.

'That is Devil's Peak; the ridge across to Table Mountain is called the Saddle. The big lump of mountain on the right is Lion's Head, and further to the right is Lion's Rump. There are good walks up the mountain. Just be careful of the wild animals and snakes.'

'Snakes? What kind of snakes?' Asked Iain.

'Poisonous snakes! They are all poisonous, except for the odd house snake,' said the captain.

'Well that counts me out of walking on the mountain,' said Iain emphatically.

They watched the lighters and rowing boats come and go from the ships in the bay, to the beach or to the wharf at Rogge Bay, ferrying passengers, light cargo and luggage.

The captain said. 'I do not know how long I'll be, but no one is allowed to leave the ship until the customs men and the authorities have boarded and talked to the passengers and crew. Then we can get everybody ashore and settled into their accommodation. Have you and Iain made arrangements to meet someone?' he asked Jamie.

'I'm sure there will be somebody to meet us, but I don't know who. Don't worry, we will sort something out. Go and get your business done with the powers that be, and we will see you later.'

'I really don't know how to thank you two enough for all you have done for the people on board this ship, especially for the girls and me. We owe you a great debt of gratitude,' said the captain.

'You owe us nothing, although we might need a ship back to Scotland if things don't work out for us,' said Iain.

'Anything I can help you boys with, just let me know.'

'Its' fine, Captain, away ye go,' Jamie said waving him away.

The boys watched the lighter take the captain to beach then joined Doctor Morgan in the saloon

'Whatever is going on you can be assured that it is not finished,' said Doctor Morgan. 'Somebody will be looking for those guns and Storer's handlers are going to be looking for answers, and probably retribution.'

'What do you think will happen to Storer?' asked Jamie.

'I asked the captain that same question. He seems to think that because Storer was smuggling guns for the natives, the military will imprison him and try him here, although because the crime was hatched in England, they may send him back for trial in London, assuming he survives his injuries of course,' said the doctor.

'It is treason, after all,' said Iain. 'That, and the murder of poor old George Knowles. He will probably be taken back so that the Government can make an example of him. We should have thrown the bastard over the side when we had the chance.'

'I agree Storer should stand trial but the government does not like the Empire's image to be damaged in any way. They may try to cover up this whole episode rather than make an example of him.'

They felt more than heard a boat come alongside the ship, Jamie and Iain swallowed the remains of their drinks and went topside to see who was there.

As they stepped on deck Captain Willard was climbing on board from the lighter followed by two civilians and six other men all in some kind of uniform. The Captain waved to the boys.

'Jamie, Iain. Just the men I am looking for. I want to

introduce you to the local law and military, they will make the arrest of Bailey, Anne Knowles and James Storer.

'Jamie Fyvie and Iain McColl, this is William Hutchison from the governor's office, who is here to meet you and arrange to get you settled, Major Walter Barclay presently stationed at military headquarters in the Cape of Good Hope Castle, and Sergeant Brian O'Donnell of the Cape Mounted Rifles, the police, stationed at the Roeland street Gaol.'

Everybody shook hands. There were two soldiers with the major and two constables with the sergeant.

'That gentleman over there is Godfrey Butler,' the captain said, pointing at a portly, red-faced man struggling up from the lighter. The soldiers walked over to help him on board the ship and he introduced himself.

'Godfrey is – was – George's partner and the company solicitor. Let us all go down to the saloon and we can get some tea,' said the captain.

As they settled down in the saloon, Lydia and Clara joined them, hugging Godfrey, as they had met him on a few occasions before he had settled in Cape Town. Then they went back to their cabin to finish packing.

'The captain has told us quite a tale of survival on your voyage from England, and you made it here because of the bravery of you two lads,' said the major, looking at Jamie and Iain.

'The doctor played a part as well,' said Iain. 'And besides, we just did what anyone would have done in the same predicament. We all did what we had to do.'

'No need to be so modest, Mr McColl. Give praise where it is due,' said the major. 'I am taking over this investigation for the military as there is gun-running involved. I have already had a meeting with Sergeant O'Donnell here and he agrees it should be a military operation, and just for your own information, O'Donnell is the only person I trust as far as policing this town goes.'

'Well, thank you kindly major,' said O'Donnell in a thick Irish brogue.

'The army will take James Storer to the military hospital at the fort under guard and tend to his wounds. Mrs Anne Knowles will also be under arrest at the fort; that's what we call the castle. There is suitable accommodation for her there. Once we have questioned everybody involved I will liaise with Mr Hutchison and he will keep the governor up to date and then send a despatch to London as to where the traitors will be tried,' said the major, consulting the notes he had with him. 'The other prisoner, Bailey, will be going with Sergeant O'Donnell to be incarcerated in the new Roeland Street jail.'

'Mr McColl, Mr Fyvie I have been notified through the Cape Government office of your arrival and I have arranged lodgings for you both in Wynberg, which are not available yet so you will be put up in a hotel in Cape Town,' said William Hutchison.

The Major stood up. 'I will have my troopers carry Storer to the fort. The Knowles woman can transfer with Bailey on another boat. You are welcome to go ashore. We can take your statements tomorrow. Doctor, I would appreciate it if you would accompany the patient.'

'Of course, major.'

It was decided to remove the prisoners first then the passengers could relax and ready their immediate personal luggage and themselves for disembarking.

Godfrey Butler kept Lydia and Clara busy in their

cabin packing bags, while the prisoners were taken on to the lighter.

Jamie and Iain were on deck with Bill Hutchison watching as the soldiers brought up Storer first through the crew's quarters and laid him on a stretcher. As they carried him past the three men to lower him on to the lighter he looked at them and suddenly sat up and tried to shout but it came out as a growling rasp.

'You… have… not heard the… last of me.'

He fell back on the stretcher, his breath wheezing but still glaring hatred in his eyes as he was loaded on the boat.

Jamie's hackles went up as did Iain's; they felt goose bumps on their skin as Storer was carried down.

'Maybe you were right Jamie,' said Iain, 'we should have done for that bastard when we had the chance.'

'Aye, you're probably right. But don't forget; you stopped me.'

They realised that Bill had been looking and listening to them with much interest.

Bill looked around and said. 'Whilst we are out of earshot of anyone else I can tell you that I am your contact for Mr Armstrong, as well as the Governor's office.'

Jamie looked at Iain. 'Do midges eat people?' He asked Bill the pre-arranged code for identification.

Bill looked from one to the other and answered. 'Only in summer if you are walking past Lock Lomond.'

Jamie and Iain looked at each other again, shaking their heads.

'That's not the answer we were looking for, Bill,' said Iain winking at Jamie, and laying his hand on the hilt of the long dagger on his belt.

'What? Of course it is,' said Hutchison looking

seriously worried.

'Bill, a *lock* is a mechanism you use to secure a door; a *loch*, on the other hand, is a body of water in Scotland,' said Iain.

As the three men laughed, Major Barclay and a trooper brought Anne Knowles out on deck to go ashore with Bailey on a separate boat from Storer.

'Major, a word to the wise,' called Jamie.

The major stopped and looked around.

'A warning to you and the men who will be guarding that woman: be aware of her wily ways and seductive charms, because she will use them solely for her own survival and to the detriment of those who would help her,' said Jamie.

'Your warning is duly noted, Mr Fyvie,' said the Major.

'If a look had the power to kill somebody, Jamie, you'd be lifeless on the deck,' said Iain.

Jamie said. 'Bill, now that we've identified everyone and we are alone, you need to know that apart from the smuggled guns and ammunition aboard, there is a shipment of gold hidden somewhere below deck that was supposed to be a down payment for the delivery of the slaves Storer was to supply.'

Hutchison looked a bit worried and said. 'I see. The major is the only person I would trust with this information. Leave it with me; the gold will be liberated.'

Only the crew remained on the ship to be questioned about the events that had unfolded on *The Flying Fish* in the time between leaving Liverpool and arriving in Cape Town.

Jamie and Iain with Bill Hutchison, Doctor Morgan, Lydia and Clara were on the Central Warf at Rogge Bay supervising the drivers and servants as to which bags and luggage had to be loaded on to which carriage.

Godfrey Butler was talking with the boys.

'I will have all your trunks, toolboxes and whatever else is in the hold belonging to you taken to a safe warehouse and stored for you. When you are ready to retrieve any of it, or you want to access it, just let me know and I will see to it personally.'

Lydia and Clara came over to them accompanied by Godfrey's wife, who had arrived with the carriage.

'Good day to you young men. I am Sarah Butler, Godfrey's wife. What a terrible business! From what I have heard it is a godsend that you two gentlemen were on that ship.'

The boys introduced themselves. 'We are just happy that Lydia and Clara are safe. I wish we could have done more for George,' said Jamie.

Lydia put her hand on Jamie's and said. 'Clara and I have discussed the loss of my father, Aunt Sarah. Jamie and Iain risked their lives for my father, and indeed for all of us, and it has been agreed that we really do not have to discuss this subject anymore.'

'Thank you, Lydia,' said Jamie.

'I will inform Bill where I'm staying. We must not lose touch,' said Doctor Morgan to Jamie and went off to his carriage.

Lydia and Clara hugged Jamie and Iain in turn. 'Please come and visit us at Aunt Sarah's house,' said Clara.

'Yes, we will, I promise,' said Iain back to her.

'Ladies, let us be off. I am sure the lads will want to get settled,' said Godfrey. 'My office is on Strand Street. I will set up a meeting. There is a lot to discuss.'

Chapter Twenty Nine

Cape Town

Nicholas Banbury was still in shock. He had been informed a few days ago by Major Barclay, of James Storer's arrest and detention at the fort, charged with gun-running, murder and treason.

He was now sitting in the major's office in the fort after being summoned for questioning. The humiliation apart, he was feeling very uncomfortable at being the focus of a military investigation.

He had started to write a letter to Earl Grayson but realised he was being a bit hasty, he had to get more information about Storer's incarceration.

As he had been assisting Storer in a Government office, he was immediately under suspicion of being party to Storer's crimes; he had been facing awkward questions for the last three hours.

'So to sum up, Mr Banbury, you had no idea of Under Secretary Storer's involvement in attempting to supply guns to the Xhosa chiefs to incite rebellion?' asked Major Barclay.

'None whatsoever, sir, and I resent the fact that you ask me to answer this question again.'

'With respect, sir, I have to ask these questions as this is a military inquiry into treasonable acts by a respected member of the colonial government, with whom you were working closely,' said the major.

'I understand you have to be thorough in your investigation, Major, but I cannot tell you any more than I have already told you,' said Banbury, clearly exasperated.

'So you did not see Storer talking with, or meeting with any unfamiliar faces, and had no suspicions of any kind that something was maybe out of place?'

Banbury thought he would give himself some credibility with his next answer.

'I must say, looking back, I did wonder about James'... er Storer's sudden urgency to return to England. I thought it rather odd at the time, as it was a rushed departure,' said Banbury. 'I suppose I now know why.'

'There have to be other people involved in this and I will get to the truth one way or another. I will be sending my report to London and will request that Storer be tried here in Cape Town, but that will ultimately be Whitehall's decision,' said the major.

Storer will not be tried in Cape Town, thought Banbury. *I will see to it that. If Storer recovers he will be sent to England, or he will perish.*

'Will he recover from his wounds, Major?' asked Banbury.

'The doctor thinks he will, but we will know for certain in the coming weeks. Thank you for coming to see me, Mr Banbury. I know you are a busy man. If there is anything else I need from you I will send a messenger to your office.'

Banbury climbed into his carriage; departed the

courtyard, drove under the portcullis at the main gate of the fort, over the moat and across the grand parade, glad to be away from the claustrophobic military scrutiny.

He was in a near state of panic as the carriage turned up Parliament Street and stopped outside the Government buildings in the grounds of the stately Goode Hoop Masonic Buildings, adjacent to the company gardens.

Hurrying to his office as best he could without drawing attention to himself, Banbury destroyed his first attempted letter and composed another lengthy communication to Earl Greyson.

He detailed everything that had transpired and reassured him that he would soon have the situation under control, and could he please send any instruction to be carried out as soon as was possible.

He sealed the letter and sealed it again in a diplomatic pouch marked 'Urgent: confidential Government business.' He then sent a servant to fetch one of his colleagues, who was a low-ranking member of the ELOS.

Robert Fairbairn knocked on Banbury's door five minutes later. An ex-army captain now employed in the Attorney General's office, he was younger than Banbury and always eager to please any time his services were required.

He was a fresh-faced happy sort of chap, with a red-cheeked complexion and boyish looks. He was everybody's friend and always had an ear to the ground. He made it his business to know everything about everybody.

He was also a killer with no conscience.

'What can I do for you, sir?' he asked Banbury, hoping he had to despatch someone from this life.

'Make sure these despatches are sent in the *special*

diplomatic pouch right away. This is very urgent, and make sure you are on call at any time. There are developments, which are moving very quickly and I may be in need of your special skills at a moment's notice.'

The special diplomatic pouch was set up to be delivered to Earl Greyson in person, for his eyes only.

Banbury told Fairbairn what little he knew about the events on *The Flying Fish*. 'I want you to find out the names of all the passengers on that ship, and who nearly killed Storer. Find out what they are doing here, then report back to me.'

'Yes sir. I would just like to inform you sir, my younger brother, Jonny, has just left the army and I'd like to recruit him to help with our expanding operational needs. I think he would be an asset to the organisation.'

'As long as you think he is trustworthy then by all means. You know the procedures of recruitment and the penalty for failure. Bring me those reports as soon as possible Fairbairn,' said Banbury.

Fairbairn went off slightly disappointed to carry out this menial duty, while Banbury pondered his next move about Storer.

If Storer survived his injuries, Banbury would need to contact him somehow, but outwardly he would condemn him as a coward and a traitor.

What was more concerning was that Fairbairn had to bring back information about the people who could get the better of James Storer to the point where they had almost killed him and how could the operation continue without Storer? The whole plot had been his brainchild.

He had to go to Storer's house to make sure the concealed cellar remained undiscovered.

The girl, Annatje, who had jumped to her death

through the trapdoor, had not been found. He and Storer's boss-boy, Williams, had ridden up to the ravine as far as the horses could go, then they had climbed and walked the last part to try and find her body, but she was nowhere to be found. Only the remains of Storer's latest victim were there, her body already unrecognisable. The scavengers had been busy.

Williams reckoned Annatje's body had been taken by a leopard to another location to be devoured. She had been small enough to be dragged off by the powerful cat. But Banbury was not convinced. He wanted proof of her death.

If she was alive and came forward to make a charge against them, it would be her word against two high-profile Government men. Besides, she would be disposed of before she could take it further. It was just the inconvenience of drawing attention to them that could be a problem. But she had never appeared so maybe she had died on the mountain.

A few days later a diplomatic pouch arrived for Banbury from his masters in Whitehall, marked for his attention only. The pouch contained official Government documents, along with sealed encrypted documents from his ELOS masters, and a letter with a clue about some ancient, hidden treasure buried by the Knights Templar somewhere in Southern Africa. The documents informed Banbury, he was now elevated into Storer's position as senior elder in the event that Storer has been compromised by two agent provocateurs on his ship sailing for Cape Town. *So the elders in England have pre-empted my letter which is still en-route to them,* thought Banbury, *they know Storer is in trouble but they don't know if he is dead or alive.*

He sent for Fairbairn and proceeded to inform him of the situation.

'The diplomatic pouch usually just comes with the mail ship, so the fact that a courier was sent highlights the seriousness of the situation,' said Banbury. 'The fact of the matter is that our people in London will only realise that Storer has survived when they receive the despatch I sent a few days ago, so we will have to wait for their instructions before we do anything else here. Understood?'

'Understood, sir,' said Fairbairn.

'What have you found out about the debacle on the ship Storer was sailing on?'

'My contact at the fort thinks the authorities are trying to cover up Mr Storer's involvement in running the guns, and intend to prove that the first mate was smuggling the guns, that he killed the owner of the shipping company and kept the captain and Storer prisoner, with help from thugs he hired in Liverpool. The problem with that is that the first mate and his helpers are all dead bar one, who is in the Roeland Street jail, and there are too many witnesses as to what really happened, I do not think Mr Storer is going to come out of this without a trial unless we get him out or kill him,' said Fairbairn matter-of-factly.

'Yes, I agree with you there. There are too many witnesses to dispose of so we will wait for instructions while Storer recuperates. This will, at least, give us some time to re-organise. From what I understand, three of the witnesses are an ex-army doctor of good standing and two other male passengers, who were the ones to thwart the take-over of the ship and dispose of Storer's henchmen. The other three are the late ship-owner's wife and daughters.'

'Quite right, sir, but the two men named on these documents are not the same men who were on the ship.' Fairbairn produced a piece of paper from his pocket and looked at his notes. 'Doctor Morgan is there, but the document from London says the other two passengers were Rattery and Black. The two men that came off the ship are Jamie Fyvie and Iain McColl, two Scotsmen who are here under the migration scheme to supply settlers with agricultural tools, wagons and such. They are also contracted to question the settlers on their progress and send reports back to the Immigration Department in London.'

'Are you sure of the names? Do you not think they are Government men?' asked Banbury.

'Quite sure, sir. Technically they do work for the Government, but not in the context that you are thinking. I think Storer and the first mate just got unlucky with these two men. They tried to get rid of the witnesses who knew what had happened to George Knowles, the ship owner, but the two Scotsmen must have retaliated and injured Storer, killed his hired help and released the captain. That is the only scenario that I can see.'

'Two men to take down six armed men? I find that highly unlikely, I think they are trained government agents,' said Banbury.

'That is conceivable sir, that being the case I think Storer made a huge mistake in trying to kill them and he has paid for that mistake; he picked on the wrong men.'

'Well, let us hope you are right and they are just here to start a business. Who knows… maybe we will recruit them. Meanwhile find out where Fyvie and McColl are staying and also the daughters of the late George Knowles and have them watched. Mrs Knowles and Storer are being detained at the fort. And keep an eye on the ship. What is it called?'

'*The Flying Fish*, sir,' said Fairbairn.

'How original! Keep a watch in case the military move it elsewhere.'

'What about the guns, sir? I know they are still on board and well-guarded.'

'I will meet with the commander at the fort, General Cunnynghame, he is one of our elders, I will impress on him the need to have a minimum guard on board to allow a quiet act of piracy,' said Banbury. 'Remember that unsavoury captain who helped us a few months ago to deliver some guns?

'Yes, sir. He is still lurking around the docks.'

'Tell him we will make it worth his while to get a small crew together to commandeer *the Flying Fish* and deliver the cargo up the east coast, then abandon the ship.'

'When will we do this, sir?'

'As soon as things calm down, I will let you know.'

'I will have the crew stand by and wait for your command, sir,' said Fairbairn.

'Also, see if you can make sense of the words in this clue about a Knights Templar treasure,' said Banbury handing Fairbairn the letter with the rhyme and the seal. 'From what I can ascertain from this letter, the elders are a bit sceptical about any treasure, but you had better investigate the possibility. Take the clue with you and report back on it. I want Fyvie and McColl followed everywhere they go until further notice. Then there is the spare witness in Roeland Street jail. I think you should arrange for him to find a final resting place in a Cape Town cemetery.'

'It will be done, sir. It will be Jonny's first kill. I do like a challenge,' Fairbairn said, getting up from his chair and leaving the room.

He is an evil man, thought Banbury. *It seems as though evil runs in the family.*

Chapter Thirty

Cape Town

Maria was selling flowers in Adderley Street with Auntie Fatima, as she had done for the past few months since waking up in Salomé's house, although she had now been taken in by Auntie Fatima, who lived next door.

Salomé and her husband Yusuf, regularly walked with Maria back up the mountain to where Yusuf and his son had found her, in a bid to try and jolt her memory.

Maria was the name she had chosen for herself because her memory had completely deserted her. They took her up the mountain on the advice of the imam at the mosque as they had established that she was of the Muslim faith and they were ready to help her. They tried in vain to find her family, if she did in fact have any family but who knew where they might be.

One evening after supper at Maria's request, Salomé and Yusuf came in from next door to sit with her and Fatima.

'I've been speaking with Aunty Fatima,' said Maria holding Fatima's hand. 'And I've explained to her that I've given a lot of thought to my situation. I have tried very hard to remember what happened to me but my memory will just not tell me what I need to know. You have all become family to me; you saved my life but in all good faith I cannot carry on living here knowing that I might have a mother and father looking for me.'

'Oh my child, you know you are welcome to stay with us, you have proved you are a good person and a hard worker. You have become part of us,' said Fatima.

Yusuf said. 'You are most welcome to stay among us until we find your family or where you come from. But what you say is correct. If there's someone looking for you then we need to try something new to bump your memory awake.'

'I've been thinking about trying something else, if you're agreeable,' said Maria.

Salomé said. 'If we can do it then we will try anything for you. What do you suggest?'

'What if we take the cart once a week or every two weeks and travel to some other communities and see if I recognise any of them or maybe someone recognises me?'

'It's certainly worth trying if we have the time to do it. I'm sure we can make the time,' said Yusuf.

'What about the police?' Said Salomé. 'Maybe we should ask them if they have had any inquiries about a missing girl.'

'The police in this town can't be trusted,' said Fatima. 'They're mostly drunken white men who find any excuse to beat the likes of us and throw us in jail. Besides, and don't take this the wrong way Maria, we must be careful, what if she's in trouble with the law?'

It was something they hadn't considered.

'The thing is. If I am in trouble with the police then it's very possible you would be as well because I'm living with you,' said Maria.

'You can be sure if they want to arrest you they will take us as well. I don't think going to the police is a good option. They're all corrupt,' said Yusuf.

'Then it's settled,' said Fatima. 'We'll find time to visit other villages and settlements and find Maria's family.'

'There's another place I would like to see as well; up on the mountain. Many times we have walked up to where you found me and a bit further up. Yusuf, you said there are only two large houses up on the slopes, I would like to go and see them; maybe I worked for one of the owners; maybe one of my family worked for them; seeing the houses might bring my memory back.'

'The owners don't like anybody going near those houses,' said Yusuf looking a bit uncomfortable. 'They say it is trespassing, which I believe is a legal word for breaking the law because you are on someone else's property and anyone caught can be jailed.'

'Can we get close without being seen?' Asked Maria.

'I'm sure we can. We will have to take the cart around to the east side of the mountain and head south then go up the slopes to where the houses are, I remember there are one or two old roads going up there. If we are seen, and I'm sure we will be, then we can hopefully say we have lost our way and be warned away. We will go to the rich houses first then we will make plans to visit the other villages,' said Yusuf.

As they approached the largest house of the two, which was adjacent to a deep ravine, Yusuf drove the cart off the road and stopped behind a thicket of small trees.

'Who lives in such a big house?' said Maria looking at the top floor above the high wall.

'There is a rumour that the man who lived here was very high up in the government. From what I've heard he was attacked by mutineers on the ship bringing him back from England and is now seriously injured in hospital, the house I suppose will be sold to some other rich white man,' said Yusuf.

Maria stared at the house for a long time trying to get some recognition.

Salomé said. 'Do you recognise anything Maria?'

Maria looked hard and closed her eyes, she started sobbing. 'No, nothing is familiar. I can't remember anything,' she said hugging Salomé.

Maria stared wistfully at the house as Yusuf drove the cart to the smaller house further down the slope with the same result, so they went home.

The following weeks proved too tiresome, time consuming and fruitless as all the places visited did not bring back any memories to Maria, and nobody recognised her.

'I will never find out who I am or where I come from,' said Maria sadly.

'You must never give up,' said Fatima softly. 'One day your memories will come back to you.'

There was, however, one small community they had overlooked.

Chapter Thirty One

Table Bay, Cape Town

Two weeks after *The Flying Fish* dropped anchor in Table Bay, another ship arrived from Liverpool. Hamish McFarland had been coming down to the jetty keeping watch for the ship over the last two days and now watched the anchor fall into the water. He waited for the Customs and Excise men to go out to the ship and do their business.

McFarland jumped into the hired whale boat and ordered the oarsmen to row out to the ship. When the boat came alongside he made a disguised signal that was recognised by one of the men standing at the gunwales of the ship, who signalled back to him in reply.

The man passed his luggage to the boatmen then climbed down into the boat and shook McFarland's hand with a secret grip of the Freemasons.

Not saying a word to McFarland he sat down and the boatmen rowed back to the beach, where they unloaded the luggage and put it on to a waiting carriage. The two brethren got into the carriage and as it moved off McFarland tested the man with three more grips, signs and three words to convince him of his identity.

'Welcome brother, I am Hamish McFarland, Master

of Lodge Southern Cross, number 398 on the Roll of the Grand Lodge of Scotland.

'Greetings, Worshipful Master. I am Rory McGregor, Master of Lodge St Claire, Edinburgh, number 349 on the Roll of the Grand Lodge of Scotland.'

'I received your letter a few days ago,' said McFarland. 'Your alarm is obviously very serious, Rory.'

'Yes, indeed it is. I wasn't sure if you would receive my letter before I got here. If we can go to a private place to talk I will tell you why I'm here.'

'You will be staying with me and my family. We'll go to the temple building first and talk in the office.'

The two men alighted from the carriage outside the Goode Hoop masonic buildings in central Cape Town and made their way to McFarland's office.

McGregor related to McFarland the tale of the Knights Templar treasure and how he had come to the decision to follow and watch over Jamie and Iain.

'Two Scots lads, Jamie Fyvie and Iain McColl, arrived here recently with the first clue to finding the treasure,' said McGregor. I anticipated them coming here and sent my letter to you a few days before they sailed. We knew about the clue and some of the contents, but the old man, a freemason in Edinburgh, who inherited it from god knows who, died before he could show it to us. You see he only realised he had it when he was going through some old documents and contacted us, but then he died without telling us where he had hidden the documents. It is not so much the treasure we want to get back, but the sacred relics that the Knights were guarding.'

'So apart from Fyvie and McColl, does anyone else, to your knowledge, have this clue?'

'I think someone else might have it. The lads sailed

from Liverpool a few days before me on the clipper, *The Flying Fish*. As you know we have a number of brethren who are in the police force and we learned through them that these two individuals had been recruited into the Government's Secret Field Police. They were being followed in Liverpool but we were already watching their back. We had to despatch one or two villains sent to kill them. We think the ELOS have the clue and hired the assassins,' said McGregor.

'The ELOS?' said McFarland immediately concerned. 'Are you sure?'

'Yes. The Secret Field Police are following the clues; first, to authenticate there are relics or treasure; second, to stop the ELOS getting their murderous hands on them. If we can follow Fyvie and McColl until they prove or disprove the existence of the treasure, then we can either leave it well alone or convince the two laddies to let us take it back to Scotland and, if we have to, discourage anyone else who wants to try and take it.'

'We're going to need reinforcements. We have brethren who are born and bred here and between them have a wealth of knowledge of the land from the Cape, to the hinterland and to Port Natal. They're all good men, and will help.'

'We need to find out where the laddies are staying and keep an eye on them. I know they have the information to retrieve the next clue and they should chase it easily after all these years,' said McGregor.

McFarland looked at the other man with a thoughtful look.

'Do you know something, Hamish?' asked McGregor.

'A ship arrived in the bay two weeks ago from

Liverpool, I believe, but nobody was allowed ashore. I waited a while and saw an army major accompanied by a police sergeant with a few other uniforms going out to the ship.'

'What ship was it?'

'I do not know, but I will find out if it was *The Flying Fish* and if Fyvie and McColl were on board,' said McFarland.

'The ELOS are not here for the treasure only. The fact is, no one really believes a treasure has survived all this time. No, they're up to some other mischief and that is partly why Fyvie and McColl are here, of that much I'm sure. But that is not our business; our priority is to recover the relics and the treasure if we can.'

'Let's get you to the house and I'll find out where these two men are.'

A day later McFarland had most of the information on what had happened aboard *The Flying Fish*: Who was being held at the fort and where the boys were staying, and reported this to McGregor.

'So, the laddies prevented a mutiny and uncovered a gun-smuggling plot,' said McGregor.

'More than that, Fyvie and McColl, must have been recruited and trained by Her Majesty's Secret Field Police to be able to overcome six armed men in a confined space,' said McFarland.

'You say a man by the name of Storer is being detained at the fort, and recovering from wounds received in a fight aboard the ship?'

'That's correct. This is a serious problem for the Cape Government. We are talking about the Colonial Secretary here. He was at death's door but seems to be responding to treatment. He is to be tried for murder and treason.'

'Is he to be tried here in Cape Town?' asked McGregor.

'I assume so. Why do you ask?'

'You say Storer is high up in Government here. Therefore we must assume, from what you have told me about the events on *The Flying Fish*, that he is the senior elder for the ELOS in Cape Town. If he is, he will be killed or spirited away by either the ELOS or the Government. You can rest assured he will never stand trial. The Government wouldn't want that and the ELOS will not tolerate a failure such as this.'

McFarland looked shocked. 'I didn't realise the enormity of the situation, Rory. I have to confess the situation is much too high up for me, but I'll take your lead and do what we have to do to protect the relics.'

'I thank you for that. So where are Fyvie and McColl staying?'

'At the Thatch Inn, in the centre of the town for the moment, until their permanent residence is ready. I already have someone watching their movements. The problem is our man has spotted another watcher.'

'The enemy have found them already,' said McGregor. 'Keep horses at the ready for a quick departure, Hamish, I have a feeling events are going to move quickly.'

'I'll let you look at an array of weapons and you can take your pick,' said McFarland.

'That'll be fine. I think I'll take a walk and have a think about things wise and wonderful. I won't go far.'

He wandered off, his woollen cap at odds with the hot climate of Africa.

Chapter Thirty Two

November/December 1855

Cape Town, the Elephant's Eye

When they disembarked the ship, Bill Hutchison had taken Jamie and Iain to his office so they could brief him on the events during the voyage.

First of all, they told him that Armstrong had to be notified as soon as possible; that Fairbrother and Armstrong's base in Liverpool were compromised.

They gave names and a detailed account of what had taken place, and where on the ship, whilst Hutchison wrote it all down, stopping to ask a question every now and then. Eventually he said he had enough information and would send a despatch to Armstrong, using a code unknown to anybody else.

After tidying up and securing the despatches in a safe, Hutchison took the boys to the warehouse where their toolboxes were stored. They removed money-belts packed with gold coins along with other valuables and documents. Hutchison then drove them to the Thatch Inn just off Greenmarket Square where they signed in and settled into their respective rooms.

Jamie knocked on Iain's door.

'Come in,' shouted Iain.

'Have you seen how much money is in these belts?' said Jamie closing the door.

'Aye... I know,' said Iain. 'Armstrong and his masters are obviously very serious about us getting to the bottom of this conspiracy if they are giving us this amount of wealth.'

Jamie opened a bottle of whisky and poured two healthy measures. 'Let's hope with Storer's demise the whole thing will blow over,' he said giving Iain his drink.

'I doubt that, Jamie. Those buggers are everywhere and we are going to have start digging for answers. Cheers.'

'Aye, cheers. Come on let's pack up and go for a walk and see the town.'

They decided to stow their money belts and sensitive documents in strongboxes provided by the hotel and secured them in the hotel's strong room. Then left the inn to go exploring.

They walked up Burg Street to the bustling Greenmarket Square, then along Shortmarket Street and right into Loop Street eventually emerging on Strand Street.

'This is the street Godfrey's business rooms are located,' said Iain.

'It feels so strange seeing all these black people and not-so-black people all over the place,' said Jamie.

'I know. I've only ever seen white-skinned people. Good afternoon,' said Iain to a brown coloured man and woman of small stature walking past them in the street.

They looked at him and kind of half-smiled as they carried on walking.

Jamie noticed some European men observing them with a look of annoyance on their faces.

'No' very friendly, are they. Maybe they don't understand my accent,' said Iain thoughtfully.

'I don't think so, Iain. I think we'd better find out more about the dos and don'ts of life here before we put our foot in it.'

They walked down the slight gradient of Strand Street and could see the fort in the distance just up from the beach, guarding Table Bay.

They turned up Adderley Street and stopped to watch divisions of soldiers marching in formation, presumably to the docks to go and fight at the frontier war as Doctor Morgan had predicted.

'Well, that kind of brings it home to you, doesn't it,' said Jamie.

'Aye, it does. It's a bit unsettling arriving in the middle of a war we know nothing about, especially when it is somewhere far away and we have never heard a shot fired in anger… well, not in a war at least.'

They continued to walk up Adderley Street and found themselves in the Company Gardens, which was laid out by the Boers many years before. They watched couples strolling in the sunshine, the ladies in their colourful frilly frocks, holding parasols to keep the sun off and the gentlemen looking uncomfortable in their stiff starched collars with lace-up ties, baking in tailed jackets and top hats.

'Bill said he would give us a tour of the town sometime in the next two or three weeks when he finds some spare time, so I suggest we find a tavern and sample the local grog,' said Iain.

Back at the Thatch Inn, Jamie said. 'I think I'm going

to like it here, Iain.'

'Christ almighty, Jamie! You've only just arrived here.'

'I know but it just feels right, I like the weather already.'

The December morning was sunny and hot with a light south-easterly wind. Jamie and Iain were sitting in the lounge of the Thatch Inn when Bill Hutchison arrived holding a couple of hats.

'I apologise for taking so long for the tour of the cape, I'm too busy by far. I brought you these Fedoras. I hope they fit you, otherwise you will burn your face and head in this sun. It can get fierce. Always cover up in the sun,' said Hutchison.

'Thanks, and don't worry yourself Bill, we've been keeping busy over the last couple of weeks familiarising ourselves with the town and the lay of the land, as it were.

The boys tried on the white, wide-brimmed hats and they fitted fairly well.

They got into an open carriage and Bill started the tour by taking them over Kloof Nek to Camps Bay.

'It's a big mountain,' commented Jamie, looking at the jutting line of buttresses following the coastline.

'The mountain is roughly 3,000 feet high. That line of buttresses is called the Twelve Apostles. There's a wagon track that goes all the way around the mountain but we will go back through Cape Town and I'll show you where your allocation of land is in Salt River.'

After they had looked at the plot of land they headed down the main road through Wynberg on the way to Simon's Town, where the Royal Navy had a safe harbour.

'I am taking you to False Bay, hopefully to see

whales, it's a bit late in the season. They come here every year for about six to eight weeks, to calve and rest before going to who knows where, but it is quite a sight seeing them sticking their tales out of the sea and leaping out of the water.'

Jamie and Iain looked at each other suddenly thinking about the Templar's clue. *As the Southeast wind howls o'er the Bay of Whales.*

The carriage took them on a coastal road through Muizenberg, which had miles of beautiful beaches.

'The old Post House was here when the British took back the Cape from the Dutch at the Battle of Blaauwberg,' said Hutchison pointing to a low thatched building on the right of the road.

As they entered the fishing village of Kalk Bay, they could see the whales frolicking out in the Bay.

'Why is it called False Bay?' inquired Jamie.

'The ships coming back from the East Indies used to mistake Hangklip, which is on the other side of the bay, with Cape Point and sail in here thinking it was Table Bay, but it wasn't; it was the false bay. Right then! Enough sightseeing today, I think we should head back to Cape Town for lunch.'

'Are there any wild animals around here?' asked Iain as the carriage approached Wynberg.

'Oh yes there are leopards and wild dogs. You will see porcupine and hundreds of monkeys called baboons.'

'Are there any elephants around?'

'No, they were hunted out years ago, as were the lions and water buffalo. As the population grew, the settlers just shot anything that moved. The hunters have to travel long distances now to get ivory and skins. It is still big business.'

'Captain Willard says that people can go walking on the mountain,' said Jamie.

'Yes, I go walking on the mountain quite often. You need a stout pair of boots and a walking stick. In fact one of the best walks is up there. The view is outstanding,' said Hutchison, pointing to a vertical, oval-shaped dark patch in the side of the mountain below the top edge that fell away to a ridge on the left.

'What is that? A cave?' asked Iain.

'More like a cavern. It's not very deep. The history enthusiasts say it was used by the Khoisan people, who were indigenous to this area before the white man arrived on these shores, and the Bantu, black people, migrated from the north and east. It is an easy walk from the bottom, or you can ride a bit of the way up the mountain and walk the rest. It is called *"Die Oliphant se Oog".*'

'*Duh… ooliesah…* what?' asked Iain.

'Die Oliphant se Oog,' said Hutchison laughing. 'It's Afrikaans for the Elephant's Eye.'

'The Elephant's Eye indeed. We will definitely be visiting there in the near future, isn't that right, Iain?'

'I can't wait,' said Iain sarcastically.

They were treated to a fine lunch at the Civil Service Club in Cape Town, then arrived back at the Inn at sunset well fed and well-watered.

'As you both are going to be working for the Immigration Department, I have written a requisition for horses, saddles and tack, which will be delivered to the stables at the inn after you have picked out a couple of horses for yourselves. I will see you tomorrow,' said Hutchison.

'Go and get the clue Jamie,' said Iain excitedly. In Iain's room Jamie spread the Templar's clue on the table.

As the Southeast wind howls o'er the Bay of Whales,
The tables' cloth is lost in the gale,
The Southern crags hold the elephant's eye,
Where the mountain echoes the eagles cry,
Find the seal the lamb is there,
To take ye on to who knows where,
The morning sun will light the eye,
There to see the way or die,
Find the way for the powers that be,
Lest you lose the heart in thee.

'This has to be it Jamie, all the pointers are there.' said Iain.

'Well, if this is the place, simply by chance we have indeed discovered the points on the clue; the bay with the whales; the elephant's eye; and the table has to be Table Mountain above us,' said Jamie.

'And I think the cloth which is obviously the tablecloth, must be the layer of cloud on top of Table Mountain which gets blown away,' said Iain.

'This might turn out to be easier than we thought it might be, after all these years the clues will probably be known to god knows how many people, albeit unwittingly. If this is the place where the second clue lies then there's only one way to find out, we need to get up there and see if we can find the sign of the seal, if it's still legible after all this time. We'll need to get horses up the mountain as far as we can and take it from there,' said Jamie.

'Time to go work,' said Iain.

The following days saw the boys concentrate all their efforts into setting up their new business in order to maintain their cover as businessmen.

They went to see Godfrey Butler and asked him if he would represent them. He duly obliged by helping them open an account with the Lombaard Bank of Cape Town.

With guidance from Bill and Godfrey they soon had letters sent out to order materials to be stored in the new fenced-off yard which was being erected at their premises in Salt River. Plans were drawn up by an architect for an office, workshop and blacksmith forges. Carpenters and labourers were hired to be ready to start work when they opened for business.

Once they were happy with the progress they were making, and the way their business plans were taking shape, they decided to ride up to the Elephant's Eye and try to find the next clue.

They set off at dawn on the chosen day with directions to the Elephant's Eye from the stable boy, the hotel supplying saddle bags filled with food, water, a flask of whisky and a bottle of wine.

Jamie was armed with his over and under pistols and daggers, as was Iain, with his blunderbusses.

They rode through Wynberg on the same road they had travelled with Bill; Jamie riding a chestnut gelding he had picked out, whilst Iain was on a dappled grey mare.

They turned right on to a road going through the suburb of Tokai straight to the side of the mountain, where, according to the stable boy, was an ancient animal path leading diagonally up the side of the mountain. Finding the path, it was easy enough to the top of that part of the mountain, but quite a bit away from the cavern as the path was angled to the left away from it.

'Well, that wasn't so hard, was it?' said Jamie.

'Not if you're a mountain goat,' replied Iain.

'The stable boy called this place Silvermine. Apparently the Dutch prospected for silver up here.'

'Jamie, I saw some movement at the bottom of the path where we started up,' said Iain.

'Aye, I thought I saw a rider, but I don't see him now. I think we're being followed.'

'We didn't expect anything less, did we? Let's carry on and find out who it is when they catch up to us.'

So following the directions they doubled back along the top of the mountain toward the cavern which was higher up, being at almost the same height as Table Mountain. The cavern could not be seen from where they were because it was perpendicular to them, overlooking a considerable part of the south peninsula.

There were boulders strewn all over the terrain which was rocky as far as the eye could see. They continued up a gradual slope until they topped a rise and went down into a shallow depression where a stream ran down from the top part of the mountain away to the left.

Following the stream as far as they could they then veered off to the right and up a steep, rocky gradient towards a ridge, trying to pick a route through the rocks which would best suit the horses. They glanced at their back trail on topping the ridge but could not see any movement.

'Can you see anybody?' asked Iain.

'No. If we are being followed they're bleddy good at it,' replied Jamie.

The terrain before them became gentler. The rocks were now wide, flat stones embedded in the earth and, further on, they encountered an expanse which could have been described as a field with long grass, the flowers in full bloom.

Flying insects were buzzing around doing their business as were birds, darting from one bush to another. Above the mountain a high screech made the boys look up to see pair of black eagles soaring on the updraft of hot air rising up from the mountain side, patrolling their territory.

'This is a better piece of land,' said Iain. 'At least we'll have a smoother ride.'

'I think we should go towards the edge of the mountain and over that wee stream flowing over the edge,' said Jamie, pointing to the spot he was talking about.

Iain took a drink from his water bottle. 'Aye, if we carry on along the edge of the mountain and then cut back over to the left of that outcrop we would be about a hundred feet below the buttress. We could leave the horses and climb up the side. It's not a vertical climb. We should find our way up and around to where the cavern is.'

'My, my, listen to the seasoned traveller,' said Jamie mockingly.

'I won't be making a habit of this. My arse much prefers the comfort of a carriage,' said Iain, nudging his horse into a walk.

Jamie follow Iain as they approached the stream. They could hear the waterfall cascading down the mountain.

Suddenly, Iain's horse pulled up snickering and whinnying trying to move backwards, bobbing her head up and down in alarm, Jamie's horse picked up on the alarm and did likewise.

'Whoa, boy! Whoa!' said Jamie to his horse, patting him on the neck. 'What's wrong, boy? Iain, calm your horse and back her up. We're right on the edge of the mountain. We don't want to let them get panicked and run off.'

They backed the horses up the path a bit and they calmed down.

'Look there on the other side of the stream,' exclaimed Iain. 'There to the right of the path on the flat rock.'

There was the reason for the horses getting skittish. A dark-coloured snake about three feet long with a frog stuck in its mouth was moving across the rock towards the path.

'Look at the size of that thing,' Iain whispered disgustedly.

'Maybe we catch a frog and stick it down the throat of the snake that's following us,' said Jamie.

'Oh yes, that is a fine idea.'

They watched with fascination as the snake disappeared from the rock into the grass only to appear again crossing the path and into the grass on the other side.

'We'll wait for five minutes and then see how the horses feel and carry on,' suggested Jamie.

'That's fine. That's a good thing.'

'What's a good thing?'

'The horses knowing that those things are around. That's a good thing. I really like that,' said Iain nervously.

'Come on, *Mrs* McColl. It should be safe to go on,' said Jamie shaking his head and laughing.

When they reached the point where they could go no further with the horses, they unsaddled them and Iain hid the saddles and bags under a bush while Jamie led the horses behind some larger bushes and tethered them.

They started up towards the buttress on a zig-zag course rather than straight up, as taught by Bradley Fairbrother, all those weeks earlier. When they eventually came to the edge of the mountain Jamie looked around the corner to see the huge cavern in the face of the cliff.

Robert Fairbairn watched as Fyvie and McColl turned right through the suburb of Tokai going towards the mountain under the cave high up on the cliff face. He pulled his horse up and summoned a local coloured man working in a vineyard.

'What is the name of that cave up there?'

'Wat? Ek verstaan nie.' *What? I do not understand.*

Fairbairn spoke Afrikaans fairly fluently.

'Wat is die naam van die grot tot daar?'

'Die olifant se oog, boss,' said the worker.

'Die olipha– The Elephant's Eye,' Fairbairn said allowed. 'Jesus, that's the name mentioned in the clue. It must be real.' He said to no one, kicking his mount forward.

He rode to where the wagon track came to a 'T' junction and took out his spy glass. He could see the boys riding diagonally up the side of the mountain and followed, taking care not to let them see him. He followed them until they dismounted and saw them climb up towards the cave and disappear round the face of the cliff.

Jamie and Iain followed a narrow animal path along the cliff face which went up and down, and meandered through the rocks and around thick bush growing out of the side of the mountain, the right side of the path was a considerable sheer drop and death to anyone who fell off.

The boys shuffled along the path hanging on to

branches when they could and hugging the side of the cliff face until they stepped on to some big flat rocks at the entrance of the cavern.

'Look at the size of this thing,' said Iain in amazement.

'It looks so small from down there,' said Jamie pointing at the main road in the distance.

'It doesn't go in very deep. I can see the back of it but the ceiling is very high. If the clue is up there then we are, as they say in the Glasgow shipyards… fucked.'

'How long do you think it will take our follower to get here?' Asked Jamie.

'If he's cautious, about an hour; maybe a bit longer.'

'Well let's take in the view and see if he arrives,' said Jamie.

Fairbairn was sure he hadn't been seen but he was wrong. He climbed up and around to the front of the cavern with his pistol drawn.

Jamie concealed himself behind an outcrop of rock with dense bush growing out the side of it on the other side of the cavern and watched Fairbairn through the branches as he walked carefully along the path to the entrance of the cavern, a pistol in his hand.

'Looking to do a bit of hunting?' asked Jamie emerging from behind the bush, gun in hand.

Fairbairn looked at Jamie, clearly surprised and said. 'No, not really,' he said looking around.

'Looking for me?' said a voice from behind.

Fairbairn looked back and saw Iain leaning behind a rock just inside the entrance with his blunderbuss pointing right at him. He knew they had been waiting for him and felt like a complete fool.

'Oh, I did not see you there. I was not expecting to

see anyone here. I often come up here for the quiet and the view,' said Fairbairn mortified.

'So you often come here with a cocked pistol in your hand?' asked Iain.

'You never know what's lurking in the cave. Besides, what business is it of yours?' said Fairbairn, angry at being caught out and having to answer questions.

'Like you, we are just up here for the view and to explore this fascinating country, but your business became ours when you followed us,' said Jamie. 'You can make your pistol safe and put it back in your belt, if you don't mind.'

Fairbairn did not like the position he had put himself in, but did as he was told and said. 'Look here, I work for the Government, in the Attorney General's office and I certainly was not following you.'

'Oh well then, it all seems to be a misunderstanding. We work for the Government as well. Are you sure you were not told by someone to follow us Mister… what's your name?'

'Fairbairn, Robert Fairbairn, and no, I was not told to follow you,' he said, raising his voice.

'I don't believe you, Robert,' said Iain. 'You don't mind if I call you Robert? The fact that you have not asked us for our names infers that you already know our names, nor did you introduce yourself when you saw Jamie, and you showed up with a cocked pistol. All this tells me that you are a liar.'

Fairbairn was about to lose control and pull out his pistol again when Iain said. 'Do not even think about it, Robert. This blunderbuss has a two-inch muzzle. Even if I point it above you it will still blow your face off your fucking head.'

'You cannot treat me in this manner. You have not heard the last of this or me,' he said suddenly calming down.

'Be sure to say hello to the Attorney General for us and maybe we will see you along the corridors of power one of these fine days,' said Jamie dismissively.

Fairbairn turned to go back along the path to his horse and Iain shouted. 'I'll be watching for your horse's arse disappearing over that ridge, Robert. Just make sure you keep going.'

Iain went around the path and watched Fairbairn ride over the ridge, then went back to find Jamie looking in the cavern. 'Tell me you found the clue and we can get off this mountain.'

They said they were out to explore and admire the view, thought Fairbairn, *but they were too professional at ambushing me and covering me with their guns. Banbury is right they must be government trained agents. It was also too much of a coincidence that they were there and the clue was real.* He was livid that a couple of amateurs had got the better of him.'

He was not a happy man and he was itching for action. His masters, the elders of the ELOS, had ordered him to recruit a corps of volunteers to fight alongside the British military forces, under the leadership of the new governor, Gerald Cuthbert. He had had a meeting with Banbury and Cuthbert, who had outlined what was expected of him and his new recruits.

He had already recruited his younger brother Jonny, who was a sergeant with the 2nd Queen's before demobbing at his older brother's request, and was now working on a list of candidates for the Fairbairn Volunteer

Corps; he was just waiting for the go-ahead. Every criminal, psychopath and murderer in Cape Town with a hatred for anyone with a black skin had volunteered to sign up.

Now he was riding on the main road through Wynberg back to Cape Town to mobilise a few of his hired cutthroats to go back and confront Fyvie and McColl.

I should report to Banbury, but if there is a treasure, he thought, *I want my share for me and my brother and they can all go to hell, including Banbury, the bloody elder.*

'You search that side and I'll search this side,' said Jamie. 'The sooner we get this done the better.'

The floor of the cavern sloped upwards and inwards until it levelled out slightly at the back. There was a lot of water running down the walls and dripping from the roof. Nooks and crannies were scattered along the walls, and moss had grown almost everywhere. They searched for the rest of the day until the sun went over the mountain and it became too dark to see without torches.

They went back to where they left their kit. 'So what do you think we should do now?' Jamie asked Iain.

'Well, are we going back down the mountain and come back tomorrow, or should we come back with more help next week?'

Jamie unravelled a piece of paper from his saddle bag and looked at it. 'The clue says; *the morning sun will light the eye, there to see the way or die.* The sun rises in the east straight in front of the cavern. I think we have to be standing at the entrance at sunrise, according to the clue.'

'It's the; *to see the way or die* bit that bothers me,'

said Iain.

'We've got plenty of food with us and we each have a blanket attached to the saddle bags. I think we build a fire and spend the night here. The weather is fine and we have a flask of Armstrong's whisky, I don't think Fairbairn will take a chance on coming up the mountain at night, if at all.'

'I knew you were going to suggest staying up here to sleep with snakes and god knows what else that wanders the mountain at night,' said Iain. 'But you're right and besides that, I would not be surprised if old Robert is waiting for us down the path somewhere. Remember Armstrong's words? *Trust no one.*'

The sun sets quickly in Africa so they collected some wood to keep them going for the night and soon had the fire burning nicely in a circle of rocks between two large boulders that the boys used for leaning against.

They ate cold mutton, cheese and bread, washed down with tea from the small boiling pot with a looping wire handle.

They never ceased to be amazed at the density of the stars in the night sky as they swigged the whisky every now and then.

Jamie made a torch and they climbed up to a vantage point below the buttress and from 3,000 feet up they watched the twinkling light from fires and lamps across the land, to Table Bay to the north and False Bay to the south.

After a while they were sitting on their blankets staring at the flames in the fire. Iain was smoking a rolled-up cigarette and Jamie lit one of his rare cheroots and the whisky tasted good.

'After what's happened, do you regret coming here?'

Iain asked Jamie.

'Not a bit. It's difficult to explain. I always wanted to be somewhere else.'

'I haven't any regrets either, I've missed Christmas and New Year and now, here I am, on top of a mountain in Africa, not knowing if I'm getting my brains blown out tomorrow. How life has changed!' he said laughing.

Chapter Thirty Three

The Elephants Eye

McFarland got the call to mobilise and roused McGregor. They passed through Salt River and met up with a brother mason called Arthur Burton, who had been alerted by the watcher. After a quick introduction to McGregor they rode off through Wynberg in pursuit of Jamie and Iain.

With Burton leading the way, McGregor and McFarland following, they rode down main rode to the turn off toward the mountain track. Burton could see through his spyglass the lone rider going up the track along the mountain.

'They have turned on to the mountain track that goes up to Silvermine. They must be going up to the Elephant's Eye,' said Burton. 'They are being followed by a white man who is in a hell of a hurry to catch up to them.'

'Are you sure there's only one man following them?' asked McFarland.

'Quite sure. We will wait for him to top the track then we will go up. He hasn't looked back once to see if he was followed,' said Burton.

When the trio reached the top of the mountain track they went off to the left of the ridge and out of sight of the track behind them. They dismounted and tethered the horses at the base of a hillock then went up to lie down at the crest looking towards the buttress.

'The person who is following your friends has left his horse and is nowhere to be seen,' said Burton peering through the spyglass.

'Can you see the laddies' horses?' asked McGregor.

'Yes, they are tethered about a hundred and fifty yards from where the other chap left his and they are unsaddled. Wait… there is someone coming around from the front of the cliff. Going by his clothes it's the chap who is following your *laddies* as you call them. He looks to be heading for his horse. Let's wait a bit.'

'Is there nobody else in sight?' this from McFarland.

'No one, but this one who is following your lads is nearly down from the cave and looks to be in a hurry. He has mounted the lone horse and is heading back to the mountain track. I did not hear any shots so I assume your laddies dealt with him and sent him on his way. Now we wait for them.'

After a few hours they saw Jamie and Iain come back to where they left their horses and saddles.

'It looks like they intend to stay up here,' said Burton. 'They've started a fire and are settling in for the night, I suggest we do the same. I don't think the other chap will come back. It will be dark soon and nobody would attempt to come up here at night.'

They went down the hill and found a secluded spot to make camp. After they had eaten and were smoking pipes around the warm fire, McFarland asked McGregor, 'Is there a reason you have not revealed yourself to these two men and offered your help, or asked them to hand over the clues, or at worst ambush them?'

McGregor puffed on his pipe and said. 'This whole thing unravelled very quickly so we had to act quickly. We did not know who we were dealing with, but that soon became clear. When I say *we,* we are a special order of only half a dozen past masters, who have all attained the highest degree in freemasonry, who were assembled to find and retrieve any lost relics or artefacts of the Knights Templar. We called a meeting of past masters who have attained the Knights Templar degree, which, as you know is now purely symbolic, along with the Grand Master at the Grand Lodge in Edinburgh, and decided to watch over these two brave young men and let them use the resources of the Government to find – or not find – the buried relics. And so far we and they are succeeding. We just need to have faith that they will let us take control at some point, but I am afraid I do not have a clue as to when that point will come about. For now we just proceed carefully.'

'It looks like these two young men don't realise what is at stake here. They have a huge burden on their broad shoulders,' McFarland said taking out a flask of whisky and passing it around.

'Well then,' said Burton, 'let's make sure they get to the end of their quest in one piece.'

Chapter Thirty Four

January 1856

The Elephants Eye

Jamie awoke before dawn and threw some wood on the fire to make some tea. He roused Iain and they finished off the remains of the picnic food and doused the fire.

By the time they had saddled up the horses and secured the saddle bags, the sky on the eastern horizon behind the Hottentot Holland Mountains had a slight bluish hue to it.

The boys tethered the horses securely and scrambled up and carefully around to the entrance of the cavern and waited for the sun.

'Jamie, look down there at the base of the mountain.'
'Fairbairn!'
'Aye, two fires. It looks like he's brought some of his friends,' said Iain.

'We're going to have to find this clue quickly, if it exists, and find another way down the mountain. We're high up here so the sun will rise and shine here long before it gets down the foot of the mountain, which should give us a small chance to find what we are looking for and get out,' said Jamie.

'The clues have been fairly easy so far simply because we know what to look for. Let's hope our luck holds.'

They watched the blaze of light burst over the distant mountains and looked up, craning to see the sun light chase the shadow down the face of the buttress to the top of the cave. As quickly as the sun had set, it now rose and filled the cavern with bright sunlight.

Jamie and Iain looked in, went left and right and then moved a bit further in and up.

Nothing.

By the time Fairbairn had found Jonny and gathered the men he sought it was getting late and the sun was already behind the mountain casting a shadow on the land.

His spy at the inn reported that the two men had not returned so they continued towards the path that led up the mountain, if they were coming back they would run into them head on.

As it turned out they did not encounter Fyvie and McColl. They must have decided to camp overnight on the mountain, but it was too dangerous to go up the path at night, and even if they reached the top safely the ground was too rocky to risk the horses, so he decided to camp at the bottom of the path until sunrise, then go up to confront them.

The next morning Fairbairn roused Jonny, to mobilise the men to start up the mountain. They were saddling their horses when Jonny shouted. 'Robert, look up there. Look up at the cave.'

The sunlight was moving down the mountain and was lighting up the entrance to the cavern.

Fairbairn extracted his eye glass from the saddle bag and focussed on the two men who he could clearly see looking at the front of the cavern. Then they disappeared.

'Mount up! Mount up right now and get moving!' shouted Fairbairn, already heading for the pathway up the mountain.

It was still dark when McGregor woke up. He put some wood on the fire and noticed Arthur was gone. He looked up the hill and could just see his outline lying at the crest. Waking Hamish he then went to join Arthur.

'See any movement yet, Arthur?'

'They have saddled up and packed up their kit, I think for a hasty departure. They are climbing to the cavern. The sun will be up soon, so whatever they are waiting for will happen soon because the horses are ready go.'

'I will ride over and take a look down the mountain path,' said McGregor.

McFarland brewed some tea and was packing the camp as McGregor saddled his horse and picked his way across to the edge of the mountain. He could see two fires off the base of the mountain and the faint movement of a camp stirring.

He re-joined Burton and McFarland at the crest of the hill. 'There's a bunch of riders breaking camp at the bottom of the path. When they get up here the laddies will have to find another way down.'

'They can only head south to find a way down. There are one or two places along the mountain where they can do that,' said Burton.

They waited until the sun's rays peeped over the mountains, bright and clear. From their vantage point they watched Fairbairn and his men coming up the track. The sun rose higher in the eastern sky.

'I don't see anything, Jamie.'

'I don't either. Move further up the cave and I'll move in to the middle,' suggested Jamie.

'There! Shite! It's gone,' exclaimed Iain. 'I thought I saw something glinting on the wall at the back of the cavern. Jamie, move up a bit and I'll move to the middle as well.'

Jamie moved up and suddenly said. 'Iain, you were right. There's a reflection.'

'I see it. Stay still. Don't take your eyes of it until I get up there,' said Iain, scrambling up the dirt floor.

When he got to where the sunlight had reflected, Jamie directed him to put his fingers on it and then came to join him.

The wall had moss growing all over it with the exception of this patch.

'It looks like a piece of glass,' said Iain. 'Scrape away the moss.'

They scraped away the moss and discovered a piece of stone shaped like an egg. A pebble with reflective elements had been inserted into a recess in the rock. Around the reflective pebble the shape of an eye was hewn into the rock, Iain and Jamie looked at each other knowing what to do without saying a word.

Jamie said. 'The clue said *the morning sun will light the eye.* But it wasn't referring to the Elephant's Eye, but the eye of the lamb.'

They scraped away the moss where they thought the outline of a lamb would be and although bits of the outline had corroded through time it eventually took the vague outline of something about the size of a large dog.

'I think they've mixed this up with a Shetland bloody pony,' said Iain.

'Very funny. See here... and here,' said Jamie pointing to the lamb's neck. 'It looks like Latin scratched into the stone, but where's the clue?'

Jamie rubbed at the area with his sleeve and saw a seam inside the shape of the head.

'Iain, give me a helping hand here. The pebble looks to be embedded in a larger piece of stone which has been shaped to fit into a larger recess in the rock.'

The used their daggers to worry the edge of the stone, but it would not move.

'Wait! Let me try something,' said Jamie.

'Make it quick. I'm sure our friends are on the move down there.'

Jamie put the point of his dirk into to the edge of the pebble at one end and, with a bit of persuasion, prised it loose. He poked the knife into the hole and it went in almost to the hilt. Then turning the knife sideways he pushed on it and the leverage moved the stone about half an inch out of the recess. He gave the knife another good push and the whole thing slid out of the wall and fell to the floor.

There, at the back of the recess, was a rolled-up mouldy piece of leather. Jamie pulled it out and put the package on the floor and looked at Iain. 'You can do the honours.'

The leather was still in fairly good condition considering the length of time it had been in there. Unravelling the leather there was a gold box still in perfect condition. Iain opened it and saw the sealed leather pouch inside and Jamie said. 'We can't make a copy and leave it for the ELOS. There's too much of a mess here to try and hide it, and we are out of time. I think you should close that and we can look at it later, because we have to get the fuck out of here.'

'Aye, you're right. Let's go!

They scrambled down to the entrance and looked down to where they had seen the fires. There was no one there. They retrieved the horses, stowed the gold box in Jamie's saddle bag, mounted up and rode off at a canter.

'We can't go back the way we came up so I suggest we head south,' said Jamie, pointing to fairly flat ground with a low hill to the left, and high ground sweeping away from the buttress to the right. 'When we came up that rocky path to the ridge, there was a wide shallow valley falling away behind that hill on the left. I think if we go around the hill and across the valley it should take us up above that wee place with the funny name…'

'Muizenberg,' said Iain.

'Aye, that's it, if we can get down there, we are home.'

'That sounds good to me. Let's go,' said Iain.

Fairbairn and his riders came up to the ridge and saw Jamie and Iain riding south, Jonny raised his rifle and took a shot at them, but the bullet went wide of the target and the boys spurred their mounts into a gallop, tearing across the veldt.

'Jonny, stop shooting for Christ's sake, now we have to chase them. Take three men, go after them, bring them down and search them thoroughly,' said Fairbairn. 'The rest of you come with me.'

The boys heard the musket shot ricochet of a rock behind

them and immediately spurred the horses into a gallop. 'Shite! They must have a sharp shooter with them,' shouted Jamie.

'Well, I hope he doesn't get any sharper than the last shot.'

Another shot rang out as they rode towards and around the hill, going up at a steep angle to the top of another ridge, then zig-zagging down the other side because of the steep gradient. They crossed the valley into a perpendicular shallow valley leading up to a flat section of the terrain. A bit further on the ground started to get very rocky again and they had to slow the horses to a walk.

As they approached the edge of the mountain overlooking Muizenberg they heard four musket shots. 'We'll have to dismount and walk the horses down there. It's too steep and too rough to ride,' said Iain.

'We'll be an easy target for any marksman above us,' replied Jamie.

'That's the old Post House there,' said Iain pointing to the small building on the main road. 'If we can keep that in sight and walk the horses down and around the base of the mountain they, or he, won't have a shot.'

'What do you want to do, Rory?' asked Burton.

'The leader has gone to check the cavern. I'll stay here and watch them if you two could give the lads a bit of help if they need it,' McGregor said.

Burton knew the terrain well and led McFarland to an animal path that took them up over a rocky outcrop, giving them a panoramic view of the direction the boys were taking. They could see the boys dismounting and leading their horses down the mountain to Muizenberg.

Burton decided to dismount and take up a position which gave them a good field of fire and wait for the pursuers. When Fairbairn's men appeared they fired two shots close to them then expertly reloaded and loosed another two shots, reloading again. The riders pulled up not knowing where the shots were coming from then turned and headed back the way they had come.

Fyvie and McColl have clearly found something and are now taking it back to Cape Town. Thought Fairbairn, after discovering the seal and the empty hole. *He had to find out what it was. He needed to see the clue to the hidden wealth.*

Returning to the horses, Jonny and the men sent in pursuit of Fyvie and McColl had returned after failing to catch them.

'What happened to them?' he asked.

'By the time we caught up to them they were already going down the mountain behind a rock face above Muizenberg. We were fired upon by someone else – maybe two people – hidden in the rocks. We couldn't make out which direction the shots were coming from so we decided to come back,' said Jonny.

'Damn it!' shouted Fairbairn. 'Are you sure it wasn't Fyvie and McColl shooting at you?'

'No. They were definitely walking their horses down the mountain.'

The fact that there was someone else on the mountain clearly watching out for Fyvie and McColl worried Fairbairn. 'Let's get off the mountain. We will catch them on the Main Road.'

Burton and McFarland re-joined McGregor who had

watched Fairbairn come back from inspecting the cavern. The riders who pursued the boys rode down to report to their leader and they all rode back over the ridge and back down the mountain.

'We'll wait a bit and then take a look at the cavern. After that we should get back to Cape Town and await the next move. We need to find out who the leader of that bunch of villains is and who he is working for,' said McGregor.

'This definitely smells of the ELOS, it may be a step to far for your laddies,' said McFarland.

Jamie and Iain made it to the main road without further incident and rode back towards Cape Town passing the road that had taken them below the Elephant's Eye the day before. They could see a group of riders in the distance coming toward them.

'That's the bastards who took a shot at us,' said Iain.

'They won't try anything here. This road is too busy. Let's ride further towards Cape Town and wait for them.'

They waited in Roeland Street just past the new jail, Jamie sitting with his leg crossed casually in front of him on his horse's neck. Fairbairn and his motley band of men came into view a few minutes later.

Fairbairn held up his hand to halt them and walked his horse over to where the boys were waiting.

'So did you find anything interesting at the cave?' he asked trying to contain his temper.

'Like what? We weren't looking for anything, were we Iain?'

'No, just taking in the splendid view and having a wee picnic, Jamie.'

Fairbairn's eyes blazed with fury. 'You think you are

a pair of clever buggers, don't you? I took my friends up to see the view and maybe shoot some vermin, but the only vermin we saw there ran away,' said Fairbairn.

'Oh, so the shots that were fired at us were just stray shots?' asked Iain.

'Yes, of course they were. Just one of the lads getting a bit excited.'

'Well, you tell your excited laddie that if I find out who he is I'll shove his rifle so far up his arse he'll need a doctor to have it removed,' said Iain, goading him.

Jonny walked his horse forward and said, 'you're welcome to try that now McColl.'

'Stand down Jonny.'

'Nobody threatens me,' said Jonny.

'Not here; another time, 'said Fairbairn still glaring at the boys. 'I will be seeing you two again,'

'I'm sure you will,' said Jamie.

Fairbairn and his brother turned and rode off, signalling their men to follow.

Fairbairn now had to report to his master.

'Fuckin' arsehole!' muttered Iain.

'We need to very wary of them,' said Jamie. 'Come on. I need a drink and we can look at the new clue.'

Chapter Thirty Five

London

Earl Greyson had received and read through the despatches from Banbury and from Major Barclay.

He immediately made arrangements to meet with his elder, then read through the report from Nicholas Banbury once more and then read through it again.

Storer had survived, but was imprisoned in Cape Town Castle, which meant the Government's prestige and credibility would be seriously damaged once the press and the public found out.

Even worse, the ELOS's plans to infiltrate the Cape Government and utilise the British Army to penetrate and annex the Southern African states outside the control of the British Empire, would be compromised. Everything would unravel now that Storer was out of the equation. After all, it had been his idea and plan from the very start.

This is a disaster, thought Greyson, wiping his hands down over his face. *It will take us years of planning to get to this stage again in the future.*

He poured himself a large brandy and sat down to mull over this setback.

'But wait!' he said out loud. 'Storer is still alive.'

He called for his carriage, made the rendezvous and was now sitting behind his elder, who was reading the correspondence from the Cape.

'This is one unmitigated mess,' the elder said with disgust.

'Elder if you will permit me, I would like to put an idea to you. This situation may yet be salvaged,' said Greyson.

'Continue.'

'According to this information, Storer will soon be fit enough to travel to England for trial. The military have him under investigation and are holding him at the fort, as smuggling guns is a treasonable offence. There are too many witnesses for this to be covered up, so, with your permission, I will send a despatch to direct the Attorney General to take the prisoner into civilian authority and have him on the next available ship back to England. The Attorney General is not one of us, but we do have a man in that office. As you know, his name is Robert Fairbairn and the commander at the fort is an elder, General Albert Cunnynghame. They will ensure that the prisoner will be transferred to civilian custody.'

'What of George Knowles' wife?' asked the elder.

'She will be put aboard a Royal Navy ship and sent back to England.'

'Does she know of us?'

'No, elder, she is merely a pawn to be sacrificed whenever we deem it fit,' said Greyson.

'Continue with your idea of a plan of action.'

'Thank you, sir. The first part of the plan is as follows; we have assets in Sierra Leone, West Africa. I suggest we order one of our ships to sail south from the capital, Freetown, to the island of St Helena and anchor there. The second part of the plan is once we have Storer in civilian custody, we make sure there is not a navy vessel available to take him to England, and secure passage for him on board a civilian ship of our choosing, with our people on board. As we know, all ships, including Storer's, sailing from Cape Town to England, stop over at St Helena. Our ship from Freetown will follow Storer's when it leaves St Helena and sails for England. Storer will then conveniently fall overboard or commit suicide by jumping into the sea, but our men will have set him adrift, to be picked up by the following ship to take him back to Freetown. Once there we will create a new identity for him and ship him back to Cape Town to continue with his operation.'

'It is a very sketchy plan. Besides, how can that work? Storer will be recognised immediately he sets foot in Cape Town,' said the elder.

'Not so, elder. According to the information in these despatches, Storer's body is so emaciated and the damage from the wounds on his face are so severe that he cannot be recognised; we have the expertise to give him the cover he needs to finish this. It would take us years to get this far again. I think it can work, sir,' said Greyson enthusiastically.

The elder lit his cigar and puffed it for a while and said. 'You know, I think this idea of yours is audacious enough to actually work, Greyson. Send your orders. I will give you a sealed letter for Cunnynghame to comply with your request. This situation could indeed, yet be salvaged.'

'Thank you, elder.'

Chapter Thirty Six

Cape Town

After the confrontation with Fairbairn, Jamie and Iain went back to the Inn and stabled the horses. They had bathed and changed into fresh clothes and were now sitting at the table in Iain's room with a glass of local beer and a whisky.

The gold box open, Iain removed a hard leather pouch, sealed with a waxy substance, probably made by the Knights. Carefully slicing through the wax, Jamie withdrew a single page of parchment with a Knights' seal stamped on it and a verse of what looked like poetry, much the same as the previous clue.

'Here we go again,' said Iain. 'We don't even know if this treasure or the relics are still there after all this time. Let's hope the next clue is as straightforward as the last one.'

'I know what you mean. We could be chasing ghosts,' Jamie replied. 'It's safe to say that the clues will be as identifiable as the Elephant's Eye was. The fact that the Knights devoted a lot of time and effort to carefully hiding the clues, tells us that something really did happen. If we don't get to the end of this puzzle or find out that it comes to a dead end, someone else will, and if there is a load of wealth waiting to be uncovered, I'd rather it wasn't the ELOS that find it.'

'Fairbairn must have seen where we dug out the clue in the cavern. Do you think he is from the ELOS?' said Iain.

'How do we tell if he is or he isn't? For our own safety we must assume that he is, but very low in the chain of command, which means he answers to someone who is in a position of power in the Cape. I think we need to establish a network of informants, but that is going to take time. Meanwhile, let's see what we can do with this clue.' Jamie read it out.

'Below the waves the rocks bare their teeth,
Two sentinels watch o'er the dark place beneath.
The eagles' seal is there, to show the way,
Past the heads, through the narrows, to the calm in the bay.
The way that you seek is there on the shore,
To the west of the stones that rise from below.
Walk fifty paces from the water's edge,
Find the path that will help to fulfil your pledge.
The dark place beckons for those to aspire,
Eager in pursuit of an object much desired.'

'Good grief,' said Iain. 'Let me have a look at it.'

Jamie passed over the clue with the eagle seal. 'It mentions waves so the location must be near the sea.'

'The sentinels, the heads and the narrows must be the entrance to a lagoon because the clue mentions a bay,' said Iain.

'And the dark place I think we can safely say is

another cave. So far so good.'

'Och, this is easy. Now all we have to do is find the location, the bay, the stones, the path, the cave and the seal. Aye, this will be easy,' said Iain with his usual sarcasm.

'God, you're such a doomsayer. We found the last one without much trouble, apart from getting shot at. All we need to do is ask around and find out if there is anywhere that resembles the description in the clue without raising any suspicions.'

'If you think back, Jamie, Armstrong told us the story from the letters discovered at the deceased mason's house... about the Knights' ships finding a safe place to do repairs and deciding to stay.'

'Yes, I remember. They sailed west along the south coast of Africa and found a safe haven through a small opening between two heads of rock. Well done, Iain. The drawing of the seal is quite crude; the two-headed eagle looks a bit deformed, but it should be enough to guide us to the next part of the puzzle, or hopefully the treasure.'

'I think we should describe the entrance to the lagoon to Captain Willard. He has been up and down this coast,' suggested Iain.

'Aye, we could tell him we need a harbour to deliver our goods and we want to go and have a look,' said Jamie. 'We'll go and find him. He did say he owes us a favour.'

Chapter Thirty Seven

February 1856

Cape Town

'My instructions were quite clear, were they not?' shouted Banbury. 'Follow them and find out where they were going and what they were doing.'

'Yes, elder, but I took the decision to muster some men and go back up the mountain because there was no time to find you, and I had to see what they were doing in the cave at the Elephant's Eye.'

'You will call me *sir* in the office. Someone may overhear you. You say one of your men started shooting at them and then your men went in pursuit of them? What on earth were you thinking you would do? Kill them and think no one would ask any questions?'

'It will not happen again, sir. The men were just a bit overzealous,' said Fairbairn, getting angry at this pompous arse.

'It had better not. You will do nothing unless I order it. Is that clear?'

'Very clear, sir.'

'What did you find at the cave?' asked Banbury.

Fairbairn wanted the treasure so badly he was close

to killing this gutless idiot right now, right here.

'I searched the cave from top to bottom and did not see anything disturbed,' he lied. 'There was only some moss lying around the earthen floor. They may have found something, so I will keep an eye on them and find out if indeed they found another clue.'

'Then do it, but we have more pressing business. Cuthbert wants you and your cutthroats out to the frontier to start with the unpleasant business of ridding the area of marauding bands of Xhosa murderers and thieves, in a way that the army cannot be seen to be doing. You will leave tomorrow and report to the governor in King William's Town as soon as you arrive. But more pressingly, I have received orders from the elders in London which will be carried out immediately. You will accompany me to the fort tonight and secure James Storer's transfer to the civilian authorities and deliver him to a waiting civilian ship to be taken to England for trial. I have managed to get two of our men to guard Storer aboard that ship.'

'But sir, isn't he under military law?' said Fairbairn.

'That has been taken care of. You will go to your superior, the Attorney General, Stephen Jeffries, who has been notified of the transfer. Bring the papers he has prepared and meet me back here. I want to see if they are in order as we will be accompanying Jeffries to see Storer safely put on a ship tonight.'

'This is all a bit sudden, sir.'

'Yes, the ELOS have the power to do this. We have brought our plans forward. After it leaves Cape Town, Storer's ship will rendezvous with an ELOS vessel off the British Island of St Helena in the Atlantic. This vessel will help him to escape. You will attempt to get Storer on his own and make him aware that arrangements have been made for him to escape his prison ship, and be picked up and taken to a safe haven. That is all you need to know at the moment, so get going and do not be late.'

Chapter Thirty Eight

Cape Town

Storer had been in and out of his delirium for weeks after being transferred from *The Flying Fish* to the fort hospital. His body was emaciated from the infection and the fever and not eating regularly. Doctor Morgan had had to use some of his precious store of chloroform to put him to sleep and with the help of a nurse had cut away the gangrenous flesh from the knife wounds on his face.

'I do not know what is keeping him alive,' he said to Major Barclay later that day. 'He should be dead, considering the infection and gangrene he has suffered, but he seems to be rallying round, so you may have a trial after all.'

'Thank you, Doctor. Although I think he should stand trial in Cape Town, I think it will be very likely he will be sent back to England for trial, along with the other two,' said Barclay. 'My commanding officer ordered me to send the appropriate despatches to London, so as soon as I receive a reply to my letters to the Colonial Secretary and the Admiralty in England, I will know what my orders are. They will probably be taken by Royal Navy ship back to Portsmouth and on to London for trial.'

'Well, the sooner the better. The scandal of a Government minister found to be caught smuggling guns is bad enough, but piracy and treason, that would shake this colony to its very core,' said the doctor. 'The quicker he is gone the better for everyone. Oh, and by the way, I will be going as well; to the Eastern Cape. An army doctor will be taking over from me. You have my statement. If you require anything else please get word to me through the Governor's office.'

Still Storer was fighting the fever that was wasting his body, caused by the horrific injuries to his head and lower chest.

Images and voices swam through his head; they kept flashing up in his subconscious, causing him to cry out in his delirium. *Guns... Knowles... die of infection... Jamie Fyvie... so much pain... fort... a wonder he is alive... Africa... Iain McColl... faces... knife... ship... storm.*

As the fever receded and his senses slowly returned he could barely remember what had happened. Where was he?

The days went by and he grew marginally stronger, he even opened his eyes. Both were open but he could only see through one. There was a doctor, he was in a hospital, but where? Which hospital? He lost consciousness.

Awake. *The Flying Fish* bringing him back to Cape Town. Secretary of Colonial Government. The fight on the ship. Storer suddenly opened his eyes and listened before trying to move. He was in so much pain. Was this real?

He closed his eyes and opened them again, seeing fuzzy images in the dim light. It was night time and the lamp cast a glow in the room. He tried to move his legs but could only move them so far, before realising they were shackled to the bed. The natural reaction to look to the bottom of the bed nearly made him faint, such was the pain in his head.

He brought up his hand and gingerly felt the bandages around his head. The nurse had left a gap for one eye to see and spaces for his nose and mouth. His torso, he felt, was covered in bandages as well. Moving more slowly he lifted his head and looked at his ankles. Definitely shackles.

His sight was clear. He lay back and saw a mosquito net covering his bed which was why objects looked fuzzy.

He closed his eyes. *Oh god, my head is going to burst with this pain,* thought Storer. *I must try to find out why I am a prisoner.* Suddenly his whole life appeared in that shaded place behind the eyelids when the eyes are closed.

'Jamie Fyvie!' he called aloud, his head exploding with pain.

He heard a key turning in a lock. The door opened and someone came in so he feigned sleep and started muttering as though having a bad dream. He heard the intruder say. 'Still delirious,' then left, locking the door.

'Fyvie,' he whispered. 'He is the reason I am here.' *He and McColl attacked us before we could take the fight to them,* thought Storer his memory returning. *Jumping through the skylight. He must be a madman. Shooting me and then throwing the knife that went through my head. No, it went through my face.* He brought his hand up to his bandaged head once more.

The seething hatred for Jamie Fyvie consumed him to the point of losing his sanity. 'Calm down, calm down, calm down,' he whispered to himself. 'The elders will know you are alive and will find a way out of this. Calm down, recuperate, mend your body and exact revenge.'

Doctors and nurses came in to change his dressings but they did not hold a conversation as they were under orders not to.

The days turned to weeks. One morning as he watched the daylight start its silent intrusion of the room, he heard a bugler blowing reveille as usual.

How long will they keep me in this damned fort? He wondered. *Whitehall cannot possibly let a trial be held. The powers that be will never allow the embarrassment.*

He would feign his partial unconsciousness for another few days until he was stronger. If they thought he was fully conscious he would be charged with god knows how many crimes. As he was in the fort, he thought he must be under a military investigation because of the gun-running. That being the case they would add treason which was punishable by hanging.

He heard someone approach the door.

The doctor came in and said. 'Hello.'

'I know you, do I not?' said Storer.

'Indeed you do, Mr Storer. I am Doctor Morgan. I was one of the unfortunate souls on the ship on which you tried to incite a mutiny.' He checked his pulse. 'I also saved your life.'

'I remember you now.'

'I was a field doctor in the army, a colonel, I have seen many horrors on the battlefield. I save what is left of my bedside manner for those who deserve it. I merely saved you for the hangman and you can stop pretending you are still sick. You are not fooling anybody,' said the doctor.

'I will not thank you for saving me in that case,' said Storer.

The doctor ignored Storer's comment and removed the bandages from his head to inspect the wounds. 'You are lucky to be alive, given the fact the fever should have killed you, but there is some disfigurement you will have to live with.'

Storer had not asked for a mirror up until now. 'I would like a mirror, Doctor. Let us get this moment of truth over with.'

'Are you sure you want to do this?' asked the doctor.

'Just get me a damned mirror!'

Doctor Morgan knocked for the door to be opened and gave the guard an instruction. A few moments later the guard came back with a reasonably sized square mirror in a wooden frame, handed it to the doctor and closed the door.

The doctor handed the mirror to Storer who held it for a few moments before looking at his reflection. He had of course felt his wounds and scars, but when he lifted the mirror and looked at the face in front of him he put it down and let out a long guttural moan.

After a while he gathered his senses and lifted the mirror again and saw what was left of his teeth through the terrible wound in his left cheek, the top and bottom jaw connected by about an inch of pale flesh where his mouth started. The eye socket above had collapsed slightly, although his eye was not damaged. He turned his head to see half of his right ear and parts of the flesh behind his jaw bone was missing. The area was heavily scarred and his hair was turning to grey. He said, 'Well, I am sure Mr Fyvie will be proud of his handy work, Doctor.'

The doctor redressed his wounds and made to leave.

'Tell me, Doctor Morgan, are Fyvie and McColl

living and prospering in Cape Town?'

'That is none of your business and the sorry state that you are in is of your own doing Storer, nobody else's. The only reason I am here is because the doctor who was attending to you had to go to Grahamstown rather urgently. I will look in tomorrow and make sure you stay alive.'

The doctor knocked on the door, the guard opened.

'Tell them from me, they will pay dearly,' Storer said quietly in a strangled rasp.

'You are the one who has paid dearly. Guard, this man can be moved to a nice comfortable cell right away,' said the doctor, then turned and left.

My hatred for Jamie Fyvie has kept me alive, thought Storer. *He has destroyed my life's work. He has disfigured me. Somehow I will escape the hangman's noose and I will kill Fyvie and all he holds dear, very slowly and painfully.'*

They came for him that night, but not to move him to another cell. He was taken by the guards to another part of the fort and given clothes to wear, then taken to the Commander's office.

With shackles on his ankles and wrists he moved very slowly, his injuries making him slightly stooped. He entered the room, his head still heavily bandaged but now with two eyes visible to see his gaolers. 'Well, well,' rasped Storer. 'Here you all are, come to see the condemned man and decide what to do with him?'

General Cunnynghame was there with Major Barclay, Nicholas Banbury with Fairbairn and the Attorney General assisted by Bill Hutchison.

Banbury caught his breath at the sight of his former colleague and friend. He could not believe that this frail and withered man in front of him was the once the tall and elegant James Storer.

General Cunninghame stood up and addressed Storer. 'James Storer, you have been charged with high treason, murder and smuggling stolen armaments, along with piracy, mutiny and god knows what else. The Attorney General here has orders from London to hand you to the civilian authorities. You will be taken henceforth to board a ship bound for England, where you will be tried for your treachery. Do you have anything to say?'

'Well, I was unaware of any smuggling, as I was merely a passenger on the ship. I was attacked by two thugs and severely injured,' said Storer.

'You can make your case in London, Mr Storer,' said Attorney General Jeffries. 'Major Barclay, will you take two soldiers and assist Mr Fairbairn to take the prisoner to the ship.'

'The prisoner is not under military jurisdiction anymore and I would like to say that this is highly irregular. For the record I object to the prisoner being transferred to civilian authority and not being made to stand trial in Cape Town,' said Barclay.

'The matter is out of my hands. London has made the decision and that is that,' said Jeffries.

'Major Barclay, your objection will be noted,' said the General, annoyed with his subordinate. 'You will assist Mr Fairbairn with the transfer of the prisoner to the ship. That is an order.'

'Yes, sir,' said Barclay, clearly not happy with the proceedings.

Two carriages were waiting in the fort courtyard to convey the contingent to Rogge Bay dock where the ship waited for its passenger.

Fairbairn assisted Storer from the jetty up on to the ship and whispered. 'Be ready for a rendezvous with a ship from Freetown, off St Helena. I do not know how the plan will be executed but you will disappear, lost at sea. I wish you god-speed, sir.'

Bill Hutchison watched Fairbairn whisper to Storer as he boarded and knew they were hatching some kind of plan.

Storer was led away to the brig by two soldiers assigned to the ship. The crew cast off the moorings and the ship drifted away into the night.

Anne Knowles, meanwhile, had sailed for England and was confined to her cabin. She would be imprisoned on her arrival to await trial and be a witness at Storer's trial.

There were no goodbyes from her stepdaughters or anyone else; nobody cared who she was when she boarded the navy ship.

Chapter Thirty Nine

Upper Wynberg

Jamie and Iain threw themselves into establishing their business. It was a natural progression that Jamie took over the running of the work force and the workshop floor, whilst Iain handled the administration, finances and advised on the carpentry from time to time.

Their permanent accommodation was now ready and so they moved into a large house with spacious grounds in the well-to-do, exclusive suburb of upper Wynberg, which was, conveniently, on the way to the wine farms of Constantia. The house belonged to Mefrou Gerda le Roux, a no-nonsense, well-dressed Afrikaans woman of slight build and sober habits. Her husband had been killed in a previous war, fighting with the local militia against the Xhosa.

She lived in a cottage on the property and rented out the furnished main house to chosen clientele, providing laundry, cooking and cleaning. She came highly recommended by Godfrey Butler's wife, Sarah.

The boys had plenty of money so they started cautiously, not taking on too much work so they could devote time to finding the new ring leader of the ELOS.

Jamie went to the fort and met with the quartermaster, who gave him an urgent order for hundreds of scythes and some wagons to be delivered for the army in King William's Town.

After discussing the finances with Iain, they hired a manager and a boss boy, who knew the local workforce.

They paid them well to bring in the best workers for testing, and soon a good working relationship was formed and production was up and running.

The boys invited Bill Hutchison for dinner to get more acquainted with him and discuss the problem of the ELOS.

After eating a superb dinner cooked by Mefrou le Roux, the three men went out to sit in cushioned chairs on the stoep to smoke and sample some fine Constantia Estate wine.

'Everybody has an informant or spies in this town. It's the only way to find out who is doing what to whom. One just has to be careful who to trust,' Hutchison said as he admired his cigar.

'Now that Storer is in custody, who will take over from him and who else is suspected of being a member of the enlightened ones, not only here in Cape Town, but anywhere north and east of here?' asked Jamie. 'We need to establish who the main players are in both camps.'

'More importantly, Bill, what is *your* feeling on who the enlightened ones may or may not be?' said Iain.

'I have been stationed here for quite a while now and working in the Governor's office makes me privy to most Government documents. I have been watching and reporting on certain individuals except one, the new Governor. The other person I have been watching is the newly promoted Secretary to the Cape Colony, Nicholas

Banbury, who was working hand in hand with Storer, but has been cleared of any involvement concerning Storer. You said you wanted my feelings on who may be the enlightened ones, well I have seen Banbury meet regularly with three other people of importance to us: General Cunnynghame, Commander of the Fort, Robert Fairbairn who works in the AG's office and Governor Cuthbert, especially when Cuthbert receives a government despatch from the Secretary of State for the Colonies, Earl Greyson, who is, as we know, a senior elder of the ELOS in London.'

'Iain, where are the documents we took from Storer's cabin?' asked Jamie.

Iain went into the house to fetch them and laid them on the table. 'You see here, Storer uses capital letters for his contacts,' said Iain.

'Not the brightest of ideas,' said Hutcheson.

'Exactly. The capital C we think is the American Chester Primeaux, whose house we broke into and found similar documents. The N must be Nicholas Banbury, but here, he doesn't write *"for B"* or *"to B"* he writes *"the B,"*' said Jamie.

'The Boers. It must be the Boers as they would have a shorter access to the Eastern Portuguese coast to hire ships and sail south,' said Hutcheson, the reality suddenly dawning on him. 'My God! So it's true. They plan to enslave the Xhosa natives and get rid of them.'

'Not if we can stop them first. We have to find out how they are planning to do this. I mean the Xhosa warriors are not going to just sit down and say, *here we are, take us away*, are they?' said Iain.

'So that leaves EG, obviously Earl Greyson' said Jamie.

Hutchison said, 'The previous governor, Garry Smyth was removed from office very quickly compared to normal procedures for replacing the head of an office of this stature. Gerald Cuthbert was sent here in a hurry and he is not taking any male prisoners in this latest war with the Xhosa. He has empowered Fairbairn to recruit a Volunteer Corp which does not operate under the same rules as the regular army.'

'Fairbairn is watching us. We went up the mountain for a day out. He followed us up but we saw him and confronted him, then he left. We decided to build a fire and camp for the night, but then Fairbairn came back in the morning with some of his henchmen and took a couple of shots at us. Thankfully we made it back in one piece,' said Jamie.

'Why would Fairbairn be after you?'

'He was obviously sent by the ELOS. They either know who we really represent and realise that we know what they are up to or, because we captured Storer, they want revenge for upsetting their plans,' said Jamie not wanting to reveal the treasure at this stage.

'Fairbairn is a psychopath, him and his brother Jonny, they're recruiting other psychopaths on orders from Cuthbert. You need to be careful of that man if he has you as a target,' said Hutcheson seriously.

'So Bill, who exactly is on our side? What is your story?' Iain said, pouring drinks.

Jamie looked at Bill for a reply.

'Both of you, your parents were killed by the ELOS,' said Hutcheson. 'Years before, my father tried to expose one of the main elders of the hierarchy in the ELOS. He was betrayed. They flayed him alive in front of my mother in our house but let her live. She went insane. I heard her repeat the horror she had watched over and over again before Armstrong and a team arrived. My mother never recovered, so I, like you, am an orphan. Maybe that's Armstrong's way of recruitment; recruiting orphaned avengers to carry out his field work. I am in this to stop these people. Revenge is secondary. We were all given a choice to serve or leave.' He lifted his whisky and threw it down in one gulp.

Iain looked at Jamie and refilled Bill's glass. 'That's no way to treat a perfectly good malt whisky,' said Iain, raising his glass to Hutcheson's story.

Jamie said. 'Fairbairn was following us because he knows we are looking for clues to uncover a treasure and ancient artefacts which the ELOS want very badly.'

Hutchison looked at the boys and said. 'You could trust me with top-secret details of the ELOS, but not with a supposed treasure?'

'No offence,' said Iain, 'but we had to be sure we could trust you not to turn into a psychopathic gold thief.'

Hutchison said. 'I know about the treasure. Armstrong sent me a coded message. I had to know how much I could trust you. If you had not told me about the clues then I would have been very worried that *you two* might turn into psychopathic gold thieves.'

'Right then. There are three of us,' said Jamie. 'Who else is to be trusted?'

'The only other undercover agent is Doctor Morgan. The Attorney General Stephen Jeffries is an incorruptible solicitor and a bit naive to be… well… anything else, but trustworthy up to a point. Everybody is innocent in his eyes. Major Barclay is straight as an arrow, regiment and all that, although his boss, General Cunnynghame, is an elder in the ELOS, as well as corrupt. That's it, apart from

Sergeant O'Donnell at the police station, who does not have a clue what we are up against. His biggest and most important case is trying to find out what has happened to some local girls who have been disappearing from around the peninsula. We may need O'Donnell's help.'

'Next question. Our company has a contract to make scythes and enough wagons to transport them and deliver them to King William's Town, wherever that is. The frontier somewhere, I suppose. But what on earth do they need all those scythes for?' asked Jamie.

'King William's Town is Governor Cuthbert's frontier headquarters where he has mustered tens of hundreds of troops. He plans to issue every soldier with a scythe to destroy any food or, in fact, anything an inch above grass level in all the Xhosa strongholds, then burn anything that is left. He will bring the chiefs to heel or kill them all and he won't stop until he fulfils his master's wishes,' said Hutcheson disgustedly.

'So we won't make the scythes or the wagons, or we could hold up production,' said Jamie.

'No, you can't do that,' said Hutcheson. 'You can't be seen to support the natives or take the chance of endangering your cover. You have to make the tools so that you both can go to the frontier without suspicion.'

'Yes, I see your point. It looks like Storer was the key to this plot, but there's something missing. There seems to be a large piece of the puzzle that has not been put in place yet and I think that piece is still with Storer,' said Jamie.

'I agree. I don't think Banbury can carry on without Storer. We will have to be vigilant and ready for the next part of their plan. When and how, I don't know. I think the timing is the key to this conspiracy,' said Hutcheson.

'Iain and I will be going to the Eastern Frontier soon. We will keep you informed Bill.'

'One last thing. Orders from Whitehall came through the diplomatic despatches that Storer will be transferred to the civilian authorities and be taken to England. Mrs Knowles has already boarded a navy ship bound for England and your only other witness, the steward, Bailey, was found stabbed to death this morning in the Roeland Street gaol. There are no suspects at the moment,' said Hutcheson.

Jamie and Iain looked at Bill.

Iain said. 'Surely this news changes everything. If Storer is transported to England to stand trial along with the Knowles woman, then the plans of the ELOS must be in disarray; maybe even come to a halt for now, as Storer is obviously central to the success of their operation.'

'But what about Banbury?' Said Hutcheson. 'Wouldn't he be privy to Storer's plans and carry on with the execution of their plans?'

'I don't know,' said Jamie. 'From what we know of the ELOS they only pass on information to their subordinates on a need-to-know basis, much like us. I don't think Banbury has been given the details of the final chapter in this conspiracy.'

'Why then do we have to put our lives in danger by continuing with this hunt for a mythical treasure, when we could hunt the members of the ELOS?' said Iain. 'They are a ship without a rudder at the moment. Fairbairn would have been taking orders from Storer probably via Banbury, but I don't think Banbury is strong enough to control him. Fairbairn is only one man. If he wants to cause trouble with us then we can handle him.'

'I agree with Iain, Bill,' said Jamie. 'We should stop,

wait and watch for any changes in the hierarchy of the ELOS in Cape Town.'

'I have already sent despatches to Armstrong on where we should direct our efforts and don't forget there is an election in Britain. If the Tories win it, and I think they will, then things could change drastically. Let us hope for the best,' said Hutcheson. 'But for now we will carry on as usual until I hear back from Armstrong.'

Chapter Forty

South Atlantic Ocean / Freetown, Sierra Leone

The ship was days into the voyage and apart from the captain, nobody else spoke to Storer save for pleasantries when delivering food and water.

When the ship set sail from Cape Town the captain informed Storer that if he behaved himself he would not clap him in irons, so he was in a comfortable cabin, which was always locked and guarded. He was taken out once in the morning for a walk around the deck and once late at night, which he thought was rather strange.

He heard the cabin door being unlocked and waited for the guard to say his monotonous sentence, *time for your walk*, as though talking to a child. Ignoring him, Storer walked past and up to the top deck for his hour of fresh air.

He stepped on to the deck shielding his eyes from the bright sunlight for a moment and walked aft around the mizzen mast and forward on the port side when he saw land dead ahead. 'Guard, are we stopping for a visit there?' he asked.

'You're not visiting anyone except the executioner. We're picking up a passenger. Works with the local government and you will be in your quarters all the time we are anchored there.'

'Where is *there*?

'We'll be anchored off Jamestown, St Helena Island,' said the guard.

Storer noticed two other ships at anchor as they got closer, then the guard took him below and locked him in his cabin.

He sat for hours wondering what was going to happen. Fairbairn had forewarned him to be ready at St Helena, but it was getting dark. Then he felt the bump of a smaller boat coming alongside. He heard the anchor being winched aboard and the crew readying the ship for departure.

What's happened? He thought. *Why did nobody attack the ship? Did they arrive on time?*

A few hours later he was still fretting about his fate when the guard opened the door to take him for his walk on deck. As he and the two guards walked astern and out of sight of the helmsman the guards grabbed him and one put his hand over Storer's mouth.

'If you want to get off of this ship, just sit on the deck next to the gunwale and stay quiet,' whispered the guard.

Storer did as ordered.

The two guards laid their rifles on the deck and lifted the mizzen hatch, pushing it back. The prow of a small dinghy appeared from below as the guards pulled it up on to the deck followed by two oars and a closed lamp.

Putting the oars in the dinghy they lifted it and lowered it over the side by two ropes attached forward and stern. Then they removed Storer's shackles and gestured for him to climb over the gunwale.

Storer stepped back terrified. 'What are you doing?'

he whispered.

The guard grabbed him by the lapel and said. 'This is your only chance to get off this ship. Your people are waiting for you. Otherwise it's the hangman.' He was so close Storer could smell his foul breath. 'I will light a lamp and cover it then lower it down to you. When you get clear of the ship by a good distance uncover the lamp, hold it high and wave it back and forth.'

The guard pushed him to the gunwale and Storer reluctantly and, because of his deformities, with difficulty climbed over and down into the small craft. The other guard lit the lamp, covered it and lowered it to Storer who looked up as they let go the ropes. The ship went off into the night, its running lights going up and down and from side to side until it disappeared leaving him very alone in the huge Atlantic Ocean.

The swells were fairly big and the odd small wave broke over the bow, soaking Storer, but the sea was not rough.

There were no visible stars and he had limited vision because of the swells. He suddenly realised there was nothing to bale water with. He felt for the oars and stopped. *What the hell is the point of rowing? I don't know where I am and how do you row in an ocean?* He thought.

He lifted the lamp and waved it back and forth for a while. He could not see anything!

What the hell am I doing? One freak wave and I'm a dead man, he thought, lifting the lamp again and waving it frantically.

He kept looking around waving the lamp when suddenly he thought he saw a ghostly-white apparition. The dinghy went down into a shallow trough and came up again. The apparition was larger.

'Sails!' he shouted to himself. 'Ship sails! Here, over here!' he shouted, waving the lamp. He wanted to stand up but he would probably capsize the boat.

He could make out the shape of the ship as some of the sails were taken in. The helmsman was good and brought the ship as close as he dared to the dinghy.

He saw figures at the gunwales. A voice shouted, 'I'll throw a rope. Tie it for'ard.'

Storer did as ordered and the small craft was pulled alongside, bouncing off the bow wave and the hull of the ship. A sailor was halfway down the side reaching out to grab his arm and help him up into waiting arms that pulled him on to the deck.

'My god, could you not have been a bit closer? You could have missed me,' Storer shouted, realising with relief he was saved and was now reinstated to his high status.

'I'll take that as a *thank you,* sir,' said a voice behind him.

Storer turned to see a large man with long hair and a bushy, well-groomed beard. He had a peaked captain's hat sitting at a jaunty angle on his head.

'And you would be?'

'Captain Dickson Forbes, out of Freetown… at your service.'

'Good evening, Captain, I am Ja–'

'My good, sir, we should go below and have a warming glass of brandy,' interrupted the captain. 'You should keep your name to yourself for now.'

The captain led the way below. Storer could see most of the crew were black, probably descendants of slaves who had escaped America to find freedom in the now

British colony of Sierra Leone.

Once settled in the small saloon next to the captain's cabin, Storer sipped his brandy and savoured the taste. 'Fine brandy, Captain.'

'We get a lot of surplus exports arriving in Freetown, Mr Storer.'

'I trust you have been well paid to rescue me, Captain, and I am grateful, though your method of rescue leaves a lot to be desired. Still, here I am. How long will it take until we arrive in Freetown?'

'More than a few days, as long as the wind stays fresh.'

'I will be in Freetown for a few weeks and then I need to go back to Cape Town,' said Storer sipping his brandy. 'Will you be available to leave in that time?'

'Forgive my stupidity, but did you not just escape form the authorities in Cape Town?' asked the Captain.

'I did, Captain, but you will be transporting someone else so please do not worry about the details. You will be well paid for your services.'

'I have other obligations to fulfil but I can be ready to go back in that time.'

Many days later as dawn was breaking the ship sailed around the southern sentinel that guarded the entrance to the large port of Freetown, and dropped anchor at White Man's Bay.

Storer went up on deck to find the captain.

'A word in private with you captain,' said Storer.

'Let us go to my small saloon, sir. I'd rather you stayed below until nightfall; prying eyes may be watching from ashore.'

'I will need you to find someone for me who lives on the outskirts of Freetown. He will be accompanying us when we sail back to Cape Town,' said Storer.

'I know many people in Freetown. What's his name? Maybe I know him,' said the Captain curiously.

Storer took another sip and watched Forbes for a reaction as he said. 'Samuel Gubotu.'

'Gubotu!' the captain exclaimed. 'Not on my ship! He runs with the devil. He's the voodoo doctor. Everybody runs scared of him. No, no not on my ship! I'd have a mutiny. Have you seen the size of him? He is a giant of a man and bad luck for a ship's crew.'

'Come, come, Captain, he is just a witch doctor with herbal brews,' said Storer.

'His mother and father practised voodoo in the West Indies off America. He has carried it on,' said the captain, genuinely fearful.

'I will double your purse and your crew's, but he will be coming with me.'

'I will take you to your cabin. I was told to bring a doctor on board. If he is not too drunk he will attend to your wounds,' the Captain said, rising from his chair. 'I will speak with the crew about Gubotu, but be advised, there will be conditions.'

'That is fine, Captain. I am sure we can come to an agreement. When we get ashore you will find out where Gubotu lives and then you can carry my message to him.'

'Finding him will not be necessary as I know only too well where he lives,' said the captain.

'Tell him to meet me where I will be staying at one hour after midnight the day after tomorrow,' said Storer.

Only when night fell did Captain Forbes lower a boat and take Storer to the beach and then to a secret location on the outskirts of the city. It was a grand old colonial house with one floor above the ground, verandas surrounding both floors.

Storer bathed and was given fresh clothes after which his wounds were dressed and checked once again, this time by an eminent doctor from the local Government hospital.

He instructed the housekeeper to buy a wide-brimmed dark hat and attach a dark veil stitched all around with a draw string at the bottom edge. When she came back with the finished product he told her to make a few changes until it was to his satisfaction and then ordered half a dozen.

The following day having donned his new head gear, Storer checked his pocket watch and seeing it was well after midnight, he wandered down stairs and out into the grounds. As he walked through the vast garden he listened to the deafening noises of insects calling out in the tropical night. He stopped. Looking through the veil he turned around sensing something.

'I know you are there, Samuel.'

Samuel Gubotu materialised from the dense bush. 'I see you master.'

He was a giant of a man, six foot seven, huge solid muscles on his body. His large head was covered in long matted dreadlocks which were tied behind his neck. He had a fuzzy beard, bright white teeth and a flat wide nose. The whites of his eyes were reddish and his skin was so black it sometimes looked purple.

In his youth Samuel and his father would go on expeditions away from home for a few days every now and then, searching in the tropical forest for the herbs and other ingredients, for the potions and medicines they used in their healing and in their rituals.

When they returned from one such expedition they

had found Samuel's mother hanging from a tree with the word *WITCH* carved on her torso.

Samuel's father had been so distraught he ran into the jungle and was never seen again. Storer, quick to see the advantages of having a witchdoctor around, had taken in the young Gubotu, knowing he had learned much of the voodoo knowledge from his parents.

During this time, as a diplomat in Freetown before taking up his post in Australia, via England, and then the Cape Colony, Storer had had delved into the mysteries of Indian hypnotism and the dark arts of voodoo and local witchcraft. He had nurtured and taken care of Samuel making sure he had some kind of education. Samuel had never forgotten this and was forever indebted to Storer.

'I hear your voice, but it is not the voice I remember and you hide behind a veil,' said Gubotu.

'I had some trouble and barely escaped with my life. I have come to ask you to sail with me to a land far to the south of here to help me avenge the terrible mutilation inflicted on my body.'

'I will go with you master. I would never refuse you.'

'Do you have an ample amount of my muti?' asked Storer.

'I have a little, but I can make up some more,' said Gubotu.

'We will need as much as you can make within the next few weeks, as that is when we will be leaving. You might want to take some ingredients with you. I will make you a very rich man, Samuel. I will send a messenger when we are about to leave. Until then, go well, my friend.'

'I will be ready master.'

Having slept for a few hours Storer dressed and went in search of breakfast. He found it being served on the stoop. The air was already muggy and hot in the late hours of the morning.

Sitting at the table was none other than Edward Carrington, sent by Earl Greyson to get a first-hand account of all that had transpired and what the future held.

Storer stopped and looked at Carrington. 'Edward Carrington, pleased to meet you again,' said Storer, extending his hand.

'Hello, James. Welcome back from the dead,' said Carrington, looking with fascination at the head dress Storer was wearing.

'The hat and veil looks a bit dramatic, but I need to keep insects and the sun away from my injuries,' said Storer. 'Let me tell you what happened as we have breakfast. There is a lot to tell and plan.'

Carrington listened for quite a long time, interrupting with a question every now and then.

When Storer finished telling what had happened to him since sailing from Liverpool, Carrington said. 'The elders, as you will know, are most displeased and have acted to try and save the situation in the Cape by notifying Nicolas Banbury that he will replace you.'

'Edward, I know if I can get back to Cape Town I can find a way to continue with our plans,' said Storer a little panicked.

'James. Let me finish. Just listen,' said Carrington firmly. 'Harold Greyson had an idea that he put to the elders. Because of your reported death and your outward appearance he would have me arrange for you to return to Cape Town with a new identity.'

'An excellent idea Edward, I am most grateful to

you,'

'James. Please. I do this for the ELOS and of course for me. So you will be going back to Cape Town with a new name and background,' said Carrington. 'Then you can carry out the final phase of our operation.'

'*My* plan,' said Storer. '*Our* plan, is still in place and still workable. When I arrive back in Cape Town I will give the impression that I am a business man with a serious skin ailment and that I am very self-conscious about it, hence the veil.'

'The elders are very worried about your condition and your state of mind and, quite frankly, the only reason you are here is because of the delicacy and situation we are in with this project,' said Carrington. 'They are not usually so forgiving.' He said, the warning very clear.

'I realise there have been setbacks. Had it not been for the two passengers on the ship, Fyvie and McColl, our plans would have been much further along than they are.'

'You say Fyvie and McColl, but the names we have for the two men, who are most certainly with the Secret Field Police, are two Scotsmen by the names of Rattery and Black. Where are they?'

'Those are the false names they used in England to throw any inquisitors off their track. I assure you these are the same men and they are well trained. I was lucky to escape with my life, unlike my men on board, who were brushed aside and killed,' said Storer.

'Then they must be dealt with as soon as possible if they have not been already.'

'If it's all the same to you, I would like to discredit them in Cape Town before eliminating them. This would cast some doubt on their story pertaining to *The Flying Fish* and possibly redeem the late James Storer's name with the Government,' suggested Storer.

'If you can make that work, so much the better,' said Carrington.

'It will be done, Edward, I promise you. I will take great delight in destroying Jamie Fyvie and Iain McColl. After all, they will be in my backyard.'

Carrington could hear the vengeance in his words. 'Your new identity,' said Carrington, sliding an envelope across the table. 'You are now Nigel Renton, born an Englishman and recently of America, now returned to England for obvious health reasons. You are very rich and looking to invest in Southern Africa where the climate is good for your health.'

'Excellent. Will Banbury be made aware of my return?' asked Storer.

'He will not, but he will be advised that James Storer's house on the mountain will be sold to Nigel Renton and he will see to Mr Renton's comfort as a major investor in the Cape Colony. Then you may reveal yourself to him,' said Carrington.

'That should give him a jolt; that he is not privy to all information.'

'As always, one needs to know what one has to, or is *allowed* to know.'

'There are two criteria which must be put in place and are vital for the final phase of the operation,' said Storer looking at Carrington carefully.

'And those are?'

'I will be taking an assistant, or you might call him a servant, with me, as he certain skills which I will need use of. His name is Samuel Gubotu and he is from Freetown.'

'That is one. And the other?'

'A question first if I may. Who is to replace Cuthbert

as governor?'

'Sir George Whyte, governor of New Zealand will be offered the governorship of the Cape.'

'An excellent choice, Edward. He is perfect for what I have in mind. When Cuthbert is replaced by Sir George Whyte as governor, Cuthbert must be transferred to a military outpost in the Empire which is at war. Gerald Cuthbert must die in battle in some obscure part of the Northern Hemisphere.'

Carrington looked puzzled. 'Killed by an assassin in our own ranks?'

'Yes, if he does not fall in battle.'

'Cuthbert is a good man. It will not be easy. May I ask why?'

'One needs to know what one has to know, Edward,' said Storer.

'Be very aware, *Nigel,* that if there are any more setbacks you may still, in reality, be the *late* James Storer.'

Chapter Forty One

March 1856

Cape Town, King William's Town, Eastern Cape

The sun was shining brightly over Cape Town as Jamie rode down into the city. He was wearing a wide-brimmed bush hat, a loose white shirt and well-fitting riding breeches. His jacket and tie were folded in a saddle bag.

He noticed more than a few admiring glances from the ladies in Adderley Street and up in Strand Street where he stopped outside Godfrey Butler's office.

He donned his jacket and tied a knot in his tie as he walked into the building and made his way to his meeting with Godfrey. He was surprised to see Bill Hutchison and another gentleman there.

'Ah, Jamie, my boy, good morning,' said Godfrey. 'Bill you know. This is Charles Blackwell who is a kind of honorary member of the Xhosa people, particularly the Ngqika tribe. I hope you don't mind; I invited him here, with Bill, to talk with you about supplying agricultural goods to the natives. He can explain the details in due course.'

'Good morning Bill. I'm pleased to meet you

Charles,' said Jamie, shaking Blackwell's hand and taking his chair.

'I am grateful for this meeting at such short notice,' said Blackwell. 'As Godfrey said, I have been living with the Ngqika since I was born. My father was a missionary from Scotland, and taught me to speak the Xhosa language fluently. The reason I am here is that I hear you are moving some equipment by wagon to King William's Town. Is that so?'

'Yes, it is,' replied Jamie. 'We will be ready to move soon. Please tell me you want to go with us, because I would dearly like someone who can speak Xhosa and has knowledge of the land to show us the way.'

'Well, Bill here has spoken to me on behalf of Governor Cuthbert to try and get the Xhosa chiefs to come in and surrender on Cuthbert's terms, but that was never going work. They rejected the proposal out of hand. The chiefs are still feeling all powerful since defeating Smyth's armies but Cuthbert, as you no doubt know, is massing thousands of troops to do battle with the Xhosa and banish them from their homelands and strongholds, and I fear this is going to be the end for the Xhosa people, especially the Ngqika tribe.'

'So how does that involve us?' asked Jamie.

'There are bands of Xhosa marauders running around the frontier, attacking anything that moves on the roads. You will need an interpreter and someone to show you the routes to take, but most of all, from my point of view, I want you to see the land and hopefully meet more of the tribespeople and maybe other chiefs. Governor Cuthbert has indicated that he is going to end this war by any means possible. When he does this, he will relocate the tribes and they will need farming equipment to feed themselves, which will be paid for by the Government and supplied by you. I want you to assess the terrain and the earth so that we can determine how much equipment will be needed to start farming, because when this war finishes there will be nothing left to eat for the natives, Cuthbert will take all the animals and destroy all the food. You see, I have seen this before; I know what is coming,' said Blackwell sadly. 'I have to be ready: I have to save as many as possible.'

'You're welcome to come with us. We would be more than happy for you to guide us and we would be delighted to respond to your request,' said Jamie.

'Thank you so much,' said Blackwell relieved.

The villains that made up Fairbairn's Volunteer Corps were riding in formation behind him and his sergeant, his brother Jonny. Fairbairn's orders were not to take a direct route to King William's Town but rather search the hills and country side for any bands of marauders hiding there, and deal with them, showing no mercy.

As they rode through the bush, Fairbairn was deep in thought.

He had watched Storer's ship sail from Cape Town for England. He desperately wanted to know what was behind Storer's rescue. *Why don't the ELOS just kill him and be done with him,* he thought, *what does he know that makes it so important for them to rescue him?*

He was leading his men on a track going inland towards the high hills some miles short of Grahamstown, looking for their first victims, relishing the idea of attacking and executing any native, Hottentot or black that looked even remotely like a rebel or a marauder.

Fairbairn held up his hand to halt the troop and

looked through his spyglass. He could see smoke rising up from a clump of trees in the valley below them. He beckoned Jonny to follow him and rode to an adjacent hill for a better view.

'Hottentot rebels with their women and whelps,' said Fairbairn handing the spyglass to his brother.

'And no sign of any sentry's. Plenty of trophy's to be had,' said Jonny. 'We ride in; shoot the men; have some fun with the women then take the prisoners to King William's Town.'

'No. No prisoners. We kill everyone to the last stinking child, said Fairbairn. 'We have to send a clear message across the land that these murdering rebels will not be tolerated.'

'In that case let's get to work. I haven't seen action for weeks and I am hungry to get to the kill,' said Jonny who was just as blood thirsty as his brother.

'Be careful little brother, don't take any chances, you are the only family I have left.'

'I will be fine Robert. Stop mollycoddling me, you're not our mother,' said Jonny angrily.

'You will follow my lead, Jonny. Do you understand?'

'Yes, *big brother*... I understand.'

'Let's get back to the men,' said Fairbairn wheeling his horse away.

'There's an encampment in a thicket of trees in the valley below us,' said Fairbairn, scratching a plan in the dirt for the circle of volunteers around him. 'We know there have been marauding Hottentot rebels in the area and it is our good fortune that we have found them. We will split up into three groups: the first group will attack on the left flank, the second through the centre and the third on the right flank. I do not have to spell it out to you. You have done this before. This uprising must come to an end. The enemy must be sent a message that they will never forget. They will not be allowed to roam the countryside, murdering and pillaging at will. Remember, we take no prisoners and no one escapes.'

They moved off riding down the valley, rifles ready to fire and pistols to follow up, with a mixture of swords, pangas, knives and cleavers to finish of whoever survived the initial volley of musket balls when they rode into the camp.

The rebels had nobody on watch, and heard the horses too late. The three-pronged attack fell upon the camp firing indiscriminately at anything on two legs. The rebels tried to get shots off in defence, but were never given a chance. They were shot down even if their hands were offered in the air in surrender. The volunteers turned their horses after the first pass and came back with pistols drawn and repeated the first attack.

Men and women holding children ran around in a blind panic screaming and shouting, *we surrender*! *Mercy*!

Their cries fell on deaf ears.

Some of the volunteers surrounded the camp, riding down those who tried to escape. Others dismounted, reloaded their guns and continued firing, using bayonets and blades to stab and cleave at the survivors. They walked through the camp killing the men and slitting the throats of the women and the children.

When, eventually, there was nobody left to kill they checked every body. Any men found wounded or alive were hanged from the nearest tree and left to rot. Some bodies were decapitated and the heads boiled until the skin fell off; the white skull taken as a trophy of war. Other body parts were removed as trophies.

That night, after taking anything of value, they feasted on slaughtered cattle and any drink they could find. The next morning, feeling very pleased with himself, Fairbairn ordered the camp to be torched and any food and drink left by the deceased destroyed. He then led his men away from his first killing ground.

They rode on past Grahamstown arriving a few days later King William's Town, where he made his report to Governor Cuthbert, who congratulated him on taking the fight to the enemy.

Fairbairn and his men made camp close to town and made the best of their time, drinking and whoring, while they waited for their orders.

The train of wagons pulled by teams of oxen, laden with scythes and other implements, left Cape Town a few days later, heading east along the road past Bellville and up the long haul through Sir Lowry's Pass over the majestic Hottentot Holland Mountains.

The wagons were accompanied by a platoon from the Cape Mounted Rifles, with Jamie, Iain, Bill and Charles all on horseback. Blackwell pointed out landmarks and explained what was growing on the farms, as they passed through lush farming and sheep-grazing country. They went through the small town of Caledon and on to Swellendam, over the Breede River carrying on till dusk.

At sunset the wagons were laagered in a semi-circle; the men from the Rifles, wagon drivers and servants sat and prepared their food around their own fires whilst the *boss*' tents were erected and fires lit. As they sat around the table in their canvas chairs Blackwell told his companions the history of years of conflict between the British and the Xhosa.

'So is this the way it's done?' asked Iain. 'We have the comforts of home while the rest of the crew sit on the ground?'

'The natives would not be comfortable sitting around a table and eating off of plates and using utensils. It's not their way,' said Blackwell. 'Maybe, in the not too distant future we will civilise them and turn them to Christian ways.'

'From what you've told us, who would want to be like us?' said Jamie.

'Since the beginning of the century the British have been trying to drive the Xhosa from the Amatolas and the Kroomie heights. More blood has been spilt over those strongholds than anywhere else in the Cape colony,' said Blackwell.

'Why don't the Government and the army just leave them to it and let them get on with their lives?' asked Jamie.

'It is plain to see you are newcomers here. I will try and explain. Over the years treaties have been made and peace deals agreed, but something always sparks a conflict and often as not it is settlers complaining they have been attacked, or the Xhosa have taken cattle or settled on land that does not belong to them. In response, the militia or mounted police go in and take cattle from the Xhosa and shoot a few of them, then the Xhosa retaliate and drive them off or take the cattle and lose themselves in the Amatolas. It takes a lot of men and money to go up there and get them out, and so it goes on and on. But I can see that with the force that Governor Cuthbert has, he is determined to once again, try and oust the Ngqika and the other Xhosa tribes from their strongholds,' said Blackwell

'I can relate to that,' said Iain. 'The English have been trying to make Scotland into a sheep farm for years. Isn't that right, Jamie?'

'Aye, and trying to turn Ireland into a potato farm.'

'The Xhosa are a very proud people. The men hunt for meat, they do not farm. The women farm and make the food. The men are warriors who want to see herds of cattle. Cattle are their wealth and their power. They will die to defend it. They will not be in a field tending corn. That would be beneath their dignity.'

'I could get very upset if someone tried to force me off my land,' said Hutcheson. 'I mean, the settlers breach the terms of a treaty, the natives take offence and start a fight, and then get blamed for inciting war.'

'The natives also have hot heads. They are not without blame,' said Blackwell. 'The problem is, there is so much bad blood and deceit that there is no trust anymore. Samkelo, the paramount chief, became chief at an early age because his father, Hintsa, was shot and killed whilst out riding with Colonel Garry Smyth, our previous governor'

'What! Smyth shot him for stealing cattle?' asked Jamie.

'Not quite. It was another war many years ago and part of the negotiation for peace was a fine of 30,000 cattle. Hintsa tried to escape on his horse but Smyth, who tried to shoot him but his gun misfired, caught up to Hintsa and pulled him off his horse. This action spooked Smyth's horse and it ran away with him. By the time Smyth got his mount under control Hintsa had run off towards the river in order to escape into the bush. Smyth ordered his men to fire on him which they did, wounding him in the leg. He got up and continued running. He was shot a second time in the body and went down again, but to everyone's surprise he got up again and reached the river. His pursuers found him in the river wounded and unarmed. One of Smyth's men took aim and shot Hintsa, point-blank in the head after he'd been heard to cry; *mercy*. One of the other officers, when left alone with his body, cut off Hintsa's ears as a souvenir.' Blackwell shook his head. 'Samkelo has never forgiven or forgotten.'

'My god, can you blame him? That's barbaric,' said Jamie. 'Taking body parts as a trophy!'

Blackwell lit his pipe and said. 'This is not civilised Britain, gentlemen. This is Africa. This is a harsh land and it will devour you if you do not conform and forget being civilised.'

The next morning they were up and on the move before the sunrise and making good time for Grahamstown. It would be many days before they arrived there, and longer again to King William's Town.

The sergeant in command of the Cape Rifles reported during the journey of more and more sightings of bands of Xhosa marauders slinking through the bush, and to be alert for ambush along the way.

When the column of wagons and troops eventually made it to Grahmstown, they decided to stay a few days, for Jamie and Iain to familiarise themselves with the town and set up a distribution point with a local trading post for their products.

One evening at dinner, Blackwell told the boys he had received some bad news.

'I have just been talking with an army officer who

has come from King William's Town. My brother James has not been heard of for some months, and we were not sure where to enquire of his whereabouts. But it seems they have found his body, along with the bodies of the party he was travelling with,' said Charles, his emotions surfacing. 'They had all been decapitated and my brother's head was presented to Sandla, one of the chiefs, as a trophy.'

'I am so sorry, Charles,' said Jamie. 'What happened?'

'They were ambushed and apparently outnumbered. They were all killed.'

'Does this mean you will be going back to Cape Town?' asked Iain.

'No! Not at all. We will leave for King William's Town tomorrow as planned and when I get there I will need to make arrangements with the local missionary there to accompany me to Sandla's kraal and ask for James's head so we can give him a decent burial,' said Blackwell.

'Will that not be a wee bit dangerous in view of the upcoming assault on the mountains by Governor Cuthbert?' said Jamie.

'No, I don't think this will be a dangerous journey at all. I know Sandla. I know how he thinks. I think he will use this tragedy to get me to go to him without him being seen to be collaborating with the white missionaries. The Xhosa people will respect the fact that I have come to get my brothers' remains. No, Sandla is clever, his intention is to glean as much information as he can from me about Cuthbert.'

'That is devious,' said Iain.

'I will leave for the mountains as soon as I can when

we arrive and hopefully I will be given an audience with Sandla before the fighting starts. He knows of me and my family. Once I have explained to him what the situation is in front of his people, he will save face and I am sure he will grant my request in exchange for information. He is not the barbarian everyone seems to think he is.'

'You can count on me to accompany you,' volunteered Jamie.

'Aye, and me,' said Iain.

'Thank you. I think it will be beneficial for you both to get the lay of the land, as it were. I will be spending some time with the Governor when we get to King William's Town, as I am to be commissioner to the Ngqika. After I speak with the missionary, I will inform you when I will leave to see Sandla. It will be at short notice, so I will try to find out when the hostilities will begin,' said Blackwell.

King William's Town was alive with nervous tension as though a thunderstorm had aimed its lightning at the town and charged the people with its power.

Blackwell went off to seek the missionary who was to take him to Sandla, while Jamie and Iain delivered the equipment to the army quartermaster under the direction of Hutchison. The wagons were then sent to East London to collect more equipment which had been sent by sea from Cape Town.

The roads between Grahmstown, King William's Town and East London were now safe as the Governor's troops had cleared the areas surrounding these places and set up regular patrols policing the roads.

The boys met Blackwell in the public bar of the inn where they were staying. They huddled around a table speaking in low tones.

'I have met with the missionary, John Rennie, an old friend of my father from the Tyhume mission. He will take us into the mountains to meet with Sandla. Apparently the chief has been made aware of the identity of his souvenir and is most anxious to have my brother's head returned.'

'Hutchison says that the military is preventing people from going to the Amatolas and there are patrols stopping and searching anyone on the roads,' said Iain.

'The Governor has given me permission for us to travel, but I think we should be careful. There are other tracks that we can use. The reverend has guides and they will show us the way, which will be under the cover of darkness tonight. Is this to your liking?'

'That's fine. Just tell us when and where to meet you and we'll be there. You have fresh horses?' asked Iain.

'There will be fresh horses at the stables and all your kit will be there. You can still change your mind if you think this could be dangerous, I would not wish anything to befall you,' said Blackwell.

'Don't you worry about us; we will help in any way we can,' said Jamie.

The boys went back to the army barracks and found the Cape Rifles sergeant who had ridden with them from Cape Town and then went to find Hutchison to ask him a favour.

'What we need,' said Jamie, 'is two of Sergeant van Bengal's best men to follow us at a reasonable distance until we reach the foothills of the Amatolas. They do not have to get involved in anything, just watch our back trail in case anyone is following us, and then come and tell us. Then they can return. We will make it worth their while.'

'I am fine to go along with that. Sergeant, can you

get two good men to go with Mr Fyvie's party?' asked Hutchison.

'I will pick a good man and go myself, sir,' said the sergeant after hearing they will make it worth their while.

'Good man. Meet us at the King's Inn at midnight. Then you can leave with us. We will tell you which way we are going when we are on the road, and split up on the way,' said Jamie.

'Very good, sir.' The sergeant saluted and went on his way.

Two days after Fairbairn reported to the Governor he was leaving the army headquarters when he saw some riders and wagons moving through town. He immediately jumped out of sight and watched in disbelief as Fyvie and McColl led a train of wagons and troopers into the army compound, stopping at the quartermaster.

What the hell were they doing here? He thought. *Are they really just businessmen delivering their products? No, they are not,* he convinced himself. *They are using this as a cover. They are following the clue they found in the Elephant's Eye to find and take the treasure for themselves.*

It would not be difficult for Fairbairn to find out where the boys were staying. The fact that Charles Blackwell, whom he knew as a bleeding heart missionary of sorts to the Xhosa people, was with them, heightened his interest. He decided to have his informants follow all three of them. He did not have to wait long.

One of his informants came back within hours to say that Blackwell had met with the Reverend Rennie according to his contact there; a Xhosa man by the name of Dunga.

'Can this Dunga be trusted?' asked Fairbairn.

'A pouch of money always buys trust, sir,' said the informant. 'Dunga says Rennie, Blackwell and two other men were making hasty arrangements to leave the town secretly this very night, with Dunga guiding them into the Amatola Mountains. He says he will take them on a track to avoid the British patrols. I can take you and your men to a safe place off that track and wait for Rennie's party to pass by, then we can follow at a safe distance.'

'You are sure they are going to the Amatola Mountains? It is not the safest place to be with war about to break out.'

'Yes, sir, they go to the Amatolas.'

Fairbairn gave his informant a bag of money. 'You have done well. Go and prepare to lead us into the bush.'

That's where the treasure must be, thought Fairbairn, *they are taking the missionaries to get past the Xhosa warriors as they speak the language.*

He summoned Jonny and the same men who had followed the boys to the Elephant's Eye and told them of this new information.

'Be ready to ride out tonight. We are going to find our treasure. I want you all to bring the assegais, shields and stabbing spears we have collected. When they make camp we will kill them in their sleep and take the information we need to find out where the treasure is buried. We will use the Xhosa weapons and make it look like they attacked them.'

The Reverend John Rennie and his guide, Dunga, led the way out of the town on to a little-known track away from the normal roads. Before they left, Jamie told the Cape riflemen which direction they would be taking and they melted into the night.

When they reached the foothills of the Amatola Mountains they decided to make camp and ascend the mountains in daylight so as not to be mistaken for anybody else. They lit a fire and ate a mutton and vegetable stew with bread washed down with tea.

The guide, Dunga, took first watch and the rest went to sleep around the fire.

Fairbairn and his men were hidden in dense bush when Dunga led Blackwell and his party along the track. This suited Fairbairn, as no one would bear witness to him following his victims to their death.

They trailed at a safe distance until their intended victims made camp. Fairbairn watched them through his spyglass and ordered his men not to light a fire themselves lest they be spotted.

At last he observed the last person to bed down. Dunga stayed up on first watch. After a while he saw Dunga slip away into the night.

As he readied his men to attack the camp, Fairbairn failed to see two men from the Cape Mounted Rifles enter the camp, unaware that he and his men had been under observation.

Jamie was woken by a hand covering his mouth. As he was bringing his dagger around to attack he heard a voice whispering. 'It's Van Bengal, sir. Please do not stab me.'

'Sergeant, what the he–?'

The sergeant motioned to him to be quiet, which he duly did.

Iain woke up and Jamie held up his hand palm outwards to keep him quiet as well.

'What has happened sergeant?'

'There are men sneaking up on your camp, sir. At first I thought it was a band of Xhosa warriors looking for a kill tonight, but they have horses and they do not move as the Xhosa do. It is very strange,' said the sergeant.

'Iain, wake up the reverend and Blackwell. Where the hell is Dunga?'

'What's happening?' asked Iain.

'The camp is being stalked. We will be attacked shortly,' said Jamie.

'We should go and talk to them,' said the reverend, 'tell them we are going to see Sandla.'

'They are not Xhosa, reverend,' the sergeant said looking for his colleague.

'How far away are they?'

'About five hundred yards, maybe less now.'

'We do not have a lot of time, so listen. Everybody put your coats and hats and anything else under your blanket. Make it look like there is someone sleeping under them,' said Jamie. 'Which direction are they coming from, sergeant?'

'From the west and north, sir.'

'Right, the firelight is weak so they will not notice the ruse until it is too late. Everybody hide behind the rocks and bushes over there,' said Jamie pointing east.

The other rifleman joined them. 'They're coming.'

Jamie had his over and under pistols cocked and ready, as did Iain with his blunderbusses. The riflemen took up position slightly south of them and they waited.

The attackers appeared suddenly from nowhere and fell on the camp, shooting at the sleeping forms under the blankets and then stabbing with assegais and short spears.

They were not Xhosa warriors, but white men

stripped to the waist covered in mud.

Jamie shouted. 'Surprise!' as he and Iain and the two Cape riflemen opened fire from their hiding place.

Three of the attackers were shot dead under the deadly gunfire; the others turned and fled into the night. Shots were fired back at them from outside the perimeter of the camp and everyone dived for cover, one shot hitting the rifleman in the leg. The sergeant pulled his colleague behind a boulder and they all reloaded.

Where did the other men come from? Thought Fairbairn, *there had been no more than four men in the camp.*

Three of his men went down, the others retreating as they were caught in the open.

Fairbairn and the remainder of his men gave their colleagues covering fire as they retreated.

'You four go around and come in behind them. We will distract them. I want them all dead,' said Fairbairn.

The defenders could only fire at the muzzle flashes and then move position as the attackers used the same tactics.

The sergeant propped his colleague up to enable him to fire his rifle then skirted around behind their position. 'They're behind us,' he shouted at no one in particular.

Jamie jumped up and went to help the sergeant as four attackers ran at them, firing their rifles wildly, missing their intended victims completely. Jamie and Van Bengal stopped, controlling their aim and opened fire, hitting two of them. Before he could get off another shot, one of the villains fell on Jamie, trying to cleave him with a panga. He managed to grab the wrist with the hideous weapon and flip the attacker over on to his back. He drew his dagger but his assailant caught Jamie's wrist in a similar fashion and they both rolled around in the bush, one trying to loosen the other's grip.

Jamie had to end this. He head-butted the villain breaking his nose and in the moment of shock pulled the villain with him as he fell back. When his back hit the ground he brought up his right leg and thrust his foot into the villain's groin and flipped him over his head. Still holding the assailant's wrist, Jamie sprang to his feet and leapt on him driving the dagger into his heart.

Jamie looked to see the sergeant pushing off the remaining attacker whose throat had been cut.

The two of them, now pumped up with adrenalin, looked around for the next attack. None came.

'These are white men trying to appear as Xhosa,' said van Bengal.

Aye, I see that; they're not very good at disguises,' said Jamie.

They retreated carefully and joined their comrades, loading their weapons as they went.

'The four men you sent behind us are all dead,' shouted Jamie. 'If that's the best you have then you are in trouble.'

Fairbairn heard the chilling voice and looked around. *There are only five of us left,* he thought.

Fairbairn said. 'Jonny, we can't risk being caught attacking white men. Tell the men to fall back.'

Jonny waved his men to fall back to the horses, mounted up and beat a hasty and humiliating retreat.

This is the second time I have been humiliated by those two Scotsmen. Thought Fairbairn, *they are obviously very dangerous men. I will not go up against them again until the odds are hugely stacked in my favour.*

All was suddenly silent. Sergeant van Bengal signalled he was going to skirt around the camp to find out if the attackers were still around. The rest of the party waited for him to report back, keeping a wary guard on the camp.

'Where's your faithful Dunga, reverend?' said Iain not sounding very happy.

'I don't know. Do you think he was killed in the melee?'

'He better have been because I'll kill him otherwise,' said Iain.

'What do you mean by that?' said the reverend defensively.

Iain walked over to the reverend and looked straight in his face. 'Dunga is obviously spying for someone, reverend. You must have told him where we were going and when.'

'But there is nothing of value here. Why would that put us in danger?'

Iain realised that he and Jamie must be the target of this attack. He knew they were in a precarious position and said, 'Reverend, there are three people working for the Cape Government in this party and it looks like someone has a big enough grudge to want to kill us all off. The mere fact that Dunga has disappeared means that he betrayed you and set us up for an ambush.'

'I have to agree with Mr McColl, reverend,' said Blackwell. 'I know, in your position, you need to show some faith, but you have to be practical and show a bit of discretion in these troubled times.'

The sergeant returned and reported. 'I heard horses retreating to the south. It looks like they have given up.'

Sergeant van Bengal looked at the bodies of the attackers with Jamie and Iain.

'I have seen these two before,' he said pointing at two of the bodies. 'They ride with those killers of Robert Fairbairn, the Volunteer Corps.'

'You sure about this?' asked Jamie.

'I am sure. I was on patrol and we came across them butchering some natives and I saw those two.'

'Dunga must have been spying for Fairbairn and told him we were in the reverend's party,' said Iain.

'Let's get your man patched up, Sergeant. Everybody try and get some sleep I'll take the watch until dawn then we will carry on into the mountains. Sergeant van Bengal will take the wounded man back to town,' said Jamie.

As the sun started its daily ritual, Jamie already had the fire going and water on the boil as the others roused themselves.

They were standing around the fire discussing where they would go into the Amatolas.

'The faithful Dunga has run away,' said Jamie glancing at the reverend. 'So it's up to you, Charles, and the reverend to guide us.'

'Between the two of us we will be able to make our way and we are both fluent in Xhosa. By this time the word will have spread among the people that I am coming for the remains of my brother. We will not be molested by the Xhosa warriors,' said Blackwell.

When they broke camp the Cape riflemen rode off back to King William's Town, the remaining four looked to the Amatola Mountains.

'This should be interesting,' said Iain.

'What?' Asked Blackwell.

'Four white men riding through Xhosaland in the

middle of a war, going to have tea with the chief of the Xhosa.'

They all chuckled at this bizarre situation.

'Thank you for lightening the mood, Iain.'

They rode through the foothills then up into the mountains led by the reverend. They were suddenly aware of shadows moving in the bush, the Xhosa warriors were now keeping watch on them and watching their back trail for any treachery.

They were walking their horses up a narrow gully when suddenly, there were Xhosa warriors on all sides of them, appearing silently and ghost-like. The leader walked down the track and spoke in Xhosa to which the reverend replied and then Blackwell.

'They want us to follow them to the top of the ridge. There is a place where we can leave the horses and later make camp for tonight.' said Blackwell.

In deathly silence the horses were tethered, with two warriors left to guard them. They followed the rest of the warriors through thick bush and narrow tracks, over short ridges and into dense forests, all designed to confuse the visitors as to where they were, or how to find their way back.

After some time they came out onto a small open plain covered in lush grass, with a river flowing through it that originated in the higher mountains. There were two large pools in the course of the river, one side with higher banks than the other, on which was a bustling village with small homesteads dotted all over.

The huts in each homestead were in a semi-circle made from a thatch woven onto a wooden framework made from thin branches. The dwellings were shaped like half an eggshell, dome side up, with an arched doorway in the side.

Immediately outside these was a circular enclosure or paddock for keeping cattle and other domestic animals safe at night. This was made from brushwood, thick acacia thorn branches and logs of wood, the entrance facing the arc of the dwellings. Inside this cattle pen could be seen cow-dung and mud-lined grain pits with stone covers at the openings to store the harvest from the fields, which were beyond the village. The reverend pointed out that the fields and gardens were tended by the women growing crops such as sweet potato, sorghum, pumpkins and melons.

It was such a beautiful and peaceful setting. It almost took their breath away.

'They live a quiet life here,' said the reverend. 'The men hunt wild animals and of course they have their cattle which provide milk, meat and skins for clothing, but we have to teach them the Christian way and civilise them from their pagan ways.'

Jamie tried to get Iain's attention because he knew he was going to say something annoying to the reverend, but he was too late.

'It seems to me, reverend, these people are perfectly happy the way they are. Why on earth would you want to change them?' said Iain.

Before the reverend could launch into a sermon they halted outside a larger homestead than the rest. This was the chief's *kraal* with a much grander hut in the middle of a compound surrounded by many smaller huts wherein lived his many wives and offspring.

Inside the kraal the tension was high. They sat on the grass outside the chief's hut and waited for Sandla to join them, watched by quiet, curious villagers.

Jamie looked around at this organised and seemingly contented community. The men were all warriors, lean muscular bodies, a straight-backed posture and tall in stature. They all had proportionate heads to their superb bodies with tight curly hair, high cheekbones, large black eyes and white teeth; they were a handsome race with beautiful women.

The warriors wore copper and ivory bangles and arm bands, necklaces and head bands of animal teeth, their main clothing nothing but a loin cloth. The women wore much the same, except they wore a skirt, a skin cap and an apron type of garment around the shoulders.

All the warriors carried at least a dozen spears – long ones for throwing, the short stabbing spears for close-contact fighting – as well as an *i-bunguza,* a fist-shaped lump at the end of a narrow shaft, the whole thing carved from the same piece of hardwood, used for breaking skulls and bringing down small game. They were a formidable people to be admired and feared in battle.

Sandla came out of the great hut and sat with his pakati beside him. Blackwell and Reverend Rennie, in keeping with protocol, asked after Sandla's great wife and children, introducing Jamie and Iain, and what they could offer in terms of agricultural advice and tools. Sandla then reciprocated with his own inquiries as to the welfare of the visitors' families, and then they got around to the question of the war trophy head of Charles's brother.

'I demand the return of the head of my brother, James, who was slain in an ambush some months ago by your warriors. He cannot have a proper and decent burial without his whole body,' said Blackwell speaking in Xhosa.

'I hear you, Chalis,' said Sandla using Blackwell's

recognised Xhosa name. 'Our warriors were at war and they did not know of your brother.'

'I realise this and I know this would not have happened otherwise. All I want is to take his remains so James can be buried and rest in peace.'

Sandla waved his hand and one of his pakati came and placed a woven basket in front of Blackwell.

'This is the head of your sacred brother.'

Sandla lifted the lid of the basket to show a grinning skull partly covered in dead skin and hair, empty eye sockets and a partial nose.

Blackwell stifled a sob and bent over almost falling over at the sight of his poor brother.

'I speak for all of my people when I say we are deeply saddened by the death of your brother. I know that you and your family have always helped the Xhosa with one hand tied behind your back by the white chiefs. It is with great sorrow I give you his remains. We are truly sorry, Chalis.'

They all sat around and talked about this and that, Jamie and Iain none the wiser of what was going on and then Sandla said, 'What of the new governor, Chalis? Has he not asked to talk with us?'

'He will not go into talks until all the chiefs surrender. As you know there are thousands of troops gathering for war and the only way to stop any more bloodshed is to surrender unconditionally. That would mean you and your people would have to leave the Amatolas. Samkelo would have to leave his lands, and Mzingisi would have to abandon the Kroomie heights for ever and resettle somewhere by the Great Kei River.'

Sandla jumped to his feet, to the consternation of Jamie and Iain.

'We will *never* give up our land again. Inkos Smyth came with his large army but we defeated him and we will defeat any army that comes to force us away from our land.'

'The new governor, Cuthbert, will start the war soon. He will not stop until he drives you out. I fear for you and your people,' Blackwell said pleading with him.

'Your heart is good, Chalis. I know that you fear for my people, but the English devils will not leave us in peace in our own land. We now have guns – many, many guns – with which we will drive the white men into the sea. The English fight for honour, for riches, for land and for power. We fight for freedom, to be free to walk on our own land, to herd our cattle and grow our crops on the fields left to us by our ancestors. We want our children to grow and prosper on their own land and we would die to fulfil this legacy.'

Blackwell looked beaten and demoralised.

Sandla said. 'Go in peace with your friends, Chalis, and bury your dead, as for the Xhosa people, tomorrow we fight for our freedom.'

The four white men stood up ready to leave the chief's kraal.

'Chalis, you will have safe passage back to King William's Town. My warriors will watch you. We will speak after the fighting is over.'

When they were taken back to the horses, they made camp and ate. It was cold being so high up in the mountains so they sat around a big fire, Blackwell and Rennie relating to Jamie and Iain what had been said at Sandla's kraal.

'I haven't, or should I say, *we* haven't been in the country long enough to understand what is up or what is down. You know… what is right or wrong,' said Jamie, gazing into the flames. 'All you hear in Cape Town is that black barbarians are murdering our people and soldiers and then you go into a village like Sandla's and come away with a different point of view all together.'

'They do not think like us or see life as we do,' said Blackwell. 'They are just…'

'Uncivilised. They are basically nice heathens and we have to help them,' said the Reverend Rennie.

Jamie and Iain looked at each other and then to a very sad Charles Blackwell, then they bedded down.

The next day they left the Amatola Mountains for King William's Town, a south-east wind carried the smell of burning wood in the air. They rode up to the crest of a hill and looked to the west and in the distance they could see smoke; thick, huge plumes of smoke, driven by the wind from the direction of the Kroomie Heights.

'It looks like the war has started,' said Jamie.

Long before they approached the town, thousands of troops had been mobilised and passed them on the way to the Amatolas to oust the chiefs who dared to oppose the British Empire in defence of their homeland.

Chapter Forty Two

King William's Town, Eastern Cape

At the same time as Jamie and his companions set off on their expedition into the Amatola Mountains, Governor Gerald Cuthbert was sitting in his office mulling over strategies on how to attack the Xhosa strongholds.

He had intended to return to Cape Town, but had decided against this as the situation on the eastern frontier was far worse than he had been led to believe.

He sent out small patrols to assess the situation, only for them to report that Mzingisi in the Kroomie Heights and Sandla in the Amatolas were sending marauders out to attack and rob farms and settlements all across the frontier. He also received reports of Hottentot rebels plundering farms and stealing cattle as well.

Nowhere was safe. The settlers were abandoning their farms and fighting their way to Grahamstown or King William's Town, some camping at Fort Beaufort. The roads between the towns were impassable

The troops that fought under Smyth were tired and ragged and needed time off to gather their strength to join up with the substantial reinforcements Cuthbert had brought with him from England.

Whilst in Cape Town, before making the decision to set up his headquarters in King William's Town, he had inquired about levies and local militias who knew the country, to bolster the campaign. He had also contacted one of the elders in the ELOS and met him and a junior elder at a house on the slopes of Table Mountain. Nicholas Banbury and Robert Fairbairn were apprised of the situation. He ordered the eccentric Englishman, Fairbairn, to raise and arm a volunteer corps, secretly funded by Banbury.

Fairbairn's Volunteers were the very dregs of humanity in Cape Town, only too eager to sign up. Any thoughts of trying to disobey Fairbairn were forgotten when one of his volunteers threatened him with a gun for reprimanding him.

Fairbairn, armed with only a knife, disarmed the man and stabbed him to death then dumped his body in the harbour.

Cuthbert needed a force to operate outside the restrictions and regulations of the British Army, to be brutal and ruthless in order to bypass the capture and trial process. He had orders from his masters in Whitehall to clean up the frontier and make peace. He had a very different set of orders from his masters in the ELOS within Whitehall, to crush the enemy without mercy, and this is what he set out to do.

All his forces, including Fairbairn's Volunteers, were mustered in King William's Town, they were almost ready to take the war to the Xhosa chiefs, but there was one more task he had to perform.

Cuthbert wanted all of Smyth's 'old school' officers gone from the colony, as per the ELOS's instructions, and so made enquiries about the conduct of General

Sommerville and summoned him to his office.

Sommerville knocked on the door and entered expecting to carry on as before, just under new management. 'Good afternoon, Governor. Welcome to the Cape Colony frontier,' he said, extending his hand in greeting.

Cuthbert stood, saluted and waited until Sommerville withdrew his hand, stood to attention and reciprocated the salute.

'This is not a social call, General, and I will make it as brief as possible. You have served here for nearly thirty years but these last few years have been, frankly, a disaster,' said Cuthbert.

Sommerville, who was still at attention, was about to say something but Cuthbert held up his hand palm outwards.

'Do not interrupt me, General. Just listen. You have made a tidy sum of money from many corrupt dealings during your years in the Cape,' said Cuthbert, watching the change in the General's face. 'Oh, you did not imagine we knew? Obviously, you can get away with certain indiscretions whilst you are on top of your profession, General, but you do not get away with it when your total incompetence in this frontier war borders on a call for an investigation and court-martial proceedings.' Said Cuthbert raising his voice.

'Your Excellency, I am s–'

'Be silent, General. I warn you, for I may be tempted to reverse what I am about to say. Apart from all else, you could have been a bit more discreet when it comes to the harem of Hottentot whores that you keep with you at all times, even when you are engaged in battle. That alone is a court-martial offence. But the British Government does not work like that, does it? You and I both know that all these offences will never see the light of day to protect the prestige of the colony, and especially the Empire. You will, in all probability, receive a knighthood when you are transferred.'

'I am to be transferred?' said Sommerville, visibly shaken at the dressing down thrown at him by this young upstart.

'Yes, your transfer has come through. You go to India. When you leave this office you will travel immediately to Cape Town where you will pack your house and leave for England as soon as possible.'

Cuthbert stood to attention and saluted. 'Goodbye, General.'

Cuthbert was now ready to launch his campaign at the Xhosa tribes and put an absolute end to this war. He promoted and hand-picked his preferred officers and commanders to lead the fighting units and made it clear what his orders were.

With his new senior commander, Colonel Eyett, he led the columns of the 73rd, 74th and 91st Regiments, along with the Cape Mounted Rifles', Fairbairn's Volunteer Corps, the Rifle Brigade and the loyal, Mfengu Regulars, from King William's Town.

On the way east, hundreds of troops peeled off and went into the valleys of the Kroomie Heights to the south, east and west.

Cuthbert carried on with 3,000 troops into the Amatola Mountains, to get a feeling of what he was up against.

When they were camped that night, Cuthbert sent out spies and patrols to give the impression that an attack in the Amatolas was imminent. Then one morning before dawn he suddenly made an about-turn and invaded the Kroomie Heights, not just Fuller's Hoek, but the whole range.

There were drought conditions in the area, had been for some time and Cuthbert had been waiting patiently for a strong south-easterly wind to blow, and blow it did on that morning. He ordered the whole of the west and south-west side of the Kroomie to be set alight.

Mzingisi watched the dust cloud get closer, stretching for miles upon miles to the south-west. He knew there were huge reinforcements but no other information had been forthcoming, but most intriguing of all was that Cuthbert had not sent out any word to ask the Xhosa chiefs to meet and discuss terms of peace, and where the Xhosa people wanted to be left to live and prosper. This was a great worry to Mzingisi.

Hundreds of troops started setting up camp on the plain below the Kroomie Heights and reports were coming to him that hundreds of troops were marching to the west of the Kroomie up Bush Neck. The same was happening at Blinkwater and hundreds more kept marching to the Amatola Mountains.

Mzingisi had 3,000 warriors as well as the Hottentot riflemen. He placed them in the cover of the forests of the Waterkloof and Fuller's Hoek, and covering the ridge between the high plateau and the lower plain on the heights. Now they waited for this new governor to attack and be driven back by the mighty Xhosa warriors.

It came a few days later when a strong south-easterly wind brought the unmistakeable smell of burning wood across the Kroomie Heights.

Next came the smoke, thick and choking, moving

ahead of the sound of crackling wood burning at a very high temperature. The speed of the bush fire took Mzingisi by surprise, the flames leaping twenty… forty feet in the air.

'My brothers, go back to Fuller's Hoek. Send runners to the others. Tell them to fall back,' shouted Mzingisi, feeling the rush of heat. 'We cannot stay here, fall back. Fall back!'

The flames, coming from all directions, devoured the tinder-dry brush and trees at an alarming speed. The wind howled from west to east, fanning the wall of flames from north to south, tearing through the valleys of the Kroomie Heights.

When Mzingisi reached his village he ordered everybody to run with what they could take. He could hear the crackle of the flames pursuing him like a demented monster. People ran in panic to try and escape the searing heat, the women taking the children, while the pakati and some warrior guards took Mzingisi through the bush away from danger.

In the valleys to the east leading to the Blinkwater, the soldiers were waiting for them. The order was given to unleash a barrage of cannon fire aimed at the fleeing Xhosa people. The bombardment went on for hour after hour. When it stopped and the smoke cleared the carnage that unfolded was catastrophic.

Mutilated bodies were strewn all over the land. The surviving women and children screamed and wailed in the confusion of horses and soldiers cutting off their escape. Any men and boys from teenage years upwards were shot or put to the cavalry sabre. The Ngqika warriors tried to fight their way through but they too were either cut down or shot.

It was a massacre.

The carnage that followed was total as the troops followed behind the devastating fire. They cut down and destroyed everything in sight that hadn't been burned to the ground. All the women and children they could find alive were captured and put in camps. Every single man they came across was shot on sight, or hanged immediately.

Mzingisi and his pakati with their followers fled, but found it difficult to hide as Cuthbert's men seemed to be everywhere they went.

Cuthbert had a small fort built at Mount Misery on the Kroomie and left a detachment of troops there to patrol the area. He then turned his attention to Gcalekaland, Samkelo's country and proceeded to decimate the land there as well. Samkelo had also fled with a small number of followers, all the cattle and other animals were taken and all remaining food burned.

The troops were ordered to take no prisoners except women and children but Fairbairn's Volunteers were particularly ruthless, cutting the throats of women and children and decapitating the men, again keeping one or two skulls as souvenirs. They took no prisoners.

Colonel Eyett then led 3,000 troops back into the Amatolas and employed the same tactics as had been used in the Kroomie. The smoke from the huge fires swept along by the south-easterly wind stretched for mile upon mile, the flames devouring the tinder-dry bush. Anything that was left standing was cut to the ground by the British forces following the fires, leaving corpses to hang and rot in the sun, all livestock confiscated.

Sandla and the other Xhosa chiefs fled before the

mighty force of the white men led by the now feared and infamous, *Ameshlomani,* the Xhosa word for 'four eyes', the name given to Colonel Eyett as he wore spectacles.

The killing and destruction went on non-stop for weeks, as Cuthbert had more than enough reinforcements and supplies to keep fresh troops rotating at all times, relentlessly sweeping backwards and forwards through the mountains until nothing and no one remained.

The Xhosa people began to hear of Fairbairn's demons killing everybody and eating them, as the rumours escalated, and of *Ameshlomani*, the four-eyed demon destroying the mountain villages, leaving rotting corpses in his wake.

Any surviving warriors of the brush fire did not last long as hundreds of soldiers came up through the valleys onto the plateau and the plains below, following the fire and cutting down any remaining resistance.

Mzingisi escaped across the valley of the Blinkwater and was on a hill to the east where he witnessed the slaughter of his people as they tried to run or fight their way out of the Kroomie.

'Inkos, we must continue to run for Sandla's country,' said Xolaxola.

Little did he know that the same destruction and slaughter was ensuing there as well.

They were huddled in a small crevasse in the side of the mountain not daring to light a fire lest it be seen by the demon soldiers.

'Who is this devil?' asked Xolaxola, looking at Mzingisi.

'I do not know, my brother. He is a demon sent to punish us for shaming the great white queen and her armies. His name is Cuthbert and he is the wrath of the white men.'

Mzingisi did not find Sandla right away for he was fleeing for his life as well. Many, many days went by. All the chiefs ran, hid and ran again, hiding in remote places known only to a few of the older members of the pakati, the locations of which had been handed down from previous generations.

The soldiers did not stop. They were relentless in their search for the chiefs and they were closing in. Soon there would be nowhere else to go. There was no shelter, no rest, and no food and they were getting sick.

Then they learned that one of the chiefs had surrendered at Fort Murray and had been dragged off in chains and imprisoned. This news alarmed the chiefs so much they threw caution to the wind and eventually managed to arrange a secret meeting.

'Is there any word from Samkelo?' asked Mzingisi, looking around the chiefs and pakati sitting around a fire in a hastily built hut.

'None of us has heard from him in many days,' said Sandla.

'We must consider crossing the Kei River to appease the demon Cuthbert,' said Mzingisi.

Cuthbert, meanwhile had no intention of letting up, he sent more troops into the Kroomie Heights to carry out another sweep of the area and burn any vegetation still standing in any of the valleys, and run to ground any survivors of the previous raid and hang them immediately.

Once the fires died down he ordered more temporary forts to be built on Fuller's Hoek: one in the Waterkloof and another in the Kroomie Heights.

He then chased down the Hottentot deserters from the Cape Mounted Rifles and the rebels from the Kat River settlement who, in the eyes of the settlers and the Government, were regarded as traitors. They were ruthlessly hunted down and shot or hanged, fresh troops again rotating all the time to keep up the momentum of the hunt, never letting up until the remainder surrendered in droves because of the proclamation of an amnesty, only to be tried and executed, or imprisoned for life.

It was reported that the leader of the rebel Hottentots, who was exempt from the amnesty, had been hiding out in Gcalekaland and had taken his own life rather than face the wrath of Cuthbert's legions of troops or, more especially, Fairbairn's Volunteers.

As the weeks went by all areas were cleared of any and all natives, Cuthbert built more small forts all over the frontier with garrisons of soldiers in each of them with reinforcements regularly changing over.

At the end of it, Cuthbert received reports from his patrols that not one Xhosa native or Hottentot could be seen anywhere. There was not a living soul in the burnt-out remains of the Amatolas nor in the Kroomie Heights. The forts reported that there were no marauders or disturbances along the roads, or in the bush around the settlements. The whole frontier had been burned and purged of all Xhosa natives.

But Mzingisi, Samkelo, Sandla and the other Xhosa Chiefs remained at large and would not surrender. Cuthbert, in his frustration, sent a despatch to all the commanders of his forces to keep up the search for the chiefs and to chase them down until they surrendered, or were captured or killed.

'We should have made a stand together and fought the British instead of running like hyenas from the lions,' said Xolaxola weakly, looking around the other faces in the hut.

The silence was broken by a messenger entering the hut and whispering to one of the pakati.

'Inkos, it is about chief Siyabulela, he has been sentenced to death. He was taken to the white man's court and tried for treason.'

'They are to hang him from the gallows?' asked Mzingisi.

No. This is worse he was to have been executed by gunfire, but the demon Cuthbert stopped this and banished him over the sea for the rest of his life, with only his great wife for comfort.'

While the chiefs and council talked about the fate of Siyabulela, the pakati councillor interrupted once again.

'Inkos, Samkelo has also surrendered to the demon Cuthbert and he has been pardoned.'

This was a shock; the Paramount Chief of the Xhosa Nation had surrendered.

Sandla broke the silence and said what everybody was thinking. 'I have lost my land and my cattle. My people are being hunted down and captured or killed. I am running every day and night for weeks. I am failing in strength to fight the British anymore. We need to talk to the demon Cuthbert and end this or he will kill us all.'

The discussions dragged on through the night, debating rights and wrongs; what was and was not the sensible thing to do for the Xhosa people. They had to make a decision soon as time was running out.

A decision was made and that decision was for all the

people to migrate across to the east side of the Kei River, as requested by the white government. They would send word to the demon Cuthbert through Captain McLean at Fort Murray that they wished to broker a peaceful settlement.

Some days later Charles Blackwell set up camp on the west side of the Kei River and sent word to Sandla to meet with him.

'Chalis, like his father before him, has always spoken for us and he can be trusted,' said Sandla.

'Siyabulela was taken and tried in the white man's court and banished from his homeland after he surrendered,' Mzingisi said, not trusting the arrangements to meet with Blackwell.

'Samkelo did not walk into a fort and surrender but sent a messenger to the demon Cuthbert that he wanted peace and he was pardoned. We have done the same and I think Chalis can be trusted to try his best for our people. We will send two men to scout the country around the meeting place to find out if we are going to a trap.'

The scouts reported that Blackwell and two other white men were waiting in the camp to welcome the Xhosa chiefs, there were no troops around at all.

The chiefs crossed the Kei River and talked with Blackwell for days before agreeing to meet with the demon Cuthbert at Yellow Wood, a place just outside of King William's Town.

A few days later the remaining chiefs, dressed in their finest regalia and each wearing the emblem of the great chiefs of the Xhosa, the leopard skin kaross, set up camp and the negotiations began with the usual social inquiries about family and wives and then they got down to business.

Cuthbert was a clever negotiator and patiently let the chiefs put forward their ideas and plan for the Xhosa nation to settle and prosper, but all the time the conversation involved the Amatola Mountains and the Kroomie Heights, and their absolute rejection of settling on the east side of the Kei River, as Cuthbert had predicted.

'I welcome the Xhosa people as part of the great community of the Cape colony and the great white queen has sent a proclamation to absolve you of any crimes or treason against her majesty,' said Cuthbert; Blackwell interpreting in Xhosa. 'I have listened to your wise words for the good of the Xhosa people and it would not be in their best interest to have them settle on the land east of the Kei River.'

This got the interest of the chiefs and they looked very pleased with themselves.

'Instead you will be settled on the fertile land between the foothills of the Amatolas to the west of the Kei River,' said Cuthbert.

Sandla was clearly shocked. 'The Amatolas and the Kroomie are our homelands. We demand to go home there.'

Cuthbert said. 'The Amatola Mountains and the Kroomie Heights have been proclaimed a *Royal Reserve.* The Xhosa people will never again be allowed to live in that region. No one will be settled in a Royal Reserve.'

Sandla made his objections clear but in the end there was no other choice than to accept the fate offered to them as he knew the demon Cuthbert would think nothing of unleashing his forces and striking down his people again.

When the Xhosa people eventually settled in their new land their cattle were returned to them and they were given farming implements to start growing crops. The land was overcrowded, flat and barren of trees.

The chiefs and the pakati were sitting in Sandla's hut, the leopard skins folded away. 'My heart pines for our homeland in the mountains. My cattle are forever looking to the west. We need a sign from our ancestors to set our people free,' said Sandla.

'Our job is done, Colonel Eyett,' said Cuthbert, holding up a scorched leopard skin kaross. 'I have skinned the Leopard.'

'You have indeed sir. Congratulations,' said Eyett.

'Whether the natives can be civilised or not is out of our hands. We must see to it that the patrols are kept up and the forts well supplied to ensure peace prevails throughout the frontier region. If you gave me the choice of the colonists or the natives I would say the Xhosa people are by far the most finest of the two. I am sick to death of these land-grabbing, mean-spirited and dishonest colonists, who want everything for nothing and wait for us to hand it to them. They have no integrity and do not care anything about the indigenous people of this land who have lost everything that they hold dear. They at least fought for their right to keep the land they have lived on for centuries until the white man came and wrenched it away.'

'It is what we do, sir. We travel the world to conquer and rule new territories. We crush all who stand in our way and all for the Empire,' said Eyett.

'Yes indeed, Colonel. We are soldiers and we do our duty. Let's have dinner and some wine, I am back to Cape Town tomorrow.'

Chapter Forty Three

May 1856

Cape Town

Nigel Renton disembarked from the ship in Cape Town with the help of his faithful companion and servant Samuel. He drew a little attention, not so much because of his stooped body and short stepping gait with the walking stick, but more because of the hat with the veil and the black gloves he was wearing to quantify the illusion of having bad skin. But the stupid people tended to humour him and pity him which he would use to full advantage.

My plans will be fulfilled, thought Storer, *as Nigel Renton, I will just be another businessman trying to make his mark. But for now I will rest and make my plans, and make discreet inquiries as to what Fyvie and McColl are doing, then find a way to destroy their reputation and eventually have them both killed.*

After speaking with the Customs and Excise men, Storer – now Renton – and Samuel Gubotu made their way to a waiting carriage. Storer recognised Nicholas Banbury talking with the driver but decided to keep his identity to himself for now.

'Welcome to Cape Town, Mr Renton. I am Nicholas Banbury with Her Majesty's Government in the Cape. It was I who transferred the house into your name and I was asked to meet you and take you there to read over and sign the documents,' said Banbury.

'Very kind of you, sir. Nigel Renton,' said Storer in a rasping voice: shaking Banbury's hand. *He does not have a clue who I really am; I am rather enjoying this,'* thought Storer. 'Please, call me Nigel.'

As the carriage drew near to his house he felt elated that against all the odds he had come back and put himself in an even better position to execute his plans for Southern Africa.

Once the Xhosa are decimated to the point where they will not cause any more wars or indeed any trouble at all, we, the ELOS, will entrench ourselves within the British administration, army and navy, and march northward to victory, riches and power, thought Storer.

'It's a fine house; is it not,' said Renton as he stared out at the high walls looming in the distance.

'One of the finest in Cape Town Nigel. I'm sure you will be very comfortable and pleased with it,' said Banbury taking a quick peek out of the window.

He noticed some coloured folk walking on the road ahead of them and said. 'There are some damned coloureds on the road, they know better than to encroach on the properties up on the mountain. I will tell the driver to warn them off.'

'Is the driver in your employ Nicolas?' asked Renton.

'No, he works for government house.'

'Then allow me.'

Renton stuck his veiled head out of the window and shouted, 'this is private property; be gone with you, don't come back or I will have you beaten and thrown in jail.'

The coloured folk ran off at the sight of the veiled apparition on the carriage.

'Well, they now know there is a new master at home,' said Banbury smiling.

The wagon following the carriage to the house on the slopes of Table Mountain was emptied of the personal belongings of Renton and Gubotu, while Banbury ushered Renton into the large library.

'It is a beautiful house,' said Renton in his rasping voice. 'I believe the previous owner was jailed and then taken to England to be tried for treason?'

Banbury immediately became very uncomfortable. 'The house is called *Arend se Kop*. It's Afrikaans, and is named after the outcrop of rock up on the mountain which is shaped like an eagle's head. I worked with that awful man and yes, he was sent to England to pay for his crimes, but was lost at sea during the voyage,' said Banbury, following Renton as he walked through the house. 'But how did you come to know about James Storer?' he asked suspiciously.

Renton ignored the question as he walked along a wide corridor with which he was very familiar and tried one of the doors. It was locked.

'Do you have the key to this door?' he asked Banbury.

'Yes, I have somewhere. It is just an old wine cellar, very damp and dingy you know.'

'Fetch the keys and open it, there's a good fellow.'

Banbury went off and returned minutes later with a wooden box and searched the labelled keys inside it.

'Ah! Here we are.'

'Bring a lamp please,' said Storer taking the key from him.

He opened the door and descended down the stone stairway with Banbury. They lit the wall lamps and Storer looked at the empty wine racks then picked up the lamp and shone it on part of the wall, which had fresh mortar and stone built into it.

'This has been recently built I see,' said Renton.

'Yes, I am afraid it had to be repaired because the stone was crumbling due to some damp seeping in,' said Banbury, wondering why Renton would be bothered with something such as this.

'You are such a poor liar, Nicholas,' said Renton really enjoying seeing Banbury squirming. 'You always were.'

'I beg your pardon?' Banbury spluttered, utterly shocked.

'I will have to restock my wine cellar and this wall will have to be removed if we are to use the real cellar below, Nicholas.'

Banbury went quite pale and looked at Renton.

'What do you mean, Mr Renton?'

'Did you ever find the girl who jumped through the trap door, Nicholas?'

Banbury took a step back and made to go up the stairs only the way was blocked by the immense Samuel with a huge scimitar sword hanging from his belt.

'What is this? Who are you, sir?' said Banbury turning back to Renton.

'You will have to contact Williams and tell him we will need some new girls.'

Suddenly Banbury had an unbelievable thought of

the wasted body that was James Storer before he embarked on the ship to England.

'James? My god, no one else could have known about what happened here. Is that really you, James?'

'My body and looks have changed somewhat, but yes, it is I, Nicholas. I have returned.'

Banbury nearly rushed over and hugged him, but restrained himself to a hearty hand shake.

'But what on earth…?'

'All in good time, Nicholas, all in good time. This *awful man* will tell you the whole story upstairs. But first we must eat and drink. We have a lot of work ahead of us, and need to start immediately.'

Banbury's face reddened but was gladdened by the return of this charismatic man who would change lives.

Storer and Banbury conferred for days on what each other knew, including Fyvie and McColl's movements, their whereabouts and what business they were involved in and where Cuthbert was with his campaign against the Xhosa.

'The local newspapers condemned Governor Cuthbert for the way he carried out his subjugation of the natives, rounding up the women and children, and hanging or shooting all the men of warrior age,' said Banbury. 'But Cuthbert brushed them aside. He did not care what was said about his tactics. He did his job and everybody could go to hell. As far he was concerned he would leave the Cape sooner or later, once he had finished the job he had come here to do.'

'So, Cuthbert is still keeping the patrols scouring the frontier?' asked Renton.

'Yes, he is. He has built a series of forts in strategic locations, which are well manned. Any renegade kaffirs still running around will be caught, or hanged and left to rot, or shot where they stand.'

'I must say it was a master stroke getting rid of Smyth and bringing Cuthbert here as governor,' Renton said, 'he certainly has given us the perfect platform to launch our final solution for the Xhosa nation. After a while in their new location the chiefs will be desperate to clutch at anything thrown to them to resurrect their fighting warriors and drive the white men out of their country.'

'It has been hinted at by the elders that Sir George Whyte, governor of New Zealand, will be offered the post of Governor of the Cape when Cuthbert has to leave for pastures new.'

'There is no hint of it, Nicolas. George Whyte *will* replace Cuthbert and he will be perfect for what I have planned.'

'Then when should we start with the final plan, James?' asked Banbury.

'You must stop calling me James. You have to get used to calling me Nigel Renton. We will start when the time is right, the timing is crucial.'

Storer settled in to his new role as the reclusive businessman Nigel Renton, enjoying being the eccentric, rich, sad man everybody thought he was.

Little do they know how strong I am, he thought. *I am now invincible. These people have no idea what I am capable of but, with some patience on my part, they will know soon enough.*

He summoned Williams and Gubotu to come up to the library.

'Samuel, Williams, take some tea with me. There are things of importance that we have to discuss,' said

Renton.

Renton took Gubotu to the side. 'Samuel, are your living quarters to your satisfaction?'

'They are good, sir. I have everything I need,'

'Do you have enough space at the back of your quarters to work on the muti?'

'Yes, sir, do not worry. I will have all the muti you need to go ahead with your plans.'

'Good, good. Williams come and join us. We are going to be very busy over the next few weeks,' said Renton.

'Williams, you know the working folk here in Cape Town, don't you?'

'I know some of the working people around the township, sir.'

'There are two white men who have a workplace in Salt River. Their names are Fyvie and McColl. They make farming tools and I believe wagons as well. I want you to find out exactly where their yard is.'

'I know of them, sir. They have a Government contract and employ a good number of people and from what I hear are very good to their workers,' said Williams.

'That is nice that they are good to their workers, but that is going to change,' said Renton, his voice suddenly louder and harsher. 'Williams, you will find out who works for them and tell them it is very bad luck to be working for Fyvie as he is cursed. Take Samuel here and tell them in no uncertain terms that death could befall their families because of the curse. I do not care what you say or do, but they will stop working for him. Is that clear?'

'Yes, sir, that is very clear, but it will not be easy;

these people do not scare easily.'

'As I say, take Samuel and threaten them. Then, to the time is right, both of you will go to the yard in the very early hours and do some mischief.'

'There are watchmen, sir. They will surely see us.'

'Samuel will leave a large enough message when he kills them, so they cannot identify you. Believe me when I tell you that their injuries will scare the people into the belief that there is a hell. I want the intimidation tactics to start immediately.'

Williams looked at the size of Samuel and the sword and tended to believe him.

'Let us proceed to the next order of business,' said Renton. 'Williams, you have been using one of Samkelo's councillors to get our guns to the Xhosa, yes?'

'I have, sir. His name is Misumzi, a long time councillor of the Chief's pakati and the clans' seer; he is now very close to Samkelo because of the guns. I have also reminded him that we have paid him a lot of money, which the chief has had no share in and would be very upset if he found out that Misumzi alone has profited from the guns and not Samkelo.'

'Well done, Williams. I like someone who shows some initiative. You say Misumzi is the seer for the clan, does he have a daughter?'

'He does not have a daughter, sir, but he has two sons, I think one by his great wife and one by another. He does have a niece, the daughter of his sister. She is learning to be a sangoma, a tribal witch doctor and she seems to have her uncle's gift as a seer. Misumzi is well known as a seer of prophecies of his clan.'

'That is perfect, Williams. You have chosen well. When the time is right you will be instructed to go to

Misumzi and inform him we are coming to speak with him and his niece. Tell him we will pay him handsomely for this meeting and we will pay even more if he carries out our instructions after we talk to his niece. Tell him he will be able to buy many, many cattle.'

'As long as I am looked after as well, sir, then I will gladly make arrangements to see Misumzi, sir.'

'Oh, you will be well rewarded when all these plans bear fruit,' said Renton not liking Williams' forwardness in demanding reward.

Gubotu and Williams left as Banbury arrived back. He poured a brandy for Renton and himself.

'I think we should organise a special party for the elite of Cape Town,' said Renton.

'You mean for the secret elite, with special sexual desires?' asked Banbury.

'Indeed, have you asked Williams to find us some fresh victims?'

'He will finish off demolishing the wall I had him build to protect the cellar and then he will start hunting,' said Banbury.

'Patience is the watchword, Nicholas' said Renton, sipping his brandy. 'We now wait for certain events to unfold, which will ultimately give us total control of the Cape Colony. Our domination from here to the native frontier will be complete and the stepping stone to Africa will be laid.'

'And you will lead us there, Ja– I mean, Nigel,' said Banbury.

'Tell Williams him to find our new, young guests quickly for I have a burning desire.

Chapter Forty Four

Cape Town

Maria was good at selling flowers. She had a knack of attracting customers, who would return again and again, and so she accepted her lot and for the last few months tried to do the best she could for these kind people who had taken her in and were helping her.

She would sit every evening and think hard on maybe a face for her mother or a father or a family member, but nothing would come to her.

The imam conferred with doctors at the hospital. One said there were doctors in England dealing with people who had been caught up in bad situations and had lost their memories to block out the ordeal they had gone through. So it may be that Maria had seen something horrific, or something really bad had happened to her, and her brain just wanted to forget it.

One morning Maria was sitting behind the flower stand preparing the new stock just arrived from the outlying farms. She was chatting about this and that when she glanced up the street and looked into the face of Williams, driving a small cart up Adderley Street.

The severe jolt that blasted through Maria's brain

threw her off the upturned wooden bucket she was sitting on and on to the ground. Auntie Fatima got such a fright it took her a moment to realise Maria had seen something, or someone, that had had a profound effect on her. She lifted Maria up and sat her on the bucket.

'Face. The man… the cart… his face… I know him,' she mumbled.

Auntie Fatima looked up. There were a few carts but she had seen the one passing by before, a few times.

'You! Hey, you,' she shouted at the driver.

Williams looked back to see what the shouting was about but could not see any disturbance.

Auntie Fatima etched his face into her brain and he turned away.

The cart went up the street and disappeared into Wale Street, but she could not worry about that now. She had to get some help and get Maria home.

Maria was able to walk but she was deep in shock at what had seen.

'Do you know that man, Maria?' asked Fatima supporting Maria up the street towards her house in the Bo Kaap.

'Yes, I do know him, but I cannot place him. I know that he is a bad man. He has done something to me.'

When they got home Fatima made tea and Maria lay down to ease the tiredness that washed over her.

'Close your eyes and take a deep breath. You are safe with us. Try and recall this man's face and where you saw him.'

Maria drank some of her tea and laid her head on the cushion. Closing her eyes she immediately saw the man's face.

'In the doorway of a small room,' she said, 'handing

me a robe… a nightgown or a loose dress… closing the door… locking it. He comes back. No, it's not the same man… another man. He has no clothes on. He takes off my clothes and touches me all over my body. I fight him off.'

Maria starts sobbing as the visions become clearer.

'He pulls me to another room and hits me. He forces me to drink… awful taste… forces more… I become… far away. He puts my hand on his thing. It is big and hard. I don't want to do it but I cannot resist him. I move my hand up and down on it.'

Fatima knew what she was describing and was horrified at what she was hearing.

The tears ran down Maria's face, her hands gripping the couch cover causing her knuckles to turn white.

'He has a pot of honey… puts some on his thing… tells me I must lick it off. He pushes it into my mouth. Somebody behind me… screaming… oh no… stop screaming…'

Maria suddenly opened her eyes, jumped up and dashed for the outside toilet and wretched her heart out. Fatima brought a damp cloth to wipe her face then took her to her bed.

'I know this is very difficult for you but can you remember or see where these things happened?'

'No, Auntie I cannot. I don't know,' she said, weeping again.

'That is alright. Do not worry, lie down and sleep, little one.'

Fatima stayed with her until she fell asleep, and then called Yusuf and Salomé to come and sit with her and sent the children out to play.

'What's wrong Auntie?'

'It's Maria. While we were preparing the flowers this morning she saw a man driving a cart past the stand and she fainted.'

'What? Who was it? A friend, a relative?' asked Yusuf.

'No, she thinks he did something to her. She was very upset, and remembered things I will not repeat. I stopped her because she was crying and losing her mind. She's sleeping now.'

'Did she know the man's name, Auntie?'

'No, and she could not say where these things happened. But you know, I have worked my flower stand there for years and I have seen that driver with that cart many times. And another thing, I have been thinking about this: a few months ago the police were looking for some young girls who mysteriously disappeared and then it seemed to stop for a while. But in the last couple of days rumours have been going around the street stalls that another two young girls have gone missing recently.'

'Yes, I remember, I think about six girls went missing,' said Yusuf.

Salomé drew in her breath. 'You think Maria was taken?'

'Yes, I do. I think she was captured but somehow she managed to escape from wherever he, or they, kept her prisoner, to have his evil way with her. She must have walked through the bush not knowing where she was and then fallen down the side of the mountain where you found her Yusuf.'

'Then she must come from somewhere far from here because nobody knows her,' said Salomé.

'Somebody somewhere is looking for her,' said Yusuf.

'There was a sergeant and a coloured policeman asking questions not so long ago. Do you remember, Yusuf? You spoke to them about any strangers around looking suspicious,' said Fatima.

'Yes, I do remember. He was Irish. His name was Donald or… O'Donnell that was it. He is new to the police force and from what I've heard people trust him because he seems to have a genuine concern for the locals.'

'You must go and find him Yusuf. He seems to be the only policeman who is looking into the disappearances. Do not talk to anyone else, just him and bring him here.'

'I will go now and see where he is stationed and ask him to come around in the morning. Let Maria sleep,' said Yusuf.

The next day another family member went to look after the flower stand for the day as the immediate family wanted to be with Maria when the police arrived.

Maria was finishing her breakfast when she heard a knock on the front door. Fatima had already told her that the policeman was coming to see her, that he was a nice man and to try and answer his questions.

Fatima told Sergeant O'Donnell and Constable Ahmed Jalala everything she knew about Maria so far and what Maria had told her, after seeing the driver of the cart.

Maria was waiting patiently in the parlour when the two policemen sat down and introduced themselves. O'Donnell knew Afrikaans fairly well but had Ahmed to help him if need be.

'So far, I know what you told Aunty Fatima, Maria, but I would like to ask you if you know the man who did these things to you. I know this is very embarrassing, but we will not repeat anything you tell us. Please do not be afraid, you could be saving another young girl's life by telling us everything you can,' said O'Donnell.

'I was lying in bed this morning thinking very hard and I have been remembering other things that happened,' said Maria, realising she was more strong-minded than she thought. She was determined to find out who she was and find the people who had done these evil deeds. 'The man who abused me was a white man, but I do not know his name. There was also another man in the room who I never saw but he was very cruel.'

'How do you know he was cruel Maria?' asked O'Donnell.

'I could hear things, sounds, and then what sounded like something being chopped or hacked, like someone using an axe… and the screaming…' Maria caught her breath and sobbed, but waved away the concern of the officers and carried on. 'The screaming of a female all through what I just told you. It was terrifying.' She was visibly shaking now.

'Ahmed, please fetch Maria some water.'

She drank some water and continued.

'My master… that's what I called him, *master*…' she thought about this for a moment. 'He would keep me from turning around, but then I would hear something heavy thump to the ground; a poor girl hitting the floor after the other man had killed her, and the sound of her being dragged away. And I remember a hole. Yes, a hole with a top on it; a metal top in the floor.'

'Could you see through the hole?' asked O'Donnell.

'No, it was closed. Wait. That was how I escaped, I remember now. I jumped into the darkness.' She tried to focus on this new part of her memory. 'My master would wait until the other man went away and then he would say, *clean up the mess and yourself Ann–*' she stopped and stood up.

O'Donnell and Ahmed were startled.

'What is it, Maria?' asked O'Donnell.

'My name is not Maria. It's Annatje.' She ran for the door. 'Aunty Fatima, my name is Annatje. It's Annatje,' she cried.

Fatima and then Salomé hugged her and started crying with her.

'Oh my, that is wonderful my child,' cried Fatima. 'Your memory is coming back.'

O'Donnell and Ahmed looked at each other and waited for Annatje to return.

When she came back she told as much as her memory would allow her.

'I am sorry, officers.'

'That's alright. Take your time,' said Ahmed, speaking for the first time.

'I would wash the floor and the tables, and then myself. Then I would be locked in a room, like a cell in a cellar. It must be a cellar. I don't know where this place is. I can't remember anything after the black hole. I am trying, but it will not come back to me.'

'You have been very brave and you have done well to remember what you have, Annatje,' said O'Donnell'

He looked at Ahmed and nodded.

'Annatje, a few months ago a family from Kalk Bay came to us to say that their daughter had gone out one day and did not come home. They reported her missing and her name is Annatje Makasar. Now, we do not want you to get your hopes up but we will go back to the police house and get a cart and take you there to meet these people.'

'Kalk Bay is where my family lives. I remember,' said Annatje. 'My father is a fisherman. I remember them and I will know if it is them.'

O'Donnell drove the cart with Ahmed in the back chattering excitedly with Annatje and Aunty Fatima as they approached Kalk Bay. The rest of the family followed behind in their small cart.

They went up the track to the fishermen's houses on the slope of the mountain above the small harbour and stopped outside one of the houses. The neighbours, seeing them coming and recognising Annatje, ran into the street, sending a child to the fishing boats to tell the men she had been found.

A woman came running out of the house shouting. 'Annatje, my daughter. Is that really you? Annatje.'

She knew immediately she was home. Annatje leapt down from the cart and ran to meet her mother, embracing her. Her father ran from his fishing boat and wrapped his arms around the two women.

The two officers sat in the cart watching the scene. Aunty Fatima and her family joined in the celebration of Annatje finding her family.

'This is what makes the job of a policeman worthwhile,' said O'Donnell.

'It does feel good, Sergeant,' agreed Ahmed.

O'Donnell turned the cart around and headed back to Cape Town.

'Now it is up to us to find the monsters that are killing our young girls,' said O'Donnell.

When they got back to the police station, Jacky O'Grady, the station commander, asked O'Donnell to come to his office.

'I believe you found one of the missing girls, Brian?' asked O'Grady. 'Did you question her about where she was being held?'

'I did, sir. The problem is she was so traumatised from her ordeal she's lost her memory. She is starting to remember things now but she's been living with a coloured family up in the Bo Kaap for months not knowing who she was. When I went to talk to her she was trying to remember what she was made to do when she was held captive and she suddenly remembered the man saying her name, so we have managed to reunite her with her family. I will go back and question her again when things calm down.'

O'Donnell related to his chief most of what Annatje had told him.

'Do you think she is telling the truth?'

'Aye, I think so. After listening to her and the people she was living with, I'm sure she's being truthful. She's lucky to be alive,' said O'Donnell. He was not going to tell the commander about the cart and driver, learning from past experience not to share any good leads lest they affected somebody with money or someone well known. Then the case would magically disappear.

'Well, I'm afraid I have some bad news for you. Another two girls have disappeared in the last three days,' said O'Grady, handing over the families' details.

'Where?' Said the sergeant.

'Go home and get some sleep. Start again tomorrow,' said O'Grady.

Tomorrow I will have to ask Annatje to sit at her stall with one of my men, thought O'Donnell. *Perhaps Ahmed. They can wait for the man on the cart to go by again and follow him to where ever he lives or works. It may take a day, it may take a month, but it will be done. I will track this suspect and his accomplices and they will be brought to book.*

Chapter Forty Five

King William's Town, Eastern Cape

Jamie and Iain had been lucky to find lodgings in King William's Town as the town was bursting at the seams with people fleeing the marauding Xhosa and Hottentot rebels. They had been there for weeks now and had used the time to set up a partnership and to find premises to store and sell their goods. During this time news was always trickling in from the war front.

The local newspaper, the Eastern Province News, was critical of Cuthbert's tactics and unproven reports of Fairbairn's Volunteer Corps' brutality with their; *no prisoner* policy, vehemently denied by Cuthbert.

The carnage went on unabated until there was barely a living soul to be found in the Kroomie or the Amatolas. The Xhosa had been utterly and decisively broken and crushed.

With the army now in control of the frontier and the roads most of the settlers started to make their way back to what was left of their homesteads.

Robert Fairbairn and his volunteers were ordered back to their camp outside town as there was no one else to slaughter but mainly because of the growing outrage of the brutality inflicted on the natives.

Fairbairn and his brother were sitting at their campfire, Fairbairn said. 'Jonny, when Fyvie and McColl leave for Cape Town, I want you to follow them and keep them under surveillance until I return. Do not do anything mind, all I want you to do is watch them; they are dangerous men.'

'I can handle them Robert, I'm not scared of them. I can take care of myself.'

Fairbairn shook his head. 'That's just the type of attitude that'll get you killed. I will send a couple of men with you so there will always be one of you following them, if anything untoward happens then send one of the men to let me know what is going on, but I don't expect to be held up here much longer. Now listen to me carefully.

Fairbairn related everything he had learned about the treasure and the clues.

'So that's what all that nonsense was about; the Elephant's Eye and the ambush at the Amatola foothills,' said Jonny.

'Yes. I was trying to get the clues from them but my immediate superior was not happy that I tried to kill Fyvie and his friend.'

'So if there is a treasure to be found we'll take it and be rich and fuck off out of this god forsaken country,' said Jonny excitedly.

'That's the plan. So just watch Fyvie and McColl; nothing more; nothing less, I don't want my boss breathing down my neck.'

'Come on, tell me who this *superior* of yours is.'

Fairbairn grabbed the front of his brothers' shirt and said. 'I've told you before, you will not know who they are. It's bad enough I'm involved with them and that they know that you are my brother; you will not be directly caught up with these people.'

'That's fine big brother; rest easy,' said Jonny, knowing what his brother was like when he lost his temper.

'Just follow my instructions to the letter; little brother,'

Bill Hutchison arranged to meet with the boys at the King's Inn. They were sitting in a quiet corner with drinks and reading the news from the frontier.

When Hutchison eventually joined them he was looking rather flustered. He sat down and ordered a drink, placing a satchel full of paperwork on the table.

Jamie said. 'I don't suppose you've found out any information on the men who attacked us on the way to Sandla's kraal.'

'Was the sergeant positive about the identity of the dead men who attacked you and that they were riding with Fairbairn?' asked Hutchison.

'He was very sure. He identified one of them and said he had seen him many times. He knew him as a ne'er do-well who would do anything for a penny.'

'I will go and speak with Sergeant van Bengal again if he ever returns from the mountains. He has given me a statement, which I will go over with him and keep to myself for the moment,' said Hutchison.

'The sergeant's a good man in a fight. See that he gets this please, Bill, we have paid them already, this is a bonus for saving our skins,' said Iain handing over a pouch of coins. 'For his wounded comrade as well.'

Hutchison hid the money in his satchel.

'As you know,' said Hutchison in a low whisper, 'the governor's despatches are coming here from Cape Town and I see quite a bit of the correspondence, although there are sealed documents for the governor's eyes only. I did a bit of snooping whilst the governor was out and I have some interesting, but disturbing news.'

'Well, what is it, Bill? Tell us the gossip from London,' said Iain.

'James Storer is presumed dead,' said Hutchison.

Jamie and Iain suddenly stopped and gave Hutchison their full attention.

'Presumed dead?' asked Jamie. 'What exactly does that mean, *presumed* dead?'

'The report says the ship on which he was sailing stopped at St Helena Island.'

'St Helena Island?' interrupted Iain.

'It's a British protectorate located in the Atlantic Ocean north-west of Cape Town. Anyway, the ship anchored there to pick up a passenger and then sailed on for England. According to the report from the sergeant of the marines guarding Storer, he was under guard the whole time they were anchored off Jamestown. When they were a few hours out of St Helena the guards took Storer for his second walk of the day on deck when he suddenly ran across the deck and dived into the sea, shouting, *I will not be taken alive*. The marines said he would only have lasted a few minutes before the shackles he had on would have tired him out and dragged him under.'

'You see. I told ye we should have chucked the bastard over the side when we had the chance,' said Iain.

'There is also a despatch from Armstrong encoded for me. The Tories have won the election. The new prime minister has suspended all operations of the Secret Field Police, under advisement of certain new ministers, until further notice.'

Jamie and Iain fell silent.

'Well, that is bad news, Bill. Does Armstrong give any reasons?' asked Jamie.

'He says, and he quotes someone else's words, *with Storer dead any cases against any other suspects would be unprovable and the conspiracy against the Cape Government has been thwarted. Certain members in the house voted that the Secret Field Police was ineffectual and too costly.*'

'That seems to be a bit flimsy,' said Iain. 'It's hard to believe Armstrong would give up solely on Storer's demise, don't you think?'

'I agree,' said Hutchison. 'But we are to stand down. We are, in effect, out of a job.'

'So Storer is dead, threw himself into the sea. I find that hard to believe,' Jamie said thoughtfully.

'Well, believe it. Also, Anne Knowles has been released and has requested to be taken back to Cape Town. She says her daughters are there, as well as all her personal belongings and assets.'

'Are you serious? After what she did to her husband and the two girls? Do Lydia and Clara know she is coming back?' asked Jamie, suddenly worried.

'Probably not, no, and I do not think Godfrey Butler will either,' said Hutchison. 'We just received these despatches today. These documents say that because of Storer's death there was not enough evidence to start proceedings for a trial and so she was exonerated and free to go.'

'I smell the hand of the ELOS here, Bill. We have

already established that the Government has been infiltrated to a greater degree than first thought,' said Jamie.

'Yes, and once again I agree. I have been keeping Armstrong aware of our findings with coded letters sent outside of the diplomatic pouches. Do not forget that the Government would have wanted to avoid a trial involving a British diplomat accused of treason and consorting with a prominent businessman's wife, to aid him in the smuggling of guns to start an insurrection in one of the empire's colonies, so Storer's death would be welcome,' said Hutchison.

'Maybe the Government had him killed, or even the ELOS,' said Iain.

'Anything is possible. We just do not know.'

The boys looked at each other and made an unspoken decision.

'We were planning on leaving in a few days now that the roads are safe, but that has changed,' said Jamie. 'We will leave tomorrow. Iain will finish up any paperwork and pay any accounts for us. We have made a few purchases, including some hardwood logs, which I will make sure are all loaded on to the wagons tonight and ready to go in the morning. We must get back to Cape Town and warn Godfrey and the girls. Bill, can you find out if there are any troops going back to Cape Town in the morning and if so, could we ride along with them?'

'I will find out for you and tell you one way or another.'

The next morning Jamie and Iain, leading the loaded wagons, left King William's Town following two wagons with maimed and wounded British soldiers accompanied by a platoon of troopers and a convoy of settlers trailing behind.

Early the same morning, Jonny was pouring coffee at the camp fire when Fairbairn rode into the camp in a bit of a hurry.

'Jonny! Fyvie and McColl have left town with an army convoy headed for Cape Town. Pick two men and follow the convoy, there are lots of settlers with them so nobody will recognise you if you just follow behind; remember what I told and not a word to anyone. Get going.'

The journey was easy-going and uneventful in the days that took them to get back to their business premises in Cape Town.

Jamie instructed the manager at the yard what to do with the wood they had purchased and then, with Iain, rode into town to Godfrey Butler's office. Arriving unannounced they waited for an hour as he had a client with him.

Butler came out of his office and said his goodbyes to the client and looked at the boys.

'This is very sudden and you two look a bit grim. My lawyer instinct tells me you are not here with good news,' said Butler.

'Well, it's good and it's bad, depending on which way you look at it,' said Iain.

Jamie and Iain took it in turns to retell the information received by Bill Hutchison; everything that is, except details of their clandestine operations.

'So Anne Knowles, *née* Fisher, is returning to Cape Town,' said Godfrey more to himself than anyone else.

'Is Anne's return going to be problematic for Lydia

and Clara?' asked Jamie.

'The girls will be well looked after, there are no problems there. Lydia and Clara never liked Anne from when they first met her and since then their dislike, I suppose, has grown into a deep hatred, especially after what happened on the ship on the way to the Cape. As for their state of mind, I would think they will be very distraught by her return.'

'You're the lawyer, Godfrey. How would she get off the charges scot free?' asked Iain.

Godfrey stood up and started to pace the width of his office, backwards and forward between the window and his chair.

'The first thing we have to look at is that on the ship nobody actually saw Anne doping George with this so-called *potion*, which by the way has been analysed by Doctor Morgan and others. Nobody knows what it is or where it comes from. They could not even hazard a guess at the ingredients, but I digress. So nobody saw her do the doping?'

'No,' said the boys in unison.

'The problem is there were two proven villains in the shape of the stewards who had access to George's cabin. They could have doped George and with Anne's cabin right next door they could easily have planted the potion where you found it. There were no witnesses to seeing Anne or, in fact, anyone taking George to the upper deck. Storer's dead, the stewards are dead and the other hired thugs are dead. Had I been the prosecutor and known Storer was dead I would never even have met her disembarking the ship to England, let alone putting her on trial.'

'Will Lydia and Clara be... look, I am not trying to

pry into their private affairs… but will the girls be financially comfortable?' asked Iain.

'Between you two, myself and these humble four walls, I am the executor for George Knowles' estate as well as his partner. I can trust you enough to tell you that in his will, George left everything, his money, his assets, his business and profits, everything to his daughters. There was no one more important to George than Lydia and Clara, and although he had a deep affection for Anne, he was not stupid enough to give away any part of his fortune to someone he had known for such a short time. His heart did not rule his head. George has bequeathed a stipend for Anne for five years, or until she re-marries. She will receive a monthly payment after which she will have to look after herself, I will probably have to tell her the bad news when she arrives back here.'

'Well, that's a relief,' said Jamie. 'We were just worried what might happen to the girls.'

'They have decided to stay in Cape Town. We have talked it over and Sarah has suggested that we extend our house and make it more comfortable for four people instead of two and still have room for visiting friends or family. Sarah and I are delighted they have decided to stay. I must say that Lydia has taken a very keen interest in her father's business. She is very astute.'

'We discovered that on *The Flying Fish*. I'm sure she could eventually run the company,' said Jamie.

'They will both still have some tutoring at home, especially Clara, as she is a bit younger, but I have no doubt that they will flourish. I will finish up here and go home and sit them down to break this news to them.'

'Well, good luck with that. Have you seen or heard from our good captain, Roger Willard?' asked Jamie.

'Yes, he has just arrived back from… I think he went to Port Natal. He was taking some cargo up there to Durban. Apparently sugar farming is growing into a huge export up there, so much so that they are considering bringing in labour from India, I believe. I will write down the captain's address for you, but you might want to try the dock at Rogge Bay. *The Flying Fish* should be there as we have secured a berth for the company ships.'

'Thanks, Godfrey, we will take a ride out to the docks and see if he is there.'

'Why don't you both come for dinner tomorrow evening, Sarah and the girls would love to see you and tell that old seadog Roger to come along as well.'

Iain said. 'Thanks, Godfrey. We'll take you up on the offer of home-cooked food. Right Jamie?'

'I would never miss a chance to sit down to Sarah's cooking.'

The boys left Godfrey and mounted up to ride home, Iain sat and looked down Strand Street.

Jamie stopped. 'What is it? D'ye think we're being followed?'

'Aye. I think so. I've just got a feeling and if we are he is good,' said Iain.

'Your feelings are rarely wrong so let's watch our back more carefully,' said Jamie as they rode off.

Jonny Fairbairn looked like any other rider in bustling Strand Street. He followed Jamie and Iain and watched them go into the lawyers' office, when they emerged he was casually looking at items on the front stoep of an ironmongers' shop, keeping them in his peripheral vision. He tensed up when they stopped and looked down the street, but they rode off eventually.

Do they know they're being followed? He thought, *Robert said they had a second clue maybe they left it with the lawyer. Christ. My nerves are getting the better of me.*
He mounted up and followed.

The boys walked their horses at a slow gait, both men deep in thought, Jamie looking up at Table Mountain, slowly passing under Devil's Peak. He said. 'I think if there is a narrow entrance between two cliffs with a channel leading to a lagoon along the coast somewhere, Captain Willard is bound to know of it.'

Iain was staring out across the suburbs of Newlands and Rondebosch. 'I was just thinking about that,' replied Iain. 'We have been ordered to stand down and not to take any more action. But you and I both know that the ELOS must be aware of us, so their elders in Cape Town must have notified their bosses in London. And now they have manipulated the Government to cause Armstrong's department to be closed down as we are a threat to them here in the Cape.'

'Aye, I cannot fault you there. We have the second clue and they're left with the now useless first clue, so I think you can guarantee that they will still be out to kill us for the second clue, which in reality still makes us active agents in order to defend ourselves, don't you think?'

'I like the way you think Jamie, my friend. Besides, I am by nature a nosey bastard, so I, for one and I think, you, for two, would like to know where the entrance to that lagoon is.'

'Aye, I do think. Let's go and see Roger.

Chapter Forty Six

June 1856

Cape Town

They could see Captain Willard on deck when they approached *The Flying Fish*. He was in deep conversation with the sailmaker and the carpenter when they dismounted and walked up the gangway. The ship was in a bit of a mess.

'Permission to come aboard, sir?' shouted Iain.

'But of course. You two never have to ask permission,' said Willard, shaking their hands warmly. 'Please excuse the mess. The Flying Fish has just returned from an unexpected voyage.'

'Oh! Where did you go to?' asked Iain.

'I was supposed to go to Durban, but I didn't go anywhere. You wouldn't know this as you have been up in the Eastern Cape for so long, but just before you departed the ship was quietly attacked at night; the solitary guard killed and the ship spirited away.'

'What! Were the guns still on board?' asked Jamie.

'Yes I'm afraid they were, needless to say they and the pirates have disappeared,' said Willard. 'The ship was spotted drifting by a passing ship and recognised; the captain put a skeleton crew on board and sailed her to East London, I sent a crew and had her brought back to Cape Town. I'm lucky to get her back in one piece.'

'It's very strange there was only one guard. So the gun-runners got their weapons after all,' said Jamie.

'Yes. There's nothing we can do as it's a military problem. Come, let us go down to the saloon, it's late enough for a sundowner.'

'A sundowner?' enquired Iain.

'Downing a drink as the sun goes down,' explained Willard.

'Storer's dead,' said Jamie and related to Willard the details of their visit to the frontier and what Hutchison said about Storer.

'Well, good riddance, it sounds as though the Governor is hell-bent on purging the Eastern Cape of all and any insurrection,' said Willard. 'But I don't think that is the main reason you came to find me.'

Jamie and Iain had discussed beforehand why they wanted the captain to take them up the coast without mentioning the next clue to the buried treasure.

'You're quite right, of course. Iain and I have started a company which manufactures farming equipment, wagons and other types of tools for different trades. We know of the docks at Port Elizabeth and East London, but we're looking for a port we've heard about, which may be smaller and better suited for us, where building a warehouse at the dockside which would be inexpensive. Do you know of a place where there is a sea entrance to a lagoon through a narrow channel between two heads of rock? It was described to me by someone in King William's Town, but he was not sure of the name.'

'A passage between two heads of rock on the Eastern Cape coast?'

'We don't know where it is exactly, but we thought you might know having sailed up there.'

The captain thought for a moment. 'I think I know where that might be. Let's have a look in the charts.'

He led the way to the charthouse and after a brief search pulled out a rolled-up chart of the coastline they wanted.

'I have never been to this place but it should be marked on here. It's an old chart, but I know the waters so well up there that I never look at it. That's it there, I think; the Belvidere and Knysna Port. It has a narrow entrance through what looks like a treacherous underwater reef into a lagoon, or more like an estuary, and if I'm not mistaken there is a small harbour there. It is navigable and it's best to sail in between those heads at high tide. There should be no problem. This would actually be to your benefit as there is a huge forest around that area which could supply timber for your business.'

'How big is the town?' asked Jamie.

'Knysna is a small town. It does not have a large population.'

'Thanks Roger, you've been more than helpful,' said Iain. 'Now that we know where to go, we'll give you plenty of notice to see if *The Flying Fish* will be available for charter when the time comes.'

'You just tell me when you want to sail and I will take you there. I would like to see Knysna for myself actually. They say it is a beautiful part of the country.'

'We must be off now. Oh, you are invited to the Butlers for dinner tomorrow evening. Eight bells sharp,' said Jamie.

'I'll be there. Thanks for stopping by.'

Jonny watched from a discreet distance as Jamie and Iain boarded The Flying Fish.

Those bastards are up to something, he thought, *maybe they're showing the clue to the captain of that ship and making arrangements to go after the treasure. I think I should relieve Fyvie of that clue and present it to my brother and prove to him that I can get to grips with challenging situations.*

As the boys rode away from the ship towards the road the sun was setting behind the mountain. It was a calm evening so they walked the horses back towards the town, stopping off for a beer along the way, getting to know more of the local people.

When they arrived at their home, Mefrou le Roux cooked up a splendid meal and they sat once again on the stoep going through the recent events.

'It is so tempting to go and follow the clue to this place, the Belvidere and Knysna lagoon, but we would attract too much attention and we would need to hire a lot of men to back us up, otherwise we will be sitting ducks,' said Jamie.

'You're right. We'll have to sit and wait to see what happens in London as I don't see Armstrong letting the ELOS get the better of him. But for now, we wait,' said Iain.

The following evening, dinner at the Butlers was superb. Everybody moved out to the stoep behind the house to enjoy the balmy evening with brandy and wine.

'You lads have been travelling quite extensively since we last saw you. Where have you been?' asked

Sarah Butler.

'We have been setting up distribution points along the route to the frontier with traders in certain towns to stock our wares. In fact, we were talking with Roger yesterday, as we may be in need of his services in the near future,' said Jamie, feeling guilty about telling half of a lie.

'We are also delivering a substantial amount of agricultural tools for the Xhosa natives after their upheaval away from their homelands, to help them start planting crops again,' said Iain. 'The Government has a structure in place to help them achieve this goal.'

'Our ships are already transporting many tools to the frontier,' said Willard.

'I am sure Jamie and Iain do not want to talk about work,' said Lydia. She turned to Clara and said. 'Let us take Jamie and Iain for a walk through the gardens.'

Clara jumped at the idea. 'Mr McColl, would you escort me through the garden please?'

'I would be honoured, Miss Knowles,' said Iain, playing along.

Jamie proffered his arm to Lydia and they wandered off, much to the delight of Godfrey and Sarah.

Jonny had sent one of his men back to King William's Town with a sealed letter for his brother telling him about the suspicious activities of Fyvie and McColl aboard the ship and urged him to get back here as quick as he can.

He followed the boys to Godfrey Butler's house and guessed they had been invited to a dinner party; they would be there for a while.

He rode back to the boys' house and, leaving his horse behind a thicket, he cautiously approached the house on foot and watched. There was a lamp burning at the front door and a glow of light in, what he presumed, would be the front parlour, but nowhere else and no sign of movement.

He walked around the side of the house and onto the stoep. He could see fairly well under the moonlight, which meant that he could also be seen. He looked through the first window and could make out a writing bureau and a desk covered in papers, obviously a library or den. Trying the window he found it to be locked so he went to the next window which was unlocked so he climbed into a small sitting room.

The wooden floor creaked and groaned as he went to the door and looked up and down the corridor; he stopped to listen. Deciding the house was empty he swiftly went to the next door down and let himself into the den and started to search for the clue. He had to scrutinise the papers under the moonlight at the window which took up a lot of time. He found nothing. He then searched the cupboards and found a strongbox behind one of the doors. He tried to pull it out but it had been fixed to the hardwood floor of the cupboard, so short of attacking it with an axe for all to hear he would have to pry it open, which could be noisy as well and almost impossible in the dark.

Just then he heard voices approaching the house.

Mefrou le Roux entered the kitchen closely followed by a scullery maid. 'It must have slipped off my finger; either in the kitchen or the den,' she said. 'My late husband saved all of his money when he was a young man to by me that wedding ring. I must find it.'

'We will find it madam, don't worry,' said the maid. 'I will start looking in the kitchen.'

'Yes you do that and I will search the den,' she said lighting a lamp.

Jonny was waiting behind the door when Mefrou le Roux walked in. He clubbed her on the head with the butt of his pistol and she fell heavily to the floor.

Hearing the noise the maid ran down the passageway.

'Are you all right mefrou?' she said, and bent down when she saw the old woman lying on the floor. 'Oh my goodness madam.'

Jonny once more stepped out from behind the door and stabbed the maid through the neck. The maid fell over dead; blood gushing from the wound as Jonny grinned and cleaned his dagger on her skirt.

He picked up the fallen lamp and heard the old woman groan.

He grabbed her by the hair and pulled her up. 'Where is the key to the strong box?' He said gruffly.

She was clearly terrified. 'The key is not in this house and even if it was I would not tell you.'

'Tell me where it is or you'll end up like the kaffir,' he said forcing her head around to see the dead maid lying in a pool of blood.

'Murderer!' shrieked the old woman.

Jonny hit her again. 'Shut up you stupid old bastard.'

As the old woman lay unconscious Jonny went to the kitchen to check if anybody heard her scream; outside nothing moved, nobody stirred.

Either Fyvie or McColl has the key for that strongbox. He thought. *Well, I'll just wait for them to return, they'll be full of the drink; they'll never expect an attack in their house. I will kill them both and I will have the clue tonight.*

Chapter Forty Seven

Cape Town

Lydia was wearing an exquisite light blue frock, which accentuated her maturing figure. Jamie could hardly keep his eyes off of her body the whole evening.

'I saw you ogling me earlier,' said Lydia.

'I was not ogling, I was admiring your dress… and your curves… and your beautiful face,' said Jamie, stopping and pulling her behind a tree. 'I have been looking forward to seeing you, Lydia. I have really missed you.' He kissed her passionately.

Pulling away from him she said. 'I have missed you as well, Jamie, so much.'

They embraced again, their tongues finding each other between their lips and their hands naturally started wandering over each other.

'This is most definitely not lady-like,' said Lydia between kisses.

'I thought you didn't want to be lady-like?'

'I don't, but society says I must.'

'Well, there is no society in these bushes and I promise I won't tell,' said Jamie moving his hands over her breasts.

Lydia moaned, she dared to reach down and cautiously felt along the front of Jamie's breeches. Feeling his erection she quickly moved her hand away.

He kissed her neck and slowly unfastened the buttons of her dress above her breasts. She moved her hand back and felt his hardness. She wanted to grip it in her hand, skin to skin, but she had no idea how to undo his breeches.

Jamie caressed the top of her breasts. Moving his mouth down, he pulled the fabric away from her nipple and took it in his mouth. She gasped with pleasure, still feeling his erection.

He uncovered her other breast, caressing and teasing the nipple with his tongue and teeth. He reached down and unbuttoned the top buttons on his breeches, Lydia slipped her hand down onto his hardness and for the first time she felt a real desire for a man, not just any man, *this* man, Jamie Fyvie. She felt an unfamiliar physical need for him.

All of a sudden they heard voices, faintly at first but getting louder.

'Oh damn and blast!' said Lydia.

'Come over here,' said Jamie.

They hid behind some bushes as they hurriedly buttoned up their clothing.

They sneaked around the bushes and then, looking calm and collected walked out from behind some trees arm in arm and saw Godfrey and Sarah with Roger Willard walking towards them.

'Is it not a beautiful evening?' said Sarah.

'Yes, it is, Aunt Sarah.'

'Will you not join us?' asked Godfrey, not understanding at all that young people would like to be alone.

'You carry on. We are going back to the house. We will see you there when you get back,' said Lydia.

When the Butlers were out of sight it was Lydia's turn to pull Jamie behind a tree and they hugged each other and kissed so passionately that they were breathless.

'I am so glad we met, Lydia. This passion I have for you is just… just… overwhelming.'

'Oh, Jamie, I can't believe how I feel. My heart is bursting, I can barely contain it. I feel like I want you… all of you. Does that make sense?'

Jamie kissed her then looked into her eyes. 'It makes perfect sense and we have all the time in the world to get to know each other, let's go back to the house.'

'Will I be seeing you more often, Jamie?'

'I will try and see you as often as possible, but bear in mind that Iain and I will be travelling quite extensively, building our business, and…'

'And what – Jamie?'

Jamie held Lydia by the shoulders and said. 'Because of the incident on the ship with Storer, we – that is, Iain and I – have been asked to keep a lookout for anything unusual and report it to a certain man in Government. More I cannot tell you as we have been asked not to discuss anything.'

'Just as we were told not to discuss anything that happened on the ship?' said Lydia.

'Yes, exactly. Our lives will eventually get back to some kind normality but for now please trust me in what I have to do, Lydia.'

'I do trust you, Jamie. Just be careful. I don't want to lose you.'

'You will not lose me,' said Jamie.

Going back to the house, Iain and Clara had just

arrived back. Clara looked a bit red around her lips and Iain was looking very flustered.

Lydia whispered to Jamie. 'Are my lips red as well?'

He looked and nodded. 'They are a little.'

Lydia saw Willard, Godfrey and Sarah walking slowly back to the house. She turned to Clara and circling her fore finger around her lips, she said. 'Clara will you help me in the house, please.'

Clara got the message and went with Lydia. When they returned they had applied some powder lightly to their faces and sat down with the guests just as the servants brought out the coffee.

The conversation carried on well into the night, whisky taking over from the coffee, the ladies sipping on sherry.

Jamie nodded at Iain.

Jamie said, 'well folks; we need to be getting home. Thank you very much for a wonderful evening.'

'Yes,' said Iain, 'work to do tomorrow. Thank you again.'

Everybody said their goodbyes and the girls walked Jamie and Iain to their carriage. It was all the two couples could do not to embrace each other.

The carriage left and wound its way through the town and on to their house in upper Wynberg.

'So how was your walk with Clara?' said Jamie.

'We couldn't get enough of each other. If we'd been elsewhere we would have ripped each other's clothes off.'

'I know what you mean. Lydia and I went through the same experience. Christ, we nearly got caught by Godfrey and Sarah. Thank god we heard them coming.'

'I wanted to ask Clara to marry me, Jamie.'

'What? Are you mad? Don't you think it's a bit early

in the relationship for something like marriage?'

'I'd hate to think I'd lose her to someone else.'

'Don't be daft. You won't lose her. Just take it slowly and make sure. That's what I'll be doing with Lydia, and believe me, I know how you feel. After tonight I have got really close to Lydia. Maybe we should take advantage of this situation with the suspension of the Field Police and carry on with our lives and forget all about this sorry business with Storer and the ELOS.'

The carriage left them at the front door of the house and then continued on to the stables at the far side of the grounds.

Iain was about to ascend the stairs to the stoep when Jamie grabbed his arm.

'Something's wrong. The old girl or the maid is usually here to meet us when they hear the carriage coming up to the house,' whispered Jamie.

Iain looked at his friend and said. 'Dae ye think somebody's in the house?'

'After all that's happened we can't take a chance that there isn't.'

'Your right. You go in the front and I'll go around the back. Give me a couple of minutes to run down to the stables and get the pistols from the carriage, then we go in,' said Iain.

'If there is someone, I'll walk on the stoep and keep their attention,' said Jamie.

Jonny heard the carriage driving up from the main road towards the house and dragged the unconscious old woman into the front hall and propped her up against the stairway then pressed his body against the wall to the side of the front door, drew his pistol and waited.

He heard the carriage stop at the front stoep and the boys descend, then the sound of the carriage moving off. Then silence.

He expected them to fall through the door but still there was silence and he waited.

What's taking them so long?

He thought he heard faint footfalls of someone running. He waited.

Where the hell are they? Christ, maybe they're coming in the back door. He thought; starting to doubt himself.

He was relieved to hear footsteps on the front stoep and expected the door to open, but the footfalls went along the front of the house casting a shadow through the window into the parlour and then the person stopped.

Jamie was sweating a bit as he walked purposely along the floorboards. He was feeling very vulnerable armed with only his daggers. He stopped at the parlour window and looked around then turned back towards the front door.

Standing to the side of the door, he unlocked it; turned the handle and violently pushed it open causing it to crash against a small table.

Jonny got such a fright he almost fired his weapon but managed to refrain.

Jamie looked around the door post and he saw Mefrou le Roux lying against the stairs. He knew it was a trap as he stepped through the door pulling out his dagger.

'Down Jamie!' shouted Iain running from the kitchen.

Jamie dived sideways into the parlour as Jonny fired, the shot thudding into the divan.

As Jonny swung his other pistol around, Iain fired, the bullet hitting Jonny in the chest under his left arm. Jamie lunged forward as Jonny fell over and grabbed his arm wrenching the pistol from his weakened grip.

'Don't move Fairbairn,' said Iain aiming his other pistol at him. 'How's the old girl Jamie?'

'She's alive but she's in a bad way. We need to get a doctor right now,' said Jamie.

'Where's that arsehole brother of yours?' Iain said to Jonny.

'Robert's dead; killed in action,' said Jonny, lying to protect his brother.

'You're a lying bastard,' said Jamie. 'There are no reports of senior arseholes being killed.'

'You'd already left King William's Town so you wouldn't have known.'

Jamie was about to say something when Mefrou le Roux let out a cry of anguish.

'I need to get her on the divan,' said Jamie.

Keeping the gun on Jonny, Iain moved around using his free hand to help lift the old woman through the wide double doors leading into the parlour.

Jonny was in a lot of pain but new he was not seriously injured and saw his chance. He jumped up and dived through the door; landing hard on the stoep. In great pain he scrambled up and over the rail and ran to where he left his horse.

Jamie was first to react and ran through the door in pursuit.

'Stop running Fairbairn; there's nowhere you can go where I won't find you,' shouted Jamie.

Jonny was running on adrenalin now but Jamie soon caught up and tackled him to the ground.

They rolled around trading punches; trying to get the better of one another when suddenly Jamie was on his back looking up at Fairbairn with a dagger in his hand plunging it down at Jamie's chest. Jamie grabbed his wrist and deflected the blow into his own arm.

Wincing, Jamie tried to hang on but Jonny pulled his arm free and made to make the killing strike when a shot rang out.

Jonny stopped for a moment; shock on his face, then fell over on top of Jamie, a hole in the back of his skull.

'Jamie, are ye all right?' shouted Iain running towards him.

Jamie pushed the dead man off. 'I'm all right, just a cut on my arm.'

Iain checked the dead body of Jonny Fairbairn and said. 'Say hello to yer arsehole brother in hell.'

Iain sent a rider to get Doctor Morgan and Bill Hutchison. The doctor patched up Jamie and was now with Mefrou le Roux, while Hutchison was talking with the boys.

'So Jonny told you that Robert Fairbairn is dead?' asked Hutchison.

'He did,' said Jamie. 'You'll have to find out if it's true.'

Iain said. 'If both the Fairbairn brothers are dead and Storer's dead then it's over. The plot aimed at the demise and slavery of the Xhosa people has been prevented, as far as we're concerned we've done what we came here to do. Whether the field police has been suspended or not, it doesn't actually effect Jamie or me anymore, we're free to pursue our own lives from here on in.'

'So you're both in agreement then, Jamie?' asked Hutchison.

'Aye. We have fulfilled our obligations here and almost paid with our lives,' said Jamie. 'Nobody can ask any more of us.'

'Well, I can't argue with that assumption. But that's a conversation that both of you will have with Hugh Armstrong if he is ever reinstated.'

'Now!' said Hutchison leaning forward. 'What about the clue to the treasure?'

'You mean, the mythical treasure, Bill,' said Jamie. 'We should destroy the clue. Even if there is any treasure to be found it should remain buried and forget about it, it will cause too much trouble.'

'I'm not so sure we should destroy the clue,' Iain said, 'maybe sometime in the future we could go and see what all the fuss is about.'

'I don't think it's our decision,' said Hutchison. 'After all it was entrusted to you by a government agency.'

'That's fine Bill, but the clue will be safe with us for now,' said Jamie.

'I'll let Armstrong know when I contact him about that and everything else that has happened and been discussed here today,' said Hutchison.

'We'll give you formal letters to the effect that we're no longer with the Secret Field Police and be getting on with our business dealings and our private lives. Thanks for all you have helped us with Bill,' said Iain.

'You'll have to remain vigilant,' said Hutchison. Keep looking over your shoulder at all times in case any remaining ELOS decide to take revenge, and keep in touch with me, I'll keep you informed of any news from London.'

'What about Fairbairn's murdering volunteers,

Bill?' said Jamie.

'If Fairbairn is dead then they will be disbanded and no doubt there will be no witnesses to bring charges, Cuthbert will see to that.'

'You are probably right,' said Iain. 'Anyway we are free of it and with any luck the whole sorry mess will be exposed and dealt with in London.'

'We've done our job, Iain,' said Jamie. We have stopped the ELOS and stopped the slavers. Let's get on with our lives,' he said lifting a glass to his friend.

Deceit of the Empire: Trilogy
Book Two
Prophets of Death
By
KD Neill
Don't miss the thrilling follow-up.

And

Book Three
Weep the Righteous Warrior
By KD Neill
The epic conclusion.

Printed in Great Britain
by Amazon